THE LADY'S MINE

 A NOVEL

FRANCINE RIVERS

Tyndale House Publishers
Carol Stream, Illinois

Visit Tyndale online at tyndale.com.

Check out the latest about Francine Rivers at francinerivers.com.

Tyndale and Tyndale's quill logo are registered trademarks of Tyndale House Ministries.

The Lady's Mine

Designed by Dean H. Renninger

Edited by Kathryn S. Olson

Published in association with the literary agency of Browne & Miller Literary Associates, LLC, 52 Village Place, Hinsdale, IL 60521

For information about special discounts for bulk purchases, please contact Tyndale House Publishers at csresponse@tyndale.com, or call 1-855-277-9400.

Library of Congress Cataloging-in-Publication Data

A catalog record for this book is available from the Library of Congress.

ISBN 978-1-4964-4757-9 (HC)
ISBN 978-1-4964-6310-4 (International Trade Paper Edition)

Printed in the United States of America

28   27   26   25   24   23   22
7   6   5   4   3   2   1

To my best friend and the love of my life, Rick Rivers
Our life continues to be an unfolding adventure

*Pure and genuine religion in the sight of God the
Father means caring for orphans and widows in their
distress and refusing to let the world corrupt you.*

JAMES 1:27

Northern California, 1875

BLEARY-EYED AND ACHING, Kathryn braced herself again as the stagecoach rattled over a stretch of rough road. Riding second-class on the transcontinental railroad had been blissfully comfortable compared to this jarring, jouncing journey into an unknown future. Two days of torture, two nights in stage stops with a slab of wood for a bed, a single much-used blanket, something resembling stew for dinner—though the proprietors had been unwilling to tell her what meat they used—and plain oatmeal for breakfast.

It might have been wiser to spend a few days in Truckee, where she had disembarked from the train, rather than hasten on with the final leg of her trip. But her options had been limited to taking this stage or waiting a week for the next one, and staying longer in the wild town with more saloons than hotels would have been too dear. Besides, the place had been a shock. The population was primarily miners, lumbermen, and railroad men, with a frightening scarcity of women. She'd never before seen a Chinese man, but she had read how they'd crossed the Pacific by the thousands, willing to take lower wages for the dangerous work of blasting and chiseling tunnels through the stone Sierra Nevada mountains for the railroad. Now that the mammoth project was complete, the despised immigrants sought other ways to eke out a living. Several had approached Kathryn the moment she alighted from the train. She hired one to transport her trunk to suitable accommodations. Though small and wiry, the man hefted her possessions to his rickety cart and headed off at a pace she was unable to match.

Hurrying after him, Kathryn stepped around steaming piles of horse dung and over puddles, nervous at the attention she attracted. Men stared. She only saw a few women, and none dressed as finely as she. And they stared, too. Kathryn caught up to her porter as he entered a riverfront hotel. A hush fell over the lobby full of men as she came through the door. Ignoring them, she went straight to the front desk and checked in, eager for privacy, a bath, a good meal, and a bed. She had spent seven days in a passenger car, her ears assaulted with the constant racket of wheels grinding on iron tracks. Ash and cinders had blown in the window from the locomotive smokestack belching embers, burning small holes in her dark-green chambray travel ensemble. The train stopped only for coal and water, barely allowing time for a meal in a local café.

Her porter hauled her trunk upstairs and left it inside a small room with a bed, a table, and a pitcher of water. Overwhelmed with disappointment and too tired to go back downstairs and ask for a better room, Kathryn untied the ribbons and removed her hat, then sprawled on the bed. She dreamed she was back in Boston, inside the Hyland-Pershing mansion, in the doorway of an upstairs suite. Her mother, radiant with happiness, cooed over a newborn son, while Kathryn's stepfather sat on the edge of the canopy bed, a proud smile on his normally scowling face. When Kathryn spoke, neither heard her. She stood, the recently disinherited daughter, observing their joy. Had they forgotten her already?

She awoke in tears, the sunrise aglow. Groggy and disoriented, she sat up, her clothing rumpled, her hair undone. Her stomach growled, reminding her she hadn't eaten since noon yesterday. She poured icy water into a bowl and washed her face. Oh, how she longed for a bath, but how much would it cost to have a tub and hot water brought upstairs? Removing and folding away her travel ensemble, she donned a Dolly Varden dress that had been delivered shortly before she'd been told she was being sent to California.

The hotel dining room was open and almost empty. Kathryn ordered scrambled eggs, bacon, fried potatoes, and biscuits with jam. Replete, she spoke to the front desk clerk, who told her she could find the services she requested at the bathhouse next door. When she saw the line of men waiting, she knew it was not a very safe place for a lady. Dismayed, she headed back to the train station to arrange transportation to Calvada. A stagecoach was parked in front, horses being put into harnesses.

"Calvada?" The clerk shook his head. "Never heard of it."

Kathryn felt a flutter of panic. "It has mail service."

"There must be a hundred or more mining towns in the

Sierras, miss. Some don't even have names. Calvada sounds like a border town, but you gotta know north or south."

The cover letter that had come with Uncle Casey's will mentioned two other towns. She handed the letter to the clerk, who read it quickly and nodded. "South, and it'll take three days to get there, barring accidents on the road. You're in luck. Stage leaves in an hour. If you miss this one, you'll have to wait another week for the next."

The stagecoach bounced again, slamming Kathryn's already-tenderized backside onto the bench. A six-foot, bushy-bearded mountain man named Cussler was the driver, and he shouted curses down on his six-horse team of bays as the coach raced along the mountain road. She wondered what she'd find waiting for her in Calvada.

Jolted and rocked, Kathryn thought back to the night before she left Boston. Her mother and stepfather had gone to the theater with friends. Kathryn dined in the kitchen with staff. Saying goodbye to people she loved had been heart-wrenching. Any hope of changing her mother's mind had ended the next morning when the judge joined her in the entrance hallway and informed her that he would be accompanying her to the train station to see her off. She had the feeling he wanted to make sure she got on the train and stayed on it.

Lawrence Pershing didn't speak to her until they had almost reached the station. Then he extracted an envelope from his inside coat pocket. "This document transfers your mother's rights to the inheritance to you. Whatever property your uncle possessed upon his death is yours. I doubt it's much. I've added enough money to give you a start. If you are frugal and wise," he added with a hint of sarcasm, "it will last until you find a suitable trade. I've paid your passage to Truckee. It will be up to you to find your way to Calvada from there."

A trade. What would that be? She had more education than most women, largely due to sneaking into the judge's library and pilfering books. But none of what she'd learned would provide her with a trade.

The stagecoach bounced abruptly, shocking Kathryn back to her present circumstances. She felt air between her and the seat, and then landed with a hard thud that drew an unladylike grunt. Cussler shouted profane insults at the horses and cracked the whip. When the coach swayed, Kathryn had to brace herself. Her midnight-blue skirt and jacket were gray with dust, her teeth gritty. Her head itched despite the hat covering her hair. How long until the next stop? Parched, she tried not to think about how good a glass of cold, clear water would taste.

Four others had ridden with her the first day, each getting off along the way. Henry Call, a bespectacled gentleman in his early thirties, met the coach at the last station. He joined her for a meal of questionable stew. The proprietor swore it was chicken, but Cussler said it tasted like rattlesnake. Kathryn preferred not to know, too hungry to care anyway. After the meal, Mr. Call handed her into the coach, where conversation ceased, both of them understanding that any attempt might result in a mouthful of road dust. He opened his satchel and extracted a file. Now and then, he removed and cleaned his glasses.

Cussler hollered, "Whoa," and the coach came to halt. He continued shouting, using words Kathryn didn't understand, but which turned Mr. Call's face red.

"You idjit! What do you think you're doing, stepping out in the road like that?"

A gruff, laughing voice replied, "How else am I gonna get a ride?"

"Buy a ticket like everyone else!"

"You gonna let me ride or leave me for bear bait?"

Kathryn looked at Mr. Call in alarm. "Are there bears out here?"

"Yes, ma'am. Plenty of grizzlies in these mountains."

As if the ratio of men to women wasn't worrisome enough! Now she had to worry about the animal life as well?

The stagecoach door popped open and a man wearing a sweat-stained, battered hat climbed aboard. Lifting his gray-streaked, bearded face, he saw Kathryn. "Holy Jehoshaphat! A lady!" His ruddy, aging face split with a grin. Still bent over, he took off his hat. "Well, I wasn't expecting to see anyone like you!"

Kathryn could have said the same.

The coach started off again, tossing the old man back. Sprawled beside Mr. Call, he expelled a foul word she had heard a hundred times from Cussler over the last forty-eight hours. He stuck his head out the window. "Hey, Cussler, when you gonna learn to drive? You tryin' to kill me?"

"I shudda driven over you and left your carcass in the road," Cussler shouted back.

The newcomer laughed, not the least insulted, and settled back in his seat. "Beggin' your pardon, ma'am. Didn't mean nothin' by it. Me and Cussler go back a long way."

Kathryn gave him a pained smile and closed her eyes. She had a headache, along with other assorted aches and pains. It had taken all her willpower at the last stage stop not to rub her backside when she'd climbed down from the coach.

The man scratched his beard. "I always hitch a ride before the road gets hairy. Tried walkin' it once and had to hang on to a tree or get runned over."

Kathryn looked out her window and pressed back with a gasp.

"If you look over the edge at the next curve, you'll see a

6

coach down there. Driver was in too much of a hurry. Happens every once in a while."

Cussler cracked the whip again, urging the horses to go faster. Kathryn gulped.

"Never know when you're gonna die." The old-timer turned philosopher. "We'll make it, dependin'."

"Depending on what?" Kathryn dared ask.

"How much Cussler drank at the last stop."

Kathryn looked at Henry Call. He shrugged. What had been in the big mug the station manager gave Cussler? She braced herself as the coach went around another curve. She couldn't help herself. She peered out. The coach lurched and the door popped open. She gave a shriek as she pitched forward. She felt someone grasp her skirt and jerk her back. The old man relatched the door. The three sat staring at one another. Kathryn didn't know who to thank and was afraid to guess.

Henry Call cleared his throat. "I was told Cussler is the best driver on the line. We have nothing to fear."

The old man snorted and tucked something into his cheek. His jaws worked like a ruminating mule deer as he studied Kathryn from her high-button shoes to the brim of her beribboned bonnet with its two dusty plumes. "What kind of bird gave up those feathers?"

"An ostrich."

"Say what?"

"Os-trich. It's an African bird."

"Musta cost you plenty." He leaned over to the window and spit a stream of brown juice.

Kathryn almost gagged. The old man wasn't finished with his perusal. Annoyed, she looked him over from his dirty hat, worn plaid shirt, weatherworn leather coat, and faded-blue canvas pants to his dusty boots. The man smelled like a muskrat, or what she imagined a muskrat might smell like. But then, who was she to turn up her nose? She hadn't had a full bath since leaving Boston. Her whalebone stays pinched. Worse, her skin itched beneath them. Her bustle felt like a log at the base of her spine.

The stagecoach sailed along smoothly, and Kathryn relaxed until Cussler shouted, "Hang on, folks! Washboard a-coming!"

Before she could ask what the driver meant, the old-timer put his dirty boots on the edge of the seat next to her and braced himself. The coach shot up, Kathryn with it. Her decorated bonnet was the only thing preventing a skull fracture. She landed with a painful thump and an *oooff.* One bounce turned into a succession. "Ah . . . ah . . . ah . . . ah . . ." She clung to the doorframe, her backside getting a beating. As quickly as the abuse started, it ended.

The ostrich plumes dangled between her eyes. Her hen-cage bustle had slipped downward. Kathryn shifted on the seat, but that made her predicament worse. Both men asked if she was all right. "Yes, of course. How long until we reach Calvada?"

"Not long, I'm thinking. Before sunset, anyway. Cussler is making good time."

Kathryn resigned herself to suffer.

Henry Call tucked his papers away. "It's a long journey for a young lady on her own, Miss Walsh. You must miss Boston."

"Indeed." So far, the journey had merely served to remind her of the heavy cost of following one's convictions.

The older man brightened. "Boston! I knew you was from back East. You've got that grand air about ya. Don't have many ladies out here." He seemed mesmerized by the flat and broken feathers. "Got plenty of the other kind though."

Henry Call cleared his throat.

The old man looked at him and chewed his cud. "She's

gonna see fer herself, ain't she?" He turned back to Kathryn. "Why are you out here?"

"Seeing to family business, sir." As if it was any of his.

The old man's brows rose and he looked her over again. "No one's ever called me *sir* before. Plenty of other names, but not that one. No, we sure don't have anyone like you in Calvada. Don't take no offense at me tellin' you that. It's a pure compliment."

"They don't have many like you where I come from either, Mr. . . ."

"No mister. Just plain Wiley. Wiley Baer."

Mr. Call took off his glasses and cleaned them again before tucking them into his breast pocket. "Do you have family in Calvada, Miss Walsh?"

"I had an uncle. He died and left an inheritance."

"In Calvada?" Wiley snorted again. "Good luck with that." His eyes narrowed. "If it's worth anything, someone's already laid claim to it."

"Perhaps I can be of assistance," Call interjected. "I'm a lawyer. If you need help making your legal claim, feel free to come to me."

"That's most kind of you, Mr. Call."

Wiley stuck another pinch of tobacco in his cheek while eyeing Henry Call. "You might as well turn around now, instead of wasting time hangin' up your shingle in Calvada. We got more lawyers than dogs got fleas. And about as welcome."

"I'm employed, Wiley. I won't be in Calvada more than a few months before I head back to Sacramento."

"Who're you working for? Morgan Sanders?" Wiley put his boot up again. "He's one mean—" he glanced at Kathryn—"bird dog."

"I'm not at liberty to say."

"Well, there's only two men in Calvada who'd have money enough to bring up a fancy lawyer from Sacramento or wherever you came from. Sanders or Beck, and I wouldn't want to get between those two."

"Who are they, Wiley?" Kathryn wanted to know something about the town that would soon become her home.

"Morgan Sanders owns the Madera Mine. Rents shacks to his workers. Owns the company store where they have to buy their supplies. Beck came lately, went into partnership with Paul Langnor. Good man, Langnor. Never watered his whiskey. Beck's been doing well with the saloon and casino since Langnor died. Added a hotel. Beck saw the elephant and got sick of buckin' the tiger, was smart enough to find somethin' else to do and make himself rich doin' it."

"Elephants and tigers?" Kathryn felt her anxiety rising.

Henry Call smiled. "Seeing the elephant means learning life the hard way, Miss Walsh. Bucking the tiger means playing faro. The game originated in Europe, and they used cards with pictures of Egyptian pharaohs on the back."

"Been playin' it since I came west in '49," Wiley confessed.

"Gambling, you mean." Kathryn understood now why the man appeared to have nothing more than his worn-out clothes and down-at-the-heels boots.

"Life's a gamble, ain't it? There's risk in anything you do."

Wiley Baer, the sage. "What can you tell me about Calvada?"

"Well, it sure ain't Boston!" He gave a snort of laughter. "I can tell you that much."

"Do you work in the Madera Mine, Wiley?"

"Work for Sanders? I ain't no fool. Once down those shafts, you never get out. Got a mine I work alone in the mountains. Claim goes way back to '52. Got papers to prove it. Good thing, 'cause the record office burned in '54. Burned again in

'58. I dig what I need to live on. That way the ore will last a lifetime." He eyed Henry Call suspiciously. "Nobody knows where it is but me." Ruminating a moment, he spit out the window again. "Every now and then, a man has just got to go to a bigger town." He winked at Henry. "Trouble is, I think I got lice . . ."

"Lice?" The mere mention made Kathryn itch.

"You bet. Some an inch long."

Mr. Call shook his head. "A tall tale, Miss Walsh."

"Who says?" Wiley Baer glowered at Call before giving Kathryn an innocent smile. "You gonna believe a lawyer over an honest man who's lived in these mountains for more'n twenty years? I'm tellin' you, we got ticks you can saddle and ride. The mosquitos carry brickbats under their wings so's they can sharpen their stingers. But you needn't worry, ma'am. There's a surefire way to get rid of them. I just draw a line down my middle, shave all the hair off one side, douse the other with kerosene, and light a match. The critters run to the clear side and I stab them with my hunting knife." He pulled one out of the sheath at his waist and held it up so she could see the nine-inch blade.

She gave him a droll look. "You'd better have good aim."

Wiley laughed. "You betcha." He winked again, at her this time.

"Are there many women in Calvada, Wiley?"

"Women? Yes, siree. About twenty, I'm guessing, if the last count stands. Not many ladies, though, and no one like you, that's for darn sure." He looked her over again. "Are you spoken for?"

"I beg your pardon?" Kathryn blushed, surprised he'd ask such a personal question.

"Are you engaged or married?" He raised his voice as though

she hadn't heard his query over the rattle of harnesses and pounding hooves.

"No."

"Well, that good news will spread like wildfire." He grinned. "If you want a husband, you can have one by nightfall."

Was that a California proposal? "No, thank you."

"Men out here are hankering for wives. And you look like a prime candidate."

She supposed he meant it as a compliment, but she felt like a juicy steak on a plate. "I didn't come out here to find a husband. I came to claim an inheritance and have charge of my own life."

"You'll need protection."

Was he offering it? "I'll buy a gun."

The stagecoach swayed sharply, and Kathryn grabbed hold of the window frame. Every muscle in her body screamed for relief.

"Wake up, folks!" Cussler shouted. "Coming round the bend to Calvada."

Mr. Call checked his case. "Will someone be meeting you, Miss Walsh?"

"I'm to contact Mr. Neumann when I arrive."

Wiley spit the plug of tobacco out the window. "Herr Neumann?"

"Yes. Do you know the gentleman?"

"Came near to cutting my ear off last time I went to his barbershop."

Judging by the length of Wiley Baer's hair, that had been several years ago.

"Lousy barber. Good man. When he's sober. If he ain't in his shop, you'll find him at Beck's Saloon."

Kathryn flinched at several loud bangs. "Was that gunfire?"

"Yep." Wiley scratched his beard. "Sounds like a Smith &

Wesson. Shooting ain't unusual in Calvada. Men get a little rambunctious with whiskey under their belts." He leaned out the coach window as it went around a bend. "Don't see any bodies lyin' in the street." He sat back. "Could be worse. I seen six men chasin' a dog down Chump Street once. They was so drunk none of 'em made the mark. 'Course, a man mindin' his own business in the dry goods store got a bullet through his head."

Kathryn didn't know whether to believe him or not. Henry Call didn't say it was a tall tale. What sort of place was Calvada? "Did the sheriff arrest the men?"

"Wasn't no sheriff."

"Surely there is some sort of law . . ."

"Yep. Men gathered at the saloon, discussed the matter. Decided his death was an act of God. A pity, but we all gotta go sometime."

Kathryn stared. "And that was all they did on the deceased's behalf?"

"Nope. Had a couple of drinks in his name, took up a collection, and had him buried in a new suit the next day."

Just as Kathryn was about to make a comment, she was struck by a stench so foul, she gagged. She covered her nose and mouth. "What on earth is that horrible smell?"

Wiley Baer's half smile turned rueful. "Like I said, Calvada ain't Boston. You'll get used to the smell in a coupla days." Three more shots rang out as the coach lurched to a stop. Had a stray bullet hit Cussler or one of the horses? Wiley opened the door and jumped down. He looked around and peered back in. "Must've rained again. Mud's past my ankles. Better get out on the other side, ma'am. Town's got sinkholes so deep men have disappeared and become part of the road."

The air was heavy with eau de sewage, mud, and horse dung. Another shot rang out. Glass shattered. Men shouted.

It sounded like a riot had broken out in the saloon across the street. Wiley sloshed through the muck. "Comin' from Beck's place. Shootin's over, is my guess."

Mr. Call climbed out of the coach and stood on the boardwalk. He offered Kathryn a hand. Trembling, knees weak, she hopped onto the boardwalk, where Wiley Baer stood scraping pounds of oozing, odiferous mud off his boots. Across the street, the swinging doors flew open and a man windmilled out. He fell backwards off the boardwalk and skidded into the middle of the street. A tall, broad-shouldered man with dark hair came through the doors after him.

"That thar is Matthias Beck. And he looks pure hostile right now."

Kathryn watched the man step off the boardwalk, stride to the middle of the street, and haul the man up from the mud. She flinched each time he punched the poor fellow: once, twice, and again before letting him drop. Men poured out of the saloon and stood along the boardwalk, cheering him on. Grabbing the man by the back of his neck, he half dragged him to a horse trough and dumped him in. The man bobbed up, sputtering. Beck shoved him down. Up and down the wretch went, as if Beck was doing laundry.

Horrified, Kathryn watched. "Why are those men laughing? Shouldn't someone stop that bully before he drowns that poor man?"

Henry Call shook his head. "Best to stay out of the situation when you don't know what happened."

When she looked at Wiley, he raised his hands. "Don't look at me. I ain't gettin' in between."

"Men!" Kathryn muttered in exasperation as she stepped to the edge of the boardwalk. *"Stop that this minute! Leave that man alone!"*

She caught the attention of every man standing outside the saloon, but Beck barely paused or glanced in her direction. The man's arms flailed as Beck pushed him under again, then pulled him up and draped him over the side and left him retching. When the man had emptied his stomach, Beck grasped the front of his shirt and spoke to him nose-to-nose.

The man managed to climb out of the trough, but his feet slipped, and he sprawled in the mud again. Rolling over, he crawled toward the boardwalk as Beck turned and looked straight at Kathryn.

Oh, dear. She gulped.

"Oh, no!" Wiley moaned. "Here he comes. Good luck, and it was nice meetin' ya." Chortling, he jumped down into the muddy street and helped a young man unharness the horses.

Kathryn's heart beat faster with each step Matthias Beck took toward her. She instinctively moved back when he stepped up onto the boardwalk. She reminded herself that she had faced down Judge Lawrence Pershing many times over the years. Beck didn't say anything. He just looked at her. She felt her lungs constrict, and her hand fluttered to her stomach. Disturbed by unaccustomed sensations, she turned away quickly, looking for her trunk.

"Well, well, Henry . . ." Beck spoke in a deep Southern drawl. "You didn't tell me you were bringing a lady."

Stiffening, Kathryn turned back and looked up. "I'm not his lady."

"Even better." He grinned in a way that made her want to slap his face, especially when it caused a rush of heat to course through her.

Henry cleared his throat. "Matthias, this is Miss Kathryn Walsh. She's come to settle—"

"I'm sure Mr. Beck isn't the least bit interested in *my* business."

"Oh, I'm interested in everything about you."

Kathryn ignored him.

"She's from Boston," Wiley volunteered.

"And looks it." Beck's gaze moved down and back up, lingering on the ostrich feathers dangling in front of her face. She controlled the urge to take off her hat and whack him with it.

"She's got a letter from Herr about some inheritance," Wiley piped up.

"Wiley Baer!" she protested. Why did her two coach companions think her business was any of Beck's?

"I'm afraid Herr Neumann isn't in a condition to talk business or anything else at present," Beck told her.

Kathryn tipped her chin. "And how would you know that, sir?"

"He passed out at my bar an hour ago. I had him carried home. He'll sleep it off by morning. In the meantime, perhaps I can be of service?" His tone was serious.

"Thank you, but I don't think so."

"You don't seem to approve of me, your ladyship."

The title grated. "I don't know anything about you other than you own that place across the street, and you beat up that poor man and almost drowned him in the trough."

"He felt like celebrating a win at the faro table and started shooting. Thankfully, he didn't kill anyone."

That information did change matters, but she still didn't approve of a public beating in response. "Wouldn't it have been better to turn him over to the constable for disturbing the peace?"

"Boston," Wiley said. "Got a sheriff yet, Matthias?"

"Not yet."

Wiley scratched his chest. "It was nice ridin' with you, missy, but I'm gonna have myself a stiff drink, bath, good meal, and go visit the Dollhouse." He turned and headed for Beck's Saloon.

Kathryn frowned. Dollhouse?

"Walsh." Beck frowned. "You couldn't be related to City Walsh."

Kathryn looked up at him. "City? My uncle's name was Casey Teague Walsh." *Casey Teague. C. T.* Maybe these people did know him as City.

All hint of humor left the man's face. "Sorry to tell you, but there's no pot at the end of the rainbow."

She blinked, feeling her stomach drop. So much for any grand dreams, not that she had been possessed of any. The judge wouldn't have handed over a gold mine.

"Well, whatever there is will have to do." She gave Henry a nod. "It was nice meeting you, Mr. Call. If you'll excuse me, gentlemen." She went into the stage office and asked if she could store her trunk and where she might find a hotel.

"My place across the street is the best in town," Beck said from behind her.

Her pulse shot up. She kept her eyes glued on the station manager. "There must be another hotel . . ."

"The Sanders Hotel is a couple of blocks down on the right, but I wouldn't recommend it for a lady like yourself." Beck stood in the doorway.

"But you think a saloon is appropriate?"

"The saloon is downstairs, your ladyship. The rooms are upstairs, fully furnished, each with a lock on the door. You'll be safe under my roof."

The heat in those eyes made her think otherwise. "No, thank you, Mr. Beck." She picked up her carpetbag and headed for the door. He didn't move.

"I'll see that Herr is sobered up while you get settled in."

Her stomach growled loudly, and she blushed.

His mouth tipped. "And I'll show you a good place to eat."

"Please move aside, sir."

His face stiffened. "You are not going to the Sanders Hotel."

Her stepfather had often used that imperious tone on her, and it always roused her own considerable temper. She gave him a cloying smile. "Is this the way you drum up business, Mr. Beck, by accosting women at the stage station?"

Beck stood aside and gave her a mocking bow. She could feel the heat from his body as she stepped around him cautiously.

"You'd be better off at your uncle's house," he said when she had taken a few steps.

Hope rose within her. "There's a house?"

"Not exactly."

"Would you kindly tell me where to go?"

"I'd like nothing better." He jerked his chin. "A few doors down to the left. Between the Bear's Head Saloon and Barrera's Fandango Hall."

She stared at him, swallowed convulsively, and gave a slight nod. "Thank you, Mr. Beck." She felt him watching her as she followed his directions.

"Say hello to Scribe for me," he called after her.

Pausing, Kathryn turned. "Scribe?"

"The boy worked for your uncle. He's been living in the place since City died. Nowhere else to go. Tell him to come to my place." He turned to Henry, said something quietly, and escorted him across the street.

2

SQUARING HER SHOULDERS, Kathryn continued down the boardwalk. Her stomach rolled at the smell. Exhausted and aching all over, she cast surreptitious glances around. This town was to be her new home. *Oh, Lord, help me.* Maybe things would look better after a good night's sleep.

The broken feathers bobbed in front of her face as she passed a boot shop. The other side of the street boasted three saloons: the Crow Bar, the Iron Horse, and What the Diggings. There was a mercantile advertising "One Thing Ore Another," an assayer's office, a small house with a red lantern in the window. A man on horseback stared at her as he rode by, colliding with two men crossing the street. A fight broke out. As she passed the

Bear's Head Saloon, she heard someone abusing the piano and glanced in. The place was packed. A man spotted her. "Holy Jehoshaphat! Take a look at that!" They did. Chairs were shoved back and booted heels beat the wooden floor like a stampede of bison across the plains.

Kathryn hastened on, trying to ignore the sound of the swinging door flying open behind her and men's voices following.

"Where'd she come from?"

"Heaven!"

"Maybe Fiona's brought in a new doll."

"You got the brains of a jackrabbit, Cody. That's a lady."

Just past the Bear's Head was a squat, run-down clapboard building with two front windows so grimy Kathryn couldn't see inside. Thankfully, the door looked solid. A nervous glance back confirmed there was a growing crowd of men on the boardwalk, all staring, all talking among themselves. She felt like a fox with a pack of hounds ready to give chase. Kathryn knocked three times, praying the boy would open the door quickly so she could duck inside.

No response. Not a sound of life inside.

"He's in there!" some man called out.

Other men were crossing the street to see what the ruckus was about. A bubble of panic rose, and Kathryn knocked again, like a woodpecker hammering a hole in a tree. She leaned her ear against the door and almost fell in when it swung open. Straightening quickly, she faced a boy a few years younger than she, but several inches taller. Lanky, with the first show of peach fuzz, brown eyes bloodshot, he swayed in front of her, wearing nothing but red long johns. His mouth opened in surprise. He blinked, rubbed his face, and stared again.

"Mr. Scribe?" She spoke weakly.

"Who are you?"

"That's what we all want to know!" a man shouted.

Now annoyed, Kathryn turned and glared at the gathering. "Go back to the bar, boys, and leave me to conduct my business."

"She's a lady all right." Most retreated.

Breathing again, she faced the young man, blushing at his state of undress. "Perhaps you could put on something more appropriate?"

His face reddened. "Oh! Sorry!" He grabbed a pair of crumpled dungarees and shoved a leg in. Leaning against a desk, he got both legs in his pants and hitched them up. When he adjusted the suspenders, the snap almost knocked him off his feet.

Mortified, Kathryn realized she had watched the whole show without blinking.

Scribe made a sweeping gesture of welcome. "Come on in and tell me who you are, when you got here, what I can do for you, and where you came from."

"I'm Kathryn Walsh, Casey Teague Walsh's niece. I've been sent from Boston to claim the inheritance."

Scribe stared at her for a moment. Then his shoulders sagged. "Well, that does it. City's life's work down a sinkhole." He waved his hand to encompass everything she could see, misery oozing out of his alcohol-saturated body. "It's all yours, Miss Walsh."

Kathryn entered, stepping over the shattered whiskey bottle and puddle of what little had remained before it was flung. Her gorge rose again. The place reeked of whiskey, male sweat, and a full chamber pot. Apple crates overflowing with paper were stacked against one wall. The room was furnished with a settee with a rumpled blanket, a big oak desk, a straight-backed pine chair, and a spittoon. In the back corner was a hulking shape covered with a tarp. At the back was an open door to a second room, probably a small apartment. This was to be her home?

She clutched her carpetbag in front of her, needing something to hang on to.

"What sort of business did my uncle have?"

"Doesn't matter now. Not a woman's trade." Scribe nodded toward the open door. "Want to see the rest of the place? Everything City owned is back there."

Kathryn followed Scribe into a cold, dank, and dusty room that smelled of tobacco and whiskey. Her heart lifted at the sight of a bookcase filled with volumes. The bed was unmade. No sheets, just a couple of Indian blankets and a chamber pot shoved beneath, thankfully covered with a fitted lid. A rough-hewn plank armoire revealed a meager collection of men's shirts, pants, a heavy coat, scuffed boots, and an old tweed Kerry cap. Not even a hint of warmth came from the ash-choked pot-bellied stove. Two straight-backed chairs faced one another over a small table, a game of solitaire spread out. Dirty pans and tin plates were stacked on a soiled counter, an empty water bucket next to the back door.

"I had City buried in his Sunday best suit and his good boots." Scribe's eyes filled and he looked away, rubbing his nose with the back of his hand. He cleared his throat. "I'm keeping the cap. If you don't mind."

Kathryn took it from the armoire and handed it to him solemnly. She tried to appear calm as she looked around the dismal room that would be her home. Even with Scribe standing in front of her, it felt empty. She would live here, alone. Her own eyes burned with tears.

"You look dead on your feet, Miss Walsh." Scribe pulled out a chair for her. "Why don't you sit down?"

Kathryn sat, dropping her carpetbag on the floor. It was a moment before she could summon her voice. "You worked for my uncle?"

"City took me in when I was seven. Taught me everything I know."

"How old are you now, Scribe?"

"Sixteen." He looked back at her. "You don't look much older."

She gave a wan smile, not that she planned to announce her age. "What happened to your parents, if I may ask?"

"Got nothing to hide. Ma died of a fever. Da in a mining accident."

An orphan, and she was putting him out of the only home he knew. Could things get any worse? "I'm sorry." Why hadn't her uncle given Scribe this house?

"It was a long time ago. I barely remember them," Scribe said, not understanding. He looked away again, mouth pressed tight. He didn't have to say more. Kathryn saw the sorrow etched on his young face. The uncle she never knew had been the only family this young man had.

"Is Scribe your real name?"

"It's the only one I go by."

"Like Wiley," she murmured.

Scribe gave a laugh of surprise. "Where did you meet that old coot?"

"On the stagecoach. Mr. Cussler picked him up on the road."

"He's got a mine around here somewhere." The boy looked tired and ill.

"I should've waited until tomorrow rather than intrude on you today." Kathryn stood and grasped the tortoiseshell handle of her carpetbag. "I'll check into a hotel for the night and come back in the morning." She bit her lip, guilt stifling her. "I don't wish to be unkind, but . . ."

"I can't live here anymore," he finished for her.

She blinked back tears. "Mr. Beck said you could stay in his hotel."

"Hope he'll give me a job, too."

"I'm so sorry to put you out, Scribe."

He straightened his shoulders. "Don't you worry about me. I'll get by."

Pausing in the doorway, she looked back at the young man standing forlornly in the front office. "Please call me Kathryn. We're practically family. I hope we'll be able to sit and talk about my uncle. I never had the privilege of meeting him. You can tell me all about him." She hadn't even known she had an uncle until the judge informed her of the unexpected inheritance.

Scribe looked at her bleakly. "I don't know much more than anyone else. Most men don't talk about where they were before they came to California. About all I know is City came in '49 like thousands of others looking for gold. He worked the streams for a couple of years. Said he didn't like the solitary, backbreaking life. So he set up shop here. Said a man had to have a purpose or he wasn't worth anything." He gave a soft, broken laugh. "One thing City loved was a purpose, and a good fight to go along with it."

Kathryn smiled. Perhaps she shared something in common with City Walsh.

Scribe's chin wobbled. "I was at the mercantile, picking up some supplies. Got to talking to a friend of mine. When I came back, I found City on the floor right there." He nodded toward the front office.

"Then it was a sudden death."

"As sudden as murder can be."

"Murder?" She put a hand to her throat.

"You didn't know?" He cursed softly. "Well, how would you? Sorry I blurted it out like that." Emotions flickered across his face—grief, anger, frustration, fear.

"Did they catch who did it?"

"No." Anger hardened his young face. "If I knew who did it, I'd do something about it!" Grief made him look like a boy again. "No one even talks about it anymore. City made some enemies. Had one man in his sights at the last, but never said who. Said he had to have all the facts before he opened his mouth."

Kathryn felt as upset as Scribe, though she'd never known City Walsh. "There should be law and order . . ."

"Yeah, well, City said the same thing, and it ain't happening anytime soon. People wanted justice for about a week. A lot of people asked questions, but no one came up with any answers, and no one saw anyone come in or out of here." Scribe ran his fingers through his dirty, matted hair. "Most of the town is drunk by dark anyway . . ." He sat, shoulders hunched. "I'll pack and get out of your hair by tomorrow morning."

The last thing Kathryn wanted to do was put this poor boy out, but what choice had she? She hoped Matthias Beck was a man of his word. "Thank you, Scribe." She stepped out onto the covered boardwalk again, closing the door quietly behind her.

Piano music came from the Bear's Head, along with men talking. Squaring her shoulders, Kathryn prepared herself to walk the gauntlet.

Matthias escorted Henry Call into the saloon to a table by a front window. Yesterday, he'd been impatient for him to arrive, eager to begin laying out plans for the project they'd discussed in Sacramento. A chance meeting and common discontent had brought them together, both veterans from the war. But right now, he was more interested in what City's niece might do. He signaled Brady, his bartender, and then looked out the window.

"She's gathering a crowd," Henry remarked. "I'm not sure this is a safe place for a girl like Miss Walsh."

"It isn't."

Brady set down a bottle of whiskey and two glasses. Bending, he peered out the window. He gave a low whistle. "I wondered what you were staring at." He caught Matthias's look, and returned to the bar.

Scribe appeared in his underwear. Matthias gave a short laugh, expecting Miss Walsh to retreat. Instead, she stood her ground. Turning, she addressed the men. Whatever she said had most heading back into the Bear's Head.

"It appears Miss Walsh can take care of herself," Henry remarked.

"I doubt that." Matthias watched her go inside the house. "What do you know about her?"

"About as much as you do."

"She didn't talk to you on the ride up?"

Henry laughed. "We were too busy hanging on for dear life. She asked Wiley Baer about Calvada. She was rather shocked when we arrived. Gunfire, you meting out justice in the street . . ."

City's door opened, but it wasn't Scribe leaving. Kathryn Walsh came out and walked toward the stage office. When she passed it and kept going, Matthias swore under his breath.

"Are you going after her?"

"I offered safe haven." He poured the whiskey. "Some people have to learn the hard way." Men came out of saloons and gawked at her. And why not? Wasn't he gawking? She was a beauty, and as out of place as a thoroughbred mare among a herd of mustangs. "I'll bet you five dollars she'll be back at the stage office tomorrow morning buying a ticket home."

Henry shook his head. "I don't think she'll be leaving anytime soon."

"Why do you say that?"

"Just a hunch. I don't think she came here by choice. She was sent."

"One telegram and her family will be calling her home. They probably thought City owned a hotel and had a gold mine."

"But why send a woman?"

An unaccompanied woman at that. Such things weren't done. It made Matthias wonder.

Henry watched her. "I haven't been here long enough to get a look around, but I think Calvada could use a lady like Miss Walsh."

"Someday. Not now. Calvada is little more than a mining camp, with all the misery that goes with it." Matthias wondered what the lady had found inside City's house. Scribe had been grieving since the man's death, and someone was giving him whiskey to drown his sorrows. He could imagine her face when she walked into that hovel. He could see those amazing green eyes widen, that creamy skin paling even more, the rushing disappointment turn down those sweet lips. If a night at the Sanders Hotel didn't send her running, a few nights in that little house between a saloon and a fandango hall would do it. She'd be willing to sell and get out of this hellhole of a town. There was only one piece of City's property Matthias wanted, and he'd offer Kathryn Walsh enough to get her to Sacramento or San Francisco, where some enterprising entrepreneur would marry her.

Kathryn Walsh had walked far enough that he couldn't see her without going out on the boardwalk. He downed his whiskey and stayed where he was. She was bullheaded, just like her uncle. Matthias found himself curious. City had never mentioned any family, let alone a niece in Boston. How did an Irish-Catholic immigrant end up related to a Protestant Bostonian

Brahmin? She looked it, anyway, from her high-button shoes and expensive traveling ensemble to that ridiculous hat that probably cost more than a year's wages for one of Sanders's miners. But he had to admit she also bore a striking resemblance to his friend. So City and that girl were related? There was a story there, and no one to provide the details except her royal highness, who was strolling into a place where there was no telling what she might see or hear.

Matthias started to get up and then sat again. She'd said no. She'd already made up her mind about him. He'd seen that look before. A muscle jerked in his jaw as he watched a parade of men heading down the boardwalk. Matthias squelched the protective instinct rising in him. She wasn't his responsibility. Then again, City had been one of his closest friends. He'd have to run to catch up, and then what? Throw her over his shoulder and haul her back here?

Henry chuckled. "She got under your skin, didn't she?" He grew serious. "Is the Sanders Hotel that bad?"

"She'll likely meet the proprietor soon after she checks in." Sanders was a bachelor, like 95 percent of Calvada's population, and of an age to be looking for a beautiful young wife to provide him with an heir to his empire. She might just fare well in that place if Sanders got word soon enough of her arrival. And Matthias bet he would.

Henry took a sip of whiskey and his brows rose. "Good Kentucky bourbon."

"I give the men what they pay for, not chain lightning or coffin varnish. It's one of the reasons I'm doing so well." He nodded toward the bar lined with men buying drinks. The faro and poker tables were full. "The best whiskey, honest tables, good accommodations."

"All you need is a restaurant."

"Gave that some serious thought, but decided against it."
Ronya Vanderstrom's business would suffer if he opened one,
and he'd been eating at her place since he came to town six years
ago. Good women should be helped, not hindered by unneces-
sary competition.

Whatever there is will have to do. What had Kathryn Walsh
meant by that statement? It didn't sound like the offhand
remark of someone who had other prospects. What would a
girl like that do to make a living in a town like this? Professions
were limited for women. There were only a handful of children,
so no teacher was needed. The minister's wife taught the few
there were.

If Herr had known anything, Matthias would have heard
about it at the bar.

One thing Matthias knew for sure: City Walsh would never
have turned over his business to a young woman. He wondered
why City hadn't left everything to Scribe. The boy was as close to
a son as any boy could be. But then, City always had his reasons.

There was one possession of City's that Matthias wanted.
And he intended to buy it tomorrow. Finishing his bourbon,
Matthias set the glass on the table. "Let's get you checked in,
Henry. We can have dinner later and talk business tomorrow."

Matthias headed across the street to check on Scribe. The
boy answered on the second knock. The place was a worse mess
than Matthias had expected. Cleaning up the house might
prove too much for a girl who looked more accustomed to giving orders to servants than doing the work of one. Good. "Just
leave everything as it is and come on over. I have a room and
work for you."

"Thanks." Scribe sounded resigned rather than grateful.

"Did Miss Walsh say anything about your housekeeping
skills?"

"No. But she did say we're practically family."

The boy already had a crush on the girl. "Don't get your hopes up." Matthias opened the door and jerked his head. "Let's go, Lothario."

The south end of Calvada proved to be no better than the north. Kathryn had passed one saloon after another, though, thankfully, she also saw a mercantile, a grocer, a bathhouse, a dry goods store, an express office, a drugstore, a tin shop, and a meat market. Holding up her skirt, she picked her way across the muddy street to the Sanders Hotel. She grimaced as she scraped her high-button shoes before going inside. To her left was a bar, overshadowed by a huge picture of a woman wearing nothing but a provocative smile. Two young women sat beneath it, both dressed in shockingly revealing knee-high dresses with low-cut necklines. Face flaming, Kathryn quickly averted her eyes. For an instant she regretted not accepting Matthias Beck's offer of a room, and then assumed his establishment would be much the same as this one.

A young, bearded clerk stared speechless as she approached the front desk. "Do you have a room available, sir?"

"We do." He looked her over. "Three dollars a night. Another dollar for dinner." He turned the register and set out a quill and inkpot.

She was too tired and depressed to quibble about prices. "Do your accommodations have baths?"

"No, ma'am, but we can have a tub brought up. It'll take a while to heat the water to fill it, and it'll cost extra."

"How much extra?"

He looked her over again. "A dollar."

After a week on a train and three days in a stagecoach, she wanted a bath more than she wanted food. And short of using a public bathhouse in a town vastly overpopulated by men, what choice had she? As soon as Scribe moved out of her humble little home and she moved in, she'd buy a tub from the mercantile.

The clerk read her name. "Walsh!" His brows shot up. "Related to City Walsh?"

"His niece."

He laughed as though at some great joke. "City Walsh's niece staying here? Mr. Sanders will want you to have the best room in the house. He'll probably come down to welcome you to town." He nodded to his left. "Restaurant is right through those doors, but it won't open until six. Do you have luggage?" He snapped his fingers and a small, dark-skinned boy appeared and took her carpetbag.

The "best room in the house" had no fireplace—only a bed, dresser, kerosene lamp, and a chair by a window offering a less than inspiring view of Calvada's main street. She saw the boy dart across the street and run up the hill where there were several large houses in a row. Apparently, even Calvada had an affluent neighborhood. Drawing the curtains, Kathryn pulled up her skirt and petticoats, untied the ribbons, and removed her bustle. The misshapen cage looked beyond repair.

When the tub arrived, it was barely big enough for her to sit in. Two steaming buckets of water filled it halfway. Seeing no towel or soap, she went downstairs to ask for them. He charged her two bits for one coarse and dingy towel and ten cents for a much-used bar of unscented soap. The water was cold by the time she returned to the room. Teeth chattering, she stood in the tub and washed quickly. Somewhat refreshed, she changed into clean unmentionables, donned a skirt and shirtwaist. Even the stench from the street below failed to obliterate her hunger.

One well-dressed gentleman sat at a table tucked in the back corner. He rose as though he'd been waiting for her. "Miss Walsh, I'm Morgan Sanders. It would be an honor if you'd allow me to host you this evening." He drew a chair back for her.

Surprised at his presumption, she almost declined, but curiosity made her approach. He was as tall as Matthias Beck, not as well-muscled, closer to forty than thirty, with dark eyes and sandy-brown hair going gray at the temples. His self-confidence bordered on arrogance, reminding her of other handsome and younger men she'd met in Boston. She had rejected more than one marriage proposal because she found the attitude repugnant. "I was told you own this hotel and the Madera Mine."

"Yes, I do, as well as other businesses in town." His mouth tipped sardonically. "I heard you met Matthias Beck upon your arrival."

"It wasn't Mr. Beck who told me." She didn't mention Wiley as she allowed Sanders to seat her. "Do you treat every guest with such generosity?"

"No, I don't." A mere lift of his hand and a waiter appeared. "Champagne. On ice." He smiled at her as the waiter left. "In celebration of your arrival. City Walsh's niece. I can see the family resemblance. He was a well-respected man in our town." His expression grew solemn. "I am sorry for your loss. It must have been a great heartache for your family."

"I never met him." Nor had he been mentioned.

"An even greater loss, then."

"I gather he was your friend."

"More a friendly adversary than friend. We didn't always agree, but we respected one another. He considered himself a man of the people, and I own and operate a large mining operation, where I employ a hundred men. I also own a general store, as well as other lucrative enterprises. I probably reminded your uncle of the imperialistic Englishmen who hold supremacy in Ireland. City came to California in '49. I came later, in '65."

"Did you fight in the war?"

He hesitated. "No, but I supplied needed goods to the Union Army."

She sensed there was more to that statement. "You've accomplished a great deal here, Mr. Sanders."

"Yes, I have. Mostly through luck and skills I gained over time. And knowing what I want in life."

Kathryn had seen that same look before. Men always seemed to measure a woman's worth by her beauty.

"You are a very lovely young woman, Miss Walsh. I imagine you have been drawing quite a bit of attention since you stepped off the stage." The waiter returned, popped the cork from the champagne, and filled two crystal flutes with the sparkling wine before placing the bottle in a bucket of ice. A slight movement of Sanders's chin and the waiter left without a word. Sanders lifted his glass in a salute. "Welcome to Calvada, Miss Walsh."

"Thank you, sir." Cautious, she barely sipped.

"There isn't another woman like you in my town."

His town? "And what kind of woman do you think I am, Mr. Sanders?"

"A lady with class and breeding. Educated, most likely, accustomed to the finer things in life. Though I do wonder why a young woman would be sent unescorted to Calvada to claim an inheritance from an uncle she's never met."

For a stranger, he knew a great deal about her. She had no intention of adding more information. Her business was her business, after all.

He waited for a moment and then smiled. "Spirited, too. You have your uncle's red hair. Perhaps you share his passionate temperament." He raised a brow. "City had spirit and convictions, but not always good sense."

"Is that why he was murdered?"

Her question seemed to surprise him. He sipped his champagne. "No one knows why he was killed. His wasn't the first violent death in Calvada. Or the last, I'm afraid."

"Considering your business holdings, it would seem in your best interest to bring law and order here."

Sanders laughed. "City said the same thing. We're not Sacramento or Placerville, Miss Walsh. But we're not Bodie either. There aren't many men in these parts who want to be a sheriff. Law and order aren't popular among men in towns like ours. But justice tends to prevail."

"As I understand it, justice did not prevail in my uncle's case."

"Sad, but true." He summoned the waiter again and ordered the venison.

"I've never had venison before," Kathryn said, annoyed that he had made her choice for her. He said she'd enjoy it. His declaration sounded more an order than confidence in her taste.

The meal wasn't up to Hyland or Pershing standards, but more than adequate to satisfy her hunger. She even had a slice of cake for dessert. Morgan talked of many things, but deeply of none. Whenever he offered more champagne, she declined. By the end of the meal, he had finished the bottle, but it seemed to have little effect on him.

"This hardly seems a town suited to a lady of your sensibilities, Kathryn. I can offer you a fair price for City's holdings, if you're of a mind to leave."

And if she said yes, where would she go? Back to Truckee? On to Sacramento or San Francisco? God seemed to have plunked her down right here in the middle of this wild and woolly town. Perhaps Calvada was penance for making herself "a public disgrace" in her stepfather's eyes. It mattered not the righteousness of the cause that got her into so much trouble. If she could go back in time, would she have made the same choices?

Her mother was right. She was impetuous. She was passionate.

Lord, make me wise. Help me to learn to speak the truth in love, not in anger.

"Thank you for the offer, Mr. Sanders, but I'd like to know more about my uncle before I make any decisions." She wanted to know why Casey Teague Walsh had left everything to her mother, a woman who despised him.

Morgan Sanders rose. "In that case, I hope you and I will get to know one another better." He drew her chair back and saw her to the staircase, where he wished her a restful night.

The night proved anything but restful. The door to the room next to her opened and closed with regularity. Rain pelted the roof. Chilled, Kathryn snuggled deep into the blankets, pulling them up over her shoulders, and remembered the fireplace in her bedroom back home. One of the servants always had it lit early so the room was warm when Kathryn entered. No fireplace here. No comforting sounds of crackling warmth. When she did finally fall asleep, she dreamed she was clinging to the stagecoach door, dangling over a cliff.

3

THE SKY WAS DOVE GRAY, the air colder than the day before. A layer of ice lay over the mud, making Kathryn's crossing treacherous. The Bear's Head was empty. Women in humble attire were about town, a few with children trailing after them. It was a weekday and after nine. Was there no school?

Her uncle's door was ajar, male voices inside: Matthias Beck, Scribe, and another, unfamiliar. Kathryn tapped and waited.

Beck opened the door. "Doesn't look like you got much sleep last night, Miss Walsh."

Was he smirking? Kathryn stepped by him and entered the house, setting her carpetbag aside and focusing on Scribe as he filled a mug with steaming coffee.

Beck introduced Herr Neumann. The man's long, dark hair was wet, parted in the middle, and freshly combed. Pale, sweat beading his forehead, he looked miserable. "Sorry I wasn't at the stage to meet you yesterday, ma'am."

She extended her hand, hoping to diminish his embarrassment. "You didn't know the day or time I would arrive, Mr. Neumann. I didn't expect to see you there." The poor man was trembling. "I was told you were indisposed. I hope you're feeling better this morning."

He blushed. "I'm alive."

Scribe invited Kathryn to sit on the settee. He offered her the coffee, which she accepted. She hesitated when she looked into the dark liquid. Doubting he had milk or sugar, she took a tentative sip. The brew was strong enough to melt a rock. She held the mug lightly on her knees, thankful for the warmth soaking through her skirt and layers of petticoats.

Beck leaned on her uncle's desk and crossed his arms, watching her.

"There's no need for you to stay, Mr. Beck. I'm sure you have business to conduct elsewhere."

"My business can wait."

The man couldn't take a hint. "I'll wait to discuss mine until you leave."

"I want to buy the press."

She stared at him blankly. "What press?"

"The one in your back corner, covered with a tarp."

She looked at the mound and back at him, then at Scribe, questions rising like a storm. No one seemed eager to enlighten her.

"You have no use for it," Beck told her.

Annoyed and curious, Kathryn set her coffee aside and stood, intending to uncover whatever was hidden beneath that tarp. "I won't know what I will or won't have use for until I have time to—"

"You don't belong here, Miss Walsh."

Turning, Kathryn glared at him. She was sick of men telling her where she belonged and what she should do with her life. The judge had been the first, followed by suitors who seemed to have her life all planned out for her.

"You're not the first man to tell me that, Mr. Beck. And you probably won't be the last." She walked to the door and opened it. "I wish you good day, sir."

Matthias Beck didn't move. Nor did she. After a moment, he straightened, walked to the door, and stood looking down at her, eyes blazing. "We aren't done."

Her pulse quickened. "Oh, indeed, we are." Why was it so hard to breathe when this man looked at her?

"Don't bet on it."

She closed the door and faced Scribe and Herr, both standing like statues in the small room. "Now, Mr. Neumann, I'd like to know whatever you can tell me about my uncle and what he might have had in mind when he named my mother as recipient of his estate."

He blanched. "Your mother?"

"The inheritance has been signed over to me for reasons I'd rather not discuss." She sat and folded her hands in her lap. "What did he hope would be done with his property?" If he'd known her mother, he would never have expected her to cross the country to this stinking mudhole they called a town.

Neumann stared at her, bug-eyed. "He didn't say. Just gave me an envelope and said to send it if anything happened to him. Something happened. I sent it with a few instructions. That's it."

"The last contact my mother had with my uncle was before

I was born and through a letter informing her that my father, his brother, had drowned in the Missouri River on his way to the California goldfields. Not a word after that."

Scribe shrugged. "Only talked about a brother once that I recall. And he was drunk and maudlin and not making much sense."

The more Kathryn learned, the less optimistic she felt. "So this building and the press are my inheritance?"

"And a mine up in the hills," Neumann added. "City did just enough work to keep the claim active."

"I forgot there was a mine." Scribe scratched his head. "He hadn't been up there for weeks."

"A mine?" Kathryn smiled, hopeful. "Is it worth anything?"

"Doubtful, Miss Walsh. City never said much about it. Just disappeared for a few days every couple of weeks, usually when he'd stirred up trouble. Probably not worth much, if anything. He must have information in his files somewhere." Neumann waved a hand at the apple crates filled with papers. He inched toward the door. "Wish I could tell you more, Miss Walsh." Reaching behind him, he opened the door and was outside before Kathryn could ask further questions. "Good luck to you." He put on his hat and headed straight for Beck's Saloon.

Kathryn sniffed. "He's very nervous for a man who knows nothing."

"You're a lady. That's enough to make the strongest man in these parts sweat bullets."

Matthias Beck hadn't been sweating. She'd barely walked in the door when he started picking a fight with her. Who did he think he was to tell her where she did or didn't belong?

Kathryn went to the back corner and pulled the tarp away to see what Beck wanted so much. A black behemoth of a machine lay beneath.

"It's a Washington handpress," Scribe told her. "Came around the Horn twenty-five years ago. Don't know how City got his hands on it."

Surprised, Kathryn looked around again. "This was a newspaper office?"

"Home of the *Calvada Voice*. Everyone in town waited for it to come out. City was always digging up something, pulling people's tails. He butted heads with almost everyone in town, including Matthias. But they were friends. City spent a lot of time at Beck's, picking his brain about the war."

Kathryn sniffed. "I imagine Mr. Beck fought for the South." His Southern drawl would have been charming if the man wasn't so annoying.

"Nope. Matthias fought for the North." Scribe half sat on the desk the same way Beck had. "He doesn't like talking about the war." He looked around. "City taught me how to set type and keep the press clean and inked. He wrote some scathing editorials. Always held to the truth. He wouldn't bend a principle no matter what it cost. I figure that's what got someone mad enough to come in here and beat him to death with the press handle."

Shuddering, Kathryn walked around the room, noticing the rust-colored stain that had soaked into the wood. Had City Walsh given the inheritance papers to Herr Neumann because he knew something was going to happen? Did he hope someone in his family might care enough to come and find out why he'd been killed and by whom? But there had been nothing in Herr's cover letter to indicate Casey Teague Walsh had met with a violent end.

Scribe sighed. "I'll get out of your hair so you can do whatever you want with the place."

Kathryn glanced at him. "Did Mr. Beck give you lodgings?"

"Yep. I have a room in the back and a job cleaning up." He looked around the office again, crestfallen. "I loved every minute working for City. He was . . ." His voice broke. He cleared it. "Better get going."

"Is my uncle the one who gave you the name Scribe?"

"My given name is Rupert Clive Fitz-William Smythe." He made a sour face. "City said it sounded as stiff as a carcass and started calling me Scribe. The name stuck."

"I'm sorry my uncle didn't leave something to you." But if he had, where might the judge have sent her? On an extended tour of Europe? More likely, he'd have sent her back to his spinster sister in New Hampshire. He'd done it once before as punishment for being expelled from boarding school.

"City always had reasons for what he did." Scribe shrugged. "And the truth is, I can set type, but I can't write the way he did." He picked up a box with his things in it. "Matthias is right, you know."

"About what?"

"Much as I hate to say it, you're too much of a lady to live in a town like this."

She thought he might be right. She didn't feel at home in Calvada, but then, she'd never felt at home in Boston either. "God works in mysterious ways." She smiled. "I'm here. I intend to make the best of it."

Before Scribe left the office, Kathryn asked him to recommend a good and inexpensive place to eat. Ronya's Café was down a few doors and across the street on the south corner. A sign stood outside: *Scrape Your Boots!* She did as instructed, dismayed by the muck that had stained the hem of her skirt.

The door opened. "Come in, Miss Walsh." A robust woman in a gingham dress and full apron stood on the threshold, her blue eyes sparkling, her graying-blonde hair braided and coiled into a crown on her head.

"You know my name," Kathryn said in surprise.

"Word spreads fast in Calvada. I'm Ronya Vanderstrom. City was a good friend. Ate breakfast and dinner here every day." Her handshake wasn't a light, polite gesture, but the firm grip of promised friendship. "I've saved a table near the stove. Make yourself comfortable."

Men occupied every table, and all of them stared when Kathryn entered. Ronya sailed between tables. "Mind your manners, gents." The men went back to eating their meals. The limited menu was written on a chalkboard. "What can I get you, Miss Walsh?"

"The miner's plate, please."

Ronya chuckled. "A young lady with an appetite."

As soon as Ronya disappeared into the kitchen, the men took surreptitious glances at Kathryn. She supposed she'd get used to the attention. One man stood and approached her table, hat in hand. Self-conscious, she looked up. He introduced himself, said he had a good claim, a sturdy cabin not far from town, and needed a wife. A chair scraped back as another man hurried over. He owned the butcher shop down the street and had a nice little house on Rome Street with a backyard big enough for a vegetable garden. When a third man pressed between the other two, loudly listing his assets, Kathryn felt trapped between the hot stove and the even hotter men blocking her escape through the front door.

Ronya appeared, a frying pan in one hand and a metal spoon in the other. She hit the pot several times. "Let's have done with this! Miss Walsh, are you looking for a husband?"

"No, I am not!"

"Well, there you are, gents. You got your answer. Now leave the girl be! Eat up, pay up, and go back to work!" Ronya went back into the kitchen.

Kathryn hastened after her. "Do you mind if I keep you company in here?"

"They don't mean you any harm."

Nervous, she glanced over her shoulder. "They seem rather desperate."

"We're short on women in Calvada. Miners' wives and widows mostly, and the other kind that keep to themselves. Nothing in between." She nodded toward a stool and went back to cracking eggs into a bowl with one hand while turning bacon with the other. "They see a pretty young lady like you and get a fire in their bellies for hearth and home."

"The last thing I want to do is get married."

Ronya looked at her. "Not to one of those roughnecks, anyway."

"Not to anyone. A woman has more rights without a husband."

"And sometimes fewer opportunities." She gave Kathryn a steady look before pouring whipped eggs into a frying pan. Bacon sizzled on the grill, making Kathryn's stomach clench with hunger. Taking a mug from a high shelf, Ronya set it in front of Kathryn and filled it with steaming, aromatic coffee.

Thanking her, Kathryn sipped, and almost moaned in pleasure. "How long have you been here, Mrs. Vanderstrom?"

"Call me Ronya. Everyone does." She scooped flour into a bowl. "I've been in California since '49. Came west by wagon train with my husband. Bernard was a good man, but didn't have a lick of sense. Neither did I, come to think of it." She chuckled as she stirred the eggs. "Bernard heard California had tropical heat, so he stocked up on panama hats and mosquito nets." She shook her head. "About as useful as a tick on a dog. With nothing worth selling, he worked the streams like everyone else, and died of fever the first winter."

Spreading bacon grease, she poured pancake batter onto the grill. "I had a Conestoga wagon, a Dutch oven, a frying pan, and enough money squirreled away to buy supplies. I know how to cook, and there were plenty of hungry men. Still are." She nodded toward the dining room. "I made enough money the first year to build a two-bedroom house. That one burned down, along with the rest of the town. We all rebuilt, but after the second fire, I moved on. Heard about a strike up here. Hoping for better luck this time." She set the eggs aside and watched the pancakes. "Filled one room with bunk beds and rented sleeping space. Charged extra for meals. Added another room, then a second floor." She flipped pancakes. "When the work got to be too much, I hired a widow. When she got married, I hired another." She laughed. "Widows don't stay single long in this town."

Ronya scooped eggs onto a plate, slid two pancakes beside them, and added four strips of crispy bacon. Setting the meal on the counter in front of Kathryn, she slid over a plate of butter, a small pitcher of blackberry syrup, and salt- and pepper shakers. She smiled as she refilled Kathryn's mug. "Do you have any skills?"

"I'm good at making trouble."

Ronya chuckled. "So was your uncle." She nodded toward the plate. "Eat hearty and give my house a good name." She lifted her chin. "I'd better check on the gents." She took the large pot of coffee into the dining room.

Kathryn sighed. What skills did she have that would do her any good here at the end of the world? What goods and services did this town lack that she could provide? She hadn't seen a single business catering to women's needs. She knew fashion trends back East, but would they be appropriate out here in the Wild West? Her mother had insisted she learn the feminine arts: fine needlework, how to play the pianoforte, how to organize and host a dinner party. She knew how to sew, though her own clothing had been made by a seamstress. The thought of spending the rest of her life at such activities gave Kathryn a headache.

Her stepfather had done his best to marry her off to the scion of a manufacturing family, but Kathryn thought Frederick Taylor Underhill was an arrogant toad who cared nothing about the women and children who worked in his father's factories. When she refused his proposal, the judge had been apoplectic.

That misdeed was merely one more added to the list of things the judge held against her.

Kathryn paid extra for the breakfast and thanked Ronya for allowing her to sit in the kitchen, then headed for Aday's General Store for supplies. She was delighted to see the homey treasure trove on display. Barrels of flour, sacks of beans, and laddered shelves laden with goods of every kind were before her. Tables filled the store—blankets on one, men's flannel shirts and dungarees on another. A glass case held a collection of knives; another, guns. Maybe she should buy a small derringer.

A thin woman in a plain brown woolen dress stood behind the counter, her hair bound beneath a handkerchief. She watched Kathryn move around the store, eyes fixed on her blue dress with matching peplum jacket and hat with lace and silk flowers. Wiping her apron, she greeted Kathryn and introduced herself as Abbie Aday. When Kathryn reciprocated, the woman sucked in her breath and called out, "Nabor! Come quick! City's niece is here!"

"Thought he didn't have any family." An angular man with a hard face and spectacles came through the back curtain. His eyes shot wide as they swept over her. "You're related to City?" Kathryn knew she was overdressed for Calvada, but there was no help for it. Everything she owned was too grand for this town. Abbie stared at her hat with blissful admiration, Nabor with open disapproval.

"I have a list of things I need." Kathryn handed the list to Abbie.

Nabor snatched it from her. "Cleaning supplies, white paint, sheets, two blankets, fabric, canned goods, a can opener . . ."

Hearing it read aloud made Kathryn wonder how much it all would cost. The envelope of money her stepfather had given her would have to last long enough for her to find an occupation.

Nabor Aday had a calculating gleam in his eyes. He thrust the list at his wife. "Call me when everything is collected, and I'll handle the rest." He disappeared behind the curtain while Abbie Aday collected and stacked items on the counter.

"Your hat is so lovely, Miss Walsh. We haven't seen anything like that around here."

Kathryn heard Nabor snort from behind the curtain.

"It was made in Boston."

"Boston." Abbie sighed, a dreamy look on her face. "We came from—"

"Stop talking, Abbie, and get to work!" Nabor called out to her.

Kathryn leaned closer. "It would be quite easy to make, with the right materials."

"Really? Could you? We don't have a millinery in town."

Her expression brightened. "We may not have what you need right now, but we can order it from Sacramento. I'd be your first customer." She beamed.

Nabor appeared, brow furrowed in anger. "No, you won't. What does any woman need with a hat like that?" He picked up the list. "Get the can of white paint and the cleaning supplies. I'll get a wheelbarrow."

"She doesn't want a wheelbarrow, Nabor."

He looked over his shoulder in disgust. "We'll need one to deliver the goods. Unless you think you can carry it all for her."

Abbie lowered her head and then looked up at Kathryn again. "We all miss City. Everyone loved his newspaper. Now all we have is Stu Bickerson's *Clarion*. He's down Champs-Élysées on the corner of Rome."

"Champs-Élysées?" Kathryn gave a soft laugh.

"Your uncle named our streets after foreign places. Of course, Champs-Élysées is more commonly known as Chump Street."

Kathryn did laugh then, and Nabor turned to glare at them.

Abbie escorted her to the bolts of cloth, and Kathryn made her selection. "Do you have any books, Abbie?"

"A few. City always had a book in his hands. He must have dozens."

Kathryn had been delighted to see the number in his collection. "Yes, but unfortunately, not what I need."

"What sort of book are you looking for?"

Blushing, Kathryn lowered her voice. "Anything on cooking, housekeeping, that sort of thing."

Abbie's gaze swept over her in a telling way. "Of course." She wove between tables. "We don't get many requests for books. Ah, here they are." She pulled a box from beneath a display table. "How about a nickel?" At that price, Kathryn wanted the entire boxful. *Leave the beans,* she wanted to say. *I'll take the books*, but knew she must be practical. While coveting Homer's *Odyssey* and Whitman's *Leaves of Grass*, Kathryn pulled out *A Treatise on Domestic Economy* by Catharine Beecher. Leafing through, she saw it held much-needed information from cooking, cleaning, and plant propagation to heating, ventilation, and waste management. Calvada could certainly do with some waste management! Snapping the book shut, she tucked it under her arm and pulled out *The Practical Housekeeper: A Cyclopedia of Domestic Economy*.

When Abbie had finished gathering all the goods and stacking them on the counter, Nabor took over tallying the prices.

"You doubled the price of the books, Mr. Aday. Abbie said one nickel for each."

"Abbie doesn't set the prices. I do. And it'll cost you another dollar to have everything delivered, unless you want to make a few trips yourself."

Furious, Kathryn paid him what he said she owed.

Nabor stayed behind to "manage the store" while Abbie pushed one wheelbarrow and a boy Nabor had drafted for ten cents pushed the other. On the way back to City's house, Kathryn stuck her head in the stage station door and asked Gus Blather, the station manager, to have her trunk delivered as soon as possible. He put it on a hand truck and followed. Men came out of saloons to watch the parade. Some joined in, one being gentleman enough to take over for Abbie when her wheelbarrow got stuck in the mud. Others traipsed behind, talking among themselves. Matthias Beck came through the swinging doors of his saloon and leaned against a front post, arms crossed, watching.

Opening the door of the humble little house she intended

to make a home, Kathryn sailed in, followed by Abbie, the boy, and Gus Blather. Kathryn thanked each one and whispered to Abbie that she would make her a hat as a gift. As they left, half a dozen men peered inside. Kathryn closed the door firmly and threw the bolt. One man tried to rub dirt off one of the windows to peer in. Kathryn decided not to wash them until she had shades and curtains.

Standing in the middle of the front office, arms akimbo, Kathryn calculated the work ahead. She'd never actually cleaned a room, let alone two, but knew how it was done. She took the bucket and went out the back door, Abbie having told her where the closest community well was located.

By midday, the whalebone stays in her corset felt like a torture device. She brushed tendrils of damp hair from her face and went back to scrubbing the front room floor. The bloodstain was there to stay. She would buy a rug to cover it. She'd already emptied the potbellied stove of ashes and refilled it with wood she'd found stacked neatly outside the back door. She hadn't lit it. The work kept her warm enough. She'd made half a dozen trips to the well, feet sore from the tight, button-up shoes caked with mud. The shoes were ruined, and the weight of the heavy mud left her legs aching. She emptied the cabinets and armoire and washed the shelves before arranging her supplies and unpacking her clothing. The Adays didn't have a bathtub for sale, but Kathryn did find a laundry washbasin big enough to serve that purpose, as well as several others. She would be washing her own clothes from now on.

By sundown, Kathryn hadn't yet finished. She wasn't presentable enough to cross the street to Ronya's Café for dinner. Washing up would mean another trip to the well. She would have to start the fire and heat the water. She would have to take down, brush, and put up her hair and dress in clean clothes. She was too tired to do any of those things, too tired to make the bed, and so dirty she didn't want to use her new sheets.

Numb with fatigue, hands raw from scrubbing, every muscle in her body aching, she sank down on the edge of the bed. Falling back, arms spread, she went to sleep.

4

MATTHIAS CORNERED SCRIBE, grudging concern for Kathryn Walsh eating away at his concentration on more important projects. "Have you seen City's niece?" He hadn't seen her out of that house in two days, though he'd heard she'd made numerous trips to the community well. That girl toting water? Hard to imagine. All she'd have to do was ask the first able-bodied man she met, and she'd have a line of them doing her bidding. Ronya told him Kathryn Walsh had received three proposals within five minutes of walking into her café.

"A butcher, a baker, and a candlestick maker." Ronya had chuckled. "All after her like bears to honey. She hid out in my kitchen. She said she has no plans to marry."

"She sat in your kitchen." The girl looked more the kind to expect a private room and personal servant.

"Sat at my worktable and visited while I cooked. She had the miner's plate and a couple cups of coffee. What's your interest in the girl, Matthias?" Ronya's mouth curved into a knowing smile.

"All I want from her is City's Washington handpress."

"Is that so?"

Since he'd been one of City's closest friends, it fell to him to keep an eye on her. The sooner she left Calvada, the sooner he could relax his vigil.

Scribe stopped sweeping the boardwalk and looked across the street like a puppy wanting to go home. "I saw Miss Kathryn yesterday. I told her I'd look in on her and make sure she was all right. I went over three times, but she wouldn't open the door."

"Why not?"

"She said she wasn't presentable. She was in the middle of something."

"In the middle of what?"

"Cleaning the house, I guess."

For two days? Two rooms in a fourteen-by-twenty? What kind of cleaning took that long?

Scribe set his broom aside. "I'll go over—"

Matthias shot a look at the lovesick lad. "Guard your heart, kid. Pretty is as pretty does. Besides, she's older than you."

Scribe stiffened. "I'll be seventeen next month."

Matthias didn't think Kathryn Walsh was much older than early twenties. She had that fresh, dewy, untouched look about her, something she'd lose quickly enough if she stayed in Calvada.

Matthias stepped off the boardwalk and headed across the street. Stamping mud off his boots, he rapped on Kathryn's door. It opened a few inches, and he got a look at her with her red hair covered, dirt and paint smudging her cheeks. She was wearing a full apron and white gloves, the kind rich girls wore to the opera.

"Oh. It's you."

Her tone riled him. "Yes. It's me. Checking to see if you're alive."

"Now that you know I am, you can go."

"Not so fast."

"I have work to do."

His mind scrambled for an excuse to linger and fixed on one. "What do you want for the press?" Her hold had relaxed enough for him to push the door open and get a peek inside. "What in blazes are you doing?"

Letting go of the door, she waved him in. "Come in, Mr. Beck. Satisfy your curiosity and then go."

City's front office was a white blur. The familiar scents of male sweat, whiskey, and tobacco had been replaced by the strong smell of whitewash paint. The old, battered oak desk had been cleared of the habitual piles of papers and polished. Three books lay open on its surface. He recognized a Bible, noticing underlining and notes in the margins. Kathryn closed the two others quickly and shoved them into a desk drawer before he could read the titles. The overflowing boxes of past issues of the *Calvada Voice* had been tidied and stacked neatly near the back wall.

"You've looked at everything but the press, Mr. Beck."

She'd covered it with flowery gingham and perched two hats, ribboned and plumed, on top, along with other feminine items: a white silk shirtwaist, a blue satin and lace dress suitable for a ball, a pair of high-button shoes, two pairs of gloves like the pair she wore, a pair of lace-trimmed bloomers, and a bustle.

"Since I can't move the press, I must make use of it."

"As a display table?" He wanted to throttle her. "Your uncle is writhing in his grave. I can get a crew and move it out of here in the next hour."

"It stays right where it is." She gave him a cloying smile. "I think it's serving a good purpose."

Matthias came closer. She stood her ground, but he saw a faint flush rise in her cheeks. "And all because I punched Toby in the street and gave him a much-needed dunking in the trough."

She looked up and drew in a soft breath. Mouth pressing tight, she tipped her chin. "I'm not that petty, Mr. Beck."

Her eyes reminded him of the new growth on spring pines. "Are you really selling those things you've put out?"

"Are you in need of a pair of bloomers?"

"What do you suppose people would say if I walked out of here with that pair wrapped around my neck?" When her eyes widened in alarm, he took pity. "Don't worry. I won't."

"There's no shop for ladies in town."

Because there weren't many ladies, but he held back saying so. The few that were in Calvada couldn't afford to wear silk and satin, or fancy hats.

"Abbie liked my hat."

Defensive. "Nabor wouldn't give her a dime to spend on a hat with feathers and flowers on it."

She looked troubled. "Well, I hope he will allow her to keep the one I gave her." She surveyed her display. "I'll do my best to offer something not already on sale, though I suppose the women's needs and desires in Calvada run deeper than what I have to offer." She walked back to her paint bucket.

"Meaning what?"

"Nothing that would interest you, I'm sure."

"Try me."

"I could make you a list, and I've only seen what's on . . . What is the main street called? Champs-Élysées?" She laughed.

"Your uncle named it."

"And Rome and Paris and—"

"Gomorrah." He hadn't meant to blurt that out.

She blinked, a frown appearing briefly before she stared at him coolly. "I think Chump Street fits better."

Someone tapped on the door. "Miss Kathryn?" Scribe peered in. He shot a dark glance at Matthias before he entered. "I just wanted to make sure you were all right."

Matthias gave a soft snort. What did the kid think he was doing? Molesting her? He gave Kathryn a wry look. "It seems you have a protector, your ladyship."

"I can bring in some more firewood, Miss Kathryn. Maybe light your fire."

Matthias rolled his eyes.

"It's already lit." She glared at Matthias. "But thank you for being such a gentleman, Scribe."

"Anything you need, anytime . . ."

Annoyed, Matthias jerked his head toward the door. "You already have a job. Get to it."

"I finished sweeping."

"Then wash shot glasses." When the boy didn't move, Matthias took a step in his direction. "Now, Scribe. You're on my payroll."

Scribe left the door half-open on his way out, glancing over his shoulder as he headed back to the saloon.

Kathryn sighed, clearly aware of the boy's affections. She looked concerned, not flattered. "Thank you, Mr. Beck."

"For chasing him out of here?"

"For putting a roof over his head and giving him a job."

"I always keep my word."

Kathryn studied him, and he found himself wondering what she thought. First impressions were hard to overcome. "How about you, Miss Walsh?"

"What about me?"

He felt himself slipping into deep water. Why had he come over here? He remembered the reason he'd given. "Will you promise to let me know when you're ready to sell the press?"

"You'll know when I've made my decision." She smoothed down her apron. "Thank you for checking on me, Mr. Beck. As you can see, all is well. Good day."

It was the second time she'd dismissed him, and he didn't like it. "You need checking on, Miss Walsh."

"I'm old enough to take care of myself, sir."

Sir. How old did she think he was? He moved closer and heard the quick intake of breath. Grinning, he slipped an arm around her waist and pulled her close. "Still think so?" When he leaned down, she ducked and twisted free and moved behind the desk. She pointed at the open door, but seemed to have lost her power of speech.

"Close the door?" He mocked. "I think we should leave it wide-open for propriety's sake."

"Out!" she croaked.

Sorry he had followed through on an impulse, he strove to be serious. "It's not a bad thing to have people know you and I are becoming friends." Men might leave her alone if they knew he had his eye on her.

"Is that what you're doing, Mr. Beck? Making friends?" Her cheeks were red, her eyes green fire. "Are you going to go, or do I have to scream?"

"That would bring a crowd. And bets as to how far I'd gotten." She looked so flustered, he took pity. "We have business to discuss."

Brushing a few strands of red hair from her forehead, she came around the desk and dipped her brush into the can of white paint. If he approached again, he knew what to expect.

"Why don't you take off the apron and headscarf and let me take you to lunch at Ronya's?" Ronya said she hadn't seen Kathryn since yesterday. The girl had to eat.

"I've already had oatmeal."

"*You* cooked?" Matthias opened the desk drawer and pulled out the books she'd hidden. "Ahhh." He chuckled. "Learning how to fend for yourself. Is that it, Miss Walsh?"

"It seems the wise thing to do." She kept an eye on him, using meticulous strokes on the board that was already coated. "Don't you have better things to do than sit and watch me paint a wall?"

He smiled, leaned back, and made himself comfortable. He let his gaze move over her at leisure. "You're going to need a bath."

Sucking in a shocked breath, she glared at him. "Thank you for telling me I stink!"

"Typical female, putting words in a man's mouth. I didn't say you stank." Her look told him to stop talking. "I'm sure you're still gritty from the stagecoach ride. And you've been cleaning up this place since you moved in. It's a reasonable assumption you'd want—"

"Are you always this offensive?"

Oh, that high tone, and all because he was trying to explain he hadn't meant to insult her. "I'll bet you had a nice bath every day back in Boston. Probably used scented soap, too."

"I have a washtub now and know where to get water. And Scribe, young gentleman that he is, has provided me with the firewood to heat it." She slapped more paint on the wall. "And there's always the bathhouse down the street."

That idea needed to be killed right now. "Oh, yes. You can go there. You'll have the privacy of a canvas partition between you and your tub mates. About twenty men, I would guess."

That got her full attention. "No walls?"

Feeling a twinge of regret for tormenting her, Matthias stood. "Outer only." He'd said more than enough to get the point across. "Sell me the press, Kathryn. Just go home where you belong."

Her expression changed. "I am home, Mr. Beck." She wiped her cheek with the back of her gloved hand, leaving a smear of paint on that smooth porcelain skin. "And just because a man wants something doesn't mean he gets it."

"Do you want to bet on that, your ladyship?"

Kathryn stripped off the gloves and tossed them into the empty paint can. "The press is not for sale."

"Everything has a price."

She lifted her head and arched a brow. "Do you want to bet on *that*?" Her eyes glittered with temper. "A press is a very powerful weapon. I wouldn't want to sell it to a man who might use it for purposes other than what is right and good. Is that clear enough, Lord Bacchus?"

Matthias's heart pounded for battle. "There's nothing worse than a self-righteous girl in a snit."

She gave him a pained smile. "Men always resort to insults when they lose an argument."

Matthias left before he said anything he'd regret.

The more work Kathryn did on her little house on Chump Street, the more she felt at home. She washed her hair and bathed in the washtub Saturday night in preparation for Sunday morning worship services. She knew people would notice her and wanted to dress as simply as she could so she wouldn't cause a stir.

The Calvada Community Church was up the hill at the end of Rome Street. The mountains loomed behind, covered with pine trees. Kathryn breathed in the scent and filled her lungs with the crisp late fall air. Snow covered the peaks and would soon be covering the town.

Surprised to find the service had already started, she slipped into the back row behind six women. There were a few other women closer to the front, with husbands and children. One of the ladies in front of her glanced back. Kathryn smiled, but the young woman turned around quickly and whispered to the lady on her right, who whispered to the next. An older woman dressed in black leaned over and gave the young women a reproving look, then glanced back at Kathryn.

Her eyes flickered in surprise. Shaking her head, she frowned and waved in a way that told Kathryn to move forward.

The last thing Kathryn wanted to do was draw more attention to herself. She whispered, "Thank you, but I'm fine right here." She could see and hear Reverend Thacker clearly.

The woman turned her back and didn't look at Kathryn again. She whispered something to the young woman beside her. Whatever she'd said was passed along to the other five women. The women rose when it was time to sing a hymn and sat in perfect unison when it ended. When the service ended, Kathryn stood, hoping to introduce herself, but the six women quickly filed out of the church without a single glance her way. Kathryn frowned. Was she being snubbed? What on earth had she done wrong?

Reverend Thacker and his wife passed by her and stood at the door to greet parishioners on their way out. Both welcomed Kathryn and asked if they might come to call. She said she'd be

pleased to have them do so. Others greeted her out front. Abbie
Aday approached, beaming, her hand touching the hat Kathryn
had given her. "It looks wonderful on you, Abbie."

Nabor looked annoyed. "We have no time to dawdle." He
took his wife by the elbow and steered her toward the gate.

Abbie glanced back over her shoulder. "You look lovely,
Kathryn." Her eyes moved over Kathryn's russet dress in admiration. Wincing, she turned away again.

Henry Call greeted Kathryn. "You're looking well. Matthias
said you've done quite a bit of work on your new home."

Nothing of which Mr. Beck would approve, she could have
said. "It's so nice to see you again." Matthias Beck was notice-
ably absent, but Morgan Sanders was in attendance. The mine
owner smiled and gave her a nod. She returned the acknowledg-
ment before addressing Henry. "Is your business going well?"

Call looked from her to Morgan Sanders and back. "As
well as can be expected. Some things take time." He hesitated.
"You've met Morgan Sanders, I hear."

"He invited me to dinner when I stayed at his hotel." Her
skin prickled uncomfortably. She had the uncanny feeling
Sanders's attention was fixed on her despite his ongoing conversation with several men. "I've been busy cleaning and organizing my little house. I plan to use the front office as a shop
for ladies." She walked out through the gate, Henry at her side.

On the way down the hill into town, Henry talked about
their stagecoach ride with Cussler and Wiley. Kathryn laughed,
enjoying his easy manner. They parted at the corner of Rome
and Chump Street, Kathryn heading to Ronya's, Henry back
to Beck's Hotel. She'd been eating oatmeal for three days and
longed for another miner's plate.

The café was packed. All conversation stopped when she
entered. A woman came from the kitchen with two plates piled

high with flapjacks. She glanced at Kathryn in surprise and set the plates down before two men who barely noticed them. Kathryn followed her into the kitchen and greeted Ronya. "May I join you ladies?"

Ronya laughed as she flipped pancakes. "Charlotte, this is Kathryn Walsh, City Walsh's niece. Kathryn, meet Charlotte, my new helper. Sit." She pointed the spatula at a stool by the worktable. "You look mighty grand this morning, Kathryn. How was church?" She didn't ask what Kathryn wanted to eat, but started filling a plate with scrambled eggs, bacon, and pancakes. She grinned at Charlotte. "This girl has an appetite."

"Reverend Thacker is a fine speaker." Kathryn admired Ronya's swift efficiency. Charlotte picked up two more plates and headed into the dining room. "You have a full house this morning. Can I help?"

"You?" Ronya sounded shocked. "Are you asking for a job?"

Kathryn considered. "Could I work for meals?"

Ronya studied her seriously. "Eat first. Then you can pitch in." She slid the loaded plate across to her, took a mug from a hook, and filled it with hot coffee. "Where have you been eating the last few days?"

"At home. Oatmeal." Kathryn grimaced. "I'm sure I could learn a great deal about cooking by working for you."

Charlotte set dirty plates on the counter near the wash pan. "Why would you work here?" She swept Kathryn's expensive ensemble with knowing eyes. "You come from wealth."

"I was an unwelcome encumbrance to my stepfather, and my mother told me her life would be much easier without me."

Both women stared at her, and Kathryn blushed, embarrassed that she had made such a slip of the tongue. "I'm wearing the remnants of my old life." She shrugged. "I wasn't sent away completely empty-handed. There is the inheritance."

"Worth barely anything," Ronya said, clearly disturbed by what Kathryn had revealed.

"My stepfather gave me money enough to support myself for a few months, if I'm frugal."

Ronya and Charlotte exchanged a look, before Charlotte spoke. "You could take your pick of any man in Calvada, Miss Walsh. Everyone is talking about you and Morgan Sanders."

"What?" Kathryn blanched. "I had dinner with the man once, and it was more a summons than an invitation."

"You'd better be careful with that man," Ronya told her.

"He owns most of the town." Charlotte sat on a stool and wiped her forehead.

Kathryn waved her hand airily. "He told me."

"So what will you do?"

"She's going to try opening a shop for ladies," Ronya told Charlotte. "Hats and unmentionables. We'll see how that goes." She chuckled. "Matthias told me. He's been eating in my café since he came to town. It seems you have the interest of two important men in Calvada."

Kathryn sniffed. "He wants to buy my uncle's press."

"Why not sell? You have no use for it."

"And he does?"

Charlotte tucked a wayward strand of hair back in her chignon. "Sure, he does. Stu Bickerson won't give him a line of print."

"Who's Stu Bickerson?"

"Editor of the *Clarion*. Morgan Sanders has him in his back pocket. Only seems fair Mr. Beck has a way to print his opinions and ideas on how to run this town."

"Run this town?" Kathryn laughed. "What's he doing? Running for mayor?"

"Not unless the men gain some guts," Ronya told her. "Right now, they're afraid of Sanders."

Kathryn couldn't believe these two women thought Matthias Beck would make a good mayor. Even so, she had her own opinions about certain things. "A newspaper should be neutral, presenting facts rather than taking sides."

Ronya gave her a wry look. "Is that how it's done in Boston?" She added seasoning to the bubbling pot of beans on the back of the big iron stove.

She sighed. "No." She'd read the blistering articles written about the suffragettes. "But one can wish." Elizabeth Cady Stanton and Susan B. Anthony had been called traitors to the natural order of God's creation. One editorial labeled their followers as "harpies"; another said they were unnatural, unfeminine, a disgrace to their sex. Many women shared that same point of view. Kathryn's own mother had ordered her never again to attend another meeting. Of course she hadn't listened. Perhaps if she hadn't lost her temper and tried to speak up at that last rally, she might still be living in Boston.

Everything had happened so fast that day. Two men had seized her like bailiffs grabbing a criminal and taken her by carriage to the front gate of the Hyland-Pershing estate. Judge Lawrence Pershing had been waiting. He had had her followed.

"And she's a public disgrace just like her father," the judge had railed at Kathryn's mother, "joining up with Susan B. Anthony and her crones, showing up at that rally, and making a scene." He'd snatched a newspaper and shaken it like a dog killing a rat. "It's all right here in the *New York Tribune*! If not for my connections, her name would be mentioned." He threw the newspaper at Kathryn. "Are you proud of yourself? Word will spread of this latest escapade. Your reputation is ruined."

Women's suffrage an escapade? Her reputation ruined? Kathryn regretted her impetuous behavior, not because she felt in the wrong, but rather that her attempt had gained nothing, certainly not the respectful hearing those women were due.

Ronya put the lid on the large iron pot. "Your uncle printed truth and look what happened to him."

Leaving Ronya's, Kathryn decided to head back up Rome toward the church. She hadn't been to the cemetery to pay her respects to her uncle. She had been so consumed with getting the little house in order that she hadn't thought of it until she saw the graveyard near the church this morning.

Simple crosses marked most graves. One large stone bore the names of men lost in a mining accident, dated October 13, 1872. Another farther on listed five more lost the previous year. Kathryn continued searching for Casey Teague Walsh's grave.

"Miss Walsh." Sally Thacker came toward her, a shawl wrapped around her shoulders. "I saw you from the parsonage. Can I help you?"

"I'm looking for my uncle's grave."

"It's over there." She pointed toward a grave off by itself, at the edge of the fenced-in boundary. "He was Catholic, you see. They usually have their own cemetery, but . . ." She left the rest unsaid.

"Did you hold a service for him?"

"Not in church, and only a few came up here when he was buried. The rest gathered at Beck's Saloon for a celebration."

Shocked, Kathryn drew back. "A celebration!"

"Of his life. He was Irish, and some of the men thought a wake more appropriate. His friends' way of showing him respect, I suppose. Your uncle spent a good deal of time at Beck's, from what I understand." She winced. "I don't mean that to sound critical in any way."

"Did you know my uncle very well, Mrs. Thacker?"

"Call me Sally, please. And no, I'm afraid I didn't know him at all. He never attended church." She accompanied Kathryn to the grave.

The cross was simple. *City Walsh*. No date, no RIP, nothing about the man who lay beneath the earth and what, if any, difference his life had made. Kathryn's eyes filled. "His full name was Casey Teague Walsh."

"I doubt anyone knew."

The grave looked bleak and lonely, the last one in a long row of the dead, with space to separate him from the others. His closest friends must have come to see him laid to rest. Who might they be? Scribe, surely. She wanted to know. "Who attended the burial?"

Sally drew her shawl more tightly around her. "Scribe. Matthias Beck."

It was a moment before Kathryn could speak. "Only two."

"There was one other."

Kathryn glanced at her, wondering at her reticence. Sally fisted the shawl at her throat. "Scribe and Matthias knew him best, Kathryn."

"Who was the other?"

"I shouldn't have said anything." Sally sighed. "Fiona Hawthorne. She stayed a long while after the others left. She was weeping."

"She must have loved him."

"Perhaps."

"Is she still here in Calvada?"

Sally shook her head. "Oh, you mustn't seek her out, Kathryn. You sat behind her this morning, but you mustn't sit back there again. It's reserved for those women. People will talk."

Talk? About what? "I sat behind six women. Which one was Fiona Hawthorne?"

"The one in black." Looking around, Sally stepped closer and lowered her voice as though ghosts might overhear their conversation. "I tell you this only so you'll understand why you should keep your distance. Mrs. Hawthorne owns a two-story brothel on Gomorrah." Sally Thacker looked too embarrassed to say more.

* * *

Kathryn returned to her house and sat at her uncle's desk. Casey Teague Walsh's closest friends had been an orphan, a saloon owner, and a prostitute. She wanted to know more about him, but that meant speaking with Matthias Beck. Their last encounter had left her shaken. Every time the man looked at her, she felt her pulse race. Best if she kept her distance.

She studied the crates of papers stacked against the wall. Perhaps the way to get to know Casey Teague Walsh was by reading the letters, notes, drafts of articles, and newspapers he'd written. It would be a monumental task, but winter nights were long and she wasn't going anywhere. She would put everything into chronological order. She'd learn the course of events as well as what her uncle thought important, what he believed in, what it was that took him out of the streams and mines and made him become a newspaperman.

She lifted a crate and set it on the desk. In her quest to know her uncle better, she might even figure out who killed him and why.

5

THE RAIN HAD LET UP when Matthias came out of Ronya's. After two stormy days, the roads were barely fit to pass. He spotted Kathryn with skirts lifted above the mud as she picked her way across the street toward the café. Her cloak dipped, gathering muck and weight with every step she took. Slipping, she spread her hands, trying to regain her balance, but slid and landed on her bustled backside in the middle of Chump Street. Her hands sank wrist-deep in mud when she tried to get up. Scribe, always on watch for her, came flying down the board-walk to the rescue. He bounded through the mud to help her up, but his earnest efforts made the situation worse, and more entertaining. Chuckling, Matthias watched the boy accidentally knock off Kathryn's hat. The morning breeze wheeled it down the street, startling a horse that reared and trampled it. One lone feather waved goodbye as a wagon wheel squashed it beneath the mire.

Determined to be her knight in shining armor, Scribe tried hefting her up. When his hands slid beneath her armpits, his fingers ventured a little too far, causing her ladyship to jerk away with a shocked squeak. She bumped him and sent him backwards as she half rose. And there the boy lay, spread-eagled.

Matthias laughed. How could he not? Despite the blistering glare Kathryn gave him, he didn't stop. He might have left her sitting on her royal rump if a wagon hadn't come around the corner, promising disaster of a different kind. Matthias caught hold of the lead horse's bridle. "Easy, now." He nodded toward the two trying to get unstuck from the street. "Have a care you don't drive over them. It would spoil the show." The driver laughed and guided the team carefully around the pair struggling to stand.

Taking pity, Matthias walked into the street and stood over them. "Need a little help, your ladyship?" Seeing Scribe's muddy handprints on her bodice made his grin widen.

Face red, Kathryn tried to rise again, but the accumulated mud on her full-length cloak held her down.

"Let me . . ." He bent forward, but she swung at him. Drawing back, he avoided the spray of mud she sent flying in his direction. The Bostonian princess looked anything but ladylike crouching with feet apart, hands spread and dripping, though she still managed to sound prissy.

"Thank you, but I'm up now and . . ." She took a step, slithered, squealed, and pitched backwards.

Though tempted to let her fall, Matthias caught her arm and steadied her. "I've seen you look better, Miss Walsh. But no need to worry now. I've got a good strong back." He released the clasp on her cloak, pulled it off her shoulders, and tossed it to Scribe.

Kathryn's eyes shot wide-open. "What do you think you're doing?"

"You'll be ten pounds lighter without it." He told Scribe to take it to Jian Lin Gong and then caught Kathryn up in his arms. "Don't rake your fingers through my hair, darlin'."

"Put me down!" She flailed. "I can walk."

"We've all seen how well you do that." His laugh died with a grunt. "You have very sharp elbows, Miss Walsh."

She rode like a captured bird, wings outstretched. "This is hardly appropriate."

"And rolling around in the mud is?"

"I wasn't rolling around in the mud."

"If you keep squirming, we'll both end up in it, and I guarantee you won't end up on top in a wrestling match with me."

Every muscle in her body stiffened. "You, sir, are no gentleman."

"I never said I was. But then, you don't look like a lady right now either."

Defeated, face crimson, she went limp. "I would thank you if I didn't know how much you're enjoying this spectacle."

Ronya stood in front of her café, hands on her hips. "Don't you dare bring her in here, Matthias. Not until she's cleaned up."

"Yes, ma'am." He changed directions. "How about the bathhouse, Miss Walsh?"

"Home. Please, Mr. Beck."

"I have a better idea." He crossed the street and strode down the boardwalk, swung around, and backed through the doors of his saloon, thankful she was too shocked to protest. He felt her stiffen again and then shrink in his arms as she looked toward the gaming tables, roulette wheels, the long, polished bar lined with staring men, the huge gilt-framed mirror he'd ordered from the East and paid a bundle to have shipped to Calvada. Matthias liked to know what was going on behind his back when he was having a chat with someone at the bar.

"Where are you taking the lady, Matthias?" a man called from the bar, then laughed.

Not answering, Matthias carried Kathryn upstairs, shouldered open a door, and set her on her feet in the middle of the best room in the hotel. All the rooms were well furnished, but this one had a big brass bed laden with down comforters, a cherrywood chest of drawers and armoire, and a marble washstand with a blue-and-white porcelain bowl and pitcher, plus other amenities. No doubt this little Bostonian was used to better, but this was luxury by Calvadan standards.

The fire had been laid but not lit. Matthias left Kathryn silent and motionless and took a match from the box on the mantel. He started the kindling beneath the logs. "I'll have hot water and soap brought up. Bathtub is behind the screen, towels on the shelf. There's a robe in the armoire. I'll send a message to Ronya. She'll pick up what you need at your house and bring it over."

Straightening, Matthias watched her look around the room. Making a comparison, no doubt. Her clothing told him she came from wealth, probably grew up in a mansion.

Unsmiling, face pale, she looked up at him with grave dignity. "Thank you for your assistance, Mr. Beck."

He saw no mockery in her expression, no hint of dissembling. "You're welcome." Even though she was covered in mud, he felt the pull of attraction. His gaze swept down over her as she glanced around again.

"This is a very nice room."

He detected no sarcasm. "Care to move in?" He saw she missed the innuendo and was glad for it.

"Tempting, but I can't afford it. And I've worked very hard to make my little house a home for myself. Don't you think?"

A home? Did she really want to know what he thought of the cluttered dump she'd walked into the day he, Scribe, and Herr gathered to talk with her about her inheritance? The place was suitable for a bachelor. But a lady? "You won't make it as a milliner. Your dress probably cost more than a miner makes in three months, Miss Walsh."

"I know." She admitted it without hesitation.

"You don't belong in Calvada."

"Perhaps not." She shrugged. "But here I am."

Matthias had the feeling she was close to tears. She clasped muddy hands together in front of her and looked every inch a chastened schoolgirl. "I'd better get cleaned up so I can leave."

"No hurry."

Closing the door behind him, he stood in the hallway, heart galloping.

Abbie Aday, and probably everyone else in town, had heard about Kathryn's mishap on Chump. "Happens to everyone," Abbie said. "It'll be worse in the height of winter. The mud freezes and then it's treacherous. Slip and fall then and you'll break bones."

"That's why I need a pair of good, sturdy boots." Kathryn's fine leather shoes with smooth soles suited Boston and carriage rides, but not a quagmire in the Sierra Nevada mountains. She needed something substantial to hold her to the ground.

Abbie clearly didn't approve. "Oh, but—"

"Shuddup, Abbie." Nabor was already pulling out boxes. "Boys' boots." It took several tries to find a pair small enough to fit Kathryn. She took note of the price. Abbie shook her head and started to say something, but Nabor silenced her with a look. "What the lady wants, the lady gets." Another customer told Kathryn to melt wax and rub it on the leather to weatherproof her purchase.

When Kathryn tried on a man's thigh-length coat, Abbie stood aghast. Kathryn was tired of shivering every time she stepped out her front door. She would shorten the sleeves, make a cap from the scraps, add a silk rose, and embroider some embellishments to give it all a feminine touch.

"You're not going to buy that, too, are you, Kathryn?"

"Woman!" Nabor snarled. "Go measure out and sack beans." His nasty tone and manner toward his wife made Kathryn bristle, but she knew saying anything would merely anger Nabor Aday and make Abbie's situation worse.

"I'd also like to purchase buttons and ribbons." She'd come up with a solution to keep her dress hems out of the mud. Brides fastened up their gowns so they could dance after the wedding. She could make the same alteration to keep her hems from dragging.

Kathryn had made sure to look at the prices of everything before making her selections, but when Nabor tallied the items, the total was several dollars more. He'd cheated her each time she'd come into the store. First it was only a few cents, then fifty, and now more. She had said nothing for the sake of her friendship with Abbie, but could not afford to allow it to continue.

Listing the cost of each item, she placed the proper amount on the counter.

"The coat was more."

"The cost of the coat is on the tag you pulled off, Nabor. It's in your pocket."

Red-faced and angry, he started to say something, but noticed other customers leaning in. He swept the money from the counter into his hand. Blushing, Abbie busied herself at the counter. She kept her head down. As Nabor turned away to help another customer, Kathryn murmured an apology to Abbie. She felt the burn of tears when she stood on the boardwalk outside the store.

On the way home, Kathryn noticed how her new coat and boots brought surprised glances, but she merely smiled in greeting and kept walking. Who designed fashions, anyway? Certainly not the women who wore them. Wasn't she wearing a whalebone corset tied tight enough to make breathing the thin mountain air difficult? How often in the past had she pored over the *Godey's Lady's Book*, sighing at the latest fashions? And Lavinia, the family seamstress, had always been quick to make a replica of whatever caught Kathryn's eye, adding her own unique touches, which stood out among all the other young women whose seamstresses were doing the same thing. Endless competition, and for what? To attract a husband?

Hands deep and warm in her coat pockets, Kathryn started when her name was called. Turning, she saw Morgan Sanders sitting high in his carriage, dressed in a fine suit and heavy wool overcoat. He pushed his hat back slightly, looking her over in some surprise. "I wasn't sure it was you. Is that a man's coat you're wearing?"

"A fine one, too. I just purchased it from Aday's. I am now warm and comfortable." She lifted the collar and smiled.

"And men's boots?"

Clearly, he didn't approve. And she didn't care. "Boys' boots, actually, and quite practical."

His smile held reproach. "I hope you won't wear either to the dinner I've arranged for us this evening. I'll come for you at six."

Who did he think he was? King of the mountain? His assumption lit her temper. "Thank you for your kind invitation, even on such short notice, Mr. Sanders, but I am otherwise engaged this evening." His expression changed. Ah, another man who didn't like being refused. And she didn't like being summoned. She kept walking.

Morgan Sanders kept the horse walking at her pace. "I have more to offer you than any other man in this town."

She'd met men like him in Boston and disliked them just as much. She believed in being honest and saving everyone time. "I'm not looking for a husband." She stopped and faced him. "I have been reading my uncle's newspapers, and your name is frequently mentioned. I'm free right now, and you appear to be heading for your mine. I would like to see it."

He looked surprised and displeased. "My mine?"

"Yes. Your mine. Above- and belowground."

"It's no place for a lady."

"I understand you're running for mayor. The mines are the lifeblood of Calvada. Shouldn't I be interested?"

He gave her a patronizing smile. "If you could vote."

Nice of him to remind her that she had no more rights in California than she had in Massachusetts. "Yes, but women have influence. Isn't your business operation what gives you so much more to offer than anyone else?"

His eyes narrowed. "Are you poking a bear, Miss Walsh?"

She'd seen that look on the judge's face, and she knew to be more cautious. Her mind scrambled for a response that wouldn't fan his temper. "I've inherited a mine, Mr. Sanders. I'm not sure what to do with it."

"Sell it to me."

She should have expected that answer, magnanimous gentleman that he was. "I might want to go into business for myself."

He laughed this time, as though she'd told a good joke. When she didn't smile, he shook his head. "A millinery is one thing, my dear. A mine is something altogether different. Your uncle barely had a pot to cook in. That should tell you something about the worth of his mine."

"Then why would you want to buy it?"

"I was showing kindness to a lovely young lady of limited means." He tipped his head. "I might drop by. You and I do have things to talk about." He snapped the reins and headed down the street.

<hr />

Kathryn spotted Wiley Baer coming out of Beck's Saloon. Hurrying into her house, she grabbed a paper from her drawer and went out to find him. He was two blocks down already, moving like a man with a destination. Walking quickly, she closed the distance, but not before he reached the end of town and turned right. When she came around the corner, she saw him going through the front gate of a two-story house.

"Wiley! Wait!"

The old man froze, gaping at her. She was panting when she reached him. Was he blushing?

"What're you doin' down here on Gomorrah?"

"Gomorrah?" She looked around with interest. Fiona Hawthorne lived somewhere along this lane, but there was no time to knock on doors and ask after the lady now. She faced Wiley. "I need to speak with you on a matter of great importance."

The front window curtain parted. Wiley coughed loudly and shook his head. Kathryn asked if he was all right. He looked exasperated as he shifted from one foot to another. "You shouldn't be down this end of town."

"One end of town looks pretty much the same as the other as far as I can see. Actually, it looks dryer here." She came up one step. "I need your expertise."

"My what?"

"Your knowledge of mines, Wiley." She lowered her voice. "You said you have a successful one and have been operating it for years. My uncle had a mine, which I've been told is worthless. But he kept it active. I'd like to know why."

The door opened a crack. Wiley grabbed the knob and yanked it closed. "I'll be back." He spoke loudly. Clearing his throat, he glowered at Kathryn. "I'd have to see it."

"Of course. I'm ready whenever you are."

He spit, shoulders drooping. "We'll go now. Since you've already put me in such a state, I wouldn't . . . Never mind." He came down the steps.

"I don't know where it is, but here is the claim." She pulled the folded paper from her coat pocket and handed it to him. "You know the area."

"Trustin' soul, ain't ya?" Sour-faced, he took the sheet and read it quickly. "Can you walk two miles?"

"Of course." She was wearing her coat and boots and fully prepared for an adventure.

"Then let's get goin'." He thrust the paper back at her. "And don't go handin' that to just anybody."

She smiled, hoping to defuse his temper. "I don't think of you as anybody, Wiley."

He snorted. "The road only goes partway to where we're goin'."

Was he worried he couldn't make it? He did smell strongly of whiskey, but he hadn't staggered on the trek down the boardwalk. He'd been like an evangelist on a mission. "Would you like me to rent a carriage, so you won't have to walk so far?"

"Me? In a carriage?" He scoffed. "Do I look like someone who rides around in a carriage? I'm askin' if *you* can make it."

Wiley wasn't much taller than Kathryn, but he was considerably older. "I think I can keep up."

An hour later, she wondered what she had been thinking. Drunk or sober, the wiry, bewhiskered little man was as hardy as a billy goat and had the temperament to match. "Come on, come on!" he shouted back at her as she paused to catch her breath. "We haven't got all day!" A cold wind came from the high mountain snows, but steam was rising off her. She would have shrugged off the coat, but then she'd have to carry it, and her legs felt like rubber.

Finally, the road ended. "Are we almost there?" Kathryn held her sides, gasping.

"No." Wiley gave her an annoyed look and headed up the mountain trail.

Her lungs burned, her head pounded, and she felt slightly nauseous. "Wiley!" she pleaded.

Glancing back, he stopped. "You're in a sorry state. It's the altitude. You'll get used to it after a while."

If she lived so long. "Don't forget. I'm from Boston. Sea level . . ." Bending over, she held up one hand in surrender. "Please. Five minutes."

Wiley took a bottle from his coat pocket and held it out. "A good swig of this will set you to rights."

If it smelled anything like he did, she didn't want to taste it. "No, thank you."

"Suit yourself." He gulped, shoved the cork in, and stuck the bottle back in his coat. "Ready yet?" He set off before she could respond, and she had no choice but to follow or give up.

What would they put on her gravestone? *Kathryn Walsh died in her corset. Couldn't untie, cut, or scorn it. Couldn't breathe and she was tired. On the mountain she expired.*

Seeing a patch of snow, she scooped up a handful and rubbed her face.

"Hurry up!" Wiley yelled. "Unless you want to get eaten by a bear!"

Heart jumping, she looked around and tried to catch up. A hundred feet ahead she saw a small but sturdy cabin beside a rocky mountainside. Beams were leaning against some rocks.

"Here it is." Wiley started shoving the beams aside, revealing a cave entrance behind them. He went inside. She heard him shuffling around, grumbling to himself. A match flared and she saw a lantern in his hand. "What're you waiting for?" He looked back at her, disgruntled.

"Are there spiders in there?"

"Sure, and snakes, too."

"Snakes?" She heard him mutter something about rattlers looking for a nice place to winter and straightened. "I'll wait here while you go in and investigate."

Wiley came to the entrance. "You made me come up here to see the durn mine, didn't ya? Interrupted a fine afternoon of entertainment I'd planned. Beggin' a favor, weren't ya?" He thumbed toward the darkness. "Git in here!"

Shuddering, eyes darting left and right, up and down, Kathryn followed Wiley into the mine. She stayed so close, she bumped into him when he stopped. He cussed and stumbled forward. Despite her profuse apology, he growled at her. "Give a man some room, will ya?" Muttering again, he moved ahead. "Nothin' but dirt and rock. That's what I see."

They kept on, Kathryn studying the timber beams bracing the walls and ceiling of the tunnel. Every little trickle of dust made her nerves jump. Wiley came to a wide room and hooked the lantern on a post. "Looks like City spent time in here." He looked closer, running his hands over the rock wall, then hunkering down to see what had been stacked in a pile. "Not silver. Sure ain't gold. But he was savin' this for some reason." He picked up a large rock and examined it. "Don't look like nothin'."

"Maybe I should take samples to an assayer."

"I wouldn't trust the two in Calvada. They both work for Sanders. You'll have to go all the way to Sacramento. Should be someone there who could tell ya what the rocks are and if they're worth anything. But I'm not sure it's worth the bother."

Kathryn picked up a large one. Her curiosity still wasn't satisfied. "Morgan Sanders offered to buy the mine."

"Don't you dare go sellin' this mine to Sanders." He stared at her in consternation. "City wouldn't want you to do that. No, siree."

"I don't intend to sell, Wiley. I'd just like to know why he held on to this claim. It must have meant something to him." She turned the rock in her hands and then held it out to Wiley.

"What're you givin' it to me fur? It's your mine."

Resigned, she tucked it into her coat pocket, where it bulged at her side. Thankfully, going down the mountain would be easier than climbing up. "I guess I'll take another stage ride." The thought was daunting. "Sacramento, here I come."

"If that's your plan, you'd better take more than one sample." Wiley picked up an empty bucket and half filled it with rocks. "They usually want more than one."

"Are you going to carry that for me?" Kathryn could only hope.

Snatching the lantern from the hook, Wiley dropped the bucket beside her on the way out. "It's your mine. You carry it."

Matthias was taking a break from reading reports when he spotted Kathryn wearing a man's coat and carrying a bucket down the boardwalk on the other side of the street. What was she doing? A few men trickled out of saloons to greet her and offer help, but she shook her head and passed them by. She stopped every twenty feet and switched hands. The closest communal well was in the other direction, so she wasn't carrying water.

Leaning forward, Matthias set the papers aside and watched, frowning. She only took five steps this time and put the bucket down. Clearly exhausted, she wiped her brow. Another man offered to help, but she waved him away. Matthias pushed his chair back. She picked up the bucket and marched across Galway, stepped up with difficulty onto the boardwalk and kept going. Her face was red with effort, but she made it to her little house, dropped the bucket, opened the door, then dragged it in and closed the door behind her.

What was she carrying? Horseshoes? "Scribe!" He jerked his chin for the boy to come over. "Go see what her ladyship just dragged into her house."

"What do you mean 'dragged in'?" He peered out the window.

"She had a bucket. It looked heavy."

"She fetches her own water. I tried to help her once, but she said she had to fend for herself."

"It wasn't water."

"How do you know?"

Holy screaming catfishes! "Never mind! I'll go see for myself."

"No! I'll go." Scribe was out the swinging doors before

Matthias could stand up. He picked his way hurriedly across the street and knocked on the door. She didn't answer. He knocked again and it opened. Matthias leaned forward, trying to get a glimpse of her, but Scribe blocked his view. The door closed. Scribe picked his way back and came inside. He walked right past Matthias, grabbed up the rag he'd discarded, and went back to washing tables.

Teeth clenching, Matthias refused to ask what Scribe found out. After a few minutes of burning frustration and telling himself it was none of his business what Kathryn Walsh had in her bucket, he gathered his papers, stacked them, and headed for his office. Why couldn't he get through one day without Kathryn grabbing his attention? Last night, he'd even dreamed about her.

Maybe he needed to get out of town for a while. Go fishing. Bad idea. He'd have too much time to think while he was waiting for a trout to take the bait. No, he had a better idea. Rather than send Henry to Sacramento to handle errands for him, why not make the trip himself? He could spend a few days checking into some businesses, see how they were doing, who was running them. There wouldn't be an opportunity to get out of town once the campaign for mayor heated up. *Thank you, City, for making me feel guilty enough to let the men talk me into running for office.* He had about as much chance of winning as a snowball in hell.

City would have laughed and told him it was about time he anted up and got in the game.

6

CUSSLER HUFFED AND PUFFED and cussed himself red in the face as he loaded Kathryn's case onto the roof of the stagecoach. "What do you have in this thing? Rocks?"

Kathryn blushed. "Just essentials I need for my trip, Mr. Cussler." Indeed, the rocks were essential and the reason for her journey to Sacramento, but she didn't want to advertise what she was doing to Cussler or to Gus Blather, the station manager, who tended to talk about where passengers were going and why. She gave Cussler a tip when he climbed down, surprising him even more by her generosity than the weight of the burden he'd just strapped down and would have to unload at the halfway station, where she'd meet another stage that would take her to Sacramento.

"Well, thanks, miss." He opened the coach door for her, flipped the coin, caught it, and tucked it into his pocket. "Blather said there's another passenger coming with us." He handed her in. "He's got five minutes to get here or we're leaving without him." He tipped his hat and closed the door. The coach dipped as he climbed up top.

Alone in the coach, Kathryn chose the middle seat to avoid splatters that might come in through the open windows. She'd chosen her brown traveling dress with the peplum jacket. She left her boots behind and wore her high-button shoes.

A thump sounded on the coach roof along with Cussler's brisk greeting. "Get in. We're off." The door snapped open, and the stagecoach dipped again as the late passenger climbed in. Kathryn's smile of greeting died when Matthias Beck took off his hat and sat opposite her, slamming the door at the same time Cussler cracked the whip. The scowling intensity of his glare made Kathryn feel she was somehow at fault. The stagecoach lurched forward and she pressed back, dismayed to find herself trapped in the coach with Beck.

"So you finally decided to leave town."

Kathryn couldn't tell whether he was relieved or indifferent. Not that it mattered to her. She saw no reason to respond since he had made a statement, erroneous as it might be. She watched the saloons and storefronts passing by. She could feel Beck's eyes fixed on her. Was he trying to be annoying? Vexed, she glared at him. "Only temporarily." The man was altogether too disturbing, especially when his gaze moved from her hat down to the toes of her shoes and back up to meet her eyes. She felt flushed with warmth. Looking away, she decided it would be best to ignore him.

They hadn't traveled more than a mile when the wretched man set his boot against the edge of her bench. Drawing her skirt closer to her thigh, she glared at him. "Would you mind removing your boot from my seat?"

"It's not on your seat. It's on the bench." He smirked. "But as you wish." He lowered his foot, shifted position, and sat beside her, bracing himself with his foot on the bench where he'd been sitting. "How's this?"

His proximity unnerved her. "I would prefer you remain on your side of the coach, Mr. Beck."

"You can't have it both ways, your ladyship."

She didn't like his tone or the title. "All right. Fine. Go back. Put your boot on my seat."

"Don't tempt me," he snarled, not budging.

The coach bounced, bumping her against Beck. Kathryn grabbed the window frame and scooted as far away from him as she could. The man was big, and there still wasn't enough space between them for her comfort. Every brush against him made her heart race faster. She had known the ride would be miserable, but being trapped inside the coach with this man taunting her would be impossible! Two days and one overnight stop in the wilderness? He glanced at her and she knew he intended to stay exactly where he was. Very well. She'd move! Kathryn started to switch sides. Another jolt and she fell back. She stood again, half-crouched, determined to get away from him.

"Careful, your ladyship. You're not picking a good time."

Cussler's whip cracked. "Hang on! Washboard coming!"

Midway between the two seats, the first bump launched Kathryn up and backwards onto Beck's lap, knocking the air out of him. "Oh!" Mortified, she tried to rise. "I beg your pardon."

Beck laughed. "Now, this is an unexpected and pleasant surprise." His warm breath in her ear raised goose bumps over her entire body.

Gasping, she tried to get up again, but the jouncing had her bouncing on his lap.

"Just relax, your ladyship. You're fine."

"You could give me some assistance."

"Of course. I should have thought of that." He encompassed her waist with strong hands and held her firmly in place. "Better?"

"I meant to help me move!" She kicked him in the shins with her heels.

"Ow! Have a care. You're safer sitting on me."

"Let go of me!" She tried to pry his fingers loose.

"Just sit tight, and it'll all be over soon." He chuckled. "Good thing you left your bustle behind. *Oww!* You have sharp little claws, don't you?"

The instant his hands loosened, Kathryn flung herself onto the opposite seat, not caring how unladylike she looked in her escape. The coach lurched up and down. Heart thundering, she tugged her jacket down and straightened her hat, all while glaring at him. They passed over the last of the washboard, and the road smoothed.

Beck put his boot up again and grinned. "I had resigned myself to a long, boring ride to Sacramento. So far, it's been quite . . . interesting."

"Why did you of all people have to be on this particular coach today?"

"Just lucky, I guess."

Aware Beck was baiting her, Kathryn looked out the window again, making every effort to ignore him. The horses galloped. Cussler shouted colorful commands every few minutes. A mile passed, then two, and Beck continued to look at her. Goading her. She clenched her jaws. Let him look. Men had looked before, and she'd paid them no attention. So why the odd sensations racing through her body? She was about to snarl at him when he spoke.

"I still want the press."

Kathryn pretended indifference. "I've decided not to sell it."

"Pure cussed stubborn, just like your uncle."

Having read quite a few copies of City Walsh's *Calvada Voice* made her feel honored to be compared to him. "Perhaps he and I share some of the same principles."

"Really!" Beck raised his brows in mock discovery. "You spend evenings cavorting with men and go to bed drunk every night, do you?"

"What?" She gaped at him.

A flicker of regret crossed his face before it hardened. "Aside from being an astute newspaper editor who possessed an uncanny and very nasty wit, City had a remarkable taste for whiskey and women. He counted Fiona Hawthorne among his closest friends, and he could drink Herr Neumann under the brass rail."

Kathryn took it all in with a growing sense of sorrow. No matter how immoral City Walsh might have been, he was still her uncle, her father's brother. Family. She had Walsh blood running in her veins. If anything, Beck's words told her how passion could flow in destructive ways. Look where passion had landed her! How many times had she seen an injustice and immediately fired off her opinions at the judge? Rather than present a problem rationally, she had provoked and antagonized him. What good had that ever done other than make him defensive and furious? Had she handled things with more grace, she might have accomplished more for others and avoided being exiled herself.

"I suppose you thought—or hoped—he was a saint."

Clasping her hands in her lap, Kathryn looked away, fighting tears. Had her father been like City Walsh? The judge certainly hadn't had anything good to say about him. *A troublemaker like all the Irish. A rebel.* Hadn't he said the same about her?

Beck sighed and muttered a soft curse. "City was a good man. He just had too much of the world under his belt. He came out in '49, during the first rush. He had no illusions about people when I met him."

"I'm fast losing mine." She met his gaze. "I thought you were his friend."

"I was." Beck leaned back. "He spent most evenings at my bar. I admired him."

"What about him did you find the most admirable? How much whiskey he could hold, or . . . ?" She stopped, ashamed she had been about to say something derogatory about a woman who had been concerned that her own reputation might taint Kathryn's if they spoke, even in church. "Never mind."

"I admired him because he believed in telling the truth, no matter the cost."

His tone captured her full attention. "You know who killed him."

Startled, he frowned. "No. No, I don't. The fact is, truth tellers tend to make a lot of enemies." He gave a bleak laugh. "I can list half a dozen men who might have wanted to shut him up."

She sensed he knew a great deal more and was regretting that he'd broached the subject of City Walsh at all. "Who is on your list?"

"Oh, no." His mouth tightened. "I have suspicions, Miss Walsh, not facts. None of which I plan to share with a woman."

"Fine." Exasperated, she shrugged. "I'll figure it out for myself."

"How? And then do what? Beat the killer with your parasol, or nail him to a wall with your hatpins?"

"Justice must prevail."

Beck gave a snort. "Sounds like a motto."

She looked at him coolly. "I've been reading my uncle's newspapers. At least, the ones left in the boxes. Old ones from four or more years ago. I'd like to know what happened to the more recent issues."

"They were confiscated."

"By whom?"

"The sheriff. He took them home to see what he could find out."

Surprised, Kathryn felt hopeful. "I thought Calvada didn't have a sheriff."

"We don't."

"But you just said . . ."

"We *had* a sheriff." Beck looked grim. "He died when his house burned down."

"Rather convenient timing, wouldn't you say?" She arched a brow, but Beck didn't say anything. "Scribe hasn't told me any of this."

"I shouldn't have, either." He said something low, his body tense, eyes dark. "One look at you when you got off the stage in your ribbons and lace, and bets were on you wouldn't last a day."

"Let alone a month." She tipped her chin. "I hope you made a very large wager on that first week, Mr. Beck."

"Not a chance. Women are capricious. But Aday did."

Hurt, Kathryn put a hand to her throat. "Abbie?"

"No, Nabor. He bet five dollars you'd be gone within ten days."

Five dollars! No wonder he tried to cheat her every time she came in the store. He wanted to make his money back from a bad wager. Kathryn crossed her arms. The man wouldn't even let his wife buy a two-dollar hat, but he wasted more than twice that gambling! Men! "Well, whether you made a wager or not, you made it clear you hoped I'd leave after the first night."

His mood lightened. "I'll bet it occurred to you."

She didn't understand the man. "Well, you can tell all the men at your bar I'm staying in Calvada." She put her hands on her knees and leaned forward. "And you can also tell them I'm going to find out who murdered my uncle."

His expression hardened again. Mirroring her position, he put his nose within inches of hers. "You go poking around and you'll get yourself into real trouble. Leave it to the men to figure out."

She sniffed and leaned back. "As if the men have done such a grand job so far. It seems no one has done anything about solving his murder. And it *is* my business. I'm City Walsh's niece. He was family."

"Family." Beck sneered, eyes blazing. "You didn't even know the man, so don't pretend feelings about him that don't exist. The only connection between the two of you is blood. And the fact that you, by some freak accident, inherited his property, instead of Scribe. I'd sure like to know how that happened. If you'd ever met City Walsh, you wouldn't have wanted to be on the same side of the street with him!"

His words felt like a beating, but she'd been judged harshly and unfairly before. It was the level of his anger that bothered her. Her own hot temper boiled up, and she had to batten it down to show a calm demeanor. She'd learned how after numerous arguments with the judge. She didn't want to make an enemy of Matthias Beck and wondered what it was about her that had him so incensed. A cool, honest answer might calm his temper. "I would have wanted to sit down with City Walsh and find out why he stayed in California when his obvious talents could have earned him a much better living elsewhere."

His eyes flickered, then narrowed. "Sure, you would." He leaned back, his body still tense.

Kathryn thought of all the things she had done over the years that had brought nothing but grief to her mother and frustration and rage to her stepfather. She had to admit there were times when her sole desire had been to goad the judge into losing his temper. Perhaps if she had been a little more circumspect and a lot less self-righteous, she wouldn't have found herself in the wilderness surrounded by people who thought whatever backbone she had was due to a whalebone corset, and the feathers in her hats indicated her intelligence. It wasn't her choice she'd been born in a mansion with a silver spoon in her mouth. Besides, it had been by her own doing that the silver spoon had been yanked from her and put back in the Hyland-Pershing mansion's kitchen drawer.

"You can't know what it means to me to have any connection to my father, Mr. Beck. I never met him. My stepfather only spoke of him with derision; my mother once, with love."

Beck searched her eyes, anger gone, a questioning look replacing it. "What would it mean?"

"Let's just say I'm not as shallow as you have judged me to be." His wry look made her add, "I'll try not to judge you on appearances either, Mr. Beck." Time and a little more research might amend her low opinion, but she doubted it.

Beck considered her and then closed his eyes as though he wanted to take a nap. He was silent so long, she thought he'd succeeded, though how anyone could sleep in a jolting, swaying coach was beyond her. She gradually relaxed, too, and then started when he spoke.

"If you're not leaving, why are you going to Sacramento?"

She didn't know him well enough to trust him. "Why are you going?"

"I wanted to get away."

"From what?"

"Trouble."

The intensity of his expression made her heart do a fillip. "A wise move, I would say."

"Would you?"

What did that sultry look mean? "Yes, I would. I most certainly would." Avoiding trouble was always a good idea. A pity she hadn't learned that lesson a long time ago. Unable to hold his gaze, Kathryn took his example and closed her eyes, pretending she needed to rest when she merely needed a respite from his disconcerting presence.

"You can try, Miss Walsh, but some things are just in the cards."

Matthias had a hard time keeping his eyes off Kathryn Walsh. He'd had a hard time keeping her out of his thoughts since she got off the stagecoach. She'd looked all woman at a distance. Close up, when she looked into his eyes, he'd felt a jolt of heat spread through his body.

He'd never felt anything like that before, not even with Alice, the woman he had loved and planned on a future with after the war. He came home and found out she'd married the son of a rich plantation owner three months after he left. Hadn't she promised to wait, even after he told her his conscience was sending him north? She'd sought him out shortly after he returned home. Still beautiful, even dressed in faded and patched clothes, real tears of regret coursing down her cheeks, she pleaded with him to forgive her and take her away with him. It wasn't love she felt, but fear and desperation, finding herself tied to a bitter, disabled veteran whose plantation was in ruins. Matthias hadn't hated her for her faithlessness. He'd pitied her.

Had he overlaid his prejudices on Kathryn Walsh? She was beautiful. She had that cultured air about her. He'd found himself observing her, listening to what people said about her, and it seemed there was more to admire about City's niece than her beauty. She might look like a featherbrained, spoiled, rich girl in her fancy clothes, but Ronya said she had no qualms about working in a kitchen or serving meals. *That girl's a hard worker.* She'd even washed dishes.

He'd seen that for himself after getting a look inside City's house.

Men talked at the bar, and "the Walsh girl" was a favorite subject. It took less than an hour to hear about Sanders inviting Kathryn to a second dinner. *Said she wanted to see his mine.* Maybe she wanted to see Sanders's assets. Ronya had taken offense at that remark. *Kathryn doesn't want to marry anyone.* What woman wasn't on the hunt for a man to take care of her? When he'd voiced that thought, Ronya had given him a look that made him taste the foot he'd just swallowed. She had been on her own since her husband died in 1850. *And doing just fine, thank you very much.*

Then there was Nabor, who clearly didn't like Kathryn, probably because she'd given his overworked, underappreciated wife a hat she wore every Sunday. Abbie told Matthias all about it when he went in to make a purchase. She thought Kathryn was the nicest lady she'd ever met, and Nabor told her to get back to work and stop talking. Matthias had heard him talking later at the bar. He said Kathryn Walsh cared nothing about her reputation. *She sat behind Fiona Hawthorne's dolls in church and even talked to her. I wouldn't be surprised if she was sent out here because . . .* A couple of men told him to shut his mouth.

If they hadn't, Matthias might have. Why was he so defensive about a girl he barely knew?

Matthias wanted to know why Kathryn had been sent to California to collect an inheritance intended for her mother, or so Scribe had said.

Cussler shouted as he pulled into the stage stop. Matthias got out, intending to assist Kathryn, but she had already opened the door on the other side. Hopping down, she brushed off her skirt and gave her jacket a tug. Cussler told them to go on inside and eat while he and the station manager changed the horses.

A bowl of stew was ready, as well as fresh hot coffee and a basket of sourdough rolls. They ate in silence and had enough time to stretch their legs and use the privy before Cussler called them back to the coach. Matthias decided to be the gentleman his mother had trained him to be, but Kathryn climbed in before he reached her. Disgruntled, he sat facing her. Neither he nor she tried to make conversation. Unlike most ladies he'd met, she didn't seem uncomfortable with silence. In fact, she seemed to be mulling something over, if that frown told him anything. He hoped it had nothing to do with City's murder. Best to get her thinking about something else. He remembered something she'd said the first day he met her.

"What did you mean when you said, 'Whatever there is will have to do'?" When she gave him a blank stare, he sought to remind her. "The day you got off the stage, I said there was no pot at the end of the rainbow in Calvada, and you said . . ."

She gave a slight shrug, hands folded in her lap. "I made myself a thorn in my stepfather's side, and a heartache to my mother. The inheritance was intended for her. The judge convinced her to sign it over to me."

"The judge?"

"My stepfather." She winced. "That's what I called him.

With the same disdain you use when calling me 'your lady-ship,' I'm afraid."

Matthias smiled slightly. "Did he deserve it?"

"I'm sure he didn't think so. And I confess I wasn't always respectful, something he deserved if for no other reason than he married my mother despite the encumbrance that came with her. Though I often thought his decision had more to do with my grandfather's fortune and need of an heir . . ." She stopped abruptly and shook her head as though catching herself in a blunder.

"Your grandfather had an estate."

"It's a long story."

"We have a long ride ahead of us." He smiled encourage-ment. "Did you misbehave?"

"No more than other children, but I look like my father."

And her uncle. "Hardly something over which you had con-trol."

"No." She smoothed her skirt, not meeting his gaze.

"But . . . ?"

"There were other reasons I'd rather not go into."

There were few reasons for a family to send a young daugh-ter away. "Ah. Star-crossed lovers."

She glanced up sharply, eyes fierce. "I have never been in love, Mr. Beck. Unlike my parents, who eloped against my grandfather's wishes." Her indignation wilted slightly. "He might have had reason to distrust my father. My parents were only married a year when my father sent her home and headed west to find his fortune. My mother wouldn't have known he died if my uncle hadn't written to her—" She spread her fingers on her skirt and looked troubled. "And why in heaven's name am I telling you all this?"

"I pried." And he wasn't finished. He had a wagonload of questions.

"All I know about you is you're good with your fists and you own a saloon—"

"A hotel and a saloon."

"I stand corrected, but the saloon came first, didn't it? And though you're a Southerner, you fought for the Union . . ."

"Who told you that?"

"Am I mistaken?"

"No, but it seems you're as curious about me as I am about you." He would've kicked himself for saying that if she hadn't turned guilty pink.

Then she had to spoil it by correcting his assumption. "I'm afraid I made a disparaging remark about you, and someone quickly came to your defense."

"Who?"

"Ronya. She thinks very highly of you."

When she wasn't lecturing him like a mother. "Gossiping about me, your ladyship? I'm warmed by your interest."

"Well, don't be too warmed by it, Mr. Beck." She tilted her head. "It only seems wise since I heard you are a candidate for mayor."

He laughed. "What does an election have to do with you? You can't vote."

"Yet." Her eyes flashed green fire. "And that's exactly what Morgan Sanders said, which makes me wonder if both of you think the same way about everything."

"I assure you we do not." Matthias sensed a frustrated suffragette, though she hardly looked the type. "And if you could, what sort of mayor might you be looking for, Miss Walsh?" He could guess. Someone handsome, well-spoken; someone well-dressed and rich. Someone who could flatter and deceive. Someone who owned a mine instead of a saloon. "A woman of your vast experience in the world must have some idea who would be best to run Calvada."

She held his mocking gaze, mouth tight, before lifting her chin. "An honest man, Mr. Beck, one of strong character who could stand on good, solid principle. A man of humility who would not bend with every political whim that blows or use his personal wealth to hold down those less fortunate. A man everyone, including women, could respect, perhaps even admire."

Her answer surprised him. "Did you say all that to Morgan Sanders when he followed you down Chump Street in his carriage, asking you to dinner?"

"He didn't ask. He—" She stopped, surprised. "How do you know about that?"

"People watch you. People talk."

"*Men*, you mean. And they say *women* gossip!"

"You should be warned that Sanders is of an age when men look for a wife to provide an heir to their empire, and he'll want someone young and beautiful, educated and charming, to dress up his parlor."

"Well, it won't be me, and as for whether I told him what kind of man I'd vote for, I didn't. But given the opportunity to talk with him again—"

"Oh, he'll make sure of that."

"I will tell him the same thing I just told you." She sniffed. "Not that either of you would listen."

A beefy man with a bushy beard helped Kathryn from the stage when they stopped for the night. Harry Pitts stammered an introduction and said he was the station manager, and his job was to make sure she was comfortable and he could provide her with whatever she might need. Ignoring Beck, Pitts escorted her inside, where a sturdy Mexican woman was setting the table. Pitts reassured Kathryn he had a private room at the back reserved for traveling ladies.

Matthias came in behind her, shrugged off his coat, and hung it on a hook by the door.

"Supper is ready," Pitts announced, holding a chair out for Kathryn as the woman plunked a large iron pot on the table and removed the lid. Kathryn smiled up at her and said it smelled delicious and asked what it was.

The woman spoke rapid Spanish as she filled a bowl and set it in front of her, then served Matthias a heaping portion. He chuckled. "Never ask what's in the pot."

"Why not?"

"You might not like the answer."

Kathryn took a cautious spoonful. She didn't like Beck's half smile as he watched her. What did he know that she didn't, and did she want to know? "It tastes even better than it smells."

The cook glanced at Pitts before leaving the room. "Shot a raccoon last night," he boasted. "Been raiding our larder."

"Raccoon?" Kathryn gulped.

"Good eating once they're tenderized. Had to pound that monster for a while, but he's all softened up now, ain't he?"

Kathryn looked down at her bowl. Beck smirked. "Have you lost your appetite, your ladyship?"

"Actually, I'm hungry enough to eat a weasel." She hesitated only slightly before taking a second bite. It tasted as delicious as the first.

"Weasels aren't worth cooking," Pitts told her, setting the basket of biscuits in front of her. "Not enough meat on the bones to bother. Now possum are good eating."

Kathryn saw her opportunity to tease Beck. "I've heard Southerners are particularly fond of them."

Pitts gave a cold laugh. "I heard they was eating rats by the end of the war, and glad of it." The idea seemed to please him.

Beck's head came up, eyes dark. He put his spoon down. The two men stared at one another. Pushing his chair back, Beck stood. Kathryn's heart pounded at the threat of violence building in the room. And it was her fault! Pitts took a step back and cleared his throat. "I'm gonna see how Cussler's doing with the horses. Showalter will be ready to leave come sunup." Beck watched him until he went out the door.

Kathryn released her breath when he sat again. "I'm sorry. I didn't intend—" His look silenced her.

"Eat your stew, Miss Walsh. It won't taste as good cold."

She wanted to ask about the war, why he'd fought for the North rather than the South. Had he joined in the conflict at the beginning when it was about states having the right to secede, or later when the rallying call was to end slavery? Had he tried to go home and found all doors closed to him? Had he been disinherited, too? She opened her mouth and then closed it, trying to gather the courage to ask. She'd answered his questions, hadn't she? She wanted to know more about him.

The anger and pain were etched in his face, though he tried to mask it. Seeing the suffering of others always hurt her, even more so when she knew she had unwittingly blundered and exacerbated it. She had meant only to tease, not to wound.

Beck finished his meal, stood, took his coat from the hook, and went outside.

Kathryn hoped he wasn't going after Pitts.

7

MATTHIAS WALKED ALONG THE ROAD to cool off. He'd seen enough in the war to know Pitts was right. It was the tone that galled and brought the echo of battle. He couldn't abide the proud disdain of the victor over the vanquished. The North had won the war, but Southern hearts were far from conquered. People could be crushed, but not defeated. Men lived not by what they were told, but by what they believed.

By the time the war ended, people in the South were starving. He'd seen the gaunt faces and hatred burning in the hollowed eyes of people he'd known since childhood. He heard Northerners revile Andersonville for starving prisoners, overlooking the surrounding neighborhoods who barely had enough to eat. What excuse had those who ran Chicago's Camp Douglas, where Rebels starved when food had been available, but withheld?

War brought out the worst in humankind. Even when the cause was just, no one came out unscathed. How many years would it take for the nation to mend? Matthias had come west to get away from the past. Along with thousands of others, he brought it with him.

Running a saloon and hotel kept him distracted, but sometimes he thought he'd have been better off a casualty of war than a survivor. Life held little satisfaction. The same soul hunger to see justice done had driven him north, then south, and finally west. Where could he go from here?

Returning to the station house, Matthias found Kathryn reading by lantern light. She glanced up. Was that pity in her eyes? That was the last thing he wanted to arouse in her. "Where'd you find a book in this place?"

"I brought it with me."

She didn't say what it was, but he could tell by the worn black leather binding. He'd seen it open on City's desk. A Bible. "You should go to bed."

"I'm not tired."

Nor was he. His blood hummed. He'd thought his heart dead after Alice. It was beating hard and fast now. Getting out of town was supposed to get him away from Kathryn Walsh. Here she was sitting within feet of him, stirring up feelings he'd rather not have. "Pitts said sunup." He shrugged out of his coat, stretched out on the bench against the wall, and covered himself with it. "Better get some sleep."

"I'd like to read awhile longer, unless the light bothers you."

He closed his eyes. "Do whatever you want."

The room was silent for a few minutes, then she got up and

went out. He thought she was going to bed, but she'd gone outside. Probably making a visit to the necessary. Matthias put his arm behind his head, waiting for her to come back. He'd sleep when she was settled in that back room reserved for ladies.

A band of coyotes yipped and barked, then howled. What was taking Kathryn so long? Was she sick? She'd seemed fine all evening. A puma screamed in the distance. Edgy, Matthias got up to check on her. As he went out the door, he spotted her standing in the middle of the road, looking up at the stars, oblivious of any danger night brought to these mountains.

She glanced back as he approached. "You couldn't sleep?"

"You shouldn't be out here in the dark alone."

"You needn't worry about me. The wolves didn't sound close."

"Coyotes, not wolves, and just as dangerous in packs."

"I thought I heard a woman scream."

"Mountain lion. And the animals are closer than you think. Probably looking at you as easy prey, a half-witted city girl standing in the open with neither fangs nor claws to defend herself."

She laughed. "Grumpy should go back to bed."

He had been rather gruff. Relaxing, he stood beside her, in no hurry now to take her back inside. Her skin was like alabaster in the moonlight, her lips slightly parted as she looked up again. "I'm sure you've seen stars before, your ladyship."

"Not like this. They feel close enough to touch." She pulled her jacket tighter, and he wished he'd grabbed his jacket so he could wrap it around her. She sighed. "The darker the night, the brighter they shine." Her mouth curved in a soft smile as she stargazed.

"We'd better go back to the house."

"Just a few more minutes. It's so beautiful."

So was she. Pulling his attention from her, he looked up. How long since he'd looked at the stars? Not since the long months of wandering, sleeping by a campfire, steeped in loneliness and sorrow. The vastness had made him feel small, forgotten. It still did.

"I could stay out here all night." She gave a soft laugh as her teeth chattered. "If it was summer."

He touched her arm so lightly she didn't feel it through her jacket. "The stars will appear again tomorrow night, regular as clockwork."

"And I'll be in Sacramento, inside a hotel, not out here in the open where I can fully enjoy them." When she looked up at him, he slipped his hand beneath her elbow.

"Now, your ladyship. You have no idea the danger you've put yourself in." And not just from coyotes and a puma. He wanted to taste that sweet mouth, and if she responded, he couldn't promise to behave himself.

"Very well, Mr. Beck." She gave him an impish smile. "I'm only going in because you seem to be afraid of the dark."

He laughed.

They walked back together. Kathryn collected her Bible and lifted the lantern as he stretched out on the bench again. Opening the door into the back room, she paused. "Good night, Mr. Beck. Sleep well." She closed the door behind her.

Matthias lay awake for a long time. When he did sleep, he dreamed, not of the battlefield as he had so many nights before, but of Kathryn.

Sacramento made Kathryn feel more at home than any other town since she had crossed the Rocky Mountains. How could she not, with streets wide and clean, buildings of brick as well as wood, men and women fashionably dressed, and a name meaning "sacrament"? Several hotels, restaurants, and numerous businesses passed by, and she could hardly wait to walk the avenue and see what else the town had to offer. The atmosphere was so much more wholesome than Calvada with its saloons and fandango halls, brothels and grinding poverty.

She saw a telegraph office. Perhaps she should send her mother another message, to follow up the one she had sent from Truckee and the long letter she'd written from Calvada about life in a mining town and the friends she'd made—Ronya, Charlotte, and Abbie. She had made no mention of Matthias Beck or Morgan Sanders. She hadn't heard a word from home and wondered if her mother was well. She had told Kathryn the day of the final battle that she was in a family way—a miracle at her age and after so many years of marriage. Kathryn's baby brother or sister was due in December. Was the judge monitoring her mother's mail? She didn't want to think so ill of him, though it was preferable to believing her own mother wanted no further commerce with her. Surely her mother would tell her whether she had a brother or sister, the first of which would satisfy Lawrence Pershing's need for an heir. Kathryn could only hope a sister would soften his heart.

Mr. Showalter called out as he pulled the stagecoach to a stop. He and Mr. Beck unloaded the luggage from the top. Frowning, Mr. Beck dropped her small trunk on the boardwalk and eyed it suspiciously before glancing her way. "What'd you bring with you? Pieces of the press?"

So that was what troubled him! "Nothing that need concern you, Mr. Beck." Let him wonder.

"Enjoy Sacramento, Miss Walsh." He tipped his hat, picked up his case, and left.

She watched him go before she went inside and asked the

clerk to put her small trunk in storage until she let him know where it would be delivered. The man hefted it onto a cart and wheeled it inside, where they talked briefly. She implied she had some nuggets in her reticule that she would like assessed and asked where she might find a reputable assayer's office. He gave her directions to Hollis, Pruitt, and Stearns. He also suggested several hotels, which, upon investigation, proved quite grand but beyond her means. She settled in less expensive accommodations and left her carpetbag in the tiny room, slipped the skeleton key into her small bag, and went out to board a horse-drawn streetcar heading toward the riverfront.

Two ladies admired her ensemble. Kathryn asked about millineries in Sacramento, and one said they were also behind fashions in the East, though there were some nice shops she might enjoy. When she mentioned Calvada, they'd never heard of it. Stepping off the streetcar at its next stop, Kathryn walked the rest of the way. A horn blew and a puff of gray steam rose as a steamboat approached the docks. Several men passed by, smiling at her and tipping their hats. The aroma of roasting meat wafted from a restaurant. She inhaled, tempted to stop, but business must come first. Help Wanted signs hung in several windows. Perhaps Sacramento would be a better place for her. Her prospects might be better in this growing city. The town certainly seemed prosperous and far more cultured than the place her uncle had called home.

But then, she'd put so much time into fixing up her little house. And she'd told Matthias Beck she was staying. Would he care if she left? Why had Uncle Casey stayed in Calvada? She'd read enough of his editorials to appreciate his talent. He could have worked for a newspaper in a far bigger town, or even a city like Boston or New York. What had held him here? Besides all that, she needed to find out about his mine.

Kathryn entered the assayer's office. Two men worked at the back of a large room, the wall covered with shelves lined with bottles. Another table had a collection of rock samples in various sizes and shapes, alongside weights and measures. Wooden bins neatly lined the side wall, each with papers attached. The youngest of the three men glanced up in surprise while the two older went on working. "Are you lost, miss?"

Kathryn introduced herself. "You were highly recommended."

The young man pushed up his glasses. "Amos Stearns, at your service, Miss Walsh." He blushed and introduced the two men behind him. Hollis and Pruitt chuckled, spoke to one another softly, and went back to work.

"I have some rocks to show you. I hope you can tell me their value." Stearns glanced at her small reticule. "Not with me, sir. I left them in a case at the stage station. When may I have them delivered for your evaluation?"

"Two to three weeks is the soonest we can get to it, Miss Walsh." Pruitt spoke firmly from the back, giving Stearns a warning look.

Kathryn thought of the cost of remaining in Sacramento for several weeks and wilted. "Are there any other assayers who might have time to look at what I've brought with me?"

Hollis snorted. "Plenty of assayers around that would have time, but not the kind you can trust."

"And those you can are just as busy as we are." Pruitt chipped away at a rock. "Everyone thinks they've found a gold mine." He tossed the rock into a big box. "Worthless."

"Well, I doubt I have gold or silver," Kathryn admitted, "but my uncle kept his claim active for some reason, and I need to know why."

Pruitt shifted rocks and bowls. "If he thinks they're worth something, why didn't he bring them himself?"

Clearly, a woman was not a normal visitor to an assayer's office. Kathryn knew these men thought she was wasting their time. Well, she might be, but she didn't want to waste hers either. "He might've done so, sir, but he was murdered." She now had their full attention. "I have no idea if the mine had anything to do with it, but I do need to know why the claim was so important to him. And if there is any reason why it might be important to anyone else."

Pruitt looked at the dozen wooden bins and gave Stearns a grim nod before going back to work. Pushing up his dusty glasses again, Stearns turned a notebook toward her. "Write the address of where you're staying, Miss Walsh, and have your samples delivered as soon as possible. We'll take a look and let you know."

Rather than pay for the streetcar, Kathryn walked back to the stage station. It didn't occur to her until after she'd made the necessary arrangements that she hadn't asked how much the assayer's report would cost.

Matthias finished speaking with Call's contacts. He was at a crossroads and knew he couldn't keep walking down the path he'd been on for the past six years. Money hadn't brought him peace. He could sell his holdings and move on, or stay and stand up for something more than lining his pockets.

City Walsh had urged him to run for mayor. Matthias told him he wanted nothing to do with politics. They argued vehemently that last night before City died. Matthias had come close to punching the older man. Since then, Matthias had been approached by a dozen other men wanting him to run. Why bother? he told them. The last two elections had been landslides, every miner at the Madera voting for Sanders. Their livelihood depended on it.

If he did decide to run, how much of his decision would have to do with City Walsh's calling him a coward the night he died? What cut deeper than being called a coward was the look of disappointment in City's eyes when he left the saloon.

It took more than one man to change a town, though City had tried.

Everyone thought Sanders had him murdered, though there had been no proof. City had aimed his criticism at all the mine owners, not just the owner of the Madera.

Tired and depressed, Matthias checked into a hotel down the street from the stage station. He wasn't in the mood for entertainment, but he wanted a good dinner in a quiet restaurant and a long night's sleep without the loud conversation of men getting drunk and rowdy or hearing the music coming from the fandango hall across the street. He wondered how Kathryn Walsh managed to sleep next to all that racket.

Where was she right now? Exploring Sacramento, probably, seeing how much better her life would be here rather than in Calvada. She said she was going back, but would she? What had she brought in that case of hers?

Matthias found a nice restaurant a few doors down from the hotel. He asked for a table in the back corner. He liked sitting where he could see the whole room—who came, who went. He ordered a glass of red wine and a steak. He'd just begun to relax when Kathryn Walsh walked in. Of all the restaurants in Sacramento, she had to pick this one.

The proprietor seated her by a front window. A beautiful girl would catch the eye of passersby. Matthias's steak, potato, and green beans came while Kathryn still sat there, undecided. No wine for her, just a tall glass of water, which she sipped while the waiter hovered nearby, eager to replenish her glass before it was one-third empty. The man couldn't take his eyes off her. When he poured, they spoke. Longer than necessary. She laughed at something the waiter said, nodded, and handed him the menu. He bowed slightly, saying something more that brought a smile to those perfect lips and did unwelcome things to Matthias's insides.

Would she feel his attention? Others were watching her, too, though more surreptitiously. He stared blatantly, willing her to look his way. She didn't. She'd probably been the center of male attention since reaching puberty. She wouldn't eat much, not with that tiny waist.

He'd finished his meal by the time hers arrived, salmon with all the trimmings. She looked at her plate as though it was a feast. She bowed her head and closed her eyes, saying grace, no doubt. After putting her napkin on her lap, she took her time eating, savoring every bite. Matthias had never seen a woman enjoy a meal so much. Where was she putting all that food? The waiter cleared her dishes and brought her a thick slice of chocolate cake and a cup of coffee.

Matthias could bet her stays were pinching by now. She ate the icing and half the cake. Most of the patrons had eaten and left before she finished. He lingered, watching her. She finally put her fork down. With regret. He signaled the waiter and told him to add the lady's bill to his own, then rose as she was informed. Surprised, she turned. Her lips parted.

"I have never seen a woman eat so much and with such pleasure." He laughed.

"The meal was heavenly." Blushing, she stood. "Thank you."

"You're welcome. Small payment for a good show."

Still embarrassed, but smiling now, she walked with him. "I'm glad you were entertained." She put her hand on her stomach. "Oh, my."

"Are you going to explode?"

She laughed with him. "No, but I do feel like a Thanksgiving turkey."

They stood outside on the boardwalk, silent in the waning sunlight. She looked at him with eyes that reminded him of magnolia leaves after a rain. His heart galloped. "Did you find a place to stay, Miss Walsh?"

"Yes, Mr. Beck."

"Shall I see you safely to your accommodations, ma'am?" Why did his Southern drawl have to sound so thick? She noticed and he saw her pupils widen.

She lowered her eyes. "Thank you for your kind offer, sir, but I can manage." She gave a slight dip. "Thank you again for my dinner." She started to step away.

"Are you heading back tomorrow?"

"No. Are you?"

"Yes. My business is done."

"Mine isn't. Have a pleasant evening, Mr. Beck."

He watched her walk away. Sacramento would be a better place for her. She would have everything she needed here, including a host of men from whom to pick a husband. Every man she passed tipped his hat or gave a nod and looked back at her. Kathryn entered a hotel a few doors from his own.

Matthias decided to find a saloon and drink something stronger than one glass of red wine.

"Copper and traces of silver," Amos Stearns told Kathryn. "Someone should come up and take a closer look. You could have yourself a bonanza, Miss Walsh." He pushed his glasses up. "As it happens, I'm planning a trip to Virginia City in the spring to see about our interests there. I could come to Calvada on my way back and inspect your mine."

Stunned, she stared at him. A possible bonanza? Why hadn't her uncle opened a mining operation? And if Wiley Baer was so knowledgeable, why had he said the mine was worthless? Maybe he wasn't the expert he claimed to be.

Stearns's gray eyes looked larger behind the lenses. "Miss Walsh? I think it warrants a closer look."

"I'm afraid I am a woman of very limited funds . . ." Though the bill today had been less than she expected, an on-site inspection might cost considerably more than she could afford.

"I've discussed it with my senior partners, and they may be interested in making an investment."

"How much of an investment depends on what Amos finds," Pruitt called out.

"You'll need capital to get started," Hollis added.

She felt overwhelmed. "Gentlemen, you are very optimistic." She saw all three were serious. "If I started a mining operation, I'd have to find someone who could manage it." She smiled. "I'm not very good with a shovel."

Amos chuckled. "No, I don't imagine you are."

Pruitt nodded toward Amos. "He might be young, but he grew up mining, and he has schooling."

Amos looked embarrassed at the praise. "With other mining operations in the area, I'm sure we could find a man qualified."

Matthias Beck popped into her head. Why had she thought of him? "Or I could sell." She thought of Morgan Sanders. She had no idea what sort of mine he ran, but she would find out when she returned to Calvada.

From the assayer's office, Kathryn went to a market near the harbor. She'd seen orchards on the way into town and wondered what she might bring back. The selection astonished her.

Oranges! An expensive luxury in Boston, but affordable here. The man said they'd been brought up from Riverside, where there had been orchards before the gold rush in '49. She purchased a small, handwoven reed basket and splurged on half a dozen, adding glossy winter apples from a neighboring booth and a pound of almonds from another.

Curious whether things were different in California than Boston, Kathryn went into a store with a Help Wanted sign in the window. She asked the bewhiskered merchant if the clerk position was still open. He said yes, and she told him she could read, write, and was good with math. She was a quick learner and a hard worker. Would he hire her? He looked flustered and said no, he'd never hire a woman. When she asked him why not, he said a woman's place was in the home, unless she was married to the owner, in which case it was proper. Oh, of course. Marry a woman and get a clerk for free. Just like Nabor Aday.

Fuming, Kathryn stood outside, her basket of oranges, apples, and nuts on her arm. Clearly life in Sacramento would not be any more to her liking than life in Calvada. It would be months before she would know anything firm about the mine, and she would need an occupation in the meantime. She bought supplies and simple hats she could embellish for the ladies of Calvada. Any income would be helpful to supplement the money her stepfather had given her.

8

KATHRYN GAVE AN ORANGE to Abbie Aday. "I'll plant the seeds in pots and pray they grow!" Abbie peeled it immediately, breaking the fruit into sections and swooning as she ate the first one. Leaning closer, she whispered, "Nabor hardly ever gets them, but when he does, he sells them at an outrageous price. He's never let me eat one . . ." She ate another section. "Oh, Kathryn, I've never tasted anything so delicious in my life." She rolled her eyes in ecstasy.

Nabor came out from the back room. "What have you got there?" One look and Abbie handed over the rest. He tucked two sections into his mouth. "Those cans still have to be stacked." He jerked his chin toward two large boxes, then took the rest of the orange into the back room. Furious, Kathryn could only glare at the curtain he pulled across the doorway.

Abbie sighed. "I'd better get to work." She smiled. "Thank you. It was a little taste of heaven." She sucked the remaining juice from her fingers before doing Nabor's bidding.

Ronya and Charlotte were both delighted to receive oranges, and Ronya was surprised by the gift of almonds. She always had apples, bartering with a grocer down the street for fruit in exchange for pastries or bread. The three women sat in the kitchen, taking a rare break between the breakfast and lunch rush.

Ronya poured Kathryn a cup of coffee. "You've been gone a few days, so I don't imagine you've heard the news. Matthias agreed to run for mayor."

"You sound pleased about it."

"I am, but I doubt he has much of a chance against Morgan Sanders. Stu Bickerson made mention of it in the *Clarion* yesterday."

When Kathryn asked about Beck's platform, Ronya shrugged. "Don't rightly know, but he'd be better for the town than Sanders." Ronya told her other news. There had been another accident at the Madera Mine. Thankfully, no one was killed or seriously injured this time. Henry Call seemed to be Matthias's business partner in some new venture, but no one knew what.

Kathryn wanted to read Stu Bickerson's article. Opening the door of the *Clarion* office, she was struck by the odor of cigar smoke and something else so foul she grimaced. A bearded man sat tipped back in his chair, boots off, stocking feet on the desk, snoring like a bear in hibernation. The office was a catastrophe of disorganization. Uncle City's house had been tidy by comparison. She stepped in and almost tripped over a spittoon overflowing with soggy cigar butts.

She cleared her throat. "Mr. Bickerson, I'm sorry to interrupt your noontime siesta." Though it was not yet noon.

Bickerson's rheumy eyes opened and then widened. His feet went up and his chair banged down. He stood on unsteady feet, thumbing his sagging suspenders into place. "Miss Walsh," he croaked. "This is a surprise."

She'd never met the man, but he clearly knew of her. "I'd like to buy the latest issue of your newspaper."

"You would?"

"The one announcing Mr. Beck's candidacy for mayor."

"Sure. Got copies here somewhere." He rummaged around on his desk. "It'll be five cents."

Five cents! "Isn't that rather high?"

"Price went up since the *Voice* shut down. Only newspaper in town."

She extracted five pennies from her drawstring purse and put them on his desk.

"Here's one." He handed over the *Clarion*.

She glanced at it, turned it over, and looked at him. "One sheet, one side? That's all?" She felt cheated.

"Not much news in Calvada."

Not when the editor slept on the job. She scanned the article about Matthias Beck, noting numerous misspellings and few answers to questions he should have asked. "This doesn't tell us very much about the candidates for mayor."

"Everyone in town knows Sanders and Beck."

"That's not the point." This was Calvada's only source of news? And why had it taken this long for her to notice?

Bickerson tucked an old cigar in his mouth and chewed on it until he found a match. "I was going to come and talk to you, Miss Walsh." He lit up and inhaled. "Heard you were trying to sell hats and such." He chortled, smoke puffing out of him like a locomotive. "City Walsh's niece setting up a ladies' shop in the *Voice*. Bet he'd be plumb happy about that."

She liked his tone even less than his newspaper. The cigar smoke was making her nauseous.

"How about I ask you some questions, write a story on you?" Bickerson's cigar bobbed up and down as he spoke, dropping ash on the front of his vest.

"Not today, Mr. Bickerson." She opened the door, desperately needing fresh air.

"A newspaper article would be good for your business."

"I'm sure word will spread." She could tell Gus Blather and the whole town would know in less than twenty-four hours.

"Didn't know women read anything but *Godey's*. But then maybe you're interested in Matthias Beck." He raised his brows.

"Only as a prospective mayor, Mr. Bickerson."

"Why? You can't vote."

"Just nosey." She smiled sweetly. "If you'll excuse me."

"Don't start a fire with it," Bickerson called after her, laughing.

She took a breath of air, preferring the stench of Calvada to the smell of Bickerson's dirty socks. She read as she walked.

Matthias Beck announced at his bar this mornin that he was proklayming hisself a candidate for mayor of Calvada. He says he is running for law and odor. When I aked him why he would wanna do suc a thing as that and he says to me well it's time I dealt myself into this game. He said he was tired of men shooting up his bar and maybe there should be a law that no man can shoot a gun in town limits. I don't lay much hope on Beck getting hisself elected. Morgan Sanders has done a fine job for us so far. No reason to change horses in mid streem.

Bickerson used space for a story about a dog howling outside the back door of the music hall and an announcement that Fiona

Hawthorne had added a new doll to her house. *Gents shud mak her feel welcome.*

"Miss Kathryn!" Scribe crossed the street, all smiles as he stepped up while she opened her front door. "You sure do look pretty today. Bets have been on that you wouldn't come back. Glad I won the bet."

She bunched the *Clarion* in her hand. Start a fire with it? Oh, it had already started a fire.

"Come in, Scribe. I'll make some tea. You and I have business to discuss."

Matthias saw Scribe coming out of Kathryn's house, a grin spread across his face as he headed across the street. He came through the swinging doors and spotted Matthias. Marching over, Scribe handed him a small, white, sealed envelope. "An invitation from Miss Kathryn Walsh." He looked like he'd been having the time of his life and couldn't conceal his glee.

"What have you been drinking?" Matthias growled.

"Tea!" Scribe laughed and headed for the bar, where he had a pile of shot glasses to wash. He stopped and turned. "Oh. I forgot to tell you. Miss Kathryn is back, and she told me to tell you that she's decided not to sell the press."

Opening the dainty monogrammed envelope, Matthias looked at the note written with the artistic flair of a calligrapher. Her words were few and to the point.

Mr. Beck,
    May I have an hour of your time to discuss your candidacy for mayor?

                            Respectfully,
                            Kathryn Walsh

What was she playing at? Matthias went to his office and wrote a response: *Your place or mine?* He sent Scribe back across the street.

Scribe returned with another little sealed envelope with *Matthias Beck* written neatly on the front. He tore it open and read. *Neither. Ronya's at 2:00 p.m. Unless you are otherwise occupied. KW.*

Matthias was beginning to enjoy himself. He wrote on the back of her note card: *I am always occupied, your ladyship, but I will gladly give you all the time you want. We will have more privacy to chat in my office. MB.*

Scribe returned quickly. *I will only meet with you in a public place. KW.*

Grinning, Matthias wrote, *People will talk, Miss Walsh. If we are seen together, they will make assumptions about our relationship. We wouldn't want that, now, would we?*

Scribe looked annoyed as he took the envelope. When he came back, he thrust Kathryn's response at Matthias and waited.

Thank you for your concern over my reputation, Mr. Beck, but I will make sure everyone understands nothing is going on between us.

How might she do that? he wondered, and decided to ask. When he knocked on the door, she called out, "Come in, Scribe." Matthias walked in. Kathryn sat at her desk, busily writing. "Just rest a minute. That man is as dense as a post. I want to add a few more questions before I forget them." Finishing, she blew on the paper as she held out her hand. "Let's see what nonsense he says this time." After a second, she glanced up. "Oh!" She dropped her pen. "It's you."

"At your service."

She walked around the desk and opened the door he'd just closed behind him. "In that case, make yourself comfortable."

She sat behind her desk again. "I read the *Clarion*." Folding her hands, she smiled. "I am hoping you have a better reason to run for mayor than 'I figured it was time I got in the game.'"

"Seems reason enough, don't you think?"

"Why do you want to be mayor? You have a lucrative saloon and hotel. And I heard you were an officer in the Union Army with a rank of captain. So you apparently have business acumen and leadership abilities, but . . ."

She sounded so earnest. "Why are you so interested?"

"I intend to write about you. Scribe has agreed to set the type and we're going to print the *Voice*."

A woman running a newspaper? He laughed. "You can't be serious."

Her eyes lit hot and fierce. "I am very serious, Mr. Beck."

She meant it. "It's a bad idea."

"I think I can do a better job than Mr. Bickerson."

"You'll get yourself into trouble."

"I've been in trouble before."

He came to his feet and planted his palms on her desk. "Open your hat shop or ladies' wear or whatever, but toss this asinine idea *now*. You have no idea what's going on."

"Then tell me."

"It's not a woman's business."

Her eyes sparked. "Well, I plan to make it my business, Mr. Beck. That press has been standing in the corner as idle as a corpse at a wake. It's about time to use it for a good purpose. I think that's what my uncle would have wanted."

Matthias gave a mirthless laugh and straightened. She had no idea the mess she could get herself into if she stuck her nose in where it didn't belong. "City wouldn't have much good to say about a girl trying to take his place behind that desk." He saw the punch hit, harder than he intended.

"I'm not a girl, Mr. Beck. I'm a woman with some education. I will do my best to honor my uncle as well as his newspaper." When he moved toward the door, she stood. "Are you leaving so soon?"

"The less you know, the better."

She sighed, but Matthias had the feeling she wasn't surprised. "I must say I was hoping for better from you, Mr. Beck." She sat and went back to whatever she was writing.

Matthias left uneasily. Slapping through the swinging door, he spotted Scribe. "In my office, kid. Now!" Scribe tossed the towel on a table and followed him.

Closing the office door, Matthias turned on him. "Don't encourage Miss Walsh to go into the newspaper business."

The boy looked rebellious and smug. "Kathryn is City's niece. Running a newspaper must be in her blood."

Bloodshed was what Matthias wanted to prevent. "Scribe, you're not doing *Kathryn* a favor by setting type for whatever nonsensical story that girl might write."

"She's not a girl. She's a lady. And she's educated."

"So she said."

"She's a lot smarter than you think she is."

"She's a young woman in a wild town where someone murdered her uncle for saying too much."

Scribe had clearly forgotten—or chose not to remember—how City had died. "We don't know for sure that was the reason." His bravado had withered slightly. "Besides, no one would hurt a lady like Kathryn."

"And you know that how?"

Scribe squared his shoulders. "Don't you worry. I'll protect her."

Great idea! Matthias almost laughed at the lunacy, but it wasn't funny. He could see the boy wouldn't listen. "Fine. Have it your way. Just remember you still work for me, and I'm running for mayor. Things are going to heat up around here, and I'll need you to run errands. Got that?"

"Yes, sir."

Matthias intended to keep Scribe working so hard, the boy would be too tired to set type, let alone operate the press. "You'll have evenings free to work for Miss Walsh. Deal?"

"Deal!" Scribe shook hands on it.

Matthias smiled and dismissed him. He was going to run that boy until his backside was dragging and then run him again.

Since Matthias Beck wouldn't cooperate, Kathryn found other sources of information. Gus Blather had a treasure trove he was only too eager to share. Ronya also proved helpful, though her friendship with Matthias made her biased. She was full of praise for the saloonkeeper.

"He could have opened a restaurant and put me out of business. Instead, he comes here for meals and encourages others to do likewise. Sanders is doing his best to shut me down."

"I didn't see many patrons when I ate in his dining room," Kathryn remarked nonchalantly.

"Two reasons for that, Kathryn. There aren't many who can afford his prices, and his French chef isn't French. He's Canadian."

"Have you met him?"

"No, but Fiona Hawthorne told me."

"You're friends?" Kathryn brightened. "I've been wanting to talk with her, but she won't even look at me in church."

"Well, she wouldn't. The last thing Fiona would want to do

is spoil your reputation." She rolled out dough. "You do know what she does for a living, don't you?"

Kathryn blushed. "Yes, and that she was one of three who attended my uncle's burial. I was told she stayed longer and cried. She must have cared for him a great deal. She's still wearing black."

"She always wears black. She's a widow like me, but she ended up on another path." Ronya punched out biscuits and put them on a greased sheet. "Matthias went to City's burial. That should give you reason to like him a little better."

"I don't dislike him, Ronya." Kathryn was surprised by the accusation. "He's been nice on occasion." She thought of their walk in the moonlight.

"On occasion?" Ronya gave her a curious look.

"He likes to make fun of me."

Ronya smiled. "You do make a fine target." She laughed. "The earnest Miss Walsh."

Stung, Kathryn defended herself. "I just want to know more about the man running for mayor."

Ronya slid a sheet of biscuits into the oven and straightened. "Are you going to be as interested in Morgan Sanders's past and character?" She looked and sounded annoyed. Was it Matthias she was defending? "I haven't heard you asking any questions about that son of a—" She pressed her lips together.

"I'll get to him soon. You seem to have a strong opinion."

"Oh, no. I'm not saying a word about Morgan Sanders."

"Why not?"

"Because I have sense." Ronya grabbed a damp rag. "And you'd better develop some quick." She wiped the worktable. "Keep your nose out of men's business."

Men's business. Kathryn bristled. She'd never expected to hear those words come out of Ronya's mouth. "I'm starting up the *Voice* again."

"A tomfool idea if I ever heard one."

Her words cut deep. "That's the sort of comment I hear from men." She stood. "Women *should* be interested in politics. A mayor makes decisions that impact all of us. Women included!"

"You're poking a hornet's nest, Kathryn."

"I intend to be truthful and impartial." She slipped her arms into her coat.

Ronya threw her rag down. "You are young and naive."

"That doesn't mean I'm stupid." She headed for the door.

"Kathryn!" Ronya came around the worktable, wearing a worried frown. "Perhaps you should read some of your uncle's newspapers."

Kathryn understood her concern. "I have. Unfortunately, the ones that might've been pertinent are missing, due to the death of a sheriff and the fire that burned down his house. Facts that give me even more reason to learn about the main players in town."

She headed for Herr Neumann's barbershop. Her uncle had let him handle the details of the inheritance. She stepped into the shop just as he was removing a man's tooth. Kathryn winced as the man in the chair yowled. "I've almost got it." Mr. Neumann planted a knee on the man's chest and yanked back. "There it is." Kathryn couldn't look, but the patient moaned in seeming relief. He got up, gave Herr a coin, grabbed his hat, put a hand to his jaw, and left.

Mr. Neumann noticed her then. "Something I can do for you, Miss Walsh?"

His bloodshot eyes told her he'd been drinking. How could any man trust him with a pair of scissors or pliers, let alone a razor? She knew better than to ask straightforward questions. She used charm and gave him the opportunity to tell his story and talk about her uncle. Then she slipped in a question here and there about Matthias Beck.

"Ho, City raked Matthias over the coals a few times. Matthias fought in the war. Like a lot of us, he came west after. Rumor has it he was under Sherman during the march through the South. Captain. That's what his partner called him."

"Langnor?"

"Paul Langnor. Matthias is good at poker. Langnor didn't have the money to expand, so Matthias went up and down Chump Street, playing cards. Bought half interest in the saloon, and then they started building. They worked well together, even though they fought on opposite sides." He wiped blood off his hand, rinsed the stained rag, and took it outside to wrap around the post to dry. "When Langnor got sick, Matthias and City tried to get him to a doctor. Burst appendix, they think. Heart gave out. A good man. Didn't water his whiskey. Neither does Beck."

"I suppose that is a very high compliment in Calvada."

"Well, it means you get what you pay for, unlike most watering holes in this town."

Shouts came from Beck's Saloon, and they both looked across the street. Kathryn frowned. "What do you suppose is going on over there?" Would Matthias be dunking another drunk in the horse's trough?

"Don't rightly know, but I think I'll find out." He paused. "Why did you come in here? Do you have a toothache?"

"No, no. I just thought I'd say hello and thank you for your help with my uncle's estate."

"Well, you are sure welcome, Miss Walsh." He closed the door to his shop and left her standing alone while he took a diagonal path across Chump Street. Dodging a horse and wagon, he made it unscathed to the other side and went through the swinging doors.

Curious about the excited shouts, Kathryn followed more cautiously. She had no intention of going into the saloon, just getting close enough to hear what was going on. What was all the banging about? Beck spoke in a loud oratory voice, but not loud enough for her to make out what he was saying. Men laughed at one point, then cheered at another.

Scribe came racing out through the swinging doors, giving her a glimpse of Beck standing on the bar. Scribe ran right by her, heading for the far end of town, his face flushed and sweating. The saloon was packed. They looked like they were celebrating a jubilee. Beck spotted her and grinned.

"And that's all I've got to say right now, gents. Belly up to the bar. Drinks on the house!"

Wondering where Scribe was, Kathryn came out and saw him crossing the street. He stumbled as he stepped up onto the boardwalk. He looked exhausted. "I have some stew ready and a few of Ronya's biscuits."

"Already ate." He muttered something else, looking ready to collapse.

"Have you been drinking?" She smelled beer as he entered the house.

He went to the chair by the desk and dropped. "Brady gave me a mug to perk me up."

"I'll make some coffee."

Scribe leaned back, legs sprawled. His body was so relaxed, he was about to slide to the floor and be a rug. She had to wake him up if they were going to get anything done. "Tell me about your day, Scribe."

"Huh?"

"I saw you running . . ."

"And running and running. Errands." His head lolled back, and he groaned like an old man. "I've been all over and around town. Been so many places I can't remember where all I've been." He yawned hugely. "I might die before the election is over." He fell asleep, mouth wide-open, and startled awake a moment later when he issued a snore loud enough to wake City Walsh from his grave. "What was that?"

"You." Kathryn couldn't help but laugh, even though she had a pretty good idea what Matthias Beck was doing. She let Scribe sleep until the coffee was ready. He leaned forward, holding one of her teacups between his hands, inhaling before sipping. "It's good."

"Always better with sugar." She'd added two heaping spoonfuls to his. "Drink some more, Scribe. You have to be awake enough to teach me how to set type."

"You write. I'll set type." He sipped.

"I'd better learn the skills of the trade, my friend. I have a feeling your boss across the street is trying to sabotage the *Voice* before it's even up and running."

That woke the boy up. "Then let's get to work." He finished the coffee, set the cup on her desk, and took the paper she handed him. He went to the cabinet and started opening small drawers of type.

Kathryn stayed close, but out of the way, watching everything he did. She asked questions as he worked. The sooner she learned how to set type herself, the better. "What was going on in the bar today? It sounded like Mr. Beck was giving a speech."

"He was. He was telling the men what he wants to do if elected. Says we need a strong town council so laws can be enacted to protect folks and settle work disputes." He shook his head. "He won't have a snowball's chance in—" He coughed. "Not a chance of that happening."

"Why not?"

"Morgan Sanders owns the biggest mining operation in town." Scribe stuck pieces of movable type into a composing stick. "And he's got the miners' votes locked tight as a Wells Fargo safe." He worked carefully, using a bodkin to pull out a piece when he made a mistake. Finishing one line of type, he started another. He dropped a couple pieces of type. Muttering under his breath, he kept working. The coffee was helping, but he looked so tired, Kathryn felt guilty. He tied a string around the two lines of type and started to transfer them to the larger galley. Fumbling, he dropped it, scattering type all over the office. Swearing, he fell to his knees and started picking up the pieces.

Kathryn laid a gentle hand on his shoulder. "It's all right, Scribe."

"No, it's not!" He swore again. "City taught me . . ." He wiped away frustrated tears with the back of his sleeve. "He said I have a talent for this." He'd filled one hand with type. "I just need more coffee."

"No. You're going back to Beck's and get some sleep." When he tried to get up, Kathryn had to help him. "When do you have a day off?"

"Matthias used to give me Monday off, but he told me today he's switching it to Sunday."

It was her custom to attend church every Sunday, have a nice lunch at Ronya's, and spend the rest of the day reading. Did Matthias Beck know that? The whole town probably knew. "We'll figure something out." She patted Scribe on the shoulder.

"Maybe I can come over early, before I go to work in the saloon."

Kathryn saw Scribe out the door. He walked across the street like a tired old man rather than a sixteen-year-old boy in good health. Beck came outside and held one swinging door open for Scribe. Then he came and stood at the edge of the boardwalk and grinned at her. "Have a nice evening, Miss Walsh?"

"Not as productive as I'd hoped, as I'm sure you know."

He went back inside, and Kathryn pulled her shawl more tightly around her. She listened to the raucous sounds of Chump Street for a moment before going back inside. Gathering up the scattered type, she separated letters into cubbies and closed the little drawers. She dipped a rag in turpentine and cleaned her inky fingers while studying the hulking press. Sitting at her desk, she uncapped her fountain pen and started to write.

9

MATTHIAS NOTICED SCRIBE COMING in the swinging doors a few minutes before eight in the morning. He'd managed to keep the boy hopping for several days. The kid looked dead tired. Jaw set, he scowled at Matthias as he headed for the bar. Matthias winced as the shot glasses rattled, wondering how many would be broken in the next hour.

Kathryn's office had been lit until well past midnight for several nights. Matthias had a feeling all his efforts to keep her out of harm's way were for naught. Once City got fired up about something, he never let up. He'd seen the same glint in Kathryn's green eyes.

Standing outside, Matthias took a long look up and down

Chump Street. Calvada was a sorry town, but it had potential. The question was, how many men would have the courage to vote against Sanders with their jobs on the line? Matthias had been talking to them day and night. Sanders went about his business as usual, so secure in his position as mayor, he didn't need to bother talking to anyone. No man should have that kind of power.

Now that Matthias was in the race, he doubted he could swing enough votes in his favor. Goodwill, free drinks, and entertainment only went so far. The incumbent had ways and means to keep a tight fist around the neck of Calvada. Something big would have to happen to overturn the plantation mentality that held Sanders's men captive.

Kathryn spent the day talking to anyone willing to share their opinions about the upcoming election, mostly women repeating what their husbands had said. Kathryn had been speaking with one of the miners' wives outside the Madera Company Store when the woman gasped and stared.

Fiona Hawthorne, stunning in black, came down the boardwalk, followed by three younger women, each wearing a full-length cape with hood. A breeze swept open one cape, revealing bare legs beneath a short red silk dress with edges of white lace showing.

Stepping aside, Kathryn gave them room to pass while other women turned away. Curious, Kathryn watched. Men grinned and followed. Nabor came out of the store and joined the parade. The women went right through the swinging doors of Beck's Saloon and were met by loud cheers of welcome. Someone pounded a lively tune on a piano. The fandango hall music was loud every night, but it didn't compare to the din coming from Beck's. He'd probably gone to Sacramento to bring back a wagonload of whiskey!

It was dark by the time the music and shouting died down. Opening the door, Kathryn heard Beck, voice raised as he gave a speech, probably standing on his bar again. She could only make out part of what he was saying.

". . . every man has the right to pursue happiness . . . time you men had a chance for a better life . . . take a hand in the way you want things run . . . law and order . . ."

Fine words, but would he back them up? She jumped when three men stumbled outside and started shooting their guns at the moon. Diving under her desk, Kathryn curled up, hands over her head. "Law and order!" she muttered, afraid some poor innocent bystander would end up with a bullet hole.

Beck was shouting and the shooting stopped. Kathryn crawled out from under her desk. By the time she peered out the window, the men had gone inside the saloon.

It seemed Beck was offering Calvada whiskey and women and little else.

She went into her apartment, put the teapot on the stove. A cup of chamomile might help her sleep.

Something had to be done to turn things right side up in this town!

Shrieking laughter drew Kathryn back to the front window. One of Fiona Hawthorne's dolls was running down the street, a drunken man in hot pursuit. Kathryn gasped. Nabor Aday, no less! Poor Abbie.

Seething, Kathryn sipped tea and looked at the fancy bonnets she'd made. Who could afford them? She felt useless, even more so when she thought of the children sitting in the drafty church with one small potbellied stove to keep them warm while shy Sally Thacker tried to teach them to read and write. She thought about the muddy streets, piles of filth in every alley, rats scurrying around in the night and carrying God-only-knew-what diseases. She thought of the lack of a sheriff and how boys like Scribe looked up to Matthias Beck. And she thought of her uncle's blood still staining the floor, despite all her scrubbing.

Crumpling the article she'd written, Kathryn started with a fresh sheet of paper.

Matthias was at Ronya's having breakfast and talking business with Henry Call when he heard Scribe hawking the *Calvada Voice*.

An hour later, Herr Neumann came across the street with a look of panic on his face. "Where have you been? Have you seen this? She's after your hide like the British after Napoleon at Waterloo! She calls you Lord Bacchus!"

Matthias took the sheet of paper from him. One page, one side. Not much of a newspaper.

BECK AND CALL

Government by Gall

If elected mayor, Lord Bacchus will most certainly see that nothing gets done in Calvada without the proper sanctification of spirits. Another headline: BAR DEBATE AND TACKLE TURNS TO BRAWL. Matthias laughed. "Seems Miss Walsh has a bit of City's sense of humor."

"Sense of humor!" Herr raged. "I don't think that woman means souls rising to heaven . . ."

"I don't think so either." Matthias grinned. "The lady is obviously angry over our innocent little social last night." Not that it had been all that innocent, as it turned out. Despite his intentions, things had gotten out of hand a time or two.

"She's after your blood!" Herr poked his finger at the offending paper. "She makes us all sound like drunken idiots."

"A slight exaggeration, Herr." There was nothing in the editorial that wasn't true.

"I'm telling you, Matthias, all it takes is one like her to ruin this town." He paced, waving his arms in agitation. "There's nothing more treacherous than a woman on a moral rampage." He jabbed his finger at the *Voice* again. "You read that editorial again. That scold makes it sound like the entire population of Calvada was drunk and chasing women down the street."

Matthias had never seen the barber with such a head of steam. "One man, Herr, and unnamed." He kept reading. A shorter article was at the bottom.

The cloven-hoofed monster recently reported in the *Clarion* was dispatched with a double-barreled shotgun. When the undertaker examined the body, it was found to be four apple crates, a pile of rags, and a rotting pumpkin. The expert marksman was unavailable for comment and last seen boasting of his kill at the Froggie Bottom Bar on the corner of Champs-Élysées Boulevard and Galway Avenue.

Scribe came across the street, a smirk on his young face. "What do you think?"

"Not bad for two novices, but not much to it."

"Better than the *Clarion*, and Kathryn's just getting warmed up."

Matthias wanted to cuff him for calling her Kathryn. "Working for Miss Walsh, are you?"

"Looks like it. Part-time, anyway."

"Good for you, kid. You can pay half the rent from now on." That dimmed the boy's expression somewhat. "Any copies left?"

"Sold 'em all in less than an hour."

Matthias jerked his chin. "You have mugs and shot glasses to wash."

Herr had been standing by, glaring at the boy like he was Judas Iscariot. "You should fire him. Kick him out."

Scribe frowned at him. "Go ahead. Kathryn will let me sleep in her front office." The boy turned to leave, but Matthias grabbed him by the scruff of the neck and sent him through the swinging doors.

Herr marched across the street and slammed into his barbershop. Matthias was about to go back inside when Kathryn Walsh stepped through her door in a blue promenade suit and a hat with Leavers lace and cabbage roses intertwined with champagne chiffon and dainty foliage. Where was she going all dressed up like that? A muscle clenched in his jaw. Let her vent her spleen on him. He could take it. But she'd better stay far away from Sanders.

Ronya's was packed. Kathryn felt the silence when she walked in the door, and it wasn't friendly. "Can I help?"

"I wouldn't if I was you," Charlotte said, taking two plates into the dining room.

Ronya looked her over. "It's not Sunday. Where are you going?"

"I'm going to conduct an interview later this morning."

Kathryn took off her hat and put on an apron. She picked up two plates as Charlotte came back in and grimaced. "Where do these go, Charlotte?"

"The two gents at the front right table by the windows."

"Be careful in there," Ronya called. "They've all been passing around the *Voice*."

Kit Cole, owner of the livery stable, and Fergus McCallum, bartender at the Rocker Box, didn't greet her. A few had things to say that made her cheeks sting, but she made no reply. Ronya raised her brows when Kathryn returned to the kitchen. "An interview, you said. With whom?"

"The incumbent candidate for mayor, Morgan Sanders. I'm going down to his hotel and see if he'll talk to me." The smell of sizzling bacon made Kathryn's stomach growl. "Then I'll go out to the Madera Mine."

Ronya scooped scrambled eggs. "Stick to hats, and leave well enough alone." She added bacon and a fluffy biscuit and slid it across the counter. "Stay and eat."

Kathryn sat. "I'll make more money printing a newspaper than making hats. Besides, the *Voice* is already better than the *Clarion*."

"Well, listen to you, all puffed up like a banty hen."

Charlotte returned to the kitchen. "Matthias and Henry just came in."

Kathryn started to rise, heart pounding. "Oh, let me serve them."

"Oh, no, you won't." Ronya pointed her spoon at the stool. "You stay right there. You want to know about Sanders?" She glowered at her. "Ask me your questions."

"It's better if I go to the man himself."

"And you think he'll give you straight answers?" Ronya cracked more eggs into a bowl. "If you want to know about the mine, you should take a walk out to Willow Creek Road." She poured milk into the bowl. "You'll get an eyeful of truth out there." She gave Kathryn directions. "Not a part of town you've explored yet, I imagine. Ask the women living out there what happens when men get crushed under tons of rock. But you'd better change into something a little less fine before you go."

"I'll go there right after I've spoken with Mr. Sanders."

Furious now, Ronya poured the eggs into the iron skillet. "Why don't you go right now? I'm sure Mr. High-and-Mighty will offer you a fancy breakfast made by his Canadian cook!"

Hurt, Kathryn stood and untied the apron. "I'm sorry you disapprove."

Charlotte put her hand on Kathryn's arm. "Be careful with that man."

Ronya slammed a skillet on the stove and muttered under her breath.

Kathryn wove her way through the dining room tables. Ignoring Matthias, she went out the front door. The Sanders Hotel was at the far end of Chump Street, and she felt like she was walking a gauntlet to get there. Men talked, some sneered. Only a few tipped their hats.

Sanders sat in his restaurant, several other men at his table, none as finely dressed as he. He didn't look happy and seemed to be doing all the talking. One of the men said something and he turned. Pushing his chair back, he stood, said something more, and the men rose and left the restaurant as he crossed the room. "Good morning, Kathryn." Before she could say anything, he signaled the waiter and ordered tea and pastries for the lady and a fresh pot of coffee for himself. "What can I do for you?"

She decided to be blunt. "I've come to ask a few questions."

"Of course you did." He chuckled. "I read the *Voice*. It was quite entertaining. I figured you'd come to me. I am mayor."

"Two terms, I've been told." Time enough to have done some good for the town. Had he? "I'd like to hear your list of accomplishments."

"You've only to look around."

"I have, and there's not much to commend."

His smile was patronizing. "You should've seen it when I arrived ten years ago. I've already improved it by offering jobs to over a hundred men and providing homes for them—and their families, if they're fortunate enough to have them."

Homes she had yet to see, but planned to visit very soon. "I'd like very much to see your mining operation." While Amos Stearns wouldn't be coming to Calvada until spring, she'd like to get some idea of what a real mining operation looked like. The Madera was the most prosperous.

"And as I said before, the mine is no place for a lady." His expression offered no hope of compromise.

She'd find another way to learn more about his business. "Calvada needs a schoolhouse and a full-time teacher. Are there any plans in that regard?"

"We haven't many children. It would be a waste of money when the church serves quite well as a schoolhouse."

"And Sally Thacker?"

"She's capable."

"Shouldn't she receive pay for carrying the responsibility of educating the children that are here?"

"Serving the community is part of her responsibility as the wife of Reverend Thacker."

He was looking less friendly, and she was striving to keep a calm demeanor. "I was informed of the municipal tax after I arrived, and I paid it." She had felt the pinch. "Where does that money go?"

"Into the city fund."

"Which is controlled by whom and used for what, exactly?"

His eyes narrowed. "Town improvements."

"Which brings me back to my first question. What have you achieved while you've been in office?"

He laughed. "Oh, my dear, you are earnest." He told her of several improvements, a new bridge and widening of a road. Other than that, he managed to talk around every question she asked, like an experienced politician. Kathryn thanked him for his time and for the tea and pastries, neither of which she had touched, and rose. Ronya had been right. But then, was Matthias Beck any better?

Morgan walked with her to the door. "I'd like you to join me for dinner this evening."

Despite her previous refusal, the man still seemed to be on the hunt. "Thank you for your kind invitation, Mr. Sanders, but I'm sure you understand that as editor of the *Voice*, it would seem I was taking one side over the other. I must remain neutral. Good day."

Kathryn decided to go to Aday's before visiting the widows on Willow Creek Road. Abbie had always proven most loquacious, and undoubtedly heard a great deal while serving customers. Perhaps she could provide some information.

Abbie turned as she came in and looked nervously toward the curtain. "What can I do for you, Miss Walsh?" The formal use of her name warned Kathryn that things had changed. Abbie glanced back again and then leaned over the counter to whisper. "Nabor doesn't want me to speak with you."

"I'm sorry about the price tags—"

"Oh, it's not over that. Your newspaper upset him."

Kathryn could guess why, though she hadn't named the man chasing one of Fiona Hawthorne's dolls down the street.

"Abbie!" Nabor growled from the back room. "Who're you talking to?"

"A customer."

He came out from behind the curtain, his face reddening when he saw Kathryn standing at the counter. "What have you been telling my wife?"

"She hasn't said anything." Abbie moved back a step, eyes wide.

"Shut up. I'm not talking to you." He pointed at Kathryn. "You're a disgrace."

Kathryn thought that better described him, but she refrained from saying so, for Abbie's sake. She left the store and went home to change into something less grand, as Ronya had advised. Then she headed for Willow Creek Road.

Matthias had been watching for Kathryn. Ronya had told him she was going to see Sanders. He spotted her coming out of Aday's. Nabor didn't like her. Nabor didn't like anyone who quibbled about his prices or disapproved of the way he treated his sweet wife. Even so, just about everyone other than Sanders's workers bought supplies from him. That would change in the days ahead. Even if he didn't win the election, Matthias intended to give the shopkeeper some competition.

Kathryn came out of the store less than a minute later. She looked upset, but quickly recovered. She went into her little house. Relaxing, he went back inside and sat with Henry by the front window. Less than half an hour later, there she was again, wearing her new coat, cap and boots, and a plain brown skirt this time. Where was she going now?

"You seem to have other things on your mind today," Henry remarked with a slight smile.

"Nothing on my mind but business, partner." Matthias looked at the paperwork. Maybe, if he wasn't worrying about her all the time, he could concentrate on ways to improve the town and bring more commerce to Calvada. He had plenty of ideas, but he had to get elected to put them into action.

Henry chuckled. "You're keeping close watch on Kathryn Walsh, aren't you, my friend?" His expression was speculative.

"I'd feel better if she wasn't so much like her uncle."

"But then she'd be a whole lot less interesting, if what I've heard about City Walsh is true." He glanced out the window. "I wouldn't worry too much. That was probably the first and last edition of the *Voice*."

"I hope so." Kathryn was heading for the north end of town.

"She looks like a woman who knows where she's going." Henry was watching, too.

"That's what worries me."

The small shanties on the far side of Willow Creek looked pieced together with remnants from abandoned shacks. One looked empty. In front of another sat a young woman hugging a blanket around her thin shoulders, her expression blank as she stared at the icy water running down from the high mountain snow. A third woman washed and hung worn clothes on a line while two small children played nearby. Smoke rose from pipes rather than chimneys. One outhouse served five houses.

Kathryn greeted the children, but they only stared at her with wide eyes, their little faces thin and sallow. Their mother straightened, watching Kathryn before she lifted another shirt. Kathryn approached and started to introduce herself.

"I know who you are. You're City Walsh's niece. I heard you came to town." The woman looked her over. "Surprised you're still here."

"Ronya Vanderstrom suggested I come talk with you."

"Did she? What about?"

"I've started up the *Voice* again and I'd like to know anything you can tell me about the Madera Mine, Mrs. . . . ?"

"O'Toole. Nellie O'Toole." She held the steaming shirt on the stick. "You want to hear what I have to say about Sanders's mine?" She gave a hard laugh. "I got trouble enough." She wrung out the shirt, shook it, and hung it on the line, every movement violent, her body rigid. She faced Kathryn. "You want plain talk, Miss Walsh? Then listen. Don't go mixing in things you got no business mixing in. Who are you to hold up our men to ridicule? What do you know about the way we live, you in your fine clothes and fancy hats?"

Kathryn's eyes smarted. She could see the abject poverty around her. "I'd like to help make things better, Mrs. O'Toole."

Nellie studied her a moment, her shoulders loosening. "We all want that. Why do you think we came to California? To live like this? We believed the newspapers that told us the West was the land of opportunity. Sanders promised us houses and good wages. Well, you see what we've got."

She wiped her brow. "My Sean talked to him about those promises he made, and when nothing come of them, he started talking to the men about organizing." She shook her head, eyes welling. "They told me a beam gave way. They didn't even try to dig him out. Not even a body to bury." She shook her head. "Take my advice. Go while you can. Back to wherever you came from."

"I was given a one-way ticket, Mrs. O'Toole. There's no going back."

"Stirred up trouble at home, too, huh?" Nellie's expression softened slightly. "I can't speak for every woman who's married to a miner, but I'd rather my Sean had gotten drunk in Beck's Saloon every night than get himself buried under a ton of rock." She called to her children, who were squabbling. "Everyone knows Matthias Beck and Morgan Sanders. I got no say in how things turn out, but if I did, I'd take Beck over Sanders any day." She turned away and then faced Kathryn again. "It wasn't just my Sean who died. Three others died with him. Now we're here, me and my young'uns and the others, barely scraping by." Her face was dark with anger and pain. "You think you can print any of that?"

Kathryn's heart squeezed tight. "I'm so sorry . . ."

"Being sorry don't do much."

Nellie O'Toole's bitter hopelessness pierced Kathryn. "A good mayor could make a great deal of difference."

"Who are you suggesting?" She gave a hard laugh. "It don't matter who runs against Sanders. Sanders always wins." She lifted her daughter and sat her on her hip. "He'll promise to make improvements in the mine, and the men will swallow the lies and vote for him because he owns them. At least here, on Willow Creek, we're not paying his rents. And he can't evict us again."

Another woman came outside, a baby asleep on her shoulder. "You shouldn't talk about him, Nellie."

Nellie's eyes flashed. "Too late now." She struggled for calm, rubbing her chin gently over her daughter's head while studying Kathryn. "I've said all I gotta say. Way too much already." Her anger wilted, fear flickering as she waved to her son. She followed him inside the shanty, yanking the canvas flap that served as a door.

The other widow's baby began to cry. She held the infant tenderly, gently patting as she spoke. "You shouldn't be asking questions, Miss Walsh. You may mean well, but you can't do anything but get yourself and others in a lot of trouble."

Kathryn didn't want to go back to Calvada. She wanted to get as far away from the mud and stench and inhumanity of the place as she could. Nellie O'Toole's despair permeated her spirit.

Sitting on the mountainside, Kathryn wept. She felt helpless and useless, a girl trained only to marry well and be a proper wife to some scion. She thought of the widows living in those shanties—Nellie O'Toole with her two children, the young mother with the sick baby, the other silent, grieving girl who seemed to have already given up. Ronya had given practical help by hiring Charlotte and moving her into one of the rooms in her boardinghouse. Kathryn wiped tears away and looked up at the snowcapped mountains. What could she do?

Chilled, she got up and walked to a higher place where she could see Calvada below. She watched horseback riders and wagons passing back and forth on Chump Street. From here, she could imagine what Calvada could be, not what it was. Up here, she felt the peace and beauty of the mountains all around her.

Even as a child, Kathryn had been enraged by injustice. Her first crime, in the eyes of the judge, had been to steal the Thanksgiving turkey from Cook and give it to a poor family who had come to beg for work at the gate. She'd been sent away to boarding school and spit back out again when she blackened a girl's eye for picking on a quiet girl from a family with new money. She'd been locked in her room a dozen times before she committed her last, unforgivable crime by joining the suffragettes fighting for women's rights. Her mother had tried to reason with her over the years. *You mustn't become so passionate over things that will never change, my darling.*

The Madera Mine Road wasn't far away. By the time she got there, the whistle had blown. Men came out in a line, armed guards doing a thorough search of each. One man seemed to be arguing with the guard in front of him. The guard shouted something, while another came up behind and hit the man with the butt of his rifle. The miner went down hard. He curled into a ball as the two guards kicked him. Other miners passed the fallen man. When one stopped to help him up, the guard who had hit him stepped forward, rifle raised. The beaten man managed to regain his feet, the guards mocking him as he stumbled away.

Kathryn went down the trail toward the road, hoping to help him. Before she reached him, two others came to his aid. She was close enough to overhear their conversation.

"You do that again and they'll kill you sure."

"You think I care anymore?"

"Don't be a fool. You want your wife scraping by like Sean's?"

One of the men spotted her. "What are you doing here?"

"I saw what happened." She approached.

The beaten man spit blood on the ground. "I read your paper. Your uncle knew what he wrote about. You don't know nothin'!"

IO

KATHRYN SPENT A SLEEPLESS NIGHT in her cozy little house and went back up the Madera Mine Road the next morning. Two rows of houses had been built not far from the mine complex, each identical, small, square, with a pitched roof, a front door with two small windows on each side, and a black pipe chimney rising at the back. Kathryn followed the sounds of children playing and found several women bundled in warm clothing, hoeing and weeding a communal winter garden behind the rows of houses. Surprised to have a visitor, they stopped working to talk with her. Most had been living in Sanders's houses since he'd built them.

"It was an improvement over what we had in Virginia City. We had to build our own there."

"At least they were ours," another said. "No rent to pay."

"We're closer. It's an easy walk for the men. The mine is just up the road."

Yes, they shopped at the company store, but the garden helped. Most of what they'd grown had already been used up or put up—butternut squash, leeks, carrots and cabbage, collard greens and onions. They hoped to have enough to get them through the winter months. "It's a hard walk to town in the snow."

How difficult it must be for these women to make do on what little their husbands made. "I see a lot of men going in and out of Beck's and the other saloons."

One woman shrugged. "My husband is happier with a drink or two in his belly."

"Some don't stop with one or two," another said as she dug the hoe into the hard soil.

The women told her most of the men working at the Madera Mine were single. After rent and a few supplies, they drank up and gambled away the rest of their pay. Some of the houses had six men living inside. There weren't many families, and only a few of the children attended Sally Thacker's lessons. With no education, Kathryn knew the boys would end up in the mine; the girls, married to miners.

After the last accident, several men had tried to sneak away in the night. "They didn't get far. Sanders's men went after them and brought them back. They were beat up bad."

"But not so bad they couldn't work." The woman hacked harder with her hoe. "They owed money to the company store. Just like the rest of us."

Kathryn went into Sanders's store when she returned to town. Everything was more expensive than Aday's: dried beans and barley, flour and sugar, calico and buttons. She thought better of Nabor after seeing the prices on boots and dungarees, coats and gloves in the Madera Company Store. Nabor had tried to cheat her, but even the altered price had been less than what Sanders charged.

Several women came to visit the next morning; all three were wives of the more affluent men in town. They showed interest in Kathryn's hats, but they were more eager to tell her what their husbands had to say about the *Voice* and its editor.

"John was furious!" Lucy Wynham, the baker's wife, fingered a pheasant feather. "He thinks women shouldn't know what goes on in a saloon and that no real lady would write about it." She gave an annoyed laugh. "As if ladies are blind and deaf and don't already know."

Vinnie MacIntosh, the undertaker's wife, peered out Kathryn's window. "You poor dear! You can see most of Chump Street from here!"

"A front-row seat to all the goings-on." Camilla Deets, the wife of one of the butchers in town, shook her head. "We live up Galway, but even up there I can hear the fandango halls every night."

"Ivan said you sound an awful lot like City." Vinnie smiled. "People waited for the *Voice* to come out when he . . ."

"Thank you." Kathryn took her words as a compliment. A bit surprised by the women's enthusiasm, she offered them tea. "I'm not sure if there will be another issue."

"You can't quit! You've only just begun!"

If she wrote what she had seen at the mine and how she had gleaned the details, what trouble might she bring on those poor women living in the row houses, or the widows on Willow Creek? But if she didn't write about it, how would anything change? She almost wished she hadn't begun at all. "You all seem pleased with what I had to say, but will it do any good? Women don't vote, and all I've managed to do is anger the men." She held up several notes that had been shoved under her door.

Camilla took one and read it aloud. "'Women are like children. They should be seen and not heard.'" She huffed. "Unless you're saying something a man agrees with."

"John probably wrote that." Lucy sighed. "Every time I raise the slightest question about anything, he says that exact same thing."

Vinnie touched Kathryn's arm. "Ivan said it was the first honest thing he's read since City . . . died. He wondered if you were going to start looking beyond Chump Street."

"I went out to Willow Creek Road two days ago, then to a hill where I could see the Madera Mine. Yesterday, I went to the row houses." What could she do to help those poor women?

"Slag Hollow." Camilla frowned. "That's what the miners call it."

Vinnie took a hat and turned it around, looking at it from all angles. "We wondered why your shop was closed for the past two days."

Kathryn had returned tired and depressed. Unable to sleep, she spent several hours making hats and seeing the cruel irony in trying to sell lovely things those poor women could never afford. She'd thought of parties she'd attended in Boston, afternoon teas, and summer gatherings where she'd danced and laughed. What good had she ever accomplished, even with her little rebellions? Had anything been for the sake of others or simply a way to antagonize her stepfather?

"Calvada needs many improvements." Camilla Deets tried on one of the hats Kathryn had made the night before. "This is lovely!" She adjusted it. "I'm sure you could suggest changes, considering you come from the East, where it's civilized. Do you have a mirror?" Kathryn brought her a small one from the back room. "Perfect," Camilla decided, admiring her reflection. "I'll take it. I can't wait to wear it to church on Sunday."

Wanting to glean more information, Kathryn offered the ladies tea and served them with her fine Minton red-and-gold china teacups and saucers. Her mother had given her a full set, but she'd only had room in her Saratoga trunk for a few special things. Though out of place in Calvada, she realized how these little shared luxuries brightened the day for these new friends.

Vinnie also purchased a hat before leaving.

The door opened again shortly after they left, and Morgan Sanders entered with one of the women who sat with Fiona Hawthorne every Sunday. She wasn't much older than Kathryn, with dark hair and brown eyes.

"Kathryn, this is Monique Beaulieu, an acquaintance of mine. Monique, this is Kathryn Walsh."

The young woman held back, silent, tense, giving Kathryn the impression that she had not been eager to come into the shop. Stepping forward, Kathryn extended her hand. *Enchantée, mademoiselle.*"

Morgan looked surprised and pleased. "You speak French."

"My mother insisted upon it, though I've seldom had the opportunity to use it." She smiled at Monique, but the girl avoided her eyes, looking around at the hats instead.

"This young lady is a friend of mine." He smiled. "A little dove I've taken under my wing."

Relieved that he would no longer be interested in her, Kathryn encouraged them to look around. She addressed

Monique in French. "I can show you samples. You've only to tell me your preferences." She took a book of designs from a desk drawer.

Morgan looked at the gingham-covered press and chuckled. Kathryn had decided to keep it covered during the morning hours when she was running her shop. "Out of business already?"

"One business will support the other." Why not be bold? "Would you like to purchase advertising space?"

"A mine doesn't need advertising, Kathryn."

She didn't approve of him using her given name, let alone the way he said it. Neither did Monique Beaulieu. "Nor, I suppose, does a company store." When his eyes narrowed, she offered an innocent smile. "However, you are campaigning for mayor, are you not?"

He laughed. "Lord Bacchus has less to offer than I do."

"You read the *Voice*."

"I found it quite amusing. Well worth the two cents I paid for it." He held Kathryn's gaze for a moment, then looked at Monique. "Have you made up your mind yet?" She shook her head and continued to look through the book. Kathryn wondered about her, how a lovely young woman ended up in a brothel.

She felt Morgan's eyes fixed on her and lifted her head. "I'm delighted to hear it was worth the price. Perhaps I should raise it to match the *Clarion*." It bothered her how little attention he was giving Monique.

"I agree with your assessment of Matthias Beck, by the way. Quite the rogue. One of my men went to hear his speech. Apparently, Beck is planning to bring more women to Calvada."

His tone left her in no doubt what kind of ladies he meant. Monique raised her head and looked at him.

Embarrassed, Kathryn didn't know what to say.

Monique closed the book firmly. "I'd like to go, Morgan. There's nothing here—"

"Not yet." Morgan cut her off and held Kathryn's gaze. "A woman can bring great comfort to a man."

Perhaps Morgan Sanders would marry Monique. Kathryn hoped he would. But she still wanted answers from the man. Her recent walks around Calvada had opened her eyes. "Madera Mine Road was improved last year, but it seems little attention has been given to Champs-Élysées."

He dismissed her concerns. "Chump Street is always a mess through winter."

"Winter comes every year, sir."

He smiled as though she was a child. "What would you suggest? Cobblestone? This isn't Boston, my dear."

"You have mountains of stone, gravel, and sand taken from your mine. Some of it could be used to make a better main street for Calvada."

"You know little about roadbuilding, Kathryn."

"I imagine the men who improved your road do."

Monique rose and slipped her hand into Morgan's arm. She said something in a low whisper. He didn't look pleased, but he demurred. He gave a nod to Kathryn. "Perhaps I will advertise. It would help you stay in business, wouldn't it? We'll talk later."

Kathryn wished she hadn't suggested it.

Matthias saw Morgan Sanders and one of Fiona Hawthorne's dolls come out of Kathryn's house. Had she realized the girl was a prostitute? With so few eligible women in town, men sometimes took a soiled dove as a wife. The other women

seldom accepted them. It had irked City that although Fiona
Hawthorne had given more money toward building the church
than anyone else in town, still the women wouldn't look at her,
let alone speak to her. How easily they judged their own sex,
without thought of what circumstances might force a woman
into selling herself. Had Kathryn asked Sanders and Fiona's doll
to leave her shop?

A bigger question was why Sanders had put Kathryn in that
situation. The man had had his eye on her since she came to
town. She'd make a fine wife for a mine owner and mother
to the son he'd want to inherit his empire. Some might say it
would be a good match. Considering the man's wealth and her
poverty, she might be tempted.

Did Kathryn understand the dark water she was tread-
ing? Thinking about Kathryn with Sanders made his stomach
clench.

Ronya said Kathryn didn't want to marry. Anyone. Ever.
Her editorial did show certain leanings toward the temperance
movement. Was she also a suffragette? He'd sure like to know.
They hadn't talked since the *Voice* came out. Maybe it was time
they did. And why not now?

Matthias tapped on her door. When she opened it, she gave
a sigh, resigned. Hardly the look he wanted to see on her face.
"May I come in?"

"I suppose you've come to take me to task for what I wrote
about you and your social event of the season." She stepped
away, letting the door drift open.

"I'm not the one you saw running down Chump Street after
one of Fiona's dolls. That man would probably like to buy you
a ticket on the next stage out of town."

"Why are you here, Mr. Beck?"

"I've come to fill in a few pieces to the story."

She frowned, looking seriously dismayed. "What pieces?"

"Whiskey loosens tongues and gets men talking about what's really going on."

She rolled her eyes. "Poppycock, Mr. Beck. What snake oil are you trying to sell me?" She sniffed. "I'll bet my conversation over a cup of tea has gained more information than your drinks-on-the-house method."

What information? he wanted to demand. "You don't know Calvada yet, your ladyship."

"It's amazing what I've learned by taking long walks, opening my eyes and ears, and listening." She looked up at him. "For example, there's a rumor that your campaign speech promised more ladies. Is it true? Mail-order brides?"

He blushed. "I plan to hire ladies to wait tables and service the hotel rooms." He winced at the last, knowing it could be misconstrued. "Making beds, that sort of thing." He clenched his teeth, telling himself to shut up. Kathryn just looked at him.

When she didn't say anything, he decided he'd better get to the point of his visit. "I came over to offer a little unsolicited advice: Too much truth at one time can hurt more than help."

"I've always thought truth the great equalizer."

"Not always. Unfortunately." He'd fought a war where both sides thought they were in the right, and little had changed that he could see, other than tens of thousands of men dying on both sides of the Mason-Dixon Line. America still wasn't unified, and men were still only equal in birth and death, nowhere in between. "I admire your passion, but while you're raking through the muck, make sure you don't fall in and drown." Would she understand the warning without him having to put a name to it?

"If you're referring to Morgan Sanders, I assure you there are many like him in the East. My stepfather wanted me to marry the son of one of them. I refused."

Saying no to a boy was easier than refusing a man like Sanders. Matthias couldn't resist asking, "Is that why you were sent west, Miss Walsh?"

"Refusing to marry was only one of my crimes."

He wanted a list, but he focused on one issue that could tell a tale. "You sound rather firm on matrimony."

"A woman has few enough rights without losing them all to a husband."

"Morgan Sanders will try to change your mind." And if he did, he'd also set out to crush her spirit.

"That might concern me, if I found the man the least bit attractive." Her eyes flickered as if she regretted revealing so much.

Matthias's mood rose. "Is that so?" he drawled with a slight smile. "I'm relieved to hear it."

She looked away first and stepped behind her desk, as though needing a barrier between them. "Was there anything else you wanted, Mr. Beck?" Her tone was calm and serious.

"Yes." Matthias looked her over slowly, met her startled eyes, and smiled. "But this isn't the time."

Scribe slouched on the settee, exhausted. "I heard Sanders and then Matthias came to call. Are we in business, or have you been talked out of it already?"

Kathryn offered him a scone from Wynham's Bakery. "O ye of little faith. Yes. We're staying in business. The sooner the *Voice* makes money, the sooner I can stop making hats. I've been working on another editorial on the other mayoral candidate."

"Sanders?" Scribe choked and coughed.

"Who else?" She slapped him on the back.

"That's sticking your neck out a little too far. You'd better be careful what you write about him."

She bristled. "What sort of newspaper are we publishing if we don't look at every candidate objectively?"

"There are only two."

"Unfortunately." She gathered her papers. "I'm not going to let a few disgruntled men and nasty notes deter me."

"And you won't make a living or be able to pay me enough to quit washing shot glasses unless we print more newspapers and raise the price to five cents, like Bickerson. And line up advertising and print jobs."

"I've already talked to most of the merchants on Chump Street. None want to do business with me. Though Morgan Sanders showed an interest."

"Oh, no. No! He doesn't need advertising." He eyed the last scone. "Are you going to eat that?"

Kathryn held out the plate so he could take it. "I offered. I wish I hadn't, but we need the money." She looked at the editorial she'd written. "Though he might change his mind after the next issue."

"I doubt he's interested in advertising. He's after you. He paid for your dinner the first night and wanted to have you up to his fancy place."

Kathryn raised her arms in exasperation. "Does everyone in town know my business?" She shook her head. "Besides, he has a lady friend." The man troubled her, but not in the same way Matthias Beck did. "If he comes, I'll tell him I've changed my mind. Advertising for him might make it look like the *Voice* is taking sides in the election."

"Offer Matthias the same deal."

When Matthias Beck had looked at her this afternoon, she'd felt like he was staking a claim. "Oh, no." Kathryn remembered the rush of sensations coursing through her body. "I think I'll leave well enough alone."

Kathryn sent Morgan Sanders a note regarding her decision. He sent a reply.

As you wish, but you won't always find it so easy to say no to me, Kathryn. I remain your devoted admirer.

Morgan

Though she couldn't sleep that night, she was no less determined to follow her course in the morning.

"What the blazes is going on now?" Shouting was coming from the bar. Matthias and Henry Call had been talking over their survey of men in Calvada, calculating whether they'd have enough votes without the Madera miners to win the election. Matthias figured he'd wasted a lot of time and money for naught.

He recognized Herr's voice. What was the barber complaining about this time?

"You've gotta see this!" Herr plowed through the throng and thrust the *Voice* at him. "Talk about gall!"

MAYOR MORGAN SANDERS

Man of the People or Man for Himself?

Matthias grabbed it out of his hand and read.

. . . empire built on the labor of miners receiving low wages and promised housing . . . six men crowded into

a cold shack . . . mining accidents . . . widows living
in poverty along Willow Creek Road . . . proposes an
expansion of town limits in order to bring in more taxes
to pay for a wider south bridge and road to benefit
the Madera Mine . . . but Sanders's mine will be just
over the line, reaping the benefits of municipal taxes
without having to pay them . . .

A chill went down Matthias's spine, and then heat shot back
up and flooded him.

"Hey! Where are you going with my newspaper?" Herr
shouted as Matthias slapped through the swinging doors and
strode across the street. Snow had come that morning, but the
ground wasn't hard yet. He took two long steps and went into
Kathryn Walsh's office. She started as he came in, jabbing herself with the needle she'd been using to stitch a cabbage rose to
a hat. Uttering a gasp of pain, she glared at him.

"For heaven's sake, Mr. Beck. Is that any way to enter a
building?" She shook her hand and sucked at the spot of blood.
Carefully putting the bonnet aside, she rose. "What's wrong?
You seem to have lost your ability to speak."

He didn't like what he felt every time he came near her. "You
and I need to have a talk."

She frowned, her nose wrinkling. Glancing down, she gave
a cry. "Look what you've tracked in!"

Matthias looked at his muddy boots and back at the foot-
prints across her threshold. He held up the newspaper.

Air hissed between her clenched teeth as she jabbed her
bloody finger at the door. "Out! Now! Go!" When he didn't
move, she advanced on him with so much fury, he took a step
back before planting his feet. He fisted the newspaper in front
of her face. She slapped it away. "I'm not talking to you until

you go outside and scrape off your boots!" She snatched the newspaper and threw it at him.

Cursing, Matthias went outside. He scraped his boots and kicked the post, rattling the boardwalk cover enough to rain snow into the street. He went back into her little office again, only to find her coming in from the back room with a bucket of water and a rope mop. She set the bucket down with a hard thunk.

"You'd better not try and hit me with that."

"Don't tempt me. My whole shop reeks of manure!" She pumped the mop up and down in the water.

"You bet it does! You decided to dive headfirst into a mine full of it!"

Flinching when he shouted, she slopped water on the mud he'd tracked in. "Go mind your own business and let me handle mine."

Matthias yanked the mop out of her hands. "You're going to listen! This is serious, Kate."

"My name is not Kate." She grabbed the mop. "Give it to me!"

"Oh, I'd like to give it to you!" Matthias ground out, letting go. "I stand corrected, your ladyship," he said through clenched teeth. "Miss Walsh." He sneered. "Stiff-necked Bostonian pain in my—"

"Remove yourself, sir!" Rigid as pine, Kathryn stood with one hand on her hip, holding the mop like a rifle at parade rest. She let out a slow breath, muscles loosening. "Or would you care for a calming cup of tea, Mr. Beck?" Her tone was sweet enough to make his teeth ache.

"Only if you can lace it with good Kentucky bourbon."

"The only lacing I have is on that shelf."

"Then I'll pass on the tea and settle for a bit of conversation." He was done playing. *"Sit down!"*

Kathryn jerked, but stood her ground. "You needn't yell." She didn't move until he took a step forward, then she sat gracefully on the settee, folding her hands demurely in her lap. "Go ahead and tell me what I already know. Mr. Sanders will be displeased with my editorial."

"Displeased? That's an understatement."

"I merely wrote what he himself shared with me and what I have observed with my own two eyes."

"You have the common sense of a rabbit!"

Her lips pressed tight. "Have you seen how his miners live? And what happens to their widows when the men get crushed under a ton of rock or blown up with dynamite?"

"I know. I've seen." He and Henry were working on plans to do something about it without turning the entire town into a war zone.

"And the prices in his company store?"

"Yes." Stooping, he picked up the *Voice* and thrust it at her. "What do you think you accomplished with this?"

"I addressed issues in direct correlation to his suitability as mayor. If past promises came to nothing, what trust should be placed in Mr. Sanders's current rhetoric?" She gave him a steely look. "Or yours, for that matter."

"For temperance, are you?"

"I doubt women would receive any rights at all, if their first act would be to take away men's liquor."

She was astute in that regard. He just wished she was wiser in other areas. "There are only two in this election—"

"And I'm not sure which of you is worse." She squared her shoulders. "Sanders employs men for less than they're worth, and then they drink up their meager earnings at your bar or gamble them away at your faro tables."

Pierced by her criticism, he didn't defend himself. She was

right, and that was why he had set a new course, though it was too early to tell anyone.

"And now you're adding women . . ." Her tone was droll, her expression watchful.

Matthias couldn't let that pass. "Men behave better when women are around." She gave a disdainful laugh. Furious, he plowed ahead. "These *ladies* will be dealing cards and working behind the bar. They're not . . ."

"Soiled doves?" She raised her brows in challenge.

"No. They're not. And there will be rules. No . . ." He wasn't sure how to say it without saying it.

"Fraternizing with clientele?" Tipping her chin, Kathryn gave him grave consideration. "And you think there will be fewer brawls, less swearing, no more shooting in the streets."

"Exactly."

She considered his idea. "And this is your method of maintaining law and order."

At least she was listening. "One of them."

Kathryn smoothed her skirt and stood. "Well, I think it's a very interesting idea, Mr. Beck. Indeed, I do."

He didn't trust her tone or the catlike smile. "I'm so glad you approve, your ladyship." He wondered what kind of editorial she'd cook up about it.

"I approve anything that will *im*prove this town." She stood in front of him. "Are we done now?"

Oh, no, lady. Not by a long shot. "Take a little friendly advice and write about something other than the election. Everyone knows Sanders. And they know me. Election Day will tell us who's going to make changes and what kind." He turned toward the door.

"And what, pray tell, would you have me write about?"

Exasperated, Matthias faced her. "Write about church functions and lodge meetings. Report on marriages, births, deaths.

Write about fashions in the East. Write about chilblains, canning, and children! I don't care! But use your head. Leave men to handle things."

She made a soft sound, as though considering his speech. "I suppose you think Stu Bickerson is a good enough newspaperman for Calvada."

She had him there. Stu Bickerson was an ignorant bumpkin and in Sanders's back pocket.

Kathryn looked completely relaxed now, her expression even softening. "I'm touched by your concern, Mr. Beck. Sincerely. Considering what I wrote about you, I'm surprised you're worried on my behalf and not raising a committee to tar and feather me and put me on the next stage out of town. Be at ease. I imagine Morgan will take what I wrote about him as seriously as you did when you read the first edition."

Morgan. He hated hearing that name on her lips. "You'd better hope so." Her eyes flickered. She wasn't as unaware of the risks as she pretended to be, which gave him further cause for worry. Courage could be reckless, and recklessness brought consequences.

"I hope Mr. Sanders reads every word and feels the conviction to change." Kathryn looked serious and slightly optimistic. "Then he will keep his original promises, raise the men's wages, improve their cabins, and help those poor widows, not to mention adding timber to prevent further cave-ins. Maybe he'll even lower the prices in his company store, at least to where Nabor Aday's are."

Matthias felt a surge of anger. And here he thought she had some sense. "What? You think you can redeem the man?"

"I wasn't talking about his soul, but now that you mention it, miracles can happen. No man is beyond redemption. Well, maybe you."

Matthias gave a bleak laugh. "So I've been told." He walked out, leaving the door open behind him.

II

KATHRYN WAITED ALL DAY for Morgan Sanders to come storming into her office the same way Matthias Beck had. He didn't come. He sent one of the foremen she had seen at the hotel. He had a gun strapped low on his hip this time. "From Morgan." He handed her an envelope and leaned down. "You'd better watch yourself, little lady." He sounded serious and looked it, too. She sat at her desk and waited for her pulse to slow before she opened the envelope.

You have wounded me deeply. You are young and naive and have much to learn about me and Calvada. Be assured I forgive you. My intentions have not changed. For now, all I want is consideration and respect. Tread more carefully in the future.

Morgan

She felt her insides shiver. What did it take to discourage a man like Sanders from pursuing her? She crumpled the note and threw it in the wastebasket.

Pulling over a piece of paper, she wrote about Matthias Beck's idea of importing women to keep the men in line. She imagined several scenarios that made her chuckle.

Pausing, she tapped her pencil on the desk and thought of the topics he had suggested. If the *Voice* was going to be relevant, she had to print more than her own editorials and rebuttals to the ridiculous tall tales Stu Bickerson invented as "news." Ronya would be a good source for cooking tips; Abbie Aday for managing a business; the miners' wives for preparing, planting, and tending gardens. Why not interview them, glean their wisdom, and share it in a weekly column? She would be the first to benefit. And the multitude of bachelors could certainly use some housekeeping tips!

Satisfied with the final draft of her editorial, Kathryn set it aside. It was too late to go to Ronya's for dinner, so she made do with a slice of bread and a cup of tea before going to work on hats. She finished the round marin anglais hat she was making as a gift for Sally Thacker, adding floral decorations and two white egret feathers. Darkness fell early this time of year, and she lit the lamp so she could keep working. As much as she preferred writing, the millinery provided income for now.

She hoped the goods she had purchased in Sacramento would bring a boom to her little shop. She decorated a plain high-crowned hat with moiré ribbon, then a sailor's round crown and brim with a simple grosgrain ribbon and bow. She finished three flat bonnets with ribbons and flowers, praying each one would cheer some woman in this cheerless town. She prayed Nabor Aday would loosen his grip on a dollar or two and give his hardworking, devoted wife a gift that would raise her spirits.

Kathryn got up early and began setting type before Scribe showed up. He looked rumpled and out of sorts and complained that he was sick of washing dishes and emptying spittoons. His spirits rose markedly when he read her editorial. Laughing, he went straight to work.

———————

A dozen men poured into Beck's the next day, all talking at once. Two had newspapers and the others tried to read over their shoulders. Henry came through the swinging doors a moment later, reading and shaking his head. Grinning, he crossed the saloon and stood beside Matthias at the bar. "You're in hot soup again, my friend. I sure wish this lady was on our side."

"What'd she say this time?"

"Read it for yourself."

The title didn't surprise him. ANGELS OF MERCY TO TAKE CALVADA UNDER THEIR WINGS was emblazoned across the top, followed by Kathryn's recounting of their conversation. She quoted him frequently and interspersed his assurances of law and order with hilarious word pictures of primly attired spinsters keeping the peace in the saloon and up and down Chump Street. Naturally, each had a highly polished silver star pinned to her bodice and a whip attached to her belt. He cringed. He'd known before he walked out her door that he was putting a target on his chest. Whatever it took, he wanted to keep her from aiming spears at Sanders.

"At least she's giving equal space to your opponent."

Matthias flipped the sheet over and swore. Clearly, she had ignored his advice. *Madera Mine has had four cave-ins in the past two years . . . five killed here . . . one missing . . . another accident . . . twice trapping a half-dozen men . . . several hours of digging before they could be rescued . . .* He spit out a foul word.

At the bottom of the back page was a blocked advertisement.

WANTED: ONE HONEST MAYOR

Qualifications: a willingness to dedicate himself
to the betterment of living conditions
for ALL citizens of Calvada.

Henry lost his smile. "You think there's going to be trouble?"

"I'd bet on it."

Trouble wasn't long in coming, and when it did, it didn't come from Morgan Sanders. It landed on the street side of the double swinging doors into Matthias's casino when a few irate wives showed up and stood on tiptoes looking into the barroom, calling for their husbands to come out. When the men refused, Matthias went to placate the women. There were only three, but they made a ruckus. He used all the Southern charm he could muster and still failed to calm the storm.

"Hogwash!" One older woman with a German accent stood toe-to-toe with Matthias, chin jutting. "We weren't born yesterday!"

"Spinsters, my eye!" a pigeon-shaped matron cried out. "Angels of mercy, my foot!" She stooped and peered under the doors. "Richaaaaaard! Come out of there if you don't want me to put rat poison in your next meal!"

"Go home, woman!" Richard shouted back, but he got up

anyway and headed for the door. Two others followed the belea-
guered Richard, intending to give him moral support. The battle
of the sexes broke out in earnest on the boardwalk, while Matthias
stood by, rubbing the back of his neck in growing frustration.

Standing beside Matthias, Henry chuckled. "And you're
bringing more women to Calvada?"

One wife wept. "How could you do this to me, Charlie?"

"I haven't done anything yet, lovey."

"Yet?"

"Now, honey . . . I didn't mean . . ."

Another man went nose-to-nose with his spouse, hollering.
"Go home right now where you belong!"

She hollered back. "And sit by while you horse around?"

"It's a man's right!"

"While I cook your meals, wash and iron your clothes, milk
your cow, feed your chickens, take care of your garden, and raise
your six children . . ."

Herr was walking a circle in front of his barbershop and
shouting. "What'd I tell you, Matthias! What'd I tell you?"

Matthias stalked back into his establishment. Grinning,
Brady set a full bottle of bourbon on the bar. "Thanks," Matthias
muttered, leaving it there. "You're a big help."

Things settled down after a couple of days.

Scribe faced verbal abuse, especially from Herr, who used to
have a soft spot for the boy, and now considered him a traitor. "We
ought to break all your fingers so you can't set any more type."

"Afraid of a little Boston lady, Herr?" Scribe smirked.

Matthias grabbed the boy by the back of his neck and hauled
him down the hallway into his office. "Don't make things
worse."

"He has no call bad-mouthing Kathryn. She's trying to make
things better!"

"You call this better?" Matthias snarled.

"Well, don't blame me. I haven't got power over her. She writes what she sees, and everything she's printed so far is right on target. And pretty funny, if you ask me."

Funny? "City was right on target, too, and got his head beat in with the handle of that press! You want to cross the street and find her the same way you found her uncle?"

That sobered the boy. Sagging onto the chopping block, he looked up with tortured eyes. "No one would do that to a lady."

Matthias remembered the war years. "Men have done worse."

Scribe's shoulders drooped. "There's nothing I can do."

"Sure there is. Stop setting type."

"She'd print it herself. She's already setting type before I get there. Might take her a little longer, but she's smart and determined."

Stepping away, Matthias raked a hand through his hair. He let out a heavy breath. "Maybe I should break her fingers before someone breaks her neck."

Scribe stood, face reddening. "You'd better not touch her! You'll have me to reckon with!"

"Oh, shut up and sit down! Do you honestly think I'd hurt her?" Matthias was trying to figure out how to keep her safe, and she was making it harder every time she put out the *Voice*.

Scribe sat, shoulders hunched. "The only one Kathryn would listen to right now is God."

Matthias glanced at him. "What'd you say?"

"God."

Matthias thought of his father and the power of the pulpit. His mother had always taught him that his father, a man of God, spoke for God.

His mother would have liked Kathryn Walsh. Though from different classes, they had a lot in common. He'd often seen his mother's Bible open. She'd encouraged him to follow his conscience, even when the cost would be great. She'd cried when he left for the war, cried in relief when he came home, cried in sorrow when he left for good.

Matthias knew what his mother would say to him now. *Nothing happens without the Lord's knowledge. Everything works together for good, Matthias. Everything is according to His plan. God brought you to Calvada and kept you here because He knew Kathryn was coming.*

If that was true, it meant God might not be finished with him after all.

Maybe it was time to have a talk with the Right Reverend Thacker. He'd ask the good reverend to have a quiet word with Kathryn. Maybe a man of God could get through to her since he couldn't make her listen. Maybe Thacker could make her shut up before someone shut her up for good.

———◦◦◦———

Kathryn's cheeks burned as Reverend Wilfred Thacker continued his hour-long sermon on a woman's place in bringing peace and comfort to the home and community. He looked straight at her several times so that she would know he blamed her for the trouble in town. He also looked pointedly at Lucy Wynham, Vinnie MacIntosh, Camilla Deets, and even poor Abbie Aday. Nabor said something and she hung her head.

"We are told in Genesis that in the very beginning of creation every trouble that befell man was the direct result of Eve giving the apple to Adam. It was Eve who was deceived. It was Eve who broke the covenant with God by offering the fruit of sin to Adam. Because of Eve, Adam was cast out of Eden."

Anger and hurt welled in Kathryn. Why did men always

harken back to this and blame women for what was wrong in the world? She wanted to cry out that Adam stood by in silence, watching and listening as Satan deceived Eve. He chose to take the fruit from Eve's hand. He chose to eat it. Closing her eyes, Kathryn clasped her hands so tightly in her lap that her fingers ached.

"... and I would remind all of you," Reverend Thacker went on with more fire than he'd ever shown before, "that God took the rib from Adam and made Eve his companion. God created woman to be nurturing and loving and *submissive*. God created woman to serve man. God did not create her to cause trouble or travail or grief for him. It would be well for some of the women within our fold to remember this. Let us have peace again."

He paused, looking straight at Kathryn. "Let us pray." The prayer was long and passionate, another sermon. The small choir sang the doxology. Sally Thacker gave Kathryn a wincing glance as she walked beside her husband to greet parishioners at the door. The congregation filed out, no one speaking. Nabor glared, a firm grip on Abbie's arm. The poor woman looked like a whipped dog.

Only Morgan Sanders spoke to her. "Quite a sermon today." His smile was sympathetic.

Reverend Thacker had always preached gentle reminders to live a good Christian life, his words filled with loving concern for his parishioners. Why the change today? He never preached on politics or the mines. It seemed to be sacred ground he dared not set foot upon. She knew this sermon was directed at her decision to start up the *Voice*. Knowing that didn't make the words less hurtful.

When Thacker extended his hand to her, she accepted the greeting. His grip was firm. "I hope you will take what I said to heart, Miss Walsh." His tone was quiet and gentle, his expression apologetic. "It was not done to hurt, but to instruct and protect not only you, but others. You mean well, but you must remember your place." He released her.

She couldn't speak past the aching lump in her throat. She would not cry here in front of all these people. She would not!

Parishioners clustered together, talking and looking at her. Nabor jerked Abbie's arm, making her turn her back as Kathryn walked by. Camilla's husband walked three feet in front of her as they headed downtown. Vinnie MacIntosh stood silent, face rigid as her husband talked to her.

Henry Call separated from a group. "Kathryn . . ."

She gave him a brief nod and kept going, back straight, chin up. She felt the censure of every person gathered in front of the church. Let them look! She went down the hill, passed by Ronya's Café, where she usually stopped for Sunday brunch, crossed the street, passed the fandango hall, now silent after the Saturday night reverie. Kathryn went into City Walsh's newspaper office and closed the door behind her.

Hands trembling, she untied the ribbons of her Sunday best hat and placed it on a stand. Sinking onto the settee, she sat silent for a moment, then burst into tears.

Matthias looked up when Henry Call came into the saloon, his expression stormy. His friend crossed the room, tossed his hat on the table, and sat. "I hope you're satisfied, Matt. Thacker wasn't content to talk with Kathryn privately as you hoped he would. Instead he crucified her in front of the whole congregation." He looked at Matthias. "I've never heard that man preach with such passion."

Matthias winced, but had to know. "Did he get through to her?"

"Get through? He might as well have used a club. She was white as a ghost when she left."

Matthias felt sick. He remembered what his father's words had done to him. "Did you speak with her after the service?"

"No. Sanders spoke to her before she left. God knows what he had to say. She didn't speak to anyone else. I imagine she was trying to hold herself together until she made it home."

Looking toward the swinging doors, Matthias debated whether he should cross the street and check on her.

Picking up his hat, Henry stood. "I know why you did it, but I can't say I approve your method."

"I don't want her to get hurt."

"You did the hurting. You hit her where she's most vulnerable. Her faith." He put on his hat. "I'll be at Ronya's." Matthias nodded. His friend and Charlotte Arnett had become quite attached to one another.

Matthias sent Scribe to check on Kathryn. He came back a few minutes later. "She wouldn't open the door. Said she was fine. Sounded hoarse."

Matthias sent him back the next morning.

"She opened the door a little, but wouldn't let me in. Her eyes are all red and puffy and she doesn't look like she's slept."

Kathryn wiped tears from her cheeks. She'd cried so much over the last two days, she felt weak and physically ill. She'd heard the same message countless times from platforms as well as pulpits, even from women, her mother included.

Remember your place . . .

Continue to speak out and you'll be seen as a scold . . .

Why can't you be silent on politics! It's not a woman's concern . . .

She couldn't eat. She couldn't sleep. She relived every word Reverend Thacker said and all the others who had spoken in angry condemnation before him.

A bruised reed, Kathryn had pored over the Scriptures, praying for enlightenment. She found words of comfort and instruction, examples of women who held positions of authority, who spoke up and gained respect. One woman, Deborah, even led an army!

Along with comfort, she found rebuke sharper than a two-edged sword cutting into her pride, exposing the cost of giving in to her temper. She felt as though a mirror had been held in front of her, and what she saw grieved her.

Memories surged back. The third and last boarding school expelled her for unladylike behavior. *You have a way with words, Miss Walsh, but words have the power to wound or heal. Retaliation never serves a good purpose.* Hadn't her temper brought on the last argument with the judge and given him just cause to exile her to this wild mining town?

The piano at Beck's competed with the guitars and squeeze-boxes at Barrera's. Kathryn's head throbbed. The men's whoops and laughter and boots pounding the dance floor sounded so carefree.

She knew she had been wrong about many things, but not everything. Nellie O'Toole, Charlotte, the wives in threadbare clothing in winter hoeing frozen ground in hope that seeds would take and there would be food in spring and summer— they were worth fighting for. She wanted to improve the plight of women in Calvada. Instead, her efforts brought criticism and shame, not only on her head, but on the head of every woman who had been sitting in a pew.

Lying sleepless in bed, Kathryn heard a knock at her front door. Men often knocked. She did her best to ignore both the decent and indecent proposals they made through the planks. Recognizing Scribe's voice, she unlocked the door and opened it. Her young friend stood swaying on the boardwalk, holding the neck of a half-empty bottle.

Snatching the bottle, she held it up before his bleary eyes. "Who gave this to you? Beck?"

"Joe down at the Watering Hole is nice to me."

"Nice," she snarled, tossing the bottle into the street, where it sank in the mud. Draping Scribe's arm around her shoulders, she helped him inside, pushing the door shut with her heel.

"We sure got 'em riled, didn't we?" the boy slurred. "Just like City. Said we were comfort the afflicted and afflict the com . . . fer . . . ble."

Leading him to the sofa, Kathryn let him sink. "I'm going to make some coffee."

"Don't want coffee." He looked up at her as though trying to focus. "Heard about what happened in church. Everyone's talking . . ."

"I'm sure they are." Kathryn felt the prick of tears.

"Guess you won't be going back there again."

Kathryn didn't respond.

"I miss him." Scribe rubbed his face. His shoulders sagged and he cried. Kathryn sat beside him and put her arm around him. Scribe looked at her. "People didn't always like what he had to say either, but they listened. They read his paper."

"Rest a while." Kathryn stood. "You need something in your stomach besides whiskey."

When Kathryn came back with coffee and some bread and cheese, she found Scribe curled on his side like a child, sound asleep. She set the cup and plate aside and spread a blanket over him. She went back into her apartment and tried to sleep. An hour later, the fandango hall was still in full swing, and she, wide-awake. She threw off the covers, put on her robe, and went back into the front office. Lighting the kerosene lamp on her uncle's desk, she pulled out one of Casey Walsh's notebooks.

Matthias had spent two hours searching for Scribe. He felt responsible for the kid, worried someone had decided to follow through on Herr's threat to break his fingers. Matthias had been to every saloon in Calvada. He'd even asked after him at Fiona Hawthorne's Dollhouse. No sign of the boy. Images of City Walsh haunted Matthias.

He'd almost started at Kathryn's house, but she hadn't been seen in public since she returned from church last Sunday, and her lantern had gone out early again. As he came down the boardwalk, he saw faint light through her window shade. The fandango hall had closed for the night. Reminded of what Henry had told him about Reverend Thacker's sermon, Matthias winced, feeling responsible for her humiliation.

At least Scribe had told him this morning that she looked better. He'd returned from her place looking relieved. "Door is open for business. She's got enough hats made to have every woman in town wearing one."

Matthias pressed the heels of his hands against eyes. He hoped he could relax now that the *Voice* was out of business. Crossing the street, he tapped at her door. "Miss Walsh. It's Matthias. Are you all right?" He heard the scrape of a chair.

"I'm fine."

She didn't sound fine. "Let me see your face so I know for sure."

"Take my word for it and go away."

"I'll stand right here until dawn . . ."

The bolt slid back, and the door cracked open. Her red hair was down and loosely braided in a long plait. "Satisfied? Now, go."

Matthias heard men coming down the boardwalk. "Let me in."

"Absolutely not!" She tried to close the door, but he pushed it open enough to step inside. "What do you think you're doing?"

"Trying to protect your reputation." The men came closer, talking and laughing. "Shhh." She'd been lambasted enough without having a group of men seeing him outside her door at two in the morning. They'd all be assuming a relationship that didn't exist. Kathryn stepped back as he bolted the door. With the lamp behind her, her body was silhouetted through the lace-trimmed white lawn nightgown and robe as she stood barefoot before him. He lost his breath.

A loud snore issued from close by. Matthias spotted Scribe sleeping on her settee. "Thank God. I've been looking all over town for him."

"He's sleeping off a bottle of whiskey Joe at the Watering Hole gave him. What's wrong with the men in this town?"

Matthias put his finger to his lips to shush her again.

She huffed. "The only men in the street this time of night are too drunk to—"

Seeing no other way to silence her, Matthias cupped the back of her head, pulled her forward, and kissed her as the men outside passed by. One hit his fist against the door and made a ribald comment before they all moved on. Matthias let go of Kathryn and she stepped back, gasping. She moved well away from him, eyes wide. She wasn't the only one affected by the kiss. He'd expected her to struggle. Instead, her hands had spread against his rib cage.

She retreated behind her desk.

"Relax, darlin'. It was the only way I could think of to shut you up." He wasn't sorry he had drawn a blank on any other method. "I need to get Scribe out of here."

"Leave him there." She looked flushed and breathless. "He's fine where he is."

"Your heart is in the right place, but he's seventeen. A man, not a boy."

"Even drunk, he's more of a gentleman than you are!"

"Maybe so, but what do you think people would say if word got out that Scribe spent the night with you?"

Kathryn's face crumpled. She uttered a soft, broken sound and sank into City's chair. "Oh, what's the blessed difference!"

Matthias felt like a mongrel dog who'd just mangled a kitten. "I didn't say it would get out." Releasing his breath, he rubbed the back of his neck, guilt gripping him. "I'm sorry, Kathryn." She didn't know how sorry he was. He never intended for Thacker to humiliate her in front of the entire congregation. When he went up to call the man to account, Thacker said it wasn't just Kathryn who could be harmed. Other women needed a firm warning, too.

"You should be sorry for—" Kathryn looked angry and flustered.

Had Thacker told her about their conversation? When she touched her lips and then her throat, he understood. "I'm not sorry about the kiss." He smiled slightly, glad she'd been stirred up. Heat still coursed through him. "I'm sorry about what happened to you in church."

"Oh." She bowed her head. "I suppose everyone in town has heard by now."

True enough, word had spread fast. "I wouldn't go back either." He hadn't stepped foot in a church since his father told him he wished he'd been stillborn.

Kathryn glanced up in surprise. "I'm going back."

"What?" Angry, he glared at her. "Why would you want anything to do with God after what Thacker said to you?" The man had preached for a solid hour, aiming words like arrows, every parishioner knowing the target. "He humiliated you in front of the whole town!"

"I'm not giving up on God because of what one man said from the pulpit." Her eyes shimmered with tears. "I'm sure Reverend Thacker thought he was doing the right thing." She shrugged. "And he did give me much to think about. I've been examining my motives, and I—" She seemed to catch herself and realize to whom she spoke. "Never mind."

Kathryn's words pierced him. *He* had given up on God because of what one man said. That man had been his father, a minister like Thacker, though a more powerful orator. Matthias had grown up believing his father spoke for God. Everyone in the congregation thought so. His sermons had changed as war became inevitable. When Matthias followed his conscience and headed north, his father had called him a fool. When Matthias returned home, his father had turned gray and bitter. *Did you think you could come back? We would have been better off if you'd been stillborn than turn out a traitor! Get out! I have no son.*

Kathryn's Bible lay open on City's desk, notes written and spread out as though she'd been searching the Scriptures for answers, instead of taking one minister's word as gospel. Matthias felt something shift inside him. Something long closed began to open.

Sitting on the edge of her desk, Matthias controlled the urge to run his hand over her bowed head. He tried to think of something to say, to make amends for what Thacker had done. He knew how words could hurt. Kathryn lifted her chin, tendrils of red hair curling against her pale forehead and cheeks. Her lips parted and his blood quickened. Words hadn't destroyed her faith, as he feared they would. She'd been crushed, but not destroyed.

She'd stopped clutching the collar of her robe, and it opened enough for him to see the smooth white skin of her throat and the throbbing pulse that matched his own. When her eyes moved down over his body, heat surged through him.

"Please move."

"Am I getting too close?" He didn't mean physically.

"My notes . . . They're under your . . . hind end."

Matthias stood abruptly. He hadn't blushed since he was a boy and was glad to see her focused on quickly gathering her papers. She stacked them, tucked them in a desk drawer, and closed it quickly. He wished he'd paid more attention to what she'd written. "Your confession?"

"My upcoming editorial."

A chill went through him. "Tell me you're not still at it!"

She folded her hands on the desk. "You should go, Mr. Beck."

"Haven't you been through enough trouble already?"

"Trouble always comes to those who fight to do what's right."

Furious, he planted his hands on her desk and leaned in. "What am I going to do about you?" He snarled in frustration. "What does it take . . . ?"

"I'm not your business."

He straightened. "I've told myself that a hundred times. But you're City's niece, and he was my friend." He needed to get out of here before he said things he'd regret. He went to the settee and stripped the blanket off Scribe. "Come on, kid." Scribe groaned. Muttering a curse under his breath, Matthias hauled him up over his shoulder. "Might be better if I take him out the back way."

Kathryn got up and came around her desk. "The front door is quicker." She opened it.

Shaking his head, Matthias did as she bade. Pausing on the threshold, he looked down at her. "Thanks for the kiss."

"I would've ducked if I'd had warning."

"Then be warned." He grinned. "There will be a next time . . . and a next . . ."

She gave him a push out the door and closed it quickly behind him. He heard the bolt slam into place. Laughing under his breath, he shifted Scribe and carried him across the street to the hotel.

12

KATHRYN WAS SURPRISED when Vinnie and Camilla came to call the next evening. She hadn't expected any of the women in church to seek her out after Reverend Thacker's verbal whacking. They didn't mention it, but talked of mundane, ordinary things. On the way out, Camilla turned to her. "James read your newspaper after church last Sunday. Your 'Angels of Mercy' editorial made him laugh until tears ran down his cheeks. I just wanted you to know." She kissed Kathryn's cheek. "Not all the men are against you."

Closing the door, Kathryn leaned her forehead against it. Her emotions were too high to face any customers. Turning her sign over, she sat at the front desk and continued reading her uncle's journals. A soft rustling and quick footsteps caught her attention. Another note pushed under her door. She'd received enough to last a lifetime. They'd been so nasty, she burned them. She picked up the folded slip. Like the others, the message was short and poorly written, but this one made her pulse quicken.

Katrin—

Thar be a unon meting tonit under soth brig. Thot you mit wanna no.

A frend

Kathryn opened the door quickly and peered out. Was that Nellie O'Toole heading toward the north end of town? Kathryn closed the door, knowing this was too important to dismiss. She couldn't send Scribe and risk having him harmed. Everyone knew he was working with her on the *Voice*. And she couldn't go herself, unless . . .

A rap on the door made her jump. Heart pounding, she thought of Matthias Beck on her doorstep last night. Her whole body flushed with heat at the memory of that kiss.

"Kathryn? I'm sorry about last night."

Scribe! She opened the door. He looked hungover and miserable. When he started to apologize again, she grabbed his arm and pulled him inside, measuring him mentally as she closed the door behind him. He wasn't much taller than she, and boyishly thin. She had a man's coat and an old scally cap she'd found among her uncle's things. "I need your clothes."

"What?" He took a step back, looking at her as though she'd lost her mind. "What for?"

"There's a meeting. I have to go, but they can't know I'm there." She pushed him through her apartment door. "You can wrap yourself in a blanket until I get back. Don't just stand there. Hurry up!"

He dug in his heels. "I'll go."

"Everyone knows you work for me. Now don't argue." She waved him in and closed the apartment door. "If I get there early enough, I can hide. They'll never know I was there."

"Hide? Where is this meeting? How're you going to hide?"

"Never mind! Just give me your pants and shirt." She could hear him muttering on the other side of the door. "You have one minute, Scribe, or I'm coming in." She heard a thud. "Are you all right?"

Scribe appeared wrapped in a blue blanket, his face red, his dark hair sticking up like pinfeathers. She tried not to laugh as she whisked around him and closed the door. Stripping off her skirt and shirtwaist, she pulled on his denim pants and plaid wool shirt. She put the scally cap on and pushed her red hair inside. When she came out, Scribe was sitting on the settee, knees together, shoulders hunched, glowering. She giggled. "How do I look?" She turned around.

"Awful."

"As long as I don't look like me. Is there any red hair showing?"

"No. This is a bad idea."

"Just go back in my room, close the door, and stay there." She blew out the lamp on her desk. "I promise I'll be very careful."

As soon as Scribe was closeted in her apartment, Kathryn slipped out the front door. The fandango hall was in full swing. So was Beck's. Hunching her shoulders, she affected an unsteady gait as she crossed Chump Street, then headed for Madera Mine Road. South Bridge was a mile outside town. Thankfully, there was a full moon to light her way.

When she saw the bridge, she headed into the woods, picking her way carefully through the scraggy pines. Three men walked on the road. She could hear them talking as they crossed the bridge and headed for town. She went under the bridge and tucked herself high behind a pylon. She had been warm on the long walk, but the chill quickly seeped in through the layers. Burrowing into her coat, she wished she'd worn gloves. Even her thin fawn suede would have been better than nothing.

One by one, footsteps approached, gravel trickling as the men arrived. Matches were lit, but no lanterns. Kathryn didn't look out from behind the pylon. She knew she wouldn't be able to see their faces, but she distinguished voices. Five men. Boots sounded on the bridge above, and another man joined them at the bottom of the ravine.

"Sorry I'm late." The man's voice was deep, a rich Irish brogue. He did the talking. She couldn't make out everything he said over the rippling stream, but enough. They were talking about the Madera Mine and Morgan Sanders.

"We'll have hoods when we get him. We throw a blanket over him and have ourselves a party. He'll be the piñata." The man had a cold laugh. "No clubs, just fists. We wanna hurt him bad and scare him. Not kill him. Understand?"

Kathryn closed her eyes and breathed softly, slowly through parted lips. She felt something claw on the exposed area of her neck, and her heart stopped, then pounded even faster as it moved around, up over her jaw. A spider! It kept moving across her brow to the cap. One of the men lit a match, and she saw beady eyes shining in the darkness. A rat! Another man swore and threw a stone at it. The rodent scurried away and disappeared behind her.

She heard her own name mentioned and focused her attention. "She's going to be on our side, boys. She's seen Slag Hollow and met some wives. One of our more poetic members is working on an impassioned letter full of hearts and flowers to explain our high principles. By the time he's finished laying out the miners' coalition, City Walsh's little niece is going to make us folk heroes."

If any name was mentioned, Kathryn couldn't hear it over the sounds of the creek or the pounding of her own heart.

"That lady sure doesn't like Beck."

"We want Sanders to be mayor. After we're done with him, he'll do whatever we say."

"And if he doesn't?"

"Then we kill him."

"Wait a minute! I didn't join the coalition to commit murder."

Silence fell for a few seconds, then the leader spoke. "It won't come to that, McNabb. But we want Sanders to think it will."

The meeting dispersed. Kathryn stayed where she was while their voices grew fainter as the men went up the slope to the road and headed for town or Slag Hollow. Two men remained under the bridge.

"What do you think? Can we trust him?"

"McNabb hasn't got the guts for this."

"He'll come around. He was up at Nellie O'Toole's yesterday."

"Doing what?"

"Hoping to take Sean's place."

Their voices dropped again. Kathryn leaned forward a few inches. "You work with McNabb. See there's another cave-in. Nothing too serious. Just make sure he doesn't make it out." The other man spoke low, and the first snarled. "It's gotta be done. We can't take chances."

Their footsteps crunched up the slope and across the bridge. Kathryn's heart was beating so fast, she felt faint. She waited a few more minutes, then slipped out of her hiding place. Whipping off the cap, she slapped her back and front and jumped around. She heard a soft squeak. The moonlight seeping through the trees along the stream didn't give enough light for her to see. Ducking down, she went out from under the bridge, crawling up the slope and peering over the heavy planks. A man stood on the other side. He took something from his pocket. She watched him roll a cigarette and tuck it between his lips. When he lit the match with his thumbnail, she saw his face clearly. The flame died quickly, leaving the red tip of his cigarette glowing bright as he inhaled. He stood for a while, smoking, then flicked the stub into the creek and headed for town.

Was he the leader or the subordinate ordered to kill McNabb? She would have followed to see where he went, but knew she needed to get to Willow Creek and warn Nellie O'Toole that her friend's life was in danger.

Kathryn knew she'd remember that man's face. She would be looking for him among the throng of men who wandered Chump Street after the whistles blew.

Calvada's nightlife was in full swing by the time Kathryn made it back to town. She told Nellie everything, and the woman gave assurance she'd warn McNabb in time. Exhausted, chilled to the bone despite her hike, Kathryn looked for a chance to get across Chump Street. Men were gathered in front of Beck's, talking loudly, laughing. Shouting drew their attention, and they headed off to watch two men slugging it out in front of the Rocker Box. As soon as their backs were turned, Kathryn ran across the street, along the boardwalk, slowed to a normal pace as she passed the fandango hall, and slipped quickly into her house. Panting, heart pounding, Kathryn put her forehead against the door, trying to get her breath back.

Someone clamped a hand over her mouth. Terrified, she

tried to scream but the sound was muffled. She twisted, bucked, and kicked to be free. He lifted her off the floor and away from the door. She dug her nails into the man's hand and bit him on the fleshy part of his thumb.

He uttered a grunt of pain. "All knees, elbows, teeth, and claws, aren't you?"

Beck! She stopped fighting and sagged, exhausted. Shifting her, he slid the bolt before he let go of her.

Lantern light silhouetted Scribe in the back doorway. He was still wrapped in the baby-blue blanket. "Don't you hurt her. I'm warning you! She's not talking. Why isn't she talking?" He came into the front office. "What're you doing?"

"Enjoying the momentary silence." Beck shook his wounded hand and glared at her. When she tried to get past him, he caught her arm and spun her around. "Where have you been, dressed up like that?"

Shaking violently, Kathryn's teeth started chattering.

Scribe spoke up when she didn't. "I told you. She went to a meeting."

Matthias studied her more calmly. "What kind of meeting is what I want to know."

"May I please sit down?" Kathryn's legs weakened.

Matthias guided her into the back apartment and put a chair near her potbellied stove. His expression changed when he got a good look at her face. "Stay put." He glanced at Scribe before opening the back door. "Keep a close eye on her."

Scribe sat on her bed, head down, knees up to his chin. He looked so ridiculous, Kathryn started to giggle and then couldn't stop. Scribe scowled at her. "What's so funny?"

"Nothing. Absolutely nothing!" She covered her mouth, fighting to regain control.

"Are you going to give me my clothes back now?" When his

eyes popped open, she realized she had half the buttons undone. Uttering a soft gasp, she grabbed her skirt and shirtwaist and fled into the front office. She was out of his clothes and into her own before she remembered to close the door. Thankfully, he was gentleman enough to look the other way. Tossing the pants and shirt to him, she paced.

"I'm decent. Tell me what happened."

Cold and still shaking, she sat by the stove again. "Put on your boots, Scribe."

He did, and then sat on her bed.

The back door opened abruptly, and Kathryn jumped up, almost falling backwards into the bookshelf.

Matthias's mouth curved sardonically. "A little jumpy, aren't you?" He looked between them, annoyed, and tossed a bundle to Scribe. "Guess I'm too late." He put a bottle of brandy on Kathryn's table. "You can take those clothes back to your room."

Scribe stood. "I'm not leaving you alone with her! It's not proper."

"Yeah, well, it wasn't exactly proper when I found you half-naked in her bed."

"Now, wait a minute." Scribe protested loudly. "I explained!"

"Save it." Matthias looked at Kathryn and smirked. "This is the second time I've caught you two in a compromising situation." Eyes still on her, he jerked his head. "Miss Walsh will be just fine, Sir Galahad. Now, get out of here and let me talk to her." When Scribe didn't move, Matthias gave him a look that galvanized him.

Kathryn sank onto the chair again. She was warm enough now, but still shivering violently.

Matthias uncorked the bottle. "You look like you need a shot of brandy."

"No, thank you."

"It's medicinal, and you're half-frozen."

"I'm thawing fast."

He chuckled. "Hot tea, then." He dipped her teapot in the bucket of fresh water by the door.

"I'm fine. Just go."

"Not until you tell me where you went."

Her whole body jerked when Matthias put a hand on her shoulder. She came to her feet and moved away from him. The room felt smaller than it had yesterday. His eyes narrowed as he studied her. "You're anything but fine, and I'm not leaving until I get some answers."

She shook her head and sat again, then stood up quickly, edgy.

"Trust me, Kathryn." He spoke so gently and with such assurance, she wanted to tell him everything. He'd been here longer and knew the town better than most. He waited in silence as though he had all the time in the world. She'd always thought herself a good judge of character, but he was a saloon owner, a profiteer. She looked at him, studying him. He gazed back as though he had nothing to hide.

"The meeting was under South Bridge."

He filled the teapot and put it on the stove. A muscle jerked in his jaw. "Were the men talking about a coalition?"

She froze, distrust rising. "How did you know that? The person who left the note said it was a secret meeting. And you are no miner."

"There are few secrets in a bar." He sounded annoyed. "You loosen tongues with tea. I find whiskey works better and faster. City heard rumors and was doing some investigating when he was killed."

Her mouth trembled and she pressed her lips together. Was he trying to frighten her? She was frightened enough already!

The pot whistled and her body flinched. Matthias used

one of her red-and-gold Minton teacups, set it in a saucer, and brought it to her like an offering. His hands were steady. Hers shook so badly, she pulled them back and tucked them beneath her arms. "I can't afford to replace them."

"This or brandy, your ladyship." His tone was gentle, teasing. He set the saucer aside and handed her the cup.

She gave him a bleak smile. The tea was strong, bracing her. "This is a dreadful town, Matthias." Tears burned. "You're right about the muck and deep holes. The rats running around are a lot bigger and meaner than the ones feasting on the garbage in the alleys."

He looked grim. "What did you hear?"

She was tempted to tell him everything, but knew the advice he'd give her. *Don't print it.* Avoiding his eyes, she gave a slight shrug. "Nothing much." Her cheeks burned at the lie.

"Were they talking about a strike?"

"No." She could feel his frustration. Finishing her tea, she set the cup carefully in the saucer. "Thank you. I feel much better now. You can go."

"You're still shaking."

"I'm cold. I'll warm up."

"That's not why you're shaking. You're scared. You're a Walsh. That's for sure. Always looking for trouble."

Suddenly inexplicably angry, Kathryn leaned forward. "I didn't go looking for trouble. I went looking for *information*."

When she got up, Matthias grasped her wrist. "And found both, didn't you?" He held firmly without hurting her. "I can feel your pulse."

She yanked free, his touch too disturbing. She grasped for excuses. "It was a long, dark walk back, and I heard something in the bushes. It might have been a bear."

"You want to try again? I can spend all night."

194

"They mentioned Morgan Sanders." She tried to make light of it.

"Mentioned him." Matthias's tone was dryer than desert sand. "I'm sure they'd like to kill him." He sounded angry now. "You needn't worry about him. He's well-armed and well-guarded."

She swung around and went to the front door. She started to open it, intending to order him out. He put his hand against it. "What's the plan?"

She moved away from him. Pacing, she glared at him. He'd never leave if she didn't tell him something. "To scare Sanders. Enough to make him give them what they want. One didn't agree." She didn't tell him why.

"I'm curious." Matthias looked furious, but spoke quietly, in a controlled voice. "Where were you when they were talking about all this?"

"Under the bridge. Behind a pylon. Where they couldn't see me." She remembered the spider crawling on her and shuddered.

Matthias swore under his breath. "Do you have any idea what they would've done to you if they'd caught you there?"

"I think so." Did she have to sound so childish and scared?

Turning away, Matthias raked a hand through his hair. Facing her, he frowned. "What about the one that didn't agree to the plan?"

"I've already seen that he'll be warned about the—" She stopped.

"The threat to kill him. Is that what you're holding back?" He swore again. "What did you do, Kate? Go up to the miners' camp and knock on doors to try to warn him?"

"No." Too late, she thought of the danger to Nellie. Her mouth trembled. "I went to someone who knows him. He'll be warned in time." She couldn't see Matthias through her tears. "I had to do something!"

"Easy." His arms came around her. "Shhhh . . ." He drew her close, resting his chin softly on the top of her head. "It'll be all right."

"No, it won't!" Her body warmed as he moved his hands over her back. Was it her heart pounding so hard, or his? She should step away.

"Please come and stay at the hotel for a few days. I want to make sure you're safe."

"I don't think so." Grabbing up her shawl from the settee, she wrapped it around herself while keeping an eye on his every movement.

His expression grew mocking. "Ah, darlin', you still don't trust me. You've seen the room. You've seen the lock."

"I'm safer here."

He looked her over and had an all too worldly look in his eyes. "You might be right about that."

She hugged herself tightly, wary. They were alone, the only light coming from a lone lantern. She wasn't cold anymore.

"What do you want to do, Kathryn?" He spoke softly.

"Make hats." The work calmed her and helped her think.

"Good idea." He sounded relieved. "Are you sure you're going to be all right?"

She gave him a wry smile. "I'm stronger than I look, Mr. Beck."

"Walk me to the door?" His tone was playful, seductive, his mouth curving.

She didn't want to get too close to him. "I'll bolt the door when you're on the other side."

"A pity." He laughed low and went through her apartment and out the back door.

Henry came in through the swinging door and sat. Matthias raised his brows. "Just coming in?" It was after midnight.

"I was seeing Charlotte home." He looked bone-tired, but relaxed. "Things are going very well."

Matthias chuckled. "I can see how well they're going."

Henry gave him a reproving look. "With the campaign."

City would be happy he'd gotten in the game, but he doubted he'd win. It wasn't just City's challenge that made him agree to run for mayor. It was wanting to make Calvada a town worth calling home.

Henry hadn't been in Calvada more than a few days before he pointed out the discouraging facts. Calvada wasn't on a main road to anywhere. If the town were to survive, businesses other than mining would have to be developed to keep people coming up the mountain and make those already living there want to stay. Matthias had come to the same conclusion. Had Henry come when originally planned, Matthias would already have sold his holdings and would have been in Truckee or Reno, Sacramento or Monterey. But Henry had been delayed. Rather than come in summer, he came in the fall, and Kathryn Walsh rode into town in the same stagecoach.

Kathryn Walsh might turn out to be Matthias's Bull Run. Instead of selling out and leaving for someplace finer, she held her ground like Robert E. Lee at Chancellorsville.

She shouldn't be living in City's house, not after she'd eavesdropped on a coalition meeting. She hadn't told him the name of the man whose life was in danger. He should have pressed her harder.

As soon as Matthias left, Kathryn sat at her uncle's desk, lit the lamp, and pulled out her writing materials. There was no time to waste. The election was only two days away. It took her less than an hour to finish two articles: one on the no-longer-secret miners' coalition, including the diabolical plans to murder a fellow miner for daring to object to murder, and then a second, encouraging the men to vote for Matthias Beck for mayor.

The fandango hall had fallen silent by the time Kathryn began opening and closing little drawers and arranging type backwards in the print tray. She'd watched and worked closely enough with Scribe to get started, though she grew frustrated with her clumsiness and lack of speed. What would have taken Scribe an hour or two took her the rest of the night. Rolling ink, she pressed the first page and proofread it. Groaning at the errors, she spent precious minutes locating the incorrect letters, prying them out with the bodkin, and reinserting them in the right place.

She'd managed to print fifty copies when someone tapped on her door. Her heart raced, and then slowed when it turned out to be Scribe and not Matthias Beck. It was just before sunrise, and he was worried. "What'd he do after I left last night?"

"Nothing. Get in here. I need you."

"You're in the same clothes. Didn't you sleep last night?"

"I'll sleep when the work is done." She waved at the press. "We have a paper to get out."

Scribe picked up a copy and started reading. She snatched it out of his hand. "Read it later, Scribe. We have no time to lose." She headed for the back apartment. "I need to freshen up."

"Holy screaming catfish!" Scribe pounded on her door. "You're not really putting this out, are you?"

She came back out, shoving strands of hair into her chignon. "Yes. I am."

"If I'd known what kind of meeting you were going to, I wouldn't have let you out the door!"

"Then it's good you didn't know. Stop dawdling, Scribe. Print more copies." She laid them on the desk to dry. "I heard every word with my own ears. The sooner everyone knows, the better. Keeping silent makes us culpable." She grabbed her shawl, worried now about Nellie O'Toole. Had she been able to warn McNabb? Had warning McNabb put Nellie in danger? Kathryn had to know. "It's not just Mr. Sanders whose life is at stake."

"Where are you going?"

"To check on someone. Don't just stand there. However many copies you print in the next hour, get them out. And I don't care if you give them away. Just make sure those newspapers get into people's hands."

"And if I don't?"

She stood in the doorway. "You will, because you know it's what City Walsh would want you to do."

Nellie O'Toole and her two children were gone. Kathryn didn't know whether to be relieved or even more worried. Those men had known McNabb visited Nellie. What if they'd come right after Kathryn had spoken to her? What if . . . ?

"Miss Walsh?" When Kathryn turned, a young woman came out of a shanty. "Nellie's gone." The woman wasn't much older than Kathryn, but was thin and worn. Her left eye was swollen shut, her cheek black-and-blue. "She left a few minutes after you did. I kept her young'uns with me until she came back with Ian McNabb. They're gone."

"Who hurt you?"

"Best I don't say. They was looking for Nellie. I told 'em she left a few days ago. They said I was lying." She touched her cheek. "I told Nellie and Ian not to tell me where they was going. If I don't know, I can't say. Better that way."

"I'm so sorry, Mrs. . . ."

"Ina Bea Cummings, ma'am."

"I'm afraid it's my fault. I'm so sorry they hurt you. You should come back to town with me. I'll make room—"

"Oh, no, ma'am. I'm safer here. Besides, I got Elvira Haines and Tweedie Witt to think about. We look out for each other. We have friends who help when they can. Hope you do, too, Miss Walsh. The men that come looking for Nellie wanted to know who warned her. I didn't know it was you until I saw you coming up the hill just now. I'm scared for you, Miss Walsh. They'll be looking for you. You know that, don't you?"

Everyone in town would know by noon. Everything she knew was in the *Voice*.

13

RETURNING TO CHUMP STREET, Kathryn heard Scribe hawking newspapers down by Aday's General Store. Exhausted, she
went inside the *Voice* office and sank onto the settee. Leaning
back, she dozed until Scribe came in the door. "Sold every copy
for five cents each." Grinning, he took the can from the bottom
drawer and emptied his pockets of nickels and dimes.

"We'll print more copies next time." She thanked him.
"Turn the sign, Scribe. I need a nap."

He flipped the sign. "You ought to bar the door."

She said she would and then promptly forgot as soon as he
left. Too tired to worry about anything, she curled onto the
settee and went to sleep. She thought she was dreaming when

the door banged open and heavy footsteps entered, then came awake abruptly when someone grabbed her arm and hauled her up. Bleary-eyed, she saw Morgan Sanders's livid face close to hers, eyes black with rage. She went cold with fear.

"Who are they? I want names."

Kathryn strove to remain calm. "Let go of me, please."

He did and stepped back, as though trying to regain control. "Everything you wrote in this is . . ." He used a foul word as he crumpled the *Voice* in front of her face, his breath hot and sour. "There isn't a man in this town that would dare come after me."

Raising her hands in a gesture of conciliation, she moved away from him. "I'm glad to know that. I wrote that piece so those men wouldn't go through with their plans."

He closed the distance, lips stretched white over bared teeth. "I don't believe any of this. I think you invented the story to swing votes to Matthias Beck."

Shocked at the accusation, her own temper rose. "I would never do such a thing!"

"Your front door swings on hinges where he's concerned."

Stunned and insulted, Kathryn glared at him. "Not in the way you suggest." And how would he know, unless . . . ? "You're having me watched? How dare you!"

"Oh, I dare a lot more. I have a man outside right now. I could call him in and a few others and take that press apart piece by bloody piece!"

Alarmed, she knew he meant it. "It wouldn't change the fact that there are men who want you dead."

"Looking out for me, are you?" He sneered. "Is that what you want me to believe?" He reached out so fast she had no time to evade him as he dug his fingers into her hair. He jerked her forward so that their faces were inches apart. Gasping in pain, she had no doubt he could easily break her neck. "Tell me who they are."

"I don't know!"

"Describe them!"

Swallowing her rising fear, Kathryn tried to appear calm. "Let go of me, Mr. Sanders."

Noise came from outside. A fight by the sounds of it. Morgan's eyes flickered, but he didn't release her. Scalp on fire, eyes watering, Kathryn didn't look away. "I only heard them. I didn't see their faces." Except one.

The fight went on outside. Kathryn could hear grunts of pain, boots scraping, more blows, and a heavy thud.

His eyes narrowed. "You're lying."

His words and the look in his eyes frightened her. "It's one thing to protect yourself, Mr. Sanders, another to take the law into your own hands."

"I am the law in this town."

The door banged open. Sanders released Kathryn so suddenly, she fell back a step. Morgan turned as she looked up. Matthias Beck stood in the doorway, mouth bleeding. Behind him on the boardwalk a man lay unconscious. Seeing the look in Beck's eyes, Kathryn knew she had to act quickly, or there would be bloodshed.

Stepping around Morgan Sanders, she put herself between the two men. "Everything is all right, Mr. Beck."

"Sure, it is." Beck's drawl came thick with sarcasm, his burning eyes fixed on Sanders.

Kathryn raised her hands. "Please don't do anything rash. Mr. Sanders was simply voicing his opinion about the article, which he has every right to do." She glanced back. "And he was just leaving. Weren't you, Mr. Sanders?"

Sanders headed for the door. "Our conversation isn't over, Miss Walsh."

Beck took a step forward. Kathryn grabbed his arm as Sanders went out the door, but she couldn't hold him back. She protested, but he followed Sanders outside, shouting now.

"Are you running away, Sanders? I'm talking to you, you son of a . . ." He used a name that brought stinging color into Kathryn's cheeks. Morgan Sanders kept walking, shoulders back, head up, ignoring him. People had come out to see what the ruckus was all about. "Come back and fight me, you yellow-bellied . . ."

"Please, stop!" Kathryn covered her flaming cheeks. "If you're trying to go after him with some notion of defending me, *don't!*" Beck looked at her, and the expression on his face made her retreat. "Fine. All right! Thank you for coming in when you did, but don't use me as an excuse for a public brawl!"

Beck wiped his mouth. She'd just stepped over a beaten man lying unconscious on the boardwalk, but the sight of Matthias Beck's blood made her weak. Turning on her heel, Kathryn fled into the *Voice* office. Beck grabbed the door before she could close it and followed her inside.

"You had to print it all, didn't you? What're you going to do when one of those men you wrote about shows up in the middle of the night?"

Kathryn didn't feel up to conversation. "Just go away, Mr. Beck." She was too scared and too tired to think straight.

"You've got Sanders on one side wanting to tear your hair out of your head and the bloody Molly Maguires on the other. Happy now?"

She understood his reference to the Molly Maguires, having pilfered the judge's newspapers as soon as he discarded them. She didn't want to be reminded of secret meetings that led to intimidation and murder and attempted mine takeovers. A Pinkerton man had infiltrated the gang and gathered enough evidence to convict them, but even after several leaders were executed, fear lingered that those who escaped might reorganize elsewhere.

Could some of them have come all the way to California?

Shaken, Kathryn grew defensive. "I took a gamble that printing what they said would stop them from following through and doing it!"

"You gamble higher stakes than I ever have."

"Well, be happy! Sanders thinks I did it for you. Calvada might just end up with a saloonkeeper for a mayor!" Realizing she was shouting, too, she strove to modulate her voice to a more ladylike tone. "If that happens, I hope you'll keep your promises to the people and hire a sheriff, so we'll have some law and order." She thought of Sanders's threat and went nose-to-nose with Matthias Beck. "Then nobody will be able to destroy my press!"

"I'd like to haul that press to the Dardenelles and dump it off a cliff!"

Scribe burst in. "Everyone in town can hear the two of you shouting."

"Let 'em hear!" Matthias roared.

His fury calmed her own. Kathryn felt more in control now. She went to her desk and shuffled papers with trembling hands. "I think we've said everything there is to say." Her voice shook.

"We're just getting started." Matthias's eyes flashed blue fire. "You're moving into my hotel."

"What?" She straightened, indignant. "I am not! I'm staying right here where I belong." She jabbed her finger at the floor. "Humble though it may be, this is my home, and *no one is going to run me out!*"

Matthias didn't say anything for a moment. His body loosened, the glaze of fury dimming. "Fine. I'll move in here with you."

Her face went hot. "Don't be ridiculous!" Embarrassed by the curling warmth at his suggestion, she turned away. Surely, he wasn't serious. She risked a look at him. Oh, yes, he was. "No. Absolutely not. Never."

"Then let's make a deal, shall we?" He spoke in a level tone, gaze fixed on her with grim determination. "If your building is still standing in a month, you can move back in."

"A month!" She chewed her lip, nervous, realized, and stopped. "One night."

"One week."

A week under his roof! Kathryn thought of what Morgan Sanders had said about her door having hinges where Matthias was concerned. She couldn't deny his attraction, but she hadn't encouraged him. What would people say if she moved into his hotel?

"No one will think the worse of you when the whole town saw Sanders storm in here."

Could the man read her mind? One look from him and her heart raced. She blushed again, annoyed that he seemed all too aware. "It wouldn't be proper."

"I could gag you, throw you over my shoulder, and carry you across the street. That way, you could claim you had no choice in the matter."

She gave a soft laugh. "That would make you look less than honorable."

His eyes warmed and a slow smile curved his mouth. "You're saying you think I'm honorable? I didn't know you had such a high opinion of me."

She ignored the sultry tone and the warmth his teasing roused. "Say I do spend one night in your hotel—"

"One week. Rent free. With someone to act as temporary bodyguard."

"Someone?" She glared at him suspiciously. "Who?"

"Not me."

She shouldn't feel so disappointed. "Do you really think this is all necessary?"

"I do. I think you know it, too."

Kathryn sank onto the settee. Sanders had walked in when the whole town could see him and manhandled her. If Matthias hadn't shown up, what might have happened?

"One week," she agreed, defeated.

He opened the door. "Let's go."

"I need to pack a few things."

"Later. You look dead on your feet."

She didn't deny it. Swinging her shawl around her shoulders, she followed him out. Her knees were shaking so badly, she stumbled and almost fell when she stepped down from the boardwalk. Matthias caught her up in his arms and headed across the street.

"Matthias!" Ronya called out. "Where are you taking Kathryn?"

"I'm putting her in protective custody." Everyone on Chump Street heard him.

Matthias backed through the swinging doors and saw the line of men at the bar staring at him as he carried Kathryn into the casino. "Hey, Beck! What do you plan on doing with your lady?" one of his customers guffawed. Several other men laughed.

They'd better understand he wouldn't tolerate anyone casting aspersions on Kathryn Walsh. "Careful, gentlemen." Matthias spoke firmly. One cold look down the line of men and their mirth died. He jerked his chin at the man standing near the back. "Come on up, Ivan." Matthias had hired the big Russian to toss any man who caused trouble. He intended to post him outside her door. He didn't trust most of the men in town, including himself. Kathryn was entirely too tempting, especially now that he had her in his arms and under his roof.

"Please put me down, Mr. Beck. I can manage."

Matthias set her on her feet, but kept his hand beneath her arm. She might be walking with back straight and chin up, but he could feel her body trembling. Delayed reaction, most likely. Just thinking about Sanders putting a hand on her made Matthias want to hunt the man down and beat the tar out of him. It might come to more than that if Sanders came after Kathryn again.

Opening the door into the best suite in the hotel, Matthias bowed. "After you, your ladyship."

She entered with some hesitation. "I shouldn't stay here." Her hand fluttered to her throat.

"Only until things cool off."

She moved away from him, clearly nervous. "I have a business to run."

A business that could get her hurt. "We'll figure it out."

Turning, she looked at him. "We?"

A pity she hadn't stuck with lady's hats. Worse luck there weren't enough women in town to buy them. Ivan stood in the doorway, waiting for orders. Kathryn noticed him. Matthias could see her mind working over the situation. The shadows under her eyes told him she'd be asleep as soon as she stretched out on that sweet feather bed. "Miss Walsh, this is Ivan." He was at a loss for a last name. "He's going to make sure no one bothers you."

Boots pounded on the stairs and Scribe came in, puffing. "The whole town is talking—"

Matthias nailed the boy with a glare. "The lady is safer here than across the street." He gave Ivan a look, and the man planted a firm hand on Scribe's shoulder and ushered him out the door. Matthias could see Kathryn changing her mind already.

"We should talk about this."

"Later. You've had a couple of long, hard days, haven't you, your ladyship? Get some rest." He headed for the door. "I'll see that a meal is brought up to you."

"Mr. Beck!" His little general looked like she was trying to plot a campaign to escape.

"The door has a good, heavy lock." He went out, closing the door behind him. He waited and heard the bolt set in place.

Ivan looked worried. "What do I do if she comes out?"

"Don't let her out of your sight."

Matthias went downstairs. As he entered the saloon, he found a throng of men celebrating. He didn't have to ask why. Herr pounded him on the shoulder. "Finally, someone was man enough to shut her up!" He raised his glass high. "To Matthias Beck, the man who should be mayor!" The men cheered.

Matthias gave a bleak laugh. They'd all learn soon enough Kathryn Walsh wouldn't be silent long.

Kathryn heard sounds of celebration, but was too tired to care what might be the reason. She went to the window and saw men rushing across the street, undoubtedly drawn by the cheering downstairs. A few looked up and saw her. Rather than draw back, she searched the upturned faces for the man she had seen lighting a cigarette after plotting cold-blooded murder. A few men leered at her, talking to their companions, who looked up as well. Imagining what they might mistakenly think, she drew back.

Pouring water into a blue-and-white porcelain bowl, Kathryn cupped her hands and cooled her face. The towel felt soft against her skin. The room had all the creature comforts, even a bathtub! A fire had been laid. She found matches in a box on the mantel, and soon flames licked the big log. Two chairs and a small table faced the hearth. She and her mother used to sit before a fire and talk. Usually after Kathryn had had an argument with the judge. When she was young, her mother had spoken words of comfort. When Kathryn turned sixteen, her mother joined in the judge's expectations. Kathryn would marry, preferably before the age of eighteen. *You're lovely, intelligent, and a well-connected young lady. Of course, you'll have suitors.* Her mother couldn't believe any girl would choose to remain single, not until Kathryn turned down her first two proposals.

Surely you don't want to be a spinster.

You can't change the world, Kathryn.

You're just like your father . . .

Their last conversation came back in a rush, and Kathryn felt the same pain she had the first time her mother said, *My life will be much easier without you.* Her mother hadn't come downstairs the day the judge took Kathryn to the train station. Had he forbidden it, worried stress might threaten the unborn child her mother carried? Kathryn couldn't blame him. She had never doubted her stepfather's love for her mother. She was the one he despised.

Why do you pit yourself against Lawrence? You know you can't win.

Why must you always be the source of discord in this house?

Kathryn didn't want trouble. She wanted to make things right! She wanted to make things better! It seemed following one's convictions and facing trouble came together. But she had to wonder. Had she made things worse by writing about what she'd heard under the bridge? Too tired to think about other possible strategies she might have followed, she sat and leaned back in the chair. What good did it do to ask questions now? What she'd done was done, and she'd have to face whatever consequences came from it.

Lawrence Pershing's face rose in her mind's eye. *Goodbye, Kathryn.* Even now, months later, she felt the stab of hurt. His tone said it all. *I'm finally rid of you. Don't come back.*

The crackle of the fire comforted her, the warmth seeping into her weary body. She struggled to keep her eyes open. When had she last slept? Day before yesterday? She couldn't remember. Her muscles loosened, her hands draping over the arms of the chair. She sank and slid as she dozed. She should get up or stretch out on the bed. Too tired to do either, she put one boot up on the edge of the small table to brace herself and fell asleep where she sat.

Matthias had stayed downstairs, not wanting men to speculate on his reasons for having Kathryn in an upstairs room. Overhearing one ribald supposition, he'd grabbed the man by the back of his collar and seat of his pants and heaved him through the swinging doors. "Anyone else want to say anything against the lady upstairs?"

Henry studied him, amused. "There are other safe places you might have taken her, my friend. Ronya's, for one."

"I didn't think of that."

"The only way you're going to keep that lady out of trouble is to marry her."

The thought had occurred to Matthias long before Henry

brought it up. The odds of getting Kathryn Walsh to agree weren't in his favor. Not yet anyway. At one point in the last few days, he'd found himself asking God how to protect her, and he hadn't prayed in years!

Ronya arrived with a tray. "She needs to eat."

"I wasn't planning to starve her."

She nodded toward the busy bar and casino. "Well, you've been a little occupied with the wild bunch."

He escorted her upstairs to Kathryn's room. Ivan stood and moved the chair blocking the door. "Haven't heard a peep out of her in a couple of hours."

Matthias tapped on the door. No answer. Taking the room key from his pocket, he unlocked the door and saw Kathryn sound asleep, sprawled in a chair near the hearth, one foot up on the table.

Ronya chuckled. "Well, she's done in." She set the tray down. "Better put her on the bed."

Matthias gently scooped Kathryn up in his arms. Her hair came loose, tumbling in a mass of red curls. Her arms hung limp, her head bobbing back. When she let out a loud snore, Ronya laughed. Chuckling, Matthias placed Kathryn on the bed. Her breathing had softened. She looked like an angel, her skin so pale and smooth. A spreading warmth tightened his chest. He wanted to hold her close and keep her safe. Unbuttoning the high, tight collar, he watched the even pulse in her throat.

Ronya slapped his arm. "What do you think you're doing?"

Straightening abruptly, Matthias blushed. "I was just loosening her collar so she can breathe."

"She's breathing just fine. You're the one who seems to be having trouble." She looked like an angry mother hen. "Let's not confuse the reasons you brought Kathryn up here, shall we?" She made a sound in her throat. "Too bad she can't be at my place."

Considering what he was feeling right now, Matthias thought that might not be a bad idea. "Do you have room?"

"No. A pity, too. The temptation of having her under your roof might be too much."

"I think she can handle it."

Ronya snorted. "I don't doubt that. Kathryn hasn't got a compromising bone in her entire body. You, on the other hand . . ."

Matthias raised a hand as though taking an oath. "I intend to keep a cool eye on her."

Ronya laughed. "I've yet to see you look at Kathryn with a cool eye, Matthias. Everyone in Calvada is watching you burn." She nodded toward the open door. "Why don't you see about fetching what she needs from her place."

He intended to bring over more than a few things.

"Oh, and, Matthias . . ." She held out her hand before he reached the door. "Hand it over."

Matthias took the key from his pocket and put it in her palm.

"Good boy." Ronya smiled up at him. "Now, see to whatever needs doing to keep our girl safe."

<hr/>

Kathryn awakened to jubilant shouting and gunfire from the street below. Groggy, she pushed the covers back. Cold air hit and she realized she had nothing on but a thin lawn shift. Who had undressed her? Looking around frantically, she spotted her skirt, shirtwaist, petticoats, red long johns, and corset neatly folded on her trunk, her boots cleaned and on the floor. No man would be so neat.

Pushing back the wild mass of red curls, she ran across the cold wooden floor, washed, and dressed quickly. Shivering, she added a log to the remaining hot coals in the grate, then went to the front window, where she peered out cautiously. A crowd of men carried Matthias Beck down Chump Street, hooting and hollering, some holding whiskey bottles high. Apparently, Matthias Beck had been elected mayor. Groaning in dismay, Kathryn realized she had slept straight through the election!

Gunshots rang out.

"So much for law and order." Grabbing her brush, Kathryn worked furiously at her hair. Her uncle's armoire had been moved into the room as well. She opened and closed each drawer, finding them filled with her unmentionables, shirt-waists, skirts, and dresses she had brought from home, all neatly folded and tucked in. Her uncle's bookshelf and books were there, along with a hat tree on which were three of her confections, her overcoat, and a shawl.

Everything had been moved except the Washington hand-press, ink, and paper supplies.

Winding her hair into a thick bun, she jammed in tortoise-shell pins and opened the door. Ivan stood. "Where do you think you're going?" He wore a holstered gun tied low on his thigh.

"I'm going outside to find out what's happened."

"Matthias got elected mayor."

"I gathered that much." When she headed for the stairs, Ivan kept pace. She paused. "I don't need your assistance, Mr. . . . ?"

"Lebedev. And I'm under orders to keep an eye on you."

He stuck close on the boardwalk as the parade gathered more followers and almost reached the Sanders Hotel. Was Morgan Sanders watching? No one likes to lose, and this parade verged on smug retaliation.

"Kathryn!" Abbie Aday called from outside the mercantile. She came quickly, a round-eyed look at Ivan and his gun before she fixed her eyes on Kathryn. "I've been so worried about you in that wild place. Nabor said Matthias had you locked in his bedroom."

"What? No!" She wanted to march down to the mercantile and smack Nabor for jumping to that false conclusion. "I'm alone in an upstairs guest room with a good lock on the door, and I'm only there because—"

"Mr. Sanders came after you and—"

"Abbie!" Exasperated, Kathryn thought it best to change the subject. "Any word on how Mr. Sanders has taken the election results?"

"No one has seen him since he left your house, and I doubt anyone wants to be near him now."

"He was mayor for two terms. He surely has something to say." She looked toward his hotel. "Someone should ask."

"It won't be you," Ivan growled.

"I'm editor of the *Voice* and have a responsibility to report what's happening in Calvada, Mr. Lebedev."

"Talk to the new mayor. Matthias Beck."

"I will as soon as he's standing on terra firma and not being carried aloft like Bacchus."

Ivan stared at her. "Huh?"

"Never mind."

Abbie pulled her shawl more tightly around herself. "I heard a dozen Madera men left the night Mr. Beck took you to his hotel. Molly Maguires from Pennsylvania, rumor has it, out here to cause trouble." Abbie stepped closer and whispered. "Nellie O'Toole came in the store last night. Nabor was down at the bar with the rest of the men, so I gave her a bag of beans, salt pork, and two jars of preserves."

Hugging her, Kathryn kissed her cheek. "You have a good heart, Abbie Aday. Don't ever let anyone tell you otherwise." She stepped away. "You can tell everyone I'm going home as soon as I find a few nice gentlemen to move my things back into my house. Mr. Beck insisted that I stay for a week, but I'm sure that's not necessary."

Abbie looked alarmed. "Oh, no, you shouldn't go back. Have you seen your house?"

Kathryn had been so intent on catching up to the parade, she hadn't even glanced across the street. Bidding Abbie good day, she hurried home. Heart sinking, she saw her window had been broken, her ripped curtains left hanging like Spanish moss. Trays of type had been yanked from the cabinet drawers and dumped on the floor. Had it been Sanders, or the men who had been thwarted in killing him?

Fearing the worst, Kathryn went to the press and examined it. "Thank God." No damage done; only the handle was missing. A wheelwright could make another. Hunkering down, she gathered type. How many hours would it take to clean up the mess and put things in order?

Ivan drew her up. "Come away, Miss Walsh. There's nothing you can do about it now."

Kathryn poured what she had into a drawer and wiped her hand on a turpentine-soaked rag. "At least they didn't burn the place down."

"No one's fool enough to do that. The whole town would burn with it."

The parade had reached Beck's. Matthias glanced her way before the men set him on the boardwalk. She wondered at his grim expression.

Scribe spotted her and ran across the street. "Matthias is mayor! No one thought he could win. It was a landslide! And it was all your doing!"

Kathryn's spirits lifted. "Well, I'm glad to know the newspaper is making some difference in Calvada."

"Oh, it wasn't the newspaper. Someone told Matthias that Sanders was in your house. He crossed the street like a shot, won the fight against Sanders's guard, and next thing everyone saw was the big man himself hightailing it out of your house and Matthias calling him a yellow-bellied son of a—"

"Yes, I heard. And that's what got Mr. Beck elected?"

"That, and he dealt with you."

"Excuse me?" Her temper rose.

"The men figured any man who could send Sanders running *and* shut you up in the space of a few minutes has to be the right man for the job!" Scribe headed back to the celebration.

Ivan chuckled and fell silent at Kathryn's glare. "You can go, Mr. Lebedev. I'm sure you'd rather join the mob bellying up to the bar than follow me around."

"I'm under orders." And didn't look happy about it.

"Fine. I'm hungry. Escort me to Ronya's, where I can have something to eat. I give my word. I'll return to my room."

Ivan glowered down at her. "You'd better." He escorted Kathryn to Ronya's and left her there.

———

Kathryn found Ronya peeling potatoes while Charlotte plucked a large wild turkey. "So! He let you out." Chuckling, Ronya nodded toward the stool.

"Under guard." She peered over her shoulder and saw Ivan heading back up the boardwalk. Charlotte tossed more feathers in a basket. Kathryn picked up a large tail feather, turning it, an idea sparking. "May I have these?" If the miners' widows could make turkey feather fans, Kathryn could send them to her mother to sell to ladies in Boston who might like something unique from the Wild West.

Ronya shrugged. "Sure. There's a basketful over there. What'll you be wanting to eat, breakfast or dinner?" She grinned. "Or both?"

"Just coffee and a biscuit, please." She intended to be gone before Matthias sent Ivan back. She'd keep her word and return. Just not yet.

Kathryn put butter and blackberry jam on her biscuit and ate half of it quickly, sipping coffee. Ronya studied her from beneath beetled brows. "Are you in a hurry to go somewhere?"

Kathryn made a grunt in response. Finishing the rest, she stood.

Ronya scowled. "Where are you going?"

"I promised to go back to the hotel."

"In that case . . ." Ronya dug in her apron pocket and took something out. "See that you keep it."

Kathryn caught the key. "Thank you." She tucked it away. "I saw my house."

Charlotte glanced up from her task. "I heard glass shatter, but by the time I came downstairs and looked out, whoever did it was gone."

"They say men were missing from their shift at the mine the day after your paper came out." Ronya sliced potatoes into a big pot, while giving Charlotte instructions to start on the corn bread stuffing. "Some say they were Molly Maguires."

"Well, whoever those men were under the bridge, I hope they're gone now."

"Sanders will take it out on the miners." Charlotte broke up corn bread in a big mixing bowl.

"Surely not." Kathryn looked between the two women and saw they both agreed. She might have to talk to Morgan Sanders. She could be charming when there was a need. "I should go." She picked up the basket and thanked Ronya for the feathers. "I'll see they're put to good use."

Covering her hair with her shawl, Kathryn left Chump Street and Beck's victory celebration behind.

14

MATTHIAS SAW IVAN come through the swinging doors alone. Scowling, he mouthed a question. *Where is she?* Ivan jerked his head and mouthed, *Ronya's,* before joining friends. Annoyed, Matthias pressed his way through the crowd. "Go back and get her."

"She's having lunch. Ronya and Charlotte are keeping an eye on her. She promised she'd come back here after she got something to eat."

Even though Matthias wanted to get away and check on her himself, the men weren't letting him. And considering how much whiskey had been consumed over the last few hours, he knew he'd better make sure the party remained one of celebration and not mayhem. Some had grudges against Sanders and saw Matthias's win as permission to go after him. Sober, they would understand things wouldn't change overnight and a riot could make them a lot worse. Matthias counseled patience and diplomacy, time and effort.

By the time dusk came, the bachelors were sitting down for a meal at Ronya's Café, the Smelting Pot, or the Sourdough Café; the married men on their way home. Ivan had left an hour ago to have supper at Ronya's before escorting Kathryn back to the hotel. Ronya told him yesterday she would be serving turkey with dressing, mashed potatoes, and chard for dinner, along with pumpkin pie. His mouth watered just thinking about it.

Pulling his coat closed against the biting chill in the air, he headed for the eatery. Someone shouted his name and he glanced over his shoulder, spotting Ivan coming from the opposite end of town. Matthias felt his stomach drop. "Where is she?"

"I don't know! Ronya said she had a biscuit and coffee and left hours ago. She never got to the hotel. I've been all over town looking for her. No one's seen her!"

Night was falling fast, bringing snow with it. Wherever she was, Matthias hoped she was indoors. The last time he'd seen her, she'd only had a shawl.

Tweedie Witt told Kathryn that Elvira Haines's baby had died, and she hadn't seen much of her in a few days. Ina Bea Cummings had spoken with Ronya Vanderstrom and would be living with Charlotte in an upstairs room, doing laundry and cleaning rooms where the men lived. Inviting Kathryn in out of the cold, they sat bundled inside Tweedie's shanty, talking for hours. Older than Kathryn by ten years, Tweedie had weathered trials. She had met her husband, Joe, in Cleveland, Ohio, when he came to work in her father's store. The youngest of five brothers, he'd left the family farm to make his own way.

"My two brothers weren't much taken with Joe Witt. Said he weren't good enough, but I thought he was grand." Her face glowed when she talked about him. They came west with a wagon train. "He was never one to pinch pennies. Bought what he wanted at Fort Laramie and Mormon Station." She smiled. "Even a yellow ribbon for me." By the time they reached Humboldt Sink with the forty-mile desert stretching out ahead, they were down to two oxen. "It was like crossing hell. Hot. No water. Alkali sand blowing. I thought I'd die, and there were days when I wished for it." When they reached Truckee, some go-backers told them the Sierra Nevada mountains were worse than anything they'd seen, and snow was coming. "I was in a family way. Seven months along. I knew I'd never make it. Joe knew it, too. Then he heard Henry Comstock found silver fifty miles south. A dozen wagons were ready to head that way, and we joined them."

There was no child in Tweedie Witt's shanty. "What happened to your baby, Tweedie?"

"Come early. Died of an evening. Two days after we was in Virginia City." She plucked at her worn, stained skirt and raised her head slowly, looking at Kathryn with sad eyes. "A little boy. Lost a girl and another boy three years later. Cholera. They's buried up there."

Kathryn took Tweedie's hand.

"'Course, Joe never found silver. He worked a couple of bonanza mines, but pay wasn't much, and silver played out quick. One mine would close and another open. Some of the owners hired Chinese. They work for almost nothing. Joe needed work. That's why we come over here. Sanders is a hard man, but he did build cabins for his men."

"But had no thought for the widows of the men who worked for him."

Tweedie shrugged. "I didn't expect nothing. Life's hard. Some are born lucky, others not. It's just the way things is." She poked the red coals and added another small log.

Kathryn moved the basketful of feathers. "I have an idea." She explained what she'd been thinking.

Tweedie's face brightened. "I'm real good at handiwork."

"You tell me what you need, and I'll provide it. We'll be partners." The little shack was drafty, with a dirt floor that felt like a slab of ice under Kathryn's bottom. "Can you come and work with me? I have a room at the hotel."

"Oh, my." Tweedie looked round-eyed with hope.

"As soon as my house is fixed up again, we can move in there." Tweedie was small and the settee would be more comfortable than sleeping on the ground.

"That would be a fine thing, Miss Walsh."

"Call me Kathryn." She gave Tweedie an impulsive hug. "I think we're going to be good friends, Tweedie."

The ground was covered with a thin layer of snow when Kathryn left Willow Creek. She had spent longer than intended talking with her new friend, but was glad for it. She would write to her mother right away. Her mother knew plenty of kind-hearted women who would buy turkey feather fans, especially knowing it was helping provide a living for a widow.

The sooner Kathryn's little house was livable, the better. She couldn't bear the thought of Tweedie spending the winter in that dreadful shack. Kathryn would also feel less vulnerable with another woman living with her. Especially if Mr. Beck decided to come barging in again.

A cold wind came up, biting her skin through her layers of clothing. She should have worn a coat. Wrapping the shawl tightly around herself, she lowered her head and headed for town.

Matthias pushed past Sanders's servant Longwei, who opened the front door, and strode into the foyer. "Sanders!"

"In here." A calm, deep voice came from the parlor. Sanders sat in a big leather wing chair, a rifle leaning against the side table. He was wearing a gun and had a half-empty glass next to a crystal decanter of brandy. "Come to gloat, Mayor Beck?"

"Where is she?"

"If you're looking for Kathryn, last I heard she was in your bedroom."

Matthias took a step and strove for control of his temper. He'd like nothing better than to knock out a few of Sanders's teeth, but he was frantic to find Kathryn. "I had her locked in a guest room to protect her from you. And from the men who were planning to murder you."

The arrogance went out of Sanders's face. He looked older. "Well, I don't have her. Check every room, if you want."

Matthias glanced at Ivan and the man headed for the stairs. He faced Sanders again. "Kathryn was trying to protect your sorry hide with that editorial."

"All I wanted was a name."

"She doesn't know."

"She had a name." Sanders spoke calmly, eyes narrowing. "I could see that in her eyes."

Matthias gritted his teeth. Had she known one of the men? If so, she hadn't trusted him with that information any more than Sanders.

"I'd offer to help find her if I didn't know there are men drunk enough on victory right now to lynch me."

"You're right about that. I've had to talk some down tonight."

"Don't expect me to thank you."

Ivan came back down the stairs. "She's not up there, boss."

Morgan looked as grim as Matthias felt. The man lifted his brandy glass. "Good luck." He gave a mirthless laugh. "To Kathryn Walsh, a woman who drives men mad." He downed the brandy in one swallow.

Matthias and Ivan left. The snow was coming fast. Matthias looked left, then right, then down the hill. He wanted to put his head back and bellow her name, but then every man in town would know Kathryn was no longer protected. She was on the loose somewhere. He hoped. He didn't want to think about what might be happening to her right now, if the men she'd overheard under the bridge had gotten ahold of her.

Ivan looked at him. "Where do we look now?"

"I wish I knew."

Kathryn couldn't feel her toes or fingers by the time she reached Calvada. Ronya's living quarters at the back of the café glowed like a beacon in a stormy sea. Shivering, her breath like smoke, Kathryn opened the garden gate, trudged through the snow, and knocked.

"Thank heavens!" She motioned Kathryn inside. "Ivan came looking for you. You said you'd go back to the hotel."

"I will." She watched Ronya looking her over and glanced down. "Oh, no! I'm so sorry." Her high-button shoes were soaked and dripping mud on Ronya's clean floor. "I'll go now."

"You're not going anywhere. You're half-frozen!" Ronya pulled Kathryn toward her fireplace. "Stay right there." She disappeared into the bedroom and quickly returned with a button-hook, a thick blanket, and a pair of woolen socks. Kathryn gasped in pain as Ronya unhooked the buttons and pulled off the wet shoes. "You'll be lucky if you don't have frostbite!" Ronya tsked. "Where did you go?"

"Willow Creek Road." She gritted her teeth as Ronya worked on her feet with warm, strong hands.

"Wandering around like everything is perfectly fine." Ronya glanced up with an accusing glare. "You haven't got a lick of sense." She wrapped soft cloths around Kathryn's bare feet and kneaded them more.

Kathryn sighed as the pain lessened. "Oh, that feels good."

"Well, don't get used to it." Ronya stood. "I've got something that will warm you up."

Kathryn hoped it was a nice, hot bowl of stew, but when Ronya returned, she held a steaming mug. Thanking her, Kathryn held it to warm her icy hands.

"Drink it!" Ronya ordered.

Obedient, Kathryn took a small sip and spit it back into the mug. Mortified at what she'd done, she apologized. She'd never tasted anything so vile. Ronya told her to take another sip and swallow it this time, then stood, hands on hips, watching to make sure she did. Shuddering, Kathryn tried again. She managed to swallow a few drops and almost gagged. "I am truly sorry, Ronya, but that coffee is revolting."

Ronya snatched the mug and marched into the restaurant kitchen. When she came back, she handed it to Kathryn again. "Now try it."

Peering into the mug, Kathryn saw cream had been added. She took a cautious sip. And lots of sugar! She took a bigger sip and tasted cinnamon and something else she couldn't identify. "It's delicious."

"Glad you like it. It's one of my winter specialties." Ronya stood over her while she sipped. "You're worse than City. Do you know that? You can't just wander around without telling anyone where you're going. He knew how to fight. You're just a girl." She took the empty mug from her. "You're still shivering. One more of these and you'll be nicely thawed out."

Kathryn's stomach felt plenty warm by the time Ronya came back, but she obeyed. The second mug of coffee was even better than the first. When Ronya demanded to know what she had been up to since leaving the restaurant, Kathryn told her about Tweedie and her feather-fan plan to bring her some income. She said the fans could become the new fashion rage in the East. She talked about the dire straits of the widows and how something had to be done and how happy she was that Ronya had given Ina Bea Cummings a job and a place to live until she matched her up with some nice eligible bachelor. She said Ronya was quite a matchmaker.

Ronya looked amused. "You don't say."

"Oh, I do say. I've heard the widows who work here all end up married. Henry Call sure has his eye on Charlotte, don't you think? Just because I don't want to get married doesn't mean I don't think others shouldn't." Kathryn giggled and went back to talking about plans she had to help Tweedie. "If everything works out as I hope, Tweedie can run the millinery while I run the *Voice*."

Ronya chuckled. "Well, you are just full of ideas, aren't you?"

"And I have a lot more." Kathryn lifted the mug and swallowed the last few drops. "I've always been full of ideas. That's what my mother used to tell me. Good ones, too, don't you think, Ronya?"

She shook her head, eyes lit with laughter. "Oh, I think your ideas are just grand."

Kathryn held the mug up. "You know, that was so good, I'd love to have another before I leave."

"Two is plenty."

Disappointed, Kathryn stood and then plopped down in the chair again. "Oh, for heaven's sake. I'm thawed, but now my legs feel like rubber." She made a second, more determined effort. "There!" She set the empty mug firmly on the table, where Ronya's lantern burned brightly and a book lay overturned. Curious, Kathryn picked it up. "*Ivanhoe* by Sir Walter Scott! Oh, one of my favorites. It's so romantic! Did you find it in the box under the table in Aday's?"

"No. I brought it from Ohio. I kept it hidden in the flour barrel so it wouldn't be dumped along the trail coming west." Ronya watched her eagle-eyed. "How are you feeling?"

Kathryn let out a contented sigh. "I feel fine. Did I tell you I took some rocks to Sacramento?" She chortled and looked around furtively as though about to tell a secret. "I was hoping I'd inherited a gold mine!" She shrugged and leaned forward. "But we'll soon see." She put her finger to her lips. "Shhhhh. Don't tell anyone." She moved to the stove and flipped up the back of her skirt. Bending, she rubbed her hind end.

Ronya laughed. "Feeling nice and warm, are you?"

"You should bottle that stuff and sell it!"

"Leave your shoes to dry and wear these boots." Ronya set them in front of the chair. Kathryn slipped her stockinged feet into them and tightened the laces, but couldn't manage to tie them properly. Stooping, Ronya brushed her hands away and tied them for her. She straightened and took Kathryn through the restaurant to the front door. "Now, my girl. You get yourself straight home." She patted Kathryn's cheek as one would a child. "You promise?"

"I promise." Kathryn threw her arms around Ronya and hugged her tight. As she withdrew, she kissed her cheek. "I'm so glad to have you for a friend."

Ronya's eyes moistened. "Now, off you go." She closed the door.

Kathryn did exactly as she had been told. She went home. Cutting across the street diagonally, she went straight in the front door of City Walsh's newspaper office.

Matthias had been up and down Rome, London, and Galway Streets and seen nothing. Ivan had headed for Gomorrah, though neither thought Kathryn Walsh would be sipping tea with a soiled dove. He'd run out of places to look. He should have kept the key instead of giving it to Ronya. If he had, Kathryn would be locked safe and sound in the upstairs bedroom. Horrific images of the war flashed in his mind. Hatred drove people to do appalling things to one another, and the men Kathryn had overheard under the bridge might want revenge.

Matthias felt sick with worry. He stood in front of the saloon and looked up and down the street. Maybe he should have left her in City's building and put a guard at the front and back doors. An evening breeze stirred the shredded curtains and Matthias thought he saw light. If the vandals were back, he'd break a few heads. The door was still off its hinges and leaning to one side. And there was Kathryn, bent over, sweeping glass into a dustpan.

She stood and smiled benignly. "Oh, hello, Matthias. How are you this evening?"

Matthias stared in consternation, the wave of relief shaking him almost as much as the anger that swiftly followed. "*Good evening?* That's all you can say when I've been looking all over tarnation for you?" He swore.

Rather than look shocked, she turned away and dumped a dustpan full of broken glass into a bucket. "There's no need for such language."

Clenching his teeth, Matthias moved into the room. "Where have you been for the last five hours?"

Kathryn waved her hand airily. "Oh, I don't want to go through all that again." She looked around. "I have a lot to do to get things in order so I can get back to work."

Matthias jerked his thumb toward the door. "Let's go, your ladyship."

She looked up at him with a beatific wide-eyed innocence. "Go where?"

"*Back to the hotel!*"

She cringed, but didn't cower. Straightening fully, she planted the broom on the floor. "You sound just like the judge."

Matthias hadn't intended to shout, and he certainly didn't intend to act like her stepfather. Kathryn went back to sweeping glass into another pile. He took another two steps, and caught a whiff of something all too familiar. Leaning down, Matthias looked at her more closely.

She drew back, eyes widening. "Don't you dare kiss me again, Matthias Beck." She wagged a finger under his nose. "No, no, no."

All the anger went out of him. "Well, well, your ladyship." He grinned. "You smell like you've had one of Ronya's winter elixirs."

"Elixir?" She frowned. "I had coffee. Delicious, creamy coffee with lots of sugar and cin . . . na . . . na . . . mon."

"And several shots of brandy." His amusement died when he

looked her over thoroughly and realized she was wearing boots instead of the high-button shoes she'd been wearing this afternoon when she had been standing beside Ivan, watching the parade. The hem of her skirt was filthy. What had she said a few minutes ago when he was so mad, he wasn't thinking straight? *Oh, I don't want to go through all that again.* His heart pounded. *All that? Again?* He doubted she'd tell him where she'd been and what she'd been doing since she'd sent Ivan back to the celebration with promises of returning to the hotel after she had something to eat. A biscuit and coffee, Ronya had told him, and she'd seemed in a hurry. Two elixirs, probably on an empty stomach. No wonder she couldn't say *cinnamon*! He was surprised she was still standing. Right now, the only thing that mattered was getting her safely to the hotel and keeping her there.

Matthias slid his hand down her arm and took her hand. "Come on, Kate. Time to get you safely home."

She blinked and looked at him with an expression he'd briefly seen the night he'd kissed her. Then she pulled her hand free, another expression closer to alarm taking its place.

"This is my home, sir."

Her mood changed faster than the weather. "Not for a while." Not ever, if he had his way. He gave a quick look around. Broken windows, smashed cabinets, mud slung everywhere. If she had her way and moved back in here, they'd be breaking her instead. "I'll have it boarded up so no further damage is done." Clearly, she didn't like that idea. He could see her trying to work out an argument. Thankfully, her mind was muddled. He took her hand again, more firmly this time. "Ronya has the key, so you needn't worry I'll lock you in again." But he would have a guard by the door with clear instructions of what she could and couldn't do. Ivan wouldn't dare let her out of his sight this time.

"All right." She gave him a slight, smug smile and went with him without protest. Her compliance gave him more cause to worry.

Men stood at the bar, drinking and talking. Others sat at tables, cards in their hands, solemn looks of concentration. He let go of her hand and took her by the arm so it would appear more proper. A few noticed them. "Hey, Matthias! Where you takin' the little lady?" Others har-harred.

"I'm escorting Miss Walsh to her room, gentlemen. Brady, when Ivan comes in, send him up." He gave a look around the room, and the laughter stopped. The men looked away.

When Matthias opened the upstairs bedroom door, Kathryn walked right in without hesitation. Watching her, he frowned. "I'll get the fire started." She thanked him and flopped into the chair. He could feel her watching him and glanced back. She dropped her eyes quickly, but not before he realized she'd been looking him over.

He struck a match. The way she'd been eyeing him produced one idea he'd best not dwell upon. He thought of another. "I could go to Stu Bickerson and tell him you made Scribe take off his clothes and spend half a night in your bedroom."

She rolled her eyes. "That's not the way it was!"

The kindling took. Straightening, Matthias gave her a cool, challenging smile. "And I could tell him I found you drunk in your front office in the middle of the night."

"I am not drunk, and it's not the middle of the night."

"Stu never worries about minor details." Matthias studied her, noticing how uncomfortable she was under his gaze. He thought he knew why. "I might even have to tell him about the kiss." He watched the color rise in her cheeks. Had she been thinking about it as much as he had?

"You wouldn't be so unkind. You're a gentleman."

"Oh, *now*, I'm a gentleman," he drawled.

A hand fluttered to her throat. "Why are you looking at me like that?"

"Like what?" When she didn't answer, he gave her a rueful smile. "Henry said the only way I can keep you safe is to marry you." He was as surprised as she when the words passed his lips. Now spoken, he knew that's what had been in the back of his mind since the day he first saw her.

For the briefest moment, he saw her eyes light up. Then a veil came down, and she shot to her feet and moved as far away from him as the room allowed. "I'm never marrying anyone."

At least she hadn't said he was the last man on earth she would marry. Her rejection included every man now or in the future. "I'm not just anyone, Kate."

She straightened, chin up, and arched a brow. "I don't care if you're the mayor and the second richest man in Calvada, I'm not marrying you."

"You sound pretty sure about that."

"It is my decision. Is it not?"

"Yes. It is. And up to me to change your mind." Matthias grinned and walked slowly toward her. "I'll bet I can." She managed to keep the same distance between them. "Just for argument's sake, what would it take to get you to agree?"

"Nothing." She frowned. "Everything." She shook her head. "A whole long list."

He kept moving and so did she. She was near the hearth, the chairs and table between them. "We could always start off this evening . . ." He teased and saw the color come up her neck and cheeks like a sunrise.

"Abso . . . loot . . . lee not!"

He tried not to laugh. "Why don't we sit and talk this over?" If she kept backing up any farther, she'd set herself on fire. "Your skirt is smoking, Kate."

"Oh, no. I'm not taking my eyes off you."

"I'm flattered." He'd carried the game far enough and wanted her to calm down. He needed to calm down, too. He took a seat and extended his hand in invitation toward the other. "Sit. Let's talk."

"I think you should leave."

"Not yet." He knew the best way to distract her. "I'm mayor now. Don't you want to ask for details of my plans for the town?"

Her lips pressed together. "What good is that, if I can't print them?"

"We can talk about that, too."

She perched on the edge of the chair, ready for flight. "What will it take for you to let me go back to my home?"

Matthias knew he couldn't expect her to be happy living in his hotel or anyone else's for that matter. "When we have a sheriff."

"Ah, yes!" She folded her hands in her lap. "Your law-and-order platform."

"Axel Borgeson will arrive within the next couple of weeks." As soon as the votes had been counted, he told Henry to send the telegram confirming the offer. "He worked for the Pinkerton Detective Agency, spying for the Union Army, then was assigned as a guard for the Union Pacific. He was at Promontory Point when the golden spike was driven in by Leland Stanford, then came out to California."

Kathryn leaned forward, excited now. "How did you find him?"

"I wasn't just going to Sacramento to buy whiskey."

Kathryn smiled at him, pleased, and thankfully relaxed. "You keep that promise and the town will thank you."

Despite her months in Calvada, she was still very naive. "Not everyone will be happy to have law and order. A lot of men come out West to get away from the rules and regulations."

"Is that why you came to California, Matthias?"

Her tone held melting curiosity. The warmth of the fire and two shots of brandy were doing their work. "No, that's not why I came." He doubted she was aware of the way her eyes moved over his body. Maybe he should open a window. But that wouldn't help. It wasn't the fire in the grate that was heating him up. It was seeing prim and proper Kathryn Walsh in a sultry mood.

"The truth is there was no hero's welcome for me when I went home." In another few minutes, she'd have one booted foot on the table and be snoring like a sailor again.

"Because you fought for the North?" Sighing, she leaned back.

Matthias didn't want to talk about Sherman's March to the Sea and what that meant to his hometown.

Kathryn blinked at him, those mesmerizing eyes like a caress. "Why did you?"

He needed to think about something else. What had she asked him? Oh, yeah. "I believed the nation would last longer unified than splintered." Allow one part of the country to break away, and soon, each state would want to become a sovereign country. They'd become like Europe, countries constantly going to war against each other. *A house divided against itself cannot stand*, he'd told his father, but even God's Word hadn't swayed Jeremiah Beck's Southern pride.

"And slavery? Where do you stand on that?"

"My best friend was the son of my father's only household slave. He went with me when I left. He was killed the first year." Kathryn listened in silence. It wasn't pity Matthias saw, but compassion. "The hardest thing I've ever had to do in my life was tell his mother. Had he stayed home, he would've lived." His voice had roughened. "She forgave me."

"She sounds like a good Christian woman."

"My father was a good Christian man. A minister, in fact." Bitterness and pain made him laugh bleakly. "He told me he wished I'd been stillborn, and then he turned his back on me and walked away."

Kathryn's eyes welled with tears. Matthias let out his breath and looked away, wishing he had given her superficial answers rather than open old wounds.

"Oh, Matthias." She gave a soft sigh. "I'm sure the Lord will deal with your father's heart. God promises to finish the work in us." She spoke softly, as one might to a troubled friend. "People say terrible things when they're hurt and angry. I know I have." A tear slipped down her pale cheek. She searched his face, her expression tender. "We seem to have something in common. My mother told me her life would be much easier without me in it."

Her words were like a gut punch. He felt her pain and knew now why she had sunk roots in Calvada.

Sleepy-eyed, she relaxed and watched the flames.

"This is nice, don't you think?" She looked at him with childlike trust. In her present mood, she was entirely too vulnerable and tempting.

Matthias knew he had already stayed too long. "I think it's time I said good night." He thought of the men downstairs, and the speculations they were undoubtedly making. He should have thought of that an hour ago.

Still seated, Kathryn looked up at him wistfully. "You know something, Matthias? I like you." She seemed pleasantly surprised by that revelation.

He chuckled. "Do you?"

"Yes. I do. You're going to be good for Calvada. You've already hired a sheriff." It took two tries for her to get out of the chair. "What will you do about the streets?" Languid, she followed him toward the door, even tucking her hand into the crook of his arm. "The children need a school. Boys and girls need an education, you know." She had some trouble pronouncing *education*, reminding Matthias how many elixirs she'd had and why she had that sultry, time-for-bed look in her eyes that was wreaking havoc with his resolve. "We haven't enough wells, either." She patted his arm. "The garbage is piled high between the buildings." Grimacing, she shuddered. "I've seen so many rats. I saw rats in Boston, too, but not nearly as many as here. Little ones and big ones. We have to do something about the garbage and the rats, Matthias."

He liked hearing her say *we*. "If I manage all that, will you marry me?"

She withdrew her hand and stepped back. "Now, don't tease. You would merely be fulfilling your duties as mayor of our fair city." She gave him a light push toward the door.

"I'll have Ivan come up and sit in the hallway."

"I'm perfectly safe."

"Not with the door unlocked."

"Oh!" Her eyes widened and she laughed. "Well! You needn't worry about that." She pushed at his chest. "Go on now."

Matthias caught her wrists and raised them. Then, letting go, he pulled her into his arms and kissed her the way he'd been wanting to for as long as he could remember. She tasted of brandy, cream, and sugar. Her eyes were closed, her lips parted. He could see the pulse throbbing in her throat, and it was almost his undoing.

"Time to say good night, your ladyship." His voice was rough with passion. He set her back from him, knowing he had taken unfair advantage. She looked at him, bemused.

Fighting temptation, Matthias opened and backed out the door, closing it quickly.

15

KATHRYN AWAKENED with a dry mouth and a headache. She debated pulling the blankets up over her head and staying in bed, but remembered Tweedie Witt would be coming to work. Rising quickly, Kathryn went through her morning ablutions and dressed. She pulled on her wool socks and boots and picked up the pair Ronya had loaned her. When she opened the door, she jumped back as Ivan's chair tipped, landing the Russian inside her room like an upside-down turtle with arms and legs whirling.

Trying not to laugh, Kathryn reached down to help the poor man. "Are you all right?"

Muttering Russian curses, Ivan managed to roll off the chair and crawl into the hallway. Still muttering, he made his feet, face red and thunderous. "Next time give me a little warning!"

She slipped out, closed and locked the door, and headed for the stairs.

Ivan caught up with her. "Where do you think you're going?"

"To Ronya's. For breakfast."

Scowling, he kept pace. "Matthias chewed me up and spit me out like bad jerky yesterday. I'm sticking to you like tree sap."

After breakfast, Kathryn went to the wheelwright to order another press handle. Patrick Flynt said he could make one, but wasn't sure he should because he'd heard she was in trouble enough already and he didn't want to give her the means to cause more. She told him if he helped her, she would put a free advertisement in the next issue of the *Voice*.

From Flynt's, Kathryn walked half a mile out of town to Rudger Lumber and inquired about glass.

Carl Rudger grinned when he saw her. "Haven't enjoyed reading a newspaper so much since City Walsh—"

"Got his head bashed in?" Ivan cut in, Mr. Rudger staring, appalled he'd be so blunt. Ivan glared, unrepentant. "Don't help her. She needs to stay put at the hotel."

Kathryn patted Ivan's arm. "Don't mind Ivan's nasty disposition. The poor man fell on his head this morning."

Ivan scowled.

Mr. Rudger had glass in stock and would install her window by end of day, at cost. "It's about time someone printed the truth around here, even if it is a woman doing it."

"Thank you for that vote of confidence," Kathryn said wryly.

"Just don't write about me in the *Voice*."

She laughed. "Don't do anything that might draw my attention."

Rudger laughed with her.

On the way back to town, Ivan's mood soured even more. "Are we done yet? Or are you planning on having tea someplace?"

"You could use a nice cup. Peppermint is good for frustration, anxiety, and fatigue."

"I could use a drink is what I could use!"

Kathryn picked out the most inexpensive fabric at Aday's, but Nabor hiked up the price so much she knew he didn't want her business. Embarrassed, Abbie busied herself with canned goods. Kathryn thanked Nabor for his time and left. She'd rather cut up one of her dresses to make curtains than buy fabric from Nabor Aday. She'd heard a new store would soon be opening at the other end of town, but right now, she had only one other option. Kathryn waited for several wagons and horseback riders to pass by, then stepped down into the muddy street.

"Where are you going now?"

"To the Madera Company Store."

He caught her by the arm. "Oh, no, you don't!"

"Let go, Ivan." When he didn't let go, she stopped in the middle of the street. "I don't think you want me to make a scene." Glowering, he released her.

Kathryn walked past the Crow Bar and the Iron Horse Saloon and into Sanders's store. Customers froze. So did she when she saw Morgan Sanders standing at the back, deep in conversation with his manager. Ivan uttered a foul word. Hesitating, Kathryn gathered her courage and walked between the rows of tables until she reached one with bolts of cloth, a larger selection than Aday's. The manager noticed her. When her eyes met his briefly, he quickly averted his gaze. Morgan was doing all the talking, telling what to order, more beans, less sugar. When the manager glanced at her again, Morgan looked back over his shoulder. His annoyed expression immediately changed to surprise.

Tensing, Ivan stepped close. "Let's go." He gripped Kathryn's arm and rested his other hand lightly on his Smith & Wesson.

Kathryn looked up at him. "Please don't do anything stupid."

"You're saying that to me?"

Morgan wove his way between tables toward them. Kathryn noticed he was also wearing a gun at his hip. Other customers moved slowly, pretending not to watch while watching. Ignoring Ivan, Morgan gave her a nod. "Good morning, Kathryn."

"Good morning, Mr. Sanders." Though her body tensed, she spoke calmly. She fingered some flowered calico and found it better quality than what Nabor stocked. Morgan stood silent, waiting, as though he was the clerk and not the store owner.

"How much for four yards of this?" She kept her tone controlled, casual.

"You can have all you want for free, along with my apology."

His tone left her in no doubt he was sincere. He seemed weary, as though he hadn't slept in a while. How could he, knowing some of his own men had been plotting murder? "Apology accepted, Morgan." Without thinking, she held out her hand. "Thank you for the kind offer, but it's only right I pay for the cloth."

His fingers closed firmly around hers. "As you wish." He named a price less than half what Nabor had demanded.

"Is that what you usually charge your customers?" When he didn't answer, she suggested a fair price. "It's what most people can afford and still make you a profit." His eyes flickered and a faint smile touched his lips. He gave a nod and signaled one of the clerks.

Rather than leave, Morgan lingered while the young man measured and cut the cloth. "You led Matthias a merry chase yesterday. He came to my house, looking for you."

"Oh." Looking for her or for a fight? "I went to visit a friend."

Morgan's eyes narrowed slightly. "Someone connected to your newspaper story?"

"Someone I met recently who needs work." She looked into his eyes, and found them warm, not cold. "She's a widow, you see. Her husband was killed in the Madera mining accident last year. She's fallen on very hard times and living in a drafty shanty by Willow Creek." She looked pointedly at his well-tailored jacket, shirt, tie, then down to the wide leather belt and black slacks. "It's the first time I've seen you wearing a gun."

"I thought it wise."

Was all this her fault? "I'm sorry for your trouble, Morgan. I heard some men left town."

His expression hardened. "Yes. I had suspicions about a few."

"I'm glad their plans came to naught."

His mouth tipped. "You might be the only person in town who would say that."

Why not tell him what she thought? "All the hard feelings could change, Morgan." When he raised his brows slightly, she went on. "You may have lost the election, but you're still a leader in this town. You could be a better one." She heard Ivan suck air between his teeth. "You have the means to do a great deal of good for the people of Calvada."

"Do I?"

"You know you do."

The clerk folded the material and rolled it in brown paper and tied with a string. She thanked him and handed over the coins. People moved around the store quietly.

Morgan inclined his head. "May I see you out?"

Kathryn gave a soft laugh. "Is that a nice way of saying you want me to mind my own business and hope I won't come back?"

"You take risks, Kathryn." His tone held no animosity as he walked with her.

"People are worth it, Morgan." When they stood outside on the boardwalk, she looked up at him. "You're worth it." She extended her hand.

Morgan took and lifted her hand, kissing it. "So are you, Kathryn."

"Are you done yet?" She could feel the steam heat coming off Ivan as they walked back to the hotel.

"I'm just getting started."

It took less than an hour for the whole town to hear about Kathryn Walsh shaking hands with Sanders and having him kiss hers. The men were all talking about it at the bar.

"He's rich. Tell me one woman who doesn't want to marry a rich man."

Matthias intended to talk to her about it, but just now he was busy setting up much-needed municipal services. He'd expected trouble from Sanders over transition of town funds, but the records had been brought in boxes to his office soon after the election. Henry Call immediately started pulling out files and going through them with a lawyer's eye. Everything looked in order. Women began answering Matthias's advertisements in Sacramento and San Francisco, but they wouldn't arrive until winter snows melted. By then, some services would be underway.

He'd fulfilled his primary campaign promise by hiring a sheriff. Axel Borgeson was due to arrive this week. Matthias planned to give him the room across from Kathryn, until the small house next to the jail was rebuilt.

Without a sheriff, the town had run wild, men handling problems with their fists or threat and sometimes use of guns.

Matthias, Brady, and Ivan always dealt with any trouble in the saloon, leaving other proprietors up and down Chump Street to follow the same rule. There hadn't been a night without some ruckus since Kathryn arrived. The truth was Matthias would be relieved to have Axel Borgeson walking the streets of Calvada with a star on his chest. The man was tough and experienced.

On the day Borgeson was expected to arrive, naturally Kathryn was at the stage to welcome him. And she couldn't have looked more pleased if he'd been President Ulysses S. Grant come to town. She launched into a list of Calvada's problems, nothing Matthias hadn't already told Borgeson in their correspondence, but the man looked all too attentive. Then Kathryn said she'd like to interview him for the *Voice*, and he said there was no time like the present. With a warm smile, she invited him to join her for coffee and a slice of apple pie at Ronya's Café.

Matthias's jaw stiffened. He could see she liked the man on first meeting. And Borgeson's gaze was a little too warm for comfort. He turned that gaze on Ivan, who had accompanied Kathryn to the station.

"Is this gentleman your beau, Miss Walsh?"

Ivan gave an indelicate snort. "No!"

"Now, Ivan," Kathryn purred, giving the big Russian a pained look, her eyes sparkling with mischief. "Alas. This is my ball and chain." She looked at Matthias. "Mr. Beck had me incarcerated—"

"Protective custody," Matthias corrected. "Ivan is her bodyguard."

Borgeson smiled. "Well, Ivan can take the day off. Miss Walsh is safe with me. I have questions to ask too. May I?"

Kathryn didn't hesitate to slip her hand through his arm. "Delighted, Sheriff Borgeson."

"Call me Axel, please."

Ivan looked at Matthias and smirked. "He's wasting no time."

"And you think I am?" Matthias growled, watching the couple walk down the boardwalk together. Borgeson had left his luggage for him to handle.

Ivan chuckled. "I guess now that *Axel* is in town and living right across the hall from the lady, I can go back to bouncing troublemakers out of the bar."

Kathryn hadn't been wasting time either. She had everything packed and ready to move back into her house. Flynt had made a new handle for the press, and Rudger had put in new windows with trim. He even added shutters, window boxes, and a fresh coat of yellow paint. City's building now looked like a daffodil in a mud heap. She had put up shades and hung curtains.

Seeing her laugh with Borgeson sent a hot rush through him. He was going to make time to talk with her, as soon as he assigned the six new civic workers their duties.

It wasn't Kathryn who answered her hotel room door later that afternoon. "Oh, hello, Mayor Beck. How are you today?"

"Fine." He stood confused in the hallway. "Who are you?"

"Tweedie Witt. I work with Kathryn. I've never been in such a lovely—"

"Where is Kathryn?" He noticed things missing from the room.

"Across the street at the newspaper office. Carl Rudger and Patrick Flynt moved her things this morning."

"Did they?" Annoyed, Matthias headed across the street. He didn't bother to knock, and she only gave him a cursory glance.

"I haven't time to argue. I'm trying to get another issue out."

Matthias strove for patience. "As I recall, we were going to discuss when you might move over here and when you'd go to press again."

She barely looked up from whatever she was writing. "I'm a free woman. It's not your decision. But now that Axel is in town, I'll be safe in my own home."

"You think so? Is *Axel* moving in with you?"

Her head snapped up at that. "Of course not. And to be clear, I wasn't living with you either."

"You were under my roof!"

"A guest in your hotel. Or so you said." She sniffed. "I'm much safer here."

He almost wished he hadn't hired Axel Borgeson. "You really should stay at the hotel a while longer."

"Be reasonable, Matthias. My things are all here now. You don't have to worry about me anymore." She gave him a guileless smile. "You know everyone will want to read about our new sheriff."

Morgan Sanders was less a worry now than Axel Borgeson. "Fine. Write the news and print it, but you're not moving out just yet."

"Axel said he'd keep an eye out for me."

Oh, Matthias could bet on that. He didn't like the feeling he got every time Kathryn said the man's name. "I'm sure *Axel* would like nothing better, but I hired him to clean up the town, not focus on one harebrained woman!"

Kathryn put her pencil down and folded her hands on the desk. "Yes, I know. And you know I can't afford a room in your hotel, and you've given me your best. Think of it from a business standpoint. It's not good for your best room to be occupied by a nonpaying guest."

"Why don't you let me worry about my own business?"

"Just as soon as you let me get back to mine!" She picked up her pencil. "Now, please go away and let me concentrate."

Matthias knew he had no other choice.

The next issue of the *Voice* was printed front and back, with
two advertisements, Flynt's and Rudger's, along with a church
announcement that a Christmas Eve service would be held at
ten in the evening, a Christmas service the following morning.
Matthias had heard Kathryn still attended services, despite the
public dressing down. He'd been surprised, but relieved. The
newspaper was hawked up and down and around town by Janet
and John Mercer's two sons, James and Joseph. The family had
fallen on hard times since the closing of the Jackrabbit Mine.
Kathryn paid the boys a penny for each newspaper they sold,
and they each earned a dollar before noon. A good day's wage
in the Madera Mine.

Matthias bought one of the first copies. The headline read
NEW SHERIFF IN TOWN. He'd figured as much. The
article was full of Axel's admirable escapades. He might have
been a spy during the war, but he clearly had nothing to hide
now. His training, his experience, his dedication to uphold-
ing the law, which included getting shot once, with details on
when, how, and why. Kathryn had done a thorough job. Her
article was better reading than a dime novel. She even included
the comforting fact that Borgeson could hit a bull's-eye three
hundred feet away every time with his Winchester rifle, and all
in the space of a few seconds.

How did she know that?

When Matthias asked, she said Axel had rented a carriage
and taken her outside town to demonstrate. Borgeson had
seemed a quiet man, but Kathryn had sure managed to loosen
his tongue. But then, she'd managed to get secrets out of him,

too. Others seemed to be falling under her spell as well—Flynt, Rudgers, and who could forget good old Morgan Sanders, more than ten years older and clearly entering his rut. Kathryn didn't want to get married. So she said. Not that it would change Sanders's mind. Not that it had changed his own.

Kathryn had City's charm and quick mind. She also had his penchant for disturbing the peace. Things seemed to be going smoothly right now, but Matthias knew it wouldn't be long before she was neck-deep in trouble again.

16

EVERYTHING BACK IN HER SNUG LITTLE HOUSE, Kathryn should have felt content. She and Tweedie spent Christmas Eve helping Ronya and Charlotte serve meals to a stream of hungry, lonely men far from home and family. Some had left wives behind, hoping to get rich quick and bring them out West by train. Now, they couldn't afford to buy a train ticket home, let alone bring family out to join them. Kathryn overheard talk of riding the rails east.

She empathized. She was homesick, too. Back in Boston, the weeks before Christmas and through New Year's had been frenetic. There had scarcely been an evening when she hadn't been attending some soiree, ball, or musical program, many of which were held right at the Hyland-Pershing mansion. Her grandfather, Charles Hyland, had been known to open the estate for lavish holiday parties, and Lawrence Pershing continued the tradition, Kathryn's mother artfully making all arrangements: string quartets, pianists, soloists, chamber orchestra with soprano. The season had been the most exciting time of the year. Guests filled the grand hall and conservatory. Kathryn had loved those evenings. She'd also loved attending the Old South Church's Christmas cantatas. Once, after she overheard the judge speaking derisively of Irish Catholics, she had snuck off the grounds and ridden a streetcar to the Cathedral of the Holy Cross just to experience a high Christmas Mass. When he found out, the judge barred her from all festivities for the rest of the season. A crushing blow, but one her mother had overcome with charm and manipulation. Her mother had often saved her from the judge's edicts. Until the last one.

Work at Ronya's done, the men off to find solace elsewhere, the women sat in the warm kitchen. Ronya offered Kathryn another of her special coffee elixirs. Kathryn laughed and said, though sorely tempted, now that she knew what was in it, she must decline. Henry came to sit a while with Charlotte in the dining room near the potbellied stove. Ronya looked weary and ready to retire. Kathryn gave her an embroidered handkerchief.

Her friend's eyes filled. "Well, now I'm sorry I have nothing for you."

"How many meals have I had here?"

"And worked for each one."

"Who made sure I didn't lose my toes to frostbite?"

"Who got you drunk?"

Kathryn hugged her. "Hush, now. You are my true friend, and I love you dearly." She turned to Tweedie. "We'd best be leaving so she can rest." Tweedie asked if Kathryn would mind if she spent the night upstairs with Charlotte and Ina Bea. Kathryn understood and tried not to feel left out. The women had been close friends long before she came to town.

Her little house felt cold and lonely. Kathryn built the fire in her stove and reread the letter from her mother, the only one she'd received since leaving Boston. Kathryn had wept the first time she read it.

My dearest Kathryn,

I apologize for not writing before this, and only sending money for the feather fans, which are very popular with my friends. Your letters describing the town left me with considerable misgivings, but Lawrence recommended time rather than sympathy. I believe he was correct. You now seem settled in your new life. You are finding your own way, which Lawrence said you would. I know how you trust in God to protect and guide you. And I share that faith.

I am well. You need not worry. Lawrence insists that I remain confined until the baby arrives, and then spend a few months resting. He is very solicitous, anticipating my every need. I do miss going out, but friends come to call. Dr. Evans comes every few days. Lawrence insists, and he remains when the doctor is with me. I feel very pampered, though there are times when I could do with less attention.

Ronya Vanderstrom sounds like a true friend and a woman of extraordinary character. Have Charlotte Arnett and Henry Call married yet? Perhaps you will find someone who suits your nature, for I find it unbearable to think of you spending your whole life alone.

Send more fans when you have them. I have not told your stepfather that I have become a saleslady. He would not approve, but it is for a good cause.

*Please send me an issue of the Voice. Consider it my
small rebellion, as we both know very well what Lawrence
would think of such a venture for a woman. That is not
to say I disagree with the decision he made on my behalf
or that you should even consider coming back to Boston.
I believe you are where God has placed you. Trust in the
Lord with all your heart, my darling, and He will lead
you into the path He has laid out for your life.*

Always my love, your mother

Restless, emotional, Kathryn couldn't sleep with guitars, squeeze-boxes, stomping feet, and laughing next door.
Saloons and another dance hall down the street would be alive
with music and patrons. She found herself tapping her foot.
She'd always loved to dance. Beck's Saloon was undoubtedly
packed, as usual. Brady would be busy at the bar, Ivan keeping his eye out for trouble, Matthias overseeing the gaming
tables. Thinking about him made Kathryn's pulse quicken.
Remembering his kisses made her wish for another. Well, that
would never do!

She picked up Homer's *Odyssey* but, after reading the same
page three times, put it down again. She went to the front window and peered out. Matthias had come outside and was looking across the street. Kathryn let go of the curtain hastily, heart
pounding. She felt hot with embarrassment, wondering if he'd
seen her looking out her new window, looking for him. She
pressed cold hands to warm cheeks.

Time passed. He didn't come. Had she hoped he would?
Fully awake, she started another letter to her mother. She
couldn't tell her distressing details, such as Reverend Thacker's
blistering public reprimand. Nor could she mention going to
South Bridge to overhear plans to commit murder, or Morgan

Sanders storming into her front office. Giving up, she put her writing tools away.

She was ready to turn down the lamp and go back to bed when someone tapped on her door. Axel often stopped by on his rounds just to check on her, but never this late. She cracked the door to tell him she was fine and faced Matthias on the stoop. Her emotions fluttered like a flock of surging swifts—pleasure, pain, fear that this was the one man who could undo her the same way Connor Walsh had undone her mother. She'd been in a tumble all evening, and seeing him was simply too much. She burst into tears. Mortified, she tried to shut the door.

Matthias pushed his way in. "What's wrong now?"

"Nothing!" She wanted to say, *It's Christmas Eve, you dolt, and I'm alone.* Worse, he was the one man who made her weak in the knees. "Just go away!" Was there anything worse than having him see her cry like a baby? When she heard him close the door, she thought he'd left, and cried harder. Then he touched her shoulder, and she jumped. "Why are you still here?" She sounded as vulnerable as she felt, and was frustrated she had so little control.

"I came over because I thought this might be a hard night for you." He spoke softly, his voice roughened. "Your first Christmas away from home."

She dashed tears away and lifted her chin. "I can manage on my own."

"I see how well you're managing." He moved closer, a sympathetic smile curving his mouth. "A pity I don't have Ronya's coffee elixir recipe." When she gave a soft laugh, he sat on the edge of her desk. "I could go back and get us a bottle of brandy . . ."

She knew he was teasing, trying to lighten her mood. "You are a rogue."

"Reformed." Something in his tone made her skin tingle. He

held out a handkerchief. She took it and thanked him. "Brady is taking over."

"Taking what over?" She shuffled papers, nervous, heart pounding, breath catching. She hoped he wouldn't notice.

"The saloon." He watched her closely. "I'm giving him the same deal Langnor gave me. Half ownership and pay for the rest over time."

Kathryn stopped what she was doing and stared at him. "But why?"

"Why?" He looked surprised. "I thought you'd be pleased to hear the news. It might even be worth an article in the *Voice*." His expression and tone hardened slightly. "Not as lengthy as Axel warranted, of course, being your hero of the moment and all."

What did Axel have to do with any of this? She tossed the papers on the desk. "Isn't the saloon what keeps the money flowing into your pockets?" she asked with sarcasm.

Matthias frowned. "And money matters to you?"

"No, but I thought it mattered uppermost to you."

He stood and moved around the desk. She sucked in a soft breath and backed up.

"I have all the money I need safely tucked away in a bank in Sacramento and some invested here. The new mercantile opens in a week."

"That's yours?"

"Part owner. There's time for all things, and a time to move on."

That announcement dropped like a stone into her stomach. She felt the tears coming again. "You were just elected mayor!" She wanted to rage and weep at the same time. "You can't leave town now!"

His eyes glowed as they moved over her face. "Oh, I'm not leaving."

She fidgeted under his perusal. "Well, that's good news because you have a lot of work to do around here." She moved toward the sofa, then changed her mind. The door to her back room was open. She should have closed it. The front office suddenly felt too small for two people, even though she and Tweedie and Scribe worked together almost every day.

"I'm already making progress," he drawled.

She wished he would look at something other than her. "Such as?"

"You'll see. I didn't come over here to be interviewed." His mouth tipped. "What's making you so nervous, Kathryn?"

"You are, if you must know."

"Why?"

There was that question again, spoken in a low, taunting tone, as if he already knew the answer, even if she didn't. "You should go."

"I think we should get married."

Her mouth opened and closed like a banked fish. "What?" She felt a rush of emotions totally inappropriate for the decision she had made about remaining single for the rest of her life. She reminded herself of what a woman lost when she let a man put a ring on her finger. "No!"

"What would it take to get you to say yes?" He moved closer. "Give me a list."

"Don't be ridiculous!"

He looked deadly serious. "A house?"

Feeling a bubble of panic, Kathryn inched back. "I have a house." When he touched her arm lightly, she faltered. Pressed and agitated, she talked fast in self-defense. "All right! You want a list?" She'd give him one he could never get through. "Collect and get the garbage out of town. We need a municipal water system. And streets easily crossed in fall and winter without mud and potholes big enough to swallow a horse and rider! A schoolhouse. A town hall for meetings and cultural events so people can hear music other than banjos, guitars, castanets, and squeeze-boxes!" What else? He kept moving closer, and she couldn't back up farther without falling on the sofa.

Matthias stood right in front of her, near enough that she could feel the warmth and smell the delicious musk scent of his body. "And if I do all that, you'll marry me."

It wasn't a question. She swallowed convulsively. "I'll think about it." She shouldn't sound so meek at a moment like this!

"Oh, no, your ladyship. You'll do more than think about it. You'll do it."

She couldn't breathe properly. "Matthias . . ." Her voice sounded raspy, uncertain, not at all like herself.

Matthias pulled her into his arms and kissed her. For half a second, she pushed against him and then found herself melting. "Consider it a deal." He looked at her, a glow of triumph in his eyes.

She panicked. "Wait just a minute."

"Everything on your list is for the town. What do *you* want from me?" Mesmerized by his eyes, so dark and penetrating, she couldn't think. Embarrassed, she felt tears coming again. When Matthias stepped back, she looked up at him, confused and hurt. Had he been making fun of her? "Sit down before you faint." He took her by the arm and sat her on the sofa. She sank, her stays keeping her from drawing a full breath. She noticed he was breathing heavily, too. What was his problem?

Muttering under his breath, Matthias snarled. "What sort of fool came up with a corset?"

"I don't know. But he must have hated women."

Matthias's laugh broke the tension. "You want me to cut the cords that bind you, darlin'?"

"Reformed, my foot."

He grinned. "Then I'd better get out of here before I forget I'm a gentleman and you're a lady." He stood and went to the door. "Lock it, in case I change my mind." He closed it firmly behind him.

Kathryn crossed the room quickly and bolted it. She heard Matthias laugh on the other side. "Sweet dreams, Kathryn."

Leaning her forehead and palms against the door, she closed her eyes. Her mother had said something about passion clouding the mind and love not being enough. Kathryn understood now. She had loved the feel and taste of Matthias's mouth. She had loved the feel of his hands on her, his body pressed hard against her.

But she couldn't marry Matthias Beck or anyone else. Sara, her mother's maid, lost all rights to the property she had brought into her marriage. Her drunken, abusive husband had willed it to a friend, leaving her destitute. What of Abbie Aday, who wasn't given so much as a penny to spend on herself after working twelve-hour days six days a week for a husband who sat at leisure in the back room, and spent evenings at the bar or playing faro? What of Ronya and Charlotte and Tweedie, all women who came west because their husbands had gold fever? Not all widows fared even as well as they had. Many ended up working in fandango halls, saloons, and brothels.

Matthias Beck was a temptation, but she wasn't going to give in to him. Thankfully, she wouldn't have to worry. He'd never be able to accomplish all the things on that list. But she wished she'd added a few more. A central park, perhaps! Besides, he couldn't have been serious. Could he? They couldn't be in the same room together for five minutes without shouting at each other.

Oh, but that kiss . . .

Kathryn didn't know it, but Matthias had, months before, made the same list she gave him. The minute she started rattling it off in panic to keep him at bay, he knew they thought alike. Everyone in town knew what Calvada lacked. It was still little more than a rough-and-tumble mining camp, but he had a vision of what it could become. City had lit the fire. Kathryn's arrival fanned the flame.

Matthias was no dreamer. Even if he accomplished everything he set out to do, it wouldn't guarantee the town's survival. Two mines had already closed. Less ore was coming out of Twin Peaks. If the Madera played out, the town was done. He found it ironic that the future of Calvada might still lie in Morgan Sanders's hands.

Kathryn received a telegram a few days after Christmas.

Mother and son in good health. L.P.

Chump Street mud froze as January snows came with high winds and low temperatures, making it hazardous to cross until midday after horses and wagons had broken up the frozen ground. Kathryn came out with a broom each morning to knock down the icicles that hung like spears from the boardwalk roof. Unemployed miners with cold-cracked faces loitered in saloons and gaming halls while others continued working at the Twin Peaks and the Madera, digging silver out of the mountainside. Ice was easily obtained for the cold rooms where men recovered from the intense heat inside the deep tunnels. The more they dug, the closer to hell they felt.

Kathryn and Tweedie stayed inside, snug and warm with a pile of firewood outside the back door. They stayed busy, Tweedie making fans, Kathryn writing articles, Scribe typesetting, and the Mercer boys selling newspapers, Calvadans waiting for new issues.

Axel Borgeson stopped by each evening on his rounds to check on Kathryn. She liked him, but didn't feel the attraction that captured her every time she glimpsed Matthias Beck going about his mayoral duties. Beck seemed to have lost interest. Kathryn told herself she was relieved.

When Kathryn asked Tweedie to attend church with her, she resisted. "Pa always said if you don't have money to give, you ain't welcome." Kathryn assured her everyone was welcome, and compulsion wasn't a reason to give. The first Sunday Tweedie accompanied Kathryn, she spotted Elvira Haines sitting in the back row with Fiona Hawthorne and the other "dolls." Tweedie sucked in her breath and stared. Kathryn paused and greeted the women, all but Elvira ignoring her. The young woman's face was pale as ash, eyes glistening. Fiona put her hand lightly over the widow's and whispered something. Elvira lowered her head.

Others close enough heard Kathryn's greeting before she and Tweedie moved farther down the aisle and slipped into a pew near the middle. Morgan Sanders came in a moment later and sat opposite. Tweedie glanced over and then leaned back, shocked. "I guess they do let anybody come in here."

When Sally Thacker went to the piano, everyone rose. Sharing hymnals, the congregation sang the hymns posted on a chalkboard. When Kathryn tried to share, Tweedie blushed and whispered, "I'll just listen." Reverend Thacker preached for over an hour. Offering plates were passed, paltry sums put in, and the doxology sung. When Morgan intercepted Kathryn, Tweedie slipped around them and hurried to catch up with Ina Bea.

"Take a little advice from someone who knows what it is to be shunned. Don't speak to Fiona Hawthorne or any of the dolls."

Kathryn found his hypocrisy surprising. "You introduced me to Monique Beaulieu as your friend."

"I wanted to see your response."

"I don't understand. Was it some sort of test? Did she know?"

"She doesn't matter. You do."

The entire conversation offended her. "You shouldn't use people, Mr. Sanders."

"You forget what she does for a living, my dear. She has her place. Even when a man is married." He walked up the aisle with her. "The world has rules, Kathryn. Break them and the world will break you."

She felt the curious looks cast at them, the whispers. She could imagine the speculations, the bets being made. She greeted Sally. Morgan shook hands with Wilfred. As they went down the front steps, she felt Morgan's hand light against the small of her back. Others noticed. It was a possessive gesture, and far too personal for comfort.

"May I see you home, Kathryn? I have my carriage and a woolen blanket to keep you warm."

"No, thank you. Tweedie and I are going to Ronya's."

He tipped his hat, his eyes mocking. "Another time."

On the way down the hill, Kathryn asked Tweedie how she liked church.

"That preacher can sure talk, and I can't say I understood a lot of what he said. Sounds like that Ezekiel had some mighty big problems." She glanced at Kathryn, cheeks and nose ruddy from the cold. "I was upset when I saw Elvira. I never thought she'd . . . end up where she is." Her eyes filled. "It ain't right she should end up that way."

Kathryn couldn't have agreed more. She wished she had known the widow sooner. Maybe she could have found a way to help her. Women needed to pull together and help one another in hard times, especially in a place like Calvada.

Tweedie dashed tears from her cheeks. "I can't say I liked sitting in the same building with Sanders." She glanced at Kathryn, troubled. "What'd he say to you?"

"Nothing of any importance."

"Better watch yourself, Kathryn."

The warning sounded similar to what Sanders had said.

Kathryn and Tweedie sat in the kitchen at Ronya's and ate venison stew and corn bread, then returned home. Kathryn always spent Sunday afternoons reading, Tweedie sewing. The young woman seemed pensive this afternoon. "You like to read, don't you? You have so many books."

"Most are what my uncle left behind."

"Pa sent my brothers to school up to the sixth grade."

Kathryn put her book aside. "What about you?"

"Oh, no, I've never been in a schoolhouse. Pa said there weren't no reason for a girl to go."

It wasn't the first time Kathryn had heard this, and it always roused her sense of injustice. "Would you like to learn to read, Tweedie?"

"Oh, I've picked up enough so's I won't get cheated." She glanced at the book Kathryn had laid aside. "But to read something like that? I'm not smart like you."

"You're very smart, Tweedie. And if you'd like, I can teach you to read." When Tweedie's eyes lit up, Kathryn retrieved some paper and a pencil. "There's no time like the present." She wrote the alphabet and explained how the letters represented sounds. "Once you learn each one, you'll be able to sound out words, put sentences together, and read books."

Tweedie grimaced in disappointment. "I don't know that I have time or enough interest."

"You just need incentive." Kathryn picked up her book. "I've been reading *Ivanhoe* by Sir Walter Scott. I'll start over and read aloud. By the end of it, you'll want to read books." She rose. "But let me get more wood first."

When she went out the back door, she spotted Scribe pushing an empty wheelbarrow down the alley and a freshly stacked pile of wood against her back wall. "Scribe! You blessed boy! It must have taken you hours out in the woods to chop all this wood! Thank you, thank you."

Scribe looked disgruntled. "I'm no boy. And I didn't chop it. I just delivered it."

"But then who . . . ?"

"Matthias."

Shivering, Kathryn picked up an armload of wood and went back inside. Stacking it by the stove, she told Tweedie she needed to talk to someone. Pulling on her boots, coat, and hat, she slammed the front door behind her and trudged through knee-high drifts of snow to Beck's Saloon. She went into the hotel lobby with cold feet and a boiling temper. "May I speak with Mr. Beck, please?"

The clerk came back a minute later and said he was in his office and the door was open. Kathryn went as far as the threshold. "Mr. Beck?"

Matthias stood and came around his desk. "I liked it better when you called me Matthias." His teasing glance danced over her. "Feeling safer now that Tweedie Witt is living with you?"

"Considerably."

"Don't think for a minute she'll keep me away from you."

She almost blurted out that she hadn't spoken to him in two weeks. He might think she missed him. Now that she was standing in his doorway, she wished she hadn't come. She should have sent a note expressing her misgivings about him supplying any of her needs. "I'll repay you for the firewood."

"It's a gift."

"One I cannot accept. People would talk."

He laughed. "Darlin', people have been talking about you since you stepped off the stage. And I'll be paying for everything you need and want as soon as we're married."

Frustrated, Kathryn entered the room. "We are not getting married. I already told you that." The man seemed to be enjoying her discomfort.

"Oh, yes, we are getting married, just as soon as I fulfill my side of the bargain." He leaned back against his desk and crossed his arms. "San Francisco for our honeymoon, I think. I'm sure you miss being in a city."

"I'll pay you back." Turning on her heel, Kathryn marched down the hall. Carl Rudger sold firewood. She'd find out from him how much she owed Matthias Beck. She was halfway to the lumberyard when she remembered it was Sunday and Rudger Lumber would be closed. By the time she returned home, she was frozen and exhausted.

"Where have you been?" Tweedie looked bewildered and concerned.

Needing to thaw, Kathryn sagged into a chair near the pot-bellied stove. "Wasting my breath."

17

IN FEBRUARY the temperatures rose slightly, pushing Ronya's daffodils up through the soil in her garden. Ronya was the first to buy an ad in the *Voice*, not that she needed one. Carl Rudger and Patrick Flynt soon followed her lead. Deets Butcher Shop bought space, thanks to Camilla. The new general store was open and doing a brisk business, but the proprietor, Ernest Walker, sought out Kathryn and bought an ad. The newspaper was beginning to make enough to pay for itself and give Kathryn a respite from worry about buying supplies.

She counted out what she owed for firewood and sent Tweedie across the street to pay Matthias Beck.

Tweedie came back. "He wouldn't take it."

The turkey feather fans had all sold. Unfortunately, the birds had gone into hiding. Tweedie took in sewing, repairing clothing for several bachelors. Kathryn knew she would soon be living alone again.

Avoiding Matthias Beck was impossible. He had created a city council and they held open meetings. As editor of the *Voice*, Kathryn knew she couldn't miss them. She waited until the meeting had been called to order before she slipped into a seat in the back. She took notes and observed everyone in the room. When Matthias asked if there was any unfinished business or questions, he looked straight at her with that mocking smile. She said nothing, her experiences in Boston having taught her that anything a woman said at a public meeting would merely agitate, not serve to improve conditions. If she had questions, opinions, or objections, she raised them in print.

Kathryn was sitting in Ronya's kitchen with Charlotte, Ina Bea, and Tweedie, when Ronya pulled a folded newspaper from her apron pocket and tossed it on the table. "Why didn't you tell me about this?"

Kathryn unfolded the *Clarion*, and there, bold as you please, the headline: MATTHIAS BECK TO WED KATHRYN WALSH. "What? No! No! No!" Bickerson's article declared that Miss Kathryn Walsh had agreed to marry Mayor Matthias Beck as soon as he fulfilled a list she'd compiled. The list followed.

Gasping, Kathryn read on. After the list came a progress report. Construction on the Mother Lode Schoolhouse would begin as soon as the snow melted. The Rocker Box Saloon had been purchased and was being converted into a town hall and event center. Gravel from the defunct Jackrabbit Mine would be hauled and dumped into the mud on Chump Street, weighted sleds used to press down and flatten the roadbed. Ditches would be dug to route drain-off out of town. By the end of summer, citizens could look forward to Champs-Élysées, Paris, Rome, and Galway Streets as hard as macadam. Any out-of-work miners with carpentry skills could apply for work on city projects at the Beck's Hotel office. The article ended with a plea for able-bodied men to apply for garbage collection and hauling. *Wage: $2 a day. Contact Matthias Beck.*

Two dollars a day was one dollar more than Madera miners made. Kathryn knew there would be a line of men from which to choose for a job no one had been willing to take on.

Not a word was misspelled, every sentence clear and concise. "Stu Bickerson didn't write this!" Kathryn wadded up the newspaper, furious.

"I figured as much." Ronya sprinkled flour on the worktable. "Did you agree to marry him?" She lifted a lump of biscuit dough from a large bowl.

"No!" She felt her face heat up. "He misunderstood."

"And what exactly does that mean? Everybody is going to be asking me since everyone knows we're friends."

Ronya was also Matthias's friend. In truth, she made friends with every person who came through the door of her café. "Just tell everyone to read the next issue of the *Voice*." She went to the stove, lifted one of the burner plates, and tossed the wadded-up *Clarion* into the fire.

Kathryn wrote furiously all afternoon, finishing an editorial on the *Clarion's* tendency to print tall tales, and admonishing the editor to check his facts before he printed a story. She went looking for Scribe to do the typesetting, but he said he couldn't. "Matthias has me running all over town delivering messages. Soonest I can get to it is—"

"Never mind." Kathryn spent the night setting the type herself. The Mercer boys hawked the *Voice* up and down Chump Street and all over town. Every copy sold.

Calvadans read that Kathryn Walsh was *not* engaged to Matthias Beck, nor did she have plans to marry at all. As for the list of civic projects, Mayor Beck seemed to be on the right path to fulfilling his promises to all Calvadans. The editor of the *Voice* had no personal involvement with Matthias Beck and no plans for such in the future. As to the agreement Bickerson described, Kathryn wrote that she had not signed, sealed, or notarized any contract with Mr. Matthias Beck. If he fulfilled the list reported, she would join other Calvadans in celebrating the first politician to ever keep his word about anything.

Stu Bickerson fired back with another issue of the *Clarion*, and none could doubt his authorship this time.

WALSH WELSHES!

No woman can keep her word and I know cause I married one onct and she said she'd never say no to me up until I put the ring on her finger and then no was the only thing that ever came out of her mouth.

Bickerson ranted front and back page, ending with advice to Matthias Beck:

Count yerself lucky that scold is welshing on her word cause if she kept it, you'd be stuck with her forever.

Kathryn wrote, typeset, and printed another issue of the *Voice*.

When a woman says, "I will think about it," that does not constitute a yes. If Mayor Beck ever does manage to keep his word to the citizens of Calvada, and all the projects he promised in his campaign are completed, I will be first in line to congratulate him on a job well done. I will keep my word and think about his casual joke regarding marriage, but I am certainly under no obligation to do anything about it.

Still fuming the day after the Mercer boys sold every copy, Kathryn sat with Ronya, pencil poised to take notes, Tweedie upstairs helping Ina Bea make beds. The savory smell of meat loaf filled the kitchen. "I'll need every step for making that scrumptious venison stew you served yesterday."

Ronya sipped coffee, taking one of her infrequent breaks. "Sounds like you're thinking about setting up a household."

"Oh, please don't tease. You know it's for my Bachelor Arts column. It's become quite popular, and not just with the ladies. Single men need housekeeping skills, too."

Charlotte chuckled. "You're right about that. Most men wear their dungarees until they can stand up by themselves. And all they know about cooking is how to open a can." She dried the last dish and put it on the shelf. "I've mended a few of Henry's shirts, but he has Jian Lin Gong do his laundry. Of course, I'll be doing it after we're married."

Tweedie and Ina Bea came into the kitchen, having finished the work upstairs. "Most men don't have the money or time to wash," Tweedie added, pulling her knitting needles out of a bag she carried when they visited. "And it's too cold now anyway. Last summer, I saw men washing in the creek. With their clothes on." Her needles clicked like fencers in a bout.

"Good thing, when some only have the clothes on their backs," Ina Bea remarked.

"That was some article you wrote, Kathryn." Ronya eyed her over her mug.

"Hopefully, that will be an end to Mr. Bickerson's nasty comments about women not keeping their word." The tip broke off Kathryn's pencil. Sighing, she pulled out her pocketknife and shaved wood, careful not to break the lead again. "I've a good mind to write another editorial on how quick some men are to forget their wedding vows and abandon their wives so they can hunt for gold!"

Charlotte shook her head. "You do that, and you'll have rocks flying through your windows again."

Tweedie sighed. "Sometimes I wish Joe and I had never left Ohio."

Ronya rose, ready to get back to work. "When a woman marries a dreamer, she'd better have a plan how she's going to keep body and soul together, even if it means hiding butter and egg money for when hard times come. I started my first café on money I'd hidden in a sock in a flour barrel."

Kathryn thought about her father abandoning his wife to join the gold rush in '49, dying within days of leaving Independence, his dream of getting rich dying with him.

"Dreamers often have a lot of charm." Ronya set bowls on the worktable. "A woman needs to guard her heart and use her head when picking a husband." She gave Kathryn a pointed look.

"Now, don't you start." Kathryn let out a breath and wrote notes.

Ina Bea brought her a basket of winter apples and set them on the counter where Ronya was working, whispering, "Hope she doesn't pick Morgan Sanders."

Kathryn heard. "I don't want a husband! I have few enough rights as a woman without handing them over to a man!"

"Depends on the man." Tweedie smiled. "Mr. Beck—"

"Never mind Mr. Beck, Tweedie." Kathryn tried to turn the conversation back to cooking, but Ronya put her hands on her ample hips.

"Did or didn't Matthias ask you to marry him?"

"No." Heat climbed into her face as Ronya, Ina Bea, and Charlotte looked at her. "His exact words were 'We should get married.' That's not a proposal."

"You could've said no."

"I said no. Repeatedly." Exasperated, Kathryn stood and paced. "He backed me into a corner and all I could think of was making a list he couldn't possibly accomplish."

The women laughed, not one of them the least bit sympathetic to her plight.

"Some men can do pretty much anything they put their mind to." Ronya grinned. "Matthias is one of them."

Charlotte peeled apples. "What's wrong with Matthias? He's handsome. He's rich. And he's Henry's business partner. There's no more honorable man in this whole world than my Henry."

Kathryn sat up straight. "Business partner? In the hotel?"

"They've started a drayage company. They've been working on it since Henry came up here. They have routes all mapped out and four wagons built already with contracts with the stage stations and horses. They'll be hauling goods by March for Cole's Market, Rowe's Tack Room, and Carlile's Apothecary, and the new general store, of course. They'll be hauling to other towns all the way up from Sacramento before you know it. We're last on the line."

"How did I not hear about this?" Kathryn wondered aloud.

Charlotte looked surprised. "I thought everybody knew. As soon as Henry and I get married, we're moving to Sacramento."

Kathryn's heart dropped. Matthias Beck planned to leave town? "Beck was just elected and now he's—"

"Oh, no. He's staying. He's still got the hotel and the new partnership with Ernest Walker. He's already taking business from Aday's." Her brows rose when she looked at Kathryn. "I thought you knew. You put that big advertisement in the *Voice*."

Ronya chuckled as she forked flour into lard for piecrust. "Beck and Call. Good name for a drayage company, wouldn't you say? And a wise choice if this town ever dies."

Kathryn wanted to kick herself for not knowing any of this. What sort of newspaperwoman was she? She'd been avoiding a man on the move. Hadn't Matthias said his time as a saloon-keeper was over? Why hadn't she questioned him more about that? Maybe she would have, if he hadn't flustered her to the point she couldn't think straight. And then Matthias Beck publishing that wedding announcement in the *Clarion* under the ruse that Bickerson had written the story. She'd been so focused on her rebuttals that she'd missed what was going on around her! Well, that had to stop.

The bell on Ronya's dining room door jangled, and Kathryn's heart leaped.

"I'll see who it is." Ina Bea quickly wiped her hands and stripped off her apron before heading into the other room. When she didn't return, Kathryn leaned back and looked. Axel Borgeson hung his hat on the rack and shrugged out of his heavy jacket. The smile he gave Ina Bea was warm with male appreciation. Kathryn looked at Ronya and raised her brows. "Another single woman bites the dust."

"Seems to me you're getting a good taste of it."

Giggling, Charlotte winked at Kathryn. "Marry Matthias. He's a good man. We'd practically be sisters."

A good man? "I've yet to see him in church." Henry hadn't

missed a service since he came to town, and even Morgan Sanders made a show of attending.

Ronya scowled at her. "You haven't seen me there either. Just because someone doesn't go—"

"Same for someone who does," Tweedie interrupted.

"Doesn't mean they're not a good person."

Kathryn felt the reprimand and knew she had no right to judge.

Ronya rolled dough. "It's not what a man says, it's what he does that matters. And Matthias is doing right well, I'd say." She looked at Kathryn. "But then, you haven't asked my opinion."

"About the venison stew," Kathryn said, trying again to focus on her column, even as she considered interviewing Matthias Beck about his new endeavors. The thought of being alone with him was unnerving. Perhaps if she took someone else with her or she only spoke to him when others were present, he would have to behave. Good heavens, she'd be safer inviting Morgan Sanders to the *Voice* office, serving tea, and interviewing him!

Maybe she *should* talk to the Madera Mine owner. She might get him to start a widows' fund.

"Kathryn? You have that look on your face again."

Kathryn glanced up at Ronya. "What look?"

"The one you always have before you get yourself into trouble."

Matthias stood inside the Rocker Box Saloon, going over plans with the lead carpenter, while two men lifted down the three-by-six-foot indecent painting. The swinging doors had been removed from their hinges, the room already cleared of gambling tables and chairs, everything sold to other saloonkeepers in town, proceeds put back in city coffers. The painting had sold for top dollar and would be shipped by Beck and Call Drayage to a saloon in Placerville. Nails screeched as two men dismantled the bar and tossed boards onto a pile.

Hoss Wrangler had never made much from the place, even though the property was in a prime location downtown. Wrangler watered his whiskey and took a cut from card sharks. Customers tended to resent that. When Matthias told the city council Wrangler was eager to sell, no one had to ask why. They all agreed the building would serve well as a public meeting hall and courthouse.

It didn't surprise Matthias to find miners skilled in carpentry eager to give up mining and return to their original trade rather than spend their lives digging in earthen bowels.

Like Hoss Wrangler, men came to Calvada and left for their own reasons. Some because they were restless and dreaming of better luck elsewhere. Some walked away from what little they owned because they couldn't stand the loneliness any longer. Matthias had seen abandoned houses with dirty dishes still on the tables. He understood. He had done his share of moving on.

City had understood that too. *You won't have any more luck than I ever did trying to outrun whatever weighs you down.* City talked a lot when he had a few drinks. But sometimes he shared wisdom gained from heartache. *Some regrets grind a man to dust. Find something worth doing with your life. A man who doesn't believe in something is no better than a corpse sitting in a chair at a wake.* The Irish rebel had spent most days working in his newspaper office, most nights drinking at Beck's bar. *Don't believe everything you think. We lie more to ourselves than anyone else.* The older man talked vaguely of things he wished he'd done, things he wished he hadn't. *Some decisions haunt you. You can change your mind, but you can't go back. And even if you could, everything would have changed by the time you made up your mind.*

City dealt with his secrets and pain by hard drinking and raising Cain, with words and fists. Matthias had never seen him back down from anything. Drunk and despairing, he picked fights for no reason. Sober, he told the truth without compromise or compassion. The one person who probably knew City better than anyone was Fiona Hawthorne. Whatever secrets City had been willing to share, she kept. Everyone in town knew when City wasn't at a bar, he was at the Dollhouse with the madam. Whatever feelings they had for each other had stayed between the two of them.

Matthias missed the man. He could use his advice. He missed City's bluntness. He missed the friendship that had grown between them, though they were years apart in age. They had understood each other. Matthias, the disinherited son of a preacher, and City Walsh, an Irish Catholic renegade who had been run out of Ireland by his own people. City had laughed about that. *It was get on a ship or end up hanged by the British, and my kin didn't like that idea.*

City told Matthias he had thought things would be different in America. So had thousands of other Irishmen who flooded the shores. They soon learned otherwise with *Help Wanted—No Irish Need Apply* signs hanging everywhere. Factories worked his countrymen like slaves, then hired others who accepted less pay. When City and his brother had spoken out against the owners, tried to organize the men to stand together and refuse to work until they got a living wage, they might as well have been back in Ireland fighting the British landowners.

The gold rush of '49 meant an opportunity to make something of himself, to have a better life, one with all the benefits of wealth. Panning for gold was hard work with little to show for it. City said life was so hard, it sucked the heart out of a man, left him hollow. *And the irony sickened me. I'd spent my whole life hating the rich, and there I was trying to be one of them.* He never told Matthias what happened to his brother or how he ended up in the newspaper business, but writing steadied him. *Truth is, I was never meant to be a rich man. God made me a thorn.* He had passion and the *Voice* gave him purpose.

The older man had been right. Seeing his friend lying in a pool of blood had awakened Matthias. While the men in the bar held a wake, he went to the cemetery. Fiona Hawthorne was already there, dressed in black, her face hidden beneath a veil. Matthias could hear her crying softly as they watched the dirt shoveled onto the pine casket.

The lawlessness had always bothered Matthias, but not enough to do anything about it. If trouble came into his saloon, he took care of it. Let the rest of the town take care of their own trouble. City had been incensed by Matthias's indifference. *Get in the game! You were a captain in the Union Army. You know how to lead men.*

The crash of wood onto the pile yanked Matthias back to the present. City wanted him in the game. Well, Matthias was neck-deep in it now, seeing the challenges on every side, making decisions every day. Calvada was like so many other Sierra Nevada mining towns. When the mines played out, the towns died. Right now, there was enough silver and gold to keep men working. But how long would it last?

Things were heating up in town, and he knew Kathryn would be digging just like City did. He'd figured announcing their engagement in the *Clarion* would keep her distracted. He hadn't gotten a yes out of her that night, but if he'd stayed a little longer, he could have. She knew it, too, or she wouldn't be avoiding him and writing fierce rebuttals. *Under duress,* she claimed. He laughed. There was some truth in that. She'd been vulnerable that night. Matthias had barely managed to keep his head with her in his arms. He wanted her yes to be a yes. And he wanted her saying it in front of God and a crowd of witnesses in the Calvada Community Church.

Maybe he should start attending church again.

Memories pulled him back, sucking him down. He remembered sitting in the empty church and listening to his father practicing the Sunday sermon from the pulpit. He'd spoken with power and eloquence. As a boy, Matthias thought his father was as close to God as any man could get. He could do no wrong. Matthias's mother said he was God's ambassador. Whatever came out of his mouth was truth.

When his father cursed him, Matthias felt the curse of God come down on him, too. But if he could go back, even now knowing the full cost, would he have chosen to fight for the Confederacy? He had asked himself that question a thousand times. And every time, after chewing on the matter from every side, the answer came out the same: The country had to hold together or the Great Experiment would fall apart.

As mayor, going back to church here, now, after the life he'd been leading, would certainly get people's attention, but attention wasn't what he was after. He wanted to feel at peace. He wanted to know he was forgiven, if not by his father, then by God. He wanted to feel his life counted for something. And he wanted to be closer to Kathryn.

He'd begun making changes right after the election, not merely to honor City Walsh or prove himself to Kathryn, but to do something worthwhile with his life. Stepping into a position of authority brought heavy responsibility. He'd found himself asking God to direct his steps and shine a light so he could see the right path to take. What he'd learned as a child was coming back to him as a man. He found himself thinking less of his father's last angry outburst, and more about his mother's faith.

When his father turned his back on him, Matthias turned his back on God. He wondered now if it had been about getting revenge against a man he always saw as an earthly representative of God. His father had been his idol but turned out to be a broken, embittered man.

Another board crashed onto the growing pile of lumber, all to be stored at Rudger's and used in the spring to build the schoolhouse. Matthias finished going over plans and left. He had work to do for Beck and Call Drayage. On the boardwalk, he spotted Kathryn coming out of Ronya's. Pulse jumping, he stopped outside the hotel and stood at the edge of the boardwalk watching her. Tweedie accompanied her. His mouth tipped. Did Kathryn really think another woman living in the house would deter him? He might not be making any more nighttime visits, but that didn't mean he wouldn't seek her out when he was ready. Kathryn glanced his way and then pretended she hadn't noticed him.

City's words echoed again. *Get in the game.*

Matthias wasn't playing cards anymore, but he was laying them on the table for all to see.

Kathryn ducked into her little house. Tweedie glanced at him and grinned before following her inside. Matthias knew he had allies in his pursuit.

―――

Kathryn sent Scribe to Morgan Sanders with an invitation to join her at his earliest convenience for tea at her newspaper office. Scribe came back scowling. "He said he's available this afternoon at two. And you are out of your mind if you go through with this! Or don't you remember what happened the last time he came in here?"

"I remember, Scribe. He apologized. He and I have matters of great importance to discuss."

"Such as?" When she didn't answer, he walked out, slamming the door behind him.

Tweedie had overheard the conversation from the apartment. "Morgan Sanders is coming here? Today?"

"Yes."

"Why?" Tweedie sounded both shocked and wary.

Kathryn shouldn't have been surprised at Tweedie's response. Her husband had died in the Madera Mine. "I want to ask him some questions, and make an appeal."

"You can't trust that man, Kathryn. And you shouldn't be alone with him."

"I know. I realize it's asking a lot, but would you stay while—?"

"No!" Tweedie paled. "No. He scares me." She gathered her shawl. "I'll be at Ronya's helping Charlotte and Ina Bea." She paused before going out the door. "Ask him why he doesn't care enough about his workers to reinforce the tunnels with more beams." Her eyes filled. "Joe would still be alive if Sanders had listened to his foremen." She went out the door.

Kathryn closed her eyes. No matter what she did, someone ended up hurt or angry.

Closing the newspaper office, she went down the street to the baker and used a few precious coins to buy a small cider cake. She moved the chair from her apartment to the front office and put a tablecloth over her desk. She brought out her Minton red-and-gold teacups and saucers. Everything was ready when Morgan Sanders knocked on the door a few minutes before two.

He had certainly dressed for the occasion and looked distinguished and handsome in his black hat, dark jacket, white shirt, and vest. Everything custom-made, probably in San Francisco. He held a gold watch in his hand, checking the time. Snapping it shut, he tucked it in his vest pocket. His white shirt was fine cotton, the red silk necktie loosely knotted with squared overlapping ends. He looked more like a Boston gentleman than a Calvada mine owner. She invited him inside.

"Thank you for the invitation." Sanders removed his hat, his gaze moving over her in appreciation. "You look lovely in lavender, Kathryn. A new dress?"

"No. Just no occasion to wear it before now." She felt an odd hitch of trepidation at his perusal and wished she'd worn her brown skirt and white shirtwaist. His presence filled the room in a way far different than Matthias Beck.

He tossed his hat on the settee as though staking territory. Smiling slightly, he looked at the white linen tablecloth draped over her desk, the Minton teacups and saucers, the cider cake. His lips curved in a wry smile. "You must want something from me to have gone to so much trouble." He raised his brows. "Do you need money, Kathryn?"

"Some," she admitted, refusing to dissemble. "Not for me. For a good cause."

"Oh, it always is." He gave a soft, mocking laugh.

She offered him a seat and poured tea, already brewed. "I hope you don't prefer cream and sugar. I have none to offer, but I was told Wynham's cider cake is very sweet."

"As are you, my dear." Morgan lifted his teacup in a salute. She cut a thick slice of cake, slid it perfectly onto a plate, added a silver fork, and set it before him. "You play mother very well. You'll make a fine hostess."

She glanced up, disturbed by the remark and not sure why.

Leaning back, he made himself comfortable. Kathryn noticed the fine black leather boots. He certainly knew how to dress like a gentleman. "I was relieved to hear there is no engagement between you and Matthias Beck."

The remark bordered too closely on the personal, but she decided to be blunt. "I think everyone in Calvada knows by now that I am not looking for a husband."

"Perhaps not, but that doesn't stop a man from looking at you as a prospective wife."

Kathryn couldn't miss his meaning and realized he might have taken this invitation as something more than she intended. "Calvada has some eligible women, Morgan." Perhaps a few facts about herself would help him look elsewhere. "I have no pedigree. I'm the daughter of an Irish Catholic immigrant who abandoned his wife after a year of marriage. My grandfather didn't approve of the marriage, though he did allow my mother to return home. I was born under his roof, not that he was happy about it or ever acknowledged me. He arranged a second marriage for my mother, to a man he did approve, and made him heir. My stepfather saw me as a burden. An opportunity came to send me away, and here I am. I didn't come to California of my own free will. I was sent." She put her teacup in her saucer.

"Calvada must have been something of a shock after Boston."

"Indeed, but I had to make a choice. I could look upon this as an exile or an opportunity. I chose the latter. Calvada is my home now."

"We have something in common, you and I." He set the cup and saucer down.

"Do we?" When he didn't say anything, she pressed. "I've shared my life story with you. I'm curious about yours."

He gave a low, mocking laugh. "Should I trust my history to a newspaperwoman?"

She offered her most charming smile. "I promise not to divulge a word, unless you admit to some heinous crime." She folded her hands and added more seriously, "I am a woman of my word."

"Matthias Beck might say otherwise."

She gasped, furious. "Did you accept my invitation merely to insult me?"

He searched her face avidly, chuckling softly. "All charm and sweetness one minute and passionate the next. No. I didn't come to insult you. Now, what small amount of money did you want, and for what?"

She supposed he wouldn't fulfill her curiosity about his past. "A donation to the church, to be set aside for widows in need."

His eyes narrowed and darkened. "Now who is being insulting? There are no widows living at Willow Creek. Ronya Vanderstrom and you have seen to that."

"That's a good thing, isn't it? But there was another, and—"

"Elvira Haines chose her path."

She fumed over his indifference. "You have some responsibility for what happened to her. Her husband died in your mine."

His eyes flashed. "Men know the hazards in the work they do, Kathryn. You asked about my life. I grew up dirt-poor. My mother died when I was a boy and left me on my own while my father worked in the Norfolk Naval Shipyard in Virginia. He died when I was fifteen. Penniless. I didn't want to end up the same way."

He leaned forward, face hard. "I went north to the capital, worked a dozen jobs, trying to find a handhold to pull myself up. I was good at sales. I knew what people wanted. It wasn't until the war that I made real money."

"In munitions?" She spoke before she thought better of it.

He gave a short laugh. "Nothing so grand. I became a sutler, authorized by the Union Army to sell goods to the troops. Not supplies, but things they wanted. The men didn't like my prices, but I wasn't in business to make friends. My father had plenty and still ended up with nothing to show for his life other than a coffin and a hole in the ground to put it in. When the war ended, I came west and bought an interest in the Madera. My partner died in a cave-in." His mouth twisted. "Some thought I killed him."

"Who said that, and why did they believe it?"

Leaning back again, he breathed out slowly. "I may be many things, Kathryn, but I am not a murderer. And you, my dear, are beginning to sound like a newspaperwoman."

"Under other circumstances, I would take that as a compliment. I'm sorry, Morgan."

"You have no idea who I am, do you? How determined I can be." He spoke quietly, his eyes so intense she blinked and felt an odd tension fill her.

"Perhaps not, on such short acquaintance."

"Oh, but you will know me. Let me be as blunt as you've been. I don't care what people think of me. If I did, I'd be as poor as my father."

She didn't agree. "Your father was rich in friends, you said, and what will you have at the end of your life if it's all about money?"

He leaned forward again, holding her eyes captive. "There are three things I've wanted since I became a man, Kathryn. Wealth; a beautiful, cultured wife; and a son to inherit what I build. I have the first. You will be the second. And from you, I will have the third."

Her heart pounded at the fierce look in his eyes. "You assume a great deal, sir."

"I assume nothing. I plan. I work for what I want. And in the end, I'll have it all."

Though frightened by his intensity, she kept a calm demeanor. "You will not have me."

Morgan Sanders looked at her until she lowered her eyes from his. Then he stood, picked up his hat, and went out the door without speaking another word.

18

MATTHIAS HADN'T BEEN IN A CHURCH since he left home
for war, but he still had the Bible his father had given him as a
boy and had read it frequently between battles. When his father
cursed him, Matthias set it on the pulpit, intending to leave
it behind, but his mother called out to him as he was riding
away and put it in his saddlebag. *Keep it for my sake, Matthias.
Promise me.*

He'd kept that promise, though he hadn't opened it or
stepped foot in a church in the last ten years.

Being cast out of her family, battered in public by Reverend
Thacker, and facing constant criticism hadn't dampened
Kathryn's faith—in God or in mankind. He'd heard about her

tea party with Morgan Sanders. The whole town knew and was talking about it. The only one not talking was Kathryn.

Matthias sat in his room, lantern lit, and paged through his Bible. He'd marked passages in Psalm 119 as a boy, so eager to be like his godly father. *"Open my eyes to see the wonderful truths in your instructions. . . . Keep me from lying to myself. . . . Help me abandon my shameful ways. . . . I believe in your commands; now teach me good judgment and knowledge."*

He'd marked other passages before and during the war. *"Create in me a clean heart, O God. Renew a loyal spirit within me."*

He could almost hear his mother's counsel: *Matthias, forgive your father, as you have been forgiven by God.*

He knew he'd never be fully at peace until he did.

Maybe being in the company of followers of Christ would help him, being in the company of Kathryn Walsh. Maybe it was time for the lost to seek fellowship with the found.

Matthias put on his best suit, vest, white shirt, and tie. When the steeple bell rang, he headed up the hill, deliberately arriving late. He sat in the last row, opposite Fiona Hawthorne and her dolls. When she glanced at him, he gave her a smile and nod. He spotted Kathryn in the middle row, Tweedie Witt beside her, and was surprised to see Morgan Sanders sitting across the aisle. Was Sanders here for the same reasons he was, or just trying to impress the lady? Annoyed, Matthias tried to concentrate on Reverend Thacker's homily. He wasn't the orator Matthias's father had been, but the man was doing a fair job preaching on the Beatitudes.

Mind drifting, Matthias thought about his father. Did he regret the curse he'd laid on his own son? And what of his mother? Did she grieve for him? Surely. Did she pray for him? He had no doubt. Maybe he should write to her. And say what? He had turned his back on God, owned a saloon in a hell-bent town in the Sierra Nevadas, and was now the mayor? That would hardly bring her comfort.

Take off the old life, put on the new.

Words he'd learned as a boy kept coming back to him.

Henry Call and Charlotte Arnett sat shoulder to shoulder near the front. They'd be married next week. Matthias would stand as best man, Ronya as matron of honor. The couple would spend their wedding night in the hotel room Kathryn had occupied for a few days, then leave the following morning for Sacramento, where Henry would manage the new Beck and Call Drayage office. Matthias would fulfill his two-year commitment to Calvada, finish the projects he'd set out for himself, and God willing, be married to Kathryn Walsh by the end of the year. He looked at the back of her head, a few soft tendrils of red hair escaping. *Be patient, Matthias.*

Thacker talked on and on. Matthias leaned back and crossed his arms. Had the man spent this much time lambasting Kathryn? Wincing, he knew the blame for that rested at his own feet. He thought he could protect her. All he'd done was hurt her.

Sanders glanced over at Kathryn again. She didn't look back. What had happened at that tea party of hers? It hadn't lasted long from what he'd been told.

The service ended and Matthias stood for the final hymn. He knew it well and sang it without opening the hymnal, earning surprised looks from parishioners close by. Reverend Thacker gave the benediction, gathered his wife, and was first up the aisle to greet people at the door. Everyone began filing out of the church. Most noticed him, some stopping to welcome him.

Kathryn stood and talked to several ladies. Clearly annoyed, Morgan stepped into the aisle. As he headed for the door, he saw Matthias. Their eyes met and held. As he passed, Matthias spoke low. "The lady's mine."

Sanders's expression hardened, a slight smirk curling his lips. "Don't bet on it."

Matthias waited until Kathryn reached the back row and then stepped out. "Miss Walsh." She knew he had been standing there, though she tried hard to pretend she hadn't noticed.

"It's good to see you in church, Mr. Beck."

"It's been a long time, but it's good to be back." He hadn't been this close to her in weeks and wasn't going to keep a distance from now on. "The wedding is next week."

Her eyes went wide, her cheeks flushed. "Wedding?"

He grinned. "Not ours, darlin'." She might have looked calm and collected, but there was a current flowing beneath the surface. Good. "Henry and Charlotte. Remember?"

Reverend Thacker greeted Matthias with pleasure. "I almost lost my train of thought when I saw you sitting in the pew. Sally and I have been praying for you since we came to Calvada."

Kathryn slipped around them and went down the front steps. When Matthias came outside, he saw her with Tweedie and several other ladies. Thankfully, Sanders had already left in his carriage.

The sky was clear, the air still crisp, spring coming on strong. People lingered, many trying to draw him into conversation. Kathryn was leaving. Matthias eased out of one conversation only to be intercepted by Nabor Aday, complaining about city taxes. Matthias had heard how the merchant had treated Kathryn. "You want improvements, Aday. They don't come without cost."

"A dollar increase is highway robbery!"

Matthias lost patience when he lost sight of Kathryn. He moved close, almost stepping on Aday's toes and lowered his voice so Abbie Aday wouldn't overhear. "You dump more than ten dollars a week at the faro tables. Then you raise your prices at random to make others bear the loss."

Red in the face, Aday jutted his chin. "And I voted for you!"

"Then you knew exactly what you were getting because I laid out all my plans."

Nabor scoffed. "The improvements aren't for the town. It's that list! You're spending our hard-earned money to get that woman."

That woman? Matthias wanted to grab him by his scrawny neck and shake him. "You have a prime downtown location, but you'll be out of business in a year, Aday."

"Are you threatening me?"

"Just telling you the truth. Ernest Walker works hard, pays a decent wage, and charges fair and consistent prices to everyone. Where do you think people will prefer to shop?"

Matthias headed for Ronya's Café, expecting to find Kathryn there. Every table was full, Charlotte and Ina Bea busy serving meals, though the latter seemed in no hurry to leave Axel Borgeson's table. Matthias headed for the kitchen. Kathryn wasn't there. Ronya looked him over as she put a pan of fresh biscuits on a trivet. "Well, don't you look grand all dressed up. Charlotte and Ina Bea said you were in church today." She laughed. "If you're looking for Kathryn, she's probably at home. Tweedie says she reads most Sundays. She ate early. I won't see her back in here until tomorrow."

She checked the bacon, turning several rashers. "What can I give you for breakfast? Pancakes, eggs, bacon, sausage?"

"Yes."

She chuckled. "You've got a hungry wolf in your belly." She eyed him. "You've been getting a lot of work done around town, Matthias. That's good. Strange that Kathryn hasn't written much about it."

"I think she's leaving all that to Stu Bickerson."

"Maybe I should put a bug in her ear."

"Suggest she talk to me here. I don't think she would want me in her office."

"Do tell." Her eyes sparkled with mischief. "And why would that be?" When he didn't answer, she filled a plate with food and slid it across to him. Ina Bea gave him utensils and a red- and white-checkered napkin, then headed back into the dining room with two plates of flapjacks. Ronya poured coffee into a mug.

"Is that a Bible you got there?" Ronya glanced at the worn black book he'd set on the counter. "First time I've seen you with one. Ever read it?"

"I was raised on it, had to memorize whole sections. My father was a preacher."

"Well, knock me over with a feather!" She gave him a steely look. "Maybe you'd better take a closer look."

He lifted his mug and glared at Ronya over the rim. "What are you trying to tell me? Just spit it out."

She stood arms akimbo. "Put a beautiful woman in front of a man, and he forgets his head is used for more than growing hair. You had better take what Kathryn says about marriage seriously." She gave a harrumph. "I'm not a good-looking woman, but I've had plenty of proposals from men over the past twenty years, including the day my husband went into the ground. And I've said no for the same reasons Kathryn is saying no."

"She doesn't trust me."

"No reason she should, is there?" Ronya gave a snort and turned to the bacon, scooping a dozen rashers with a spatula and flipping them over.

"Now, wait a minute, Ronya . . ."

She eyed him again. "You've been trying to shut down the *Voice* since she opened it." She waved her hand. "But it's not about you. It's about the laws. Kathryn is in love with you, Matthias. I'm not sure she even knows it, but she's fighting hard against it." She gave a slight laugh. "And I see how much you like hearing that. Of course, you would. It gives you the advantage, doesn't it? Trouble is you don't know Kathryn Walsh at all. She's not like Charlotte or Ina Bea or most women wanting nothing more than a husband and babies."

Matthias had listened long enough. "You talk like I'm trying to take everything away from her."

"Aren't you? You tried to buy the press when she got here, didn't you?" She put both hands on the worktable and glared at him. "If you don't love her, leave her alone. If you do, let her be the woman she is. You'll find a good description in that Bible of yours. Proverbs 31, if I remember rightly."

"A woman of virtue . . ."

"Just like a man to focus on the woman. Take a good, hard look at the husband that woman had." She shook her head. "If I ever met a man who treated me with that kind of respect, I might even marry again."

Though Kathryn had made the decision never to be a bride, she loved weddings. Charlotte was lovely in peach, and the look on Henry's face when he saw his bride brought tears to Kathryn's eyes. Matthias stood taller than his friend, every inch the handsome Southern gentleman, as Reverend Thacker guided Henry and Charlotte through their vows. And that sweet, chaste kiss at the end, so far removed from the one Matthias had given her.

Stirred, she sat up. That man popped into her head constantly. He was a fever she couldn't shake. She caught herself watching him as he remained with the newlyweds, seeing they had whatever they needed. Oh, how easy it would be to let her heart rule over her head, but she had too much to lose to allow that to happen.

Ronya had made the wedding cake, and Kathryn stayed close, helping serve guests. When the couple cut the cake, Kathryn couldn't help but feel a twinge of envy, even if only for a moment. Charlotte hugged her afterwards, gushing. "Oh, I'm so happy, I could burst." Her eyes were moist with tears.

"You'll be leaving in the morning?"

"First thing. I'll miss you, Kathryn. And Ronya and Ina Bea and Tweedie. You must come to Sacramento and visit us."

The musicians began playing. Henry drew his bride into a dance. Matthias spoke, startling her. "So what do you think?" Heart racing, she didn't know what he meant, and thought it would be better not to ask.

"They're very happy. Sacramento will be a wonderful place for them to live. I heard farms are doing well around the city and all down into the Central Valley. Eastern markets will be hungry for the produce, and it'll have to be transported to the railway stations. I hear they're working on refrigerated cars." She babbled on and on. "It's a good hub for a drayage company." She couldn't seem to stop herself.

"Yes, it is." He looked down at her with a wry smile, making her blush. She looked away, annoyed.

"Have you thought about what you'll do if Calvada fails?"

Surprised at such a suggestion, she glanced up. "Fails? You're the mayor and you think the town will fail?"

"When the ore plays out—and it will—the town will die."

She didn't want to think about that and what it might mean to all the people living here. "One day's trouble is enough, without worrying about what may or may not happen tomorrow."

"It's always good to have a contingency plan. Tweedie is moving in with Ina Bea, I hear."

She didn't dare look at him. Who had told him? "I guess I'll have to bolt my front and back doors every night. Axel stops by to check on me each evening and Scribe works most days."

"Yes, I know. But you were safer with Tweedie living with you."

Her heart hammered, and the warm melting sensation swimming through her body reminded her of one memorable kiss. Better if she never thought about that again, and certainly not with Matthias standing so close. "Well, don't concern yourself, Mr. Beck. I won't be letting anyone in my door at night." He didn't say anything. "I've been hearing good reports on progress around town. Would you be willing to meet me for coffee at Ronya's?" Her friend had asked her why she never wrote about what the new mayor was accomplishing. It was about time she put personal feelings aside and did her job as a newspaperwoman.

Matthias smiled. "Name the day and time, and it will be my pleasure." His gaze was warm. "After we talk, I'd like to show you some of the work that's going on."

Kathryn felt on firmer ground. "The town hall, I hope."

"It'll be finished by the end of the week. The town council plans an open house, but I think the editor of the *Voice* should make that announcement after she sees everything. The building will also serve as our courthouse, until we have enough money to buy and renovate another saloon." He gave her a rueful grin. "I imagine you like the idea of closing a few more down."

She laughed, feeling at ease. "Yes, well, there will still be a dozen from which the men can choose."

"I'm betting you'd shut them all down, if you could."

So, he thought she was a temperance fighter. "That's not a battle I intend to wage. I doubt men would want to give women the right to vote if the first thing they did was shut the saloons."

His brows flicked up. "A careful answer from a woman who doesn't imbibe." He gave her a roguish grin. "With the exception of one rather memorable evening."

"Must you remind me?" She knew he was teasing. "Though tempted, I haven't had another of Ronya's elixirs since."

"A pity. We had a good talk that night, Kathryn. Your guard was down."

She remembered every word he said and had never felt closer to a man. But was it wise? Best to change the subject to something safer. "Do you really think the mines could fail?"

"You wrote about the demise of the Jackrabbit." He didn't speak for a moment. "What does Morgan Sanders have to say about the Madera?"

News spread quickly in Calvada. "I didn't ask him to tea to interrogate him about the Madera." Sometimes she wondered if the town even needed a newspaper.

"Why not? Other things to talk about?"

His tone let her know he was not happy about her little tête-à-tête with the mine owner. "It was nice to see you in church last Sunday." She felt his annoyance, but he didn't press her.

"First time in a long time. Brought back a lot of memories."

Good ones, she hoped, remembering what he had said about his last conversation with his father.

His mouth flattened. "I notice you got Morgan Sanders to attend."

"He was attending before I—"

"No, he wasn't. He started the week you came to town. Big news, but then you weren't in the business yet."

Lips parting, she looked up, and there was no doubt this

time. "You're angry with me. I wanted to ask him to start a widows' fund—"

"And thought tea and cider cake would—" He stopped. "Actually, I'm jealous. You trust him more than you trust me."

"Well, I won't anymore."

Matthias's eyes blazed. "Did he try something?"

"No." She spoke in a quiet, fierce voice. "And isn't it rather hypocritical for you to be offended for my sake when you . . . ? Never mind."

"Having a hard time forgetting that kiss, too, are you?"

Heat spread through Kathryn's entire body. She saw Henry look toward them. "I think you're wanted elsewhere."

"If you'll excuse me, Miss Walsh."

Matthias didn't approach her again.

Kathryn told herself she was glad of it.

⸺⸺⸺

Ina Bea and Axel left the reception together. Tweedie left soon after. Kathryn helped Ronya load dishes and serving bowls into two carts and pushed one back to the café. Ronya sent her home after that. When she came into the house, Tweedie was sitting on the settee, her things in a gunnysack beside her.

"I've been waiting for you. Thank you for all you've done for me, Kathryn. I'll never be able to repay you. It's just that Ina Bea and I went through such hard times on Willow Creek, and became good friends . . ."

Kathryn cut her off. "I understand." She hugged her.

Tweedie withdrew, eyes full. "I'll have the room to myself when Ina Bea is working. I can get so much more work done . . ."

"Without people coming in and out the door." Kathryn nodded. She knew Tweedie expected Morgan Sanders to be one of the visitors. Kathryn feared she might be right. Still, it was the nature of her business to keep her door open. "I'd like to write an article about you and your business."

"Oh, would you? That would be grand!"

"With pleasure, Tweedie. You're an independent woman. Will you be making any more fans to send east?"

"Oh, no, I don't think so. I already have more sewing than I can manage. I hope your mother won't mind." She lifted her gunnysack to her shoulder.

"I'm sure she'll be pleased you're doing so well." Kathryn opened the door and watched her head for Ronya's. She would see Tweedie each day when she went to the café to eat, but it wouldn't be the same.

Depressed, Kathryn made herself a cup of tea and sat at her desk, nibbling at the slice of wedding cake Ronya had sent home with her. The sun was going down and the fandango hall starting up. What would it be like to rollick with abandon, to have the freedom to stomp your feet and dance and sing? She sighed. A lady wasn't allowed such luxury.

Axel tapped on her door at nine. She cracked it open, and they exchanged a few words before he continued his rounds. Kathryn bolted the door and went into her apartment to get ready for bed. The place felt empty without Tweedie. Somehow the revelry next door exacerbated her loneliness. She picked up *Ivanhoe*, remembering how Tweedie had been enraptured by the story. She had learned the rudiments of reading quickly. Kathryn hoped she would continue learning on her own.

Half-asleep, Kathryn heard a noise at the back door. Heart jumping, she listened intently, but it was only sniffling, scratching, and whining. Pushing off her covers, Kathryn lit the lamp and cautiously opened the door. A scruffy, mottled dog sat looking up at her with pitiful brown eyes. She'd seen the dog around town numerous times. It didn't seem to belong to anyone. "You poor thing. Are you hungry?" The dog wagged its tail. "Well, you wait right here." Looking over her small larder, she opened a can of baked beans and ham.

The dog dug his nose in. Kathryn scratched him behind the ears and then closed the door and bolted it again.

When Kathryn got up in the morning, he was still there.

Ronya told Kathryn to bathe the dog in vinegar and rub him with a concoction of ground rosemary, fennel, witch hazel, and eucalyptus oil. The poor animal looked miserable, ears down, shivering. Once all the dirt and grime washed away and she towel dried him, she discovered the dog had a healthy coat of black, golden-brown, and white fur. He gazed at her with adoring brown eyes ringed with black, his muzzle and cheeks white.

"You look like a bandit." Kathryn scratched him under the chin. "That's what I'm going to call you. Bandit."

When Kathryn headed to Ronya's, Bandit stayed at her side. "I'm sorry, my furry friend, but you can't come inside. I'll save some of my dinner for you."

Matthias came in a few minutes before the appointed hour of their interview. Kathryn intended to keep the conversation focused on civic improvements and pelted him with questions.

He surveyed her pile of notes with a sardonic smile. "What I thought was going to be a nice conversation feels like an interrogation."

"I'm just doing my job." She dug in her small drawstring bag and put a dime on the table.

His eyes narrowed. "What do you think you're doing?"

"Paying for our coffee." She pushed her chair back and rose before he could protest. "You promised to show me the town hall. Shall we go?"

"All business today, aren't you?" Matthias remarked dryly.

"All for the people, Mr. Beck."

Bandit rose when she came out the door. Matthias raised a brow. "A new friend? What did you do? Feed him?"

"A can of pork and beans, and Ronya is giving me scraps."

Matthias laughed. "You'll never get rid of him."

"I don't want to get rid of him. He's good company."

"Why? Because he lets you do all the talking?"

She couldn't help but smile. "There is that."

"Or are you hoping to keep visitors away?"

"That, too." Kathryn gave Matthias an impish smile. "He's quite protective. He almost took a chunk out of Scribe's leg this morning when he walked into the office without knocking."

"Thanks for the warning." Matthias smirked. "I'll bring a meaty bone when I come to call."

The renovated saloon looked functional for both a court and town hall, rows of chairs, two tables, the judge's bench, and a jury box, all movable pieces of furniture. Kathryn was impressed with the workmanship. Matthias talked about how things could be shifted to serve multiple purposes, all the while running a hand over Bandit's upturned head. The dog sat with mouth open in a canine grin, tongue lolling.

Kathryn watched, annoyed. "Making friends with my guardian?"

"Thought it might be wise." Matthias gave her a teasing look. "He seems to like me."

"There's no accounting for taste."

"Now don't be jealous."

She laughed. "You're incorrigible, Mr. Beck, but you've done a good job for the town. You mentioned a site for the school-house."

"Just down the hill from the church. We start building next month."

"The Mother Lode Schoolhouse?" she said dryly.

"Seemed an appropriate name. And I'm advertising for a teacher. Unfortunately, we only have thirty children in Calvada. People will protest the cost for so few."

"There will be more children as the town grows."

He smiled at her. "One can hope."

Kathryn's heart quickened. As they came out of the building, Gus Blather called out to Kathryn. "I've been looking all over for you, Miss Walsh." He held out a slip of yellow paper. "A telegram from Sacramento. Someone named Amos Stearns?" Kathryn thanked him and opened the folded slip.

```
Arriving April 10 by stage. Would like to
discuss your mine. Amos Stearns
```

Kathryn folded the message and tucked it into her reticule. Blather stood waiting. She thanked him again and said no response was necessary. Matthias raised his brows after Blather left. "Good news?"

"One can hope."

Kathryn met Amos Stearns at the stagecoach office. When he stepped down from the coach, dust-covered and weary, his face lit up. "What a pleasure to see you again, Miss Walsh." Cussler tossed him a carpetbag and he fell into step beside Kathryn. She recommended Beck's Hotel. They headed that way along the boardwalk. "I have the report, Miss Walsh, and will go over everything with you as soon as possible. This evening, if you're free. I know it's short notice."

"Ronya Vanderstrom opens for dinner at five." She'd be delighted if he met her at her house so they could walk to Ronya's together. She started to point across the street and froze as a four-horse team pulling a Hall and Debree Trash wagon mounded with garbage rolled on by. When had that service started?

"The *Voice?*"

"A newspaper."

"A woman running a newspaper? Times are certainly changing."

She couldn't tell whether he approved or not. "Yes, they are, and about time they do."

Matthias came through the swinging doors. She made quick introductions, said she looked forward to seeing Amos later, and headed across the street. When she glanced back before going inside, the two men were talking. She opened the door and Bandit jumped up, circling her.

Scribe had already set the type for her column on housekeeping. "Sanders sent you a message." He didn't look happy about it. "It's on your desk."

She opened the envelope.

My dearest Kathryn,

I fear I made you uncomfortable with my recent declaration. May I have the pleasure of your company for dinner this evening to clear any misgivings you might have? I will come for you at six.

Fond regards,
Morgan

Scribe stood scowling at the press. "A love note?"

"No." It felt more like a summons. She sat at her desk and pulled out her writing materials.

Dear Morgan,
  Thank you for your kind invitation, but I have a previous engagement this evening.

                                                        Kathryn

She folded and tucked the note into an envelope, sealed it, wrote *Mr. Morgan Sanders* on the front, and held it out. "Would you please take this—?"

"Now I'm running errands for you, too?"

"I'm sorry, Scribe, but I can't be the one to deliver it."

Yanking off the printer's apron, he snatched it and headed for the door. "Some people don't know when to leave well enough alone." He slammed the door behind him.

When he came back, he was even more annoyed. "He asked me about some man you met at the stage station."

Good grief! Did he have someone watching her every movement?

"What man?" Scribe stood in front of her desk.

She realized he was jealous. "Amos Stearns. He's one of the assayers I spoke with in Sacramento."

"Assayer? Is he here about City's mine?"

Kathryn wished she hadn't said anything. "Yes, but I don't know what he has to say yet."

"Well, he wouldn't make a trip all the way up here if it was bad news. He could wire that." He headed for the press, then stopped. "Whatever you do, don't sell that mine to Sanders!" Scribe went back to fitting tied lines into place. They both worked in silence, until Scribe inked the press and made one copy for her to proofread. "So? Can I come along and hear what this assayer has to say?"

Amos Stearns didn't seem overjoyed to have Scribe join them for dinner. Kathryn assured him that anything he had to say could be said in front of her friend. Ronya's dining room was busy, as usual, and the three of them drew attention when they walked in the door. Thankfully, there was a table near the back. Ina Bea had replaced Charlotte and served them venison stew and fresh biscuits. Amos tucked into his meal like a miner who'd worked a full day. For a thin man, he had a big appetite. Kathryn didn't ask questions until Ina Bea came back with three bowls of bread pudding with raisins and cream sauce, and mugs of rich, hot coffee. "About the report . . ."

"Copper." Amos dipped his spoon into the bowl. "The samples you brought are rich in copper and traces of silver. I'd like to examine the mine tomorrow, if—"

"Yes, of course." Kathryn looked at Scribe.

He stared back at her, eyes wide and bright with excitement. "We have a bonanza!"

Kathryn clamped a hand on Scribe's wrist. "Hush."

Scribe looked around and then leaned forward, eyes fixed on the assayer.

Kathryn squeezed. "I'm sure it's not as simple as finding copper. You have to dig it out of the mountain and process it. Which means you need equipment, supplies, men to work. You need knowledge and management skills . . ."

Amos nodded. "We'll take things one at a time, Miss Walsh. My father was superintendent over a coal mine in Kentucky. After my mother died, I spent more time underground with him than I did in open air. I did my schooling at night. Mining fascinates me, always has. I trained two years at the School of Civil and Mining Engineering before coming out to California.

If your mine shows what I think it will, we can talk about whether you want my help or someone else's."

Amos's manner surprised Kathryn. He had seemed such a mild, quiet young man in Sacramento, but he was full of confidence now. Talking geology made his eyes glow. Scribe looked like he had a fever. Her heart jumped when Matthias came in the door. When he glanced around the room, she knew he was looking for her. Their eyes met and she felt a punch of sensations in her stomach. He crossed the room.

"Kathryn." He greeted her casually and focused on Amos. "Stearns. Hope you're enjoying your stay in Calvada."

"I've been looking forward to the visit for some time." He smiled at Kathryn.

Scribe grinned up at Matthias. "He says City's mine is loaded with copper. Oww." He frowned at Kathryn. "What'd you kick me for?"

Several men nearby showed a sudden interest in their conversation. "That is not what Mr. Stearns said, Scribe."

"Sure is!"

Leaning toward him, she snarled, "Be quiet. Don't make me sorry I invited you." Conversation seemed to have died around them.

Matthias was grim. "It seems your luck is turning, Kathryn." He gave Amos another look. "If you've the means, you'd better jump in before another hears the news."

She knew he meant Morgan Sanders. "I think everyone is getting a little ahead of themselves."

"Mining isn't a woman's business."

Kathryn stiffened. "You said the same thing about running a newspaper."

"Two very different enterprises, your ladyship."

She couldn't agree more, but she had no intention of

admitting that now, not when facing his dismissive attitude about a woman's abilities. "We'll see."

Matthias chuckled. "I'm sure you will." He gave a slight bow. "I'll leave you to your fact-finding expedition." He joined Herr Neumann, Patrick Flynt, and Carl Rudger at a front table.

When Scribe opened his mouth, Kathryn cut him off. "We will not discuss this further while in a café for all to hear." She glared at her young friend. She addressed Amos. "We can meet tomorrow morning at Cole's Livery Stable. I'll see about renting a buggy."

19

REMEMBERING HER FIRST VISIT TO THE MINE, Kathryn dressed in a simple brown skirt, peplum jacket, cream shirt-waist, and boots. A straw hat with ribbon ties covered her hair. She had a cloth tucked into a side pocket. Amos and Scribe had already arrived at the livery stable, both in denim pants and plaid flannel shirts, Amos holding a tool belt with rock pick, hammer, small shovel, crevice tool, and compass. Scribe was peppering the man with questions, and Kit Cole listened to every word while harnessing the horse.

Rolling her eyes, Kathryn joined them. "Blowing a bugle, Scribe? Letting the whole town know where we're going and why?"

Contrite, he blushed and said he'd meet them at the mine. "City showed me a shortcut."

"A shortcut?" Kathryn called after him, but he was already out the door and out of sight. She gave Amos a shrug. "There's still a lot I don't know about this town."

She insisted upon driving the carriage and noted how tense Amos was on the ride. She wasn't going that fast, but then men always liked to have the reins. At the end of the road, she hopped down before Amos could come around the carriage to assist her and tied the reins to a thick pine branch.

"You'll need a road," Amos puffed a few minutes later, his breath a mist in the cold air. The uphill walk and thin mountain air had them both breathless.

Kathryn wondered where the money would come from to build one.

Scribe stood at the mine entrance. "Took you long enough!" He lit the lantern, grabbed a shovel, and went inside. "Watch out for snakes! The last time City and I came up here, we found a whole den of six. It's warming up, so they'll be on the move."

Snakes? How could she have forgotten Wiley Baer's warning when he brought her up here last fall? She hadn't come pre-pared for snakes. Hanging her hat on the lantern hook, Kathryn covered her hair with the cloth. At least she'd have no spiders crawling into her hair.

"Are you coming?" Scribe yelled back.

"Hold your horses, Scribe!" She entered and hadn't gone six feet before she felt sticky silken strands touch her face. She waved, slapped, and wiped them away.

Amos glanced back. "Why don't you wait at the entrance, Miss Walsh? Might be safer."

She gave a nervous laugh. "And miss all the excitement?" She proceeded, eyes darting up, down, and all around. She heard an eerie sound fill the tunnel ahead. "What is that?"

"Rattler!" Scribe thrust the lantern to Amos. "Stay back! I'll take care of him." Raising the shovel, Scribe lunged forward and brought it down with a bang. The sound continued. He swore. *Bang, bang, bang.* "Got him! Don't go near the head. They can still sink their fangs into you after they're dead."

She saw the snake writhing on the floor. "It looks alive to me."

"Just the throes of death." *Bang, bang, bang.* "He's a goner."

Amos pointed. "There's another one over there."

Kathryn wanted to turn and run out of the tunnel, but stayed planted where she was as Scribe dispatched the second. Insides churning and quaking, Kathryn stuck close to the two men as they went farther in, the walls feeling closer, the air dank. "I can tell you right now, Amos, I'm not going to make a good miner."

He laughed. "Men will do the digging."

Scribe snorted. "But she'll be giving all the orders."

She giggled. "I rather like that arrangement." Her voice sounded strange in the confined space.

Amos paused, held up the lantern, and ran his hand along the wall. He took his time, studying the tunnel. When they reached the chamber where City had stopped digging and stacked up rocks, he set the lantern in the center. Using a rock pick, he took more samples. Hunkering down by the light, he turned them over in his hands. "You've got high-grade silver in here. And look at this! A small vein of gold." He straightened and went back to work. "Your uncle put a lot of work into this tunnel and chamber."

Kathryn looked at Scribe and he shrugged. "City never really worked it. Not as long as I've known him. Came up every couple of weeks, but usually only for a day or two. Mostly to get out of town."

"Well, someone did."

Kathryn had a suspicion who.

"I didn't see this place until two years ago." Scribe looked around, frowning. "City said we were going prospecting. Told me to bring canteens and food and showed me the shortcut. The shelter, picks, and shovel were already here, and a case of whiskey. He worked like he was mad at somebody. Just threw rock in those piles. Seemed a waste of time to me. Next time we came up, most of the rocks were gone and we started building the pile again."

"Wiley Baer." Kathryn intended to talk to that man the next time she saw him in town. So much for her ability to judge a man's character.

Amos looked at her. "Who's Wiley Baer?"

Picking up a rock, she looked at the shine in the lantern light. "An old miner who bragged about his secret mine. I think this is it." Hurt and disillusioned, she tossed the rock back. She'd liked Wiley. "I suppose he's been stealing."

"I doubt that." Scribe shook his head. "More than likely he's been keeping this place secret because City wanted it that way."

"If Wiley was a partner, why was there only one name on the claim?"

"I don't know." Scribe shrugged. "They were friends from way back. City said they came west on the same wagon train. Wiley saved him from drowning at a river crossing."

She frowned. "Really? That must have been when my father died." So Uncle Casey had almost drowned, but Wiley managed to save him. If only someone had been able to save her father as well. "You're saying Wiley came to Calvada with my uncle?"

"I think he just comes and goes. I've been in Calvada since I was five, and I never saw Wiley around until City took me in." He scratched his head. "It was Wiley told Herr that City had family back East. He didn't know who or where, but thought Fiona Hawthorne would know. That's how Herr found your mother."

Amos slid his rock pick back into his tool belt. "Whatever your uncle's reasons for not developing this mine, he should have. Looks like a bonanza. Let's get back to town. Nothing more we can do right now, but we have a lot to talk about. Scribe, if anyone asks what we found, tell them a lot of rock and dirt. The less you talk, the better."

Scribe's eyes shone like twin points of light.

"And try not to look like we've found the pot at the end of the rainbow."

On the way out, Amos whispered to Kathryn, "If this was my claim, I'd have guards posted."

"Now?"

"The sooner, the better. Word will spread fast, and there are men who will do just about anything to take this from you."

Matthias was standing in the street, talking with the road crew, when Kathryn and Amos Stearns returned the buggy to the livery stable. He'd seen Scribe a few minutes before, flushed from a run, eyes bright. He went straight into the newspaper office. Kathryn and Amos came down the boardwalk. Kathryn was dusty and somewhat ruffled. The man was doing all the talking. Something serious, judging by the intensity of the young assayer. He must have felt Matthias's interest, for he looked his direction and lifted his chin in greeting as he opened the door for Kathryn. She glanced back over her shoulder. Matthias raised his brows in question. She seemed disturbed, as though whatever Amos had to say unsettled her. Would she talk to him about it? Doubtful. Matthias returned his attention to the road crew shoveling gravel from the defunct Jackrabbit Mine into the street.

"Two more loads today," the foreman told him. "Sanders will raise the price." Matthias figured as much when he heard Sanders had bought the property. If there was a way to make money, Sanders would be at the front of the line. But then, he couldn't fault the man on that when he was doing the same thing.

Kathryn turned the Open sign to Closed.

She might look as though her hopes had been dashed, but Scribe's demeanor and Amos Stearns's watchful eye told another story.

⸱⸱⸱⸱⸱⸱⸱⸱⸱⸱⸱⸱⸱

Overwhelmed with Amos's talk of underground mining methods, engineering, machinery, ventilation, explosives, and rock mechanics, Kathryn raised her hand in surrender. "I need time to think, Amos."

"Unfortunately, time isn't on our side. Word is probably already spreading, thanks to our young friend. I came up to Calvada hoping to find exactly what we did. My partners are waiting for word from me, ready to give you the capital you need to start operations."

This quiet man certainly had a streak of determination. "I appreciate that, but—"

"I can act as mine superintendent and get things rolling. You're going to need an underground foreman, mine engineer, maintenance supervisor, and crew . . ."

He wasn't listening to her at all. "Stop! Now!"

She knew Amos Stearns was knowledgeable and eager, but did

he have experience enough to superintend a mine? He wanted to be in charge. That was clear enough. Despite the way Matthias's comment raised her hackles, Kathryn couldn't agree more that mining was not a woman's business. One minute inside the dark, dank, spiderwebbed snake den had told her that much. She never wanted to set foot inside that tunnel again. Nevertheless, the mine belonged to her. She couldn't shirk responsibility and dump all management decisions on someone else.

Not a woman's business, she thought again, annoyed. Well, neither was the newspaper business, and the *Voice* was now making enough money to support her. It wasn't much, but it paid her bills and kept a roof over her head.

With the Jackrabbit Mine shut down, men needed work. Some had already left for other towns. More would follow if another mine didn't open.

A bonanza.

Morgan Sanders would probably have heard by now of her meeting with Amos at Ronya's and their venture out of town this morning.

"Kathryn . . ."

Her hand shot up again. "Please."

Amos wanted to offer his help. Help? No, he had come to run a mine, undoubtedly thinking a woman incapable of managing. He hadn't even thought her capable of driving the buggy!

When word got out, she knew she could expect offers for the mine. She stood. "We'll talk again in the morning."

Amos didn't look pleased, but he rose. "May I have your permission to contact my associates and tell them what I've seen?"

"Yes, but let them know I'm not ready to enter into any contract with them just yet."

His brows rose slightly. "I understand, but you're already in the thick of it. If you decide to sell, they could advise what price to put on the mine. If you decide to keep it, I'm sure they'd invest. As I told you, they have interests in Virginia City. They also hold shares in mines in Sutter Creek, Jackson, and Placerville. They've been at this longer and have more financial resources than I. Frankly, the only thing I have to offer is the experience I gained working with my father. He was a foreman. The truth is, I miss it. I've got a fire in my belly right now to do something more than work in an assayer's office."

Kathryn liked him. "I can tell how excited you are, Amos, but you're going to have to be patient and wait for me to catch up."

"Then I'll say no more and leave you to it, Kathryn." He picked up his hat. "You could find yourself a very wealthy young woman in the next few months."

They agreed to meet again at Ronya's for dinner. Kathryn made one stipulation: no more talk of mines. She saw him out the door.

<hr />

Matthias didn't like seeing Kathryn with another man, especially two nights in a row, and one who had her full attention. The assayer from Sacramento had made the trip all the way up to Calvada just to deliver a report and see a mine? Stearns might well see a business opportunity, but anyone watching the two of them, heads together, could see the man was charmed by the woman holding the claim. Ina Bea stopped at their table and talked with the couple. The two women laughed and chatted while Stearns, silent, had his eyes fixed on Kathryn. Well-dressed, lean, dark-blond hair, trimmed beard, he looked more like a clerk than a miner. When Ina Bea walked away, Kathryn spoke to Stearns again, warmly, like two friends. She seemed perfectly at ease with him. Anytime Matthias came near her, she clothed herself in formality and caution. Not that he hadn't provided cause.

He'd behaved like a gentleman the last few times they'd met. He'd shown her everything he'd been doing since the election, pleased to see how pleased she was. Not for herself, she made clear, but for the benefits to all Calvadans. He was done standing back.

Axel Borgeson joined Matthias. Thankfully, the town had quieted considerably since he'd put on the badge. Borgeson had no tolerance for tomfoolery. Two who had tested his mettle found themselves bruised and bloody and locked up until dawn, when they were herded out to shovel lye into public outhouses and clear Chump Street of horse manure.

Borgeson gave Ina Bea his order, his gaze fixed on the sway of her hips as she walked away. "Broke up a brawl down at the Red Lantern. Drunk jackrabbits. No damage done except to each other. Told them they could behave or get out of town."

Borgeson looked across the room, then back at Matthias, eyes crinkling with amusement. "Your mind seems to be elsewhere. And I can understand why. You don't see many women like Kathryn in a town like this, do you?"

"No. You don't."

Ina Bea set two mugs on the table and poured coffee. She came back with two plates piled high with corned beef, potatoes, carrots, and steamed cabbage glistening with butter. She asked Axel if all was going well on his rounds. He said the town was quiet, and he heard there was a dance at Rocker Box Hall Friday night and was she interested. Blushing, she said yes, that would be lovely. Matthias gave him a wry look as Ina Bea headed back to the kitchen.

Axel picked up his knife and fork. "How's Kathryn's list coming along?" Grinning, he took a bite of corned beef.

Kathryn and Amos had long since finished their dinner and now got up to leave. They both gave him a smile and nod as they went out the door together.

"Another conquest," Axel remarked. "Seems emotions run high where Miss Walsh is concerned. Some men have nothing good to say about her while others admire her spunk."

"She's taken a lot of guff since she came to town, most of it from me."

"So I've heard." Axel laughed. "Did you really throw that girl over your shoulder and carry her into your hotel?"

"No! She came willingly. Although . . ." Heat surged into Matthias's face. "I did carry her across the street. It seemed the only way to keep her out of trouble at the time."

———

Later that night, Matthias decided to check in on Kathryn and was surprised when she invited him in. She said she'd been wanting to discuss something with him. "I have to decide what to do with City's mine." She seemed to be waiting for him to say something. "No opinion?"

"It's not my mine." Was she leaning toward him or was he just hoping?

Drawing a sudden breath, Kathryn got up and moved away from him. "Now that word is out, thanks to Scribe's big mouth, I'll have to do something."

Matthias watched her move restlessly around the room. "What does Amos Stearns have to say about it?" He didn't like bringing the assayer into their conversation, but needed to know what was going on between them.

Kathryn sat at her desk and shuffled notes. "He thinks his partners will want to invest, and he'd like to run it."

"And how do you feel about that?" He tried to keep the edge out of his voice.

"I don't know anything about mining. He has training, expertise, and is confident he could do the job."

Matthias didn't know anything about mining either, but he knew about business. "Do you trust him?"

"I like him, and he seems trustworthy."

"But?"

She gave a slight shrug. "I think he's very interested in the mine, but I think he is also interested in . . . other things."

"You." Matthias and everyone else who'd seen them at Ronya's recognized a man infatuated with a woman.

"It could make for a difficult working relationship. And I'm not sure I want someone taking over and running things the way I've seen mines run around here."

"The Madera." He felt some relief she wasn't as naive about Morgan Sanders as some thought.

"How does your partnership with Henry work?" She pulled over some paper and picked up a pencil. "Would you mind telling me?"

He laughed. "Interviewing me *now*?" She'd like to keep things all business. He stood and turned a straight-backed chair around and set it beside her desk. "What do you want to know, your ladyship?"

"Everything."

"Thinking of going into a partnership with Amos Stearns?" If she said yes, he wasn't sure he wanted to help.

"I might consider it, but I'll still have to think about other options."

Matthias wished he had the money to invest, but he'd already put money into Walker's General Store and Beck and Call Drayage. He told her his partnership with Henry was simple.

A solid plan, prospective customers, equal capital invested in building wagons, buying horses, setting up the office in a hub city.

"Sacramento," Kathryn said flatly. "You'll be leaving Calvada, won't you?" She didn't try to hide her disappointment. "After your time as mayor ends."

"Maybe, maybe not." He wasn't leaving without her. "I'll go to Sacramento every three months and Henry and I will go over all the accounts. He's a friend and I trust him, but I still need to know what's going on."

Kathryn wrote rapidly. Leaning back, she wove the pencil between her fingers.

He could see her quick mind working. "What's going on in that head of yours?"

"Just an idea."

"If you trust Stearns, and he and his partners make an offer, it might be wise to sell. Mining isn't—"

"For a lady?" She tossed the pencil onto her desk, annoyed now. "So I've been told. Repeatedly. Which makes me want to do it, just to prove every man in Calvada wrong. And I know that's not a good enough reason." She paused. "But it is my inheritance. I need to make a responsible decision about what to do with it. I've seen firsthand the dangers of being rich."

"Wealth isn't evil, Kate. It's the love of money that is. When no matter how much you have is never enough."

She picked up her pencil again and tapped it. "Amos said I could become a very rich young woman, but I'm not sure I want to be rich. Though there are times when I wish I had the money to buy whatever I want." She gave him a wan smile. "The crate of books at Aday's. I pushed it under the table so no one else would notice it. And there's always the question of whether I'm up to the task of managing anything."

He was surprised at her lack of confidence. "You've run two businesses."

"I was a poor milliner, but the *Voice* is doing well."

"Maybe those enterprises were meant to prepare you for what was coming." What was he saying?

Kathryn laughed, amazed and amused. "Is this Matthias Beck seriously telling me he thinks I could run a mine?"

"*Could* doesn't necessarily mean *should*, Kate. Depends on what you want the outcome to be."

"Oh!" Her eyes widened and grew bright, as though his words had unwittingly triggered an explosive idea.

Frowning, he studied her. She was already lost in whatever had come into her fertile brain. A long red tendril had escaped her chignon. He lifted it and curled it around his finger. She felt the gentle tug and looked at him, her breath coming softly. When her lips parted, he felt the heat surge up. Time to remove himself from temptation. Letting go of the soft red curl, he stood. "Walk me to the door?" His voice was rough.

As Kathryn came around the desk, Matthias lowered the wick on the lantern. She drew in her breath slowly. "Best that no one sees me leaving your place at this hour. We don't want anyone making the wrong assumptions."

"I've stopped worrying about what people think."

Matthias looked at her with a teasing grin. "Are you saying I can stay?"

She gave him a light push. "Just when I thought I could trust you."

Matthias wanted to kiss her. When she opened the door and looked up at him again, he had the feeling she wanted that, too. But something stopped him.

"For everything there is a season, a time for every activity under heaven."

They stood so close together, Matthias could feel Kathryn's warmth, smell the scent of her. He could breathe her in. When he reached out slowly, she didn't move away. He ran his hand along her arm and took her hand, squeezing it gently. Leaning down, he kissed her cheek. "Good night, your ladyship."

20

ANOTHER NOTE WAS SLIPPED under Kathryn's door Wednesday morning. She recognized the handwriting.

My dear Kathryn,
    There is an important meeting of the mine owners this afternoon. I'll send the carriage for you at five, unless I hear otherwise.

                                        Yours,
                                        Morgan

Kathryn felt no hesitation. Of course she wanted to attend. Of course she wanted to know what was going on. She was ready when the driver came for her, but questioned his route when he drove to the end of town and turned up Gomorrah. "Where are you taking me?"

"To Mr. Sanders. Just taking this route 'cause the horse was turned this way."

Then why was he slowing the carriage as he came to Fiona Hawthorne's house? Kathryn saw Monique peering at them from an upstairs window. The driver stared at her. Monique stepped back, yanking the curtain closed. Kathryn leaned forward. "Did Mr. Sanders tell you to come this way?"

"The boss told me to bring you to him, and the horse was pointed south. Besides, it's good for people to know where they stand."

She didn't know if he was talking about Monique Beaulieu or her. "My visit is strictly business."

"None of my business if it wasn't." He turned right at the top of the hill where the mine owners lived. Morgan's place was the largest, a three-story house with a low decorative iron fence surrounding it. Two men, obviously servants, worked in the garden.

The driver stopped by the gate, jumped down, and offered her a hand. She went up the steps and knocked. Another servant, a Chinese man, opened the door. He bowed and then stepped back as Morgan, dressed in all his sartorial splendor, came out from beneath an arched doorway. "Kathryn." He spoke warmly, his gaze moving over her with open appreciation. The servant closed the front door behind her and headed down the shadowed hallway, hands slipping inside his loose-sleeved black silk tunic.

As Morgan ushered her toward the arched doorway, Kathryn glanced at the triple arches of mahogany crown molding, one leading up a stairwell to the second story, another down a long hallway. The third led to a parlor, beautifully furnished with a burl mahogany empire sofa upholstered in plush blue with pink fleur-de-lis velvet, a freshly oiled carved walnut settee and chairs, marble-topped tables with curving legs, and chintz draperies and lace curtains. A gold-framed mirror over the Georgian fireplace with a polished brass peacock screen made the room seem larger. In the corner near the windows stood a grand piano. She had seen more elaborate homes in the East, but by Calvada standards, this was a mansion with all the luxurious trimmings.

"Well? What do you think of my house?"

"It's lovely." And it was silent. "Where is everyone? You said there was a meeting."

"There was. At three. We adjourned an hour ago."

Her heart did a fillip and she felt sudden trepidation. What game was he playing with her? Kathryn took a step back. "You led me to believe—"

"I said there was a meeting I thought you might find interesting. We'll talk about it over dinner."

"I don't like being tricked, Morgan."

She turned to leave, but he caught her arm and swung her back, eyes dark. "And I don't like being dismissed like a schoolboy." He propelled her toward a wing chair and practically pushed her into it.

"What do you think you're doing?" She tried to stand, but Morgan stood in front of her, his expression such that she sank down, frightened.

"We're going to spend the evening together, you and I. And we're going to have an understanding at the end of it."

Something about his smile made her stomach clench. Her mind whirred. How many people had seen her get into his coach and be driven down Chump Street? "I shouldn't be here in your home alone with you. It's highly improper."

He smirked. "We were alone when you invited me to tea."

"The front door remained partially open so that anyone passing by could see we were talking. I should have a chaperone."

Morgan laughed. "And who would that be? Tweedie Witt? She moved into Ronya's Café, didn't she? A falling-out perhaps? Because you invited me into your inner sanctum for tea and cake?"

Kathryn didn't like his tone and felt unnerved by the smug satisfaction radiating from him.

He studied her. "Are you afraid of me?"

She *was* afraid, but felt an instinctive restraint about admitting it. Morgan had not yet taken a seat. Would he try to stop her from leaving if the opportunity opened? What did he intend? People already thought her unconventional. If word spread about this, they would think her immoral as well.

Folding her hands in her lap, Kathryn tipped her chin and met his eyes. She had to remain calm, or at least appear to be. "This behavior is beneath you, Morgan."

"You think so? Would you have come if you knew we would be alone?"

"No." She rose sedately, hoping he would allow her to leave. "And I must go now to preserve my reputation."

"This from a young woman who has cared little for convention since getting off the stagecoach." He spoke dryly, the warmth receding from his dark eyes. "You and I have things to discuss. Subjects best not overheard by others."

Her heart hammered. She dared not move toward the door, for that would bring her closer to him. Striving to remain calm and think, she sat and smoothed her skirt. "Very well. What is it you wish to discuss that would make you go to such lengths?"

Morgan sat on the edge of a chair as though ready to rise if she did. "I've been told Amos Stearns brought you a report on City's mine."

She could guess where this was going. "Do you know Mr. Stearns?"

"I can't say I've had the pleasure, but Hollis and Pruitt are well-known in Sacramento. What did he tell you?" Morgan eased back in the chair, though she felt his coiled tension. "Come, come, my dear."

Kathryn remained silent. She had been naive to think a friendly visit over tea and cider cake would sway this man. She didn't want to tell him anything, but conversation was preferable to the increasing threat she felt by remaining silent. "Mr. Stearns did bring a report. Scribe was precipitously excited about the possibilities." She gave him a demure smile, knowing he would have heard all that information already. "You offered to buy the mine when I first came to Calvada. Had you already seen it?"

"No, but I thought the claim worthless. And I offered to buy it to help a poor young lady in need."

"Did you? Why?"

His eyes narrowed. "Don't be impertinent. It's not becoming of a lady. Hollis and Pruitt wouldn't have sent Stearns if they hadn't found something worth pursuing." He seemed amused. "I always wondered why City never let go of the claim, though I now wonder even more why he didn't work it." He raised his brows. "Has Stearns told you what the mine is worth?"

"Mr. Stearns didn't mention a price, but whatever price he gives, I have no plans to sell."

Morgan scoffed. "You certainly can't manage it."

A fire blazed inside her. She was sick of having men tell her what she could and couldn't do. "Why not?" She kept her tone light though anger heated her blood.

"Don't be ridiculous, Kathryn. You're a lady."

She was a woman, and most men seemed to think women incapable of anything more than cooking their meals, washing their clothes, catering to their every need, all the while birthing and tending their babies. "Everyone says the same thing, but I won't be bullied into selling."

"That has never been my intent." His eyes moved across her face and down over her body. "I'm far more interested in you than in City's mine. I made that clear long before anyone knew City's mine might be worth something. But if I have you, I have it all, don't I?"

She must not show fear, though it was flooding her body. How far would this man go to get what he wanted? "This is hardly the behavior of a gentleman."

"You are very young, my dear. A gentleman knows what he wants, and I want you."

Why not be frank? Since he seemed to hold such high value on it. "You don't want me. You want City's mine."

"You underestimate your charms. I made up my mind about you the first night we had dinner together."

When Morgan rose, she fought down panic. Footsteps approached in the hall, and the Canadian chef from Morgan's hotel entered the room with a plate of fancy hors d'oeuvres. Kathryn took one. "Did you close your restaurant this evening?" She hoped to delay his departure with questions.

The chef smiled. "No, mademoiselle. Phillippe—"

"That will be all, Louis." Morgan jerked his head in dismissal. The man nodded and left. Morgan gave her a stern look. "A lady never addresses the servants."

"Perhaps I'm not the lady you thought I was." As soon as the words passed her lips, she wished she hadn't said it, for he could take it in the wrong way.

He chuckled, clearly aware of her unease and enjoying it. "Your innocence is a delight. We are going to have a pleasant evening together."

"Is that a command?"

"If it needs to be." He poured two glasses of red wine and held one out to her.

"I don't imbibe."

"Tonight you will. Because I offer it."

Kathryn took a shaky breath, but didn't accept the glass.

"Try the wine. I assure you, it is of the finest quality, purchased in San Francisco, shipped all the way from France."

"No, thank you."

"Such a polite little hypocrite."

"I beg your pardon?"

"As you should. You rather enjoyed Ronya's famed elixir one night, I hear."

Her mouth fell open, but she saw no point in defending herself. "People take far too much interest in my life, Mr. Sanders. Especially you." With three thousand men and less than a hundred women, it was difficult to keep anything private, even with doors locked and window shades down.

Morgan took a leisurely sip of wine. "I know quite a lot about you. Matthias Beck is in and out of your house at all hours." His mouth twisted unpleasantly. "Isn't he?"

She blushed. "Not for the reasons you are clearly insinuating. Mr. Beck is more a friend than you are proving to be." Taking the opportunity as he set his glass aside, Kathryn ran for the doorway. She hadn't even reached the archway when Morgan caught hold of her arm and swung her around to face him.

He gripped her chin, his eyes blazing. "You're not going anywhere."

Kathryn gasped at such rough treatment. Truly frightened now, she tried desperately to feign indignation. "Let me go! You're hurting me!"

His fingers tightened as he leaned closer. "So, Beck is your *friend.* I can't help but wonder how close your relationship is." He brought her back to the chair and pressed her into it. Planting his hands on the arms, he leaned down over her. "Look at me, Kathryn. I said *look at me!*" She did as he commanded, hating herself for it. "Are you still a virgin?" He mocked her, searching her face with feigned concern. He gave a soft laugh and straightened. "Yes. You are." He brushed his fingers along her cheek, his touch sending a chill through her. "So soft. So pure." He moved away and sat facing her again, now fully relaxed, in control. "You are going to be my wife. I made up my mind about that months ago."

She swallowed convulsively. "I have some say about that, and the answer is no."

"I didn't ask." Morgan gave a derisive laugh. "I need a wife, and you're ripe for marriage. I want a son. Marry me and you will have everything a woman could desire. Refuse and I'll have word spread that you spend time on Gomorrah."

His cold assurance unnerved her. "I'm quite sure if you made the same proposal to Miss Beaulieu, you would find her most agreeable."

"Monique knows her place." His mouth curved. "She'll remain my mistress."

The Chinese servant stood in the doorway. "Dinner is served."

Morgan stood, the pleasant host once more. "Shall we?" When Kathryn didn't rise, he hauled her up and whispered, "Don't try my patience." When she looked toward the door, he pressed her ahead of him before letting go. She followed the servant, feeling Morgan's looming presence behind her, blocking escape.

Morgan seated her. He took his place at the head of the table. He studied her for a moment, silent, contemplative, as though imagining how he expected the rest of the evening to play out. She was thankful for the eight-foot table between them. The silverware laid out foretold five courses. As serving dishes were brought in, Morgan shook out his napkin and placed it on his lap. Kathryn did as well. The knife for the main course looked sharp enough to be used as a weapon.

Morgan's chef offered the first course and told them he had prepared a sumptuous beef Wellington with glazed carrots and warm wilted winter greens. Kathryn declined wine as a stuffed mushroom was placed before her. Annoyed, Morgan told Louis to bring the lady a tumbler of spring water. When he picked up his knife and fork, she bowed her head. *Lord, help!* Raising her head, she found Morgan looking at her with sardonic humor. She fingered the silverware before selecting the knife. The first taste resurrected her appetite. She hadn't eaten since breakfast, too busy with the newspaper to go down to Ronya's. After the appetizer came a green salad with sweet dressing, followed by the main course, and it was, indeed, delicious.

"Your chef has outdone himself." She remembered the over-cooked venison steak she had been served at the hotel.

"I've never seen a lady with such an appetite."

She smiled, having eaten enough to feel her stays cutting into her, and possibly enough to make herself sick. If Morgan touched her, she might just surprise him in a way that would dampen his ardor.

"You will eat like this every day, my dear."

She couldn't help herself. "A pity so many who work for you can only afford two simple meals a day." She cut another small bite. "Are you interested in buying my mine because yours is playing out?"

Morgan glowered at her. "You have a sharp tongue."

Kathryn hoped the knife she planned to slip into her lap would be far sharper.

"The Jackrabbit closed down," she informed him as though

he didn't already know. "Twin Peaks is showing less profit . . ." She raised a brow.

"I assure you, the Madera has plenty of ore yet to mine."

His vehemence told her she had touched a nerve. Of course, he would be eager to buy her uncle's mine, or find a way to gain control of it. Morgan plowed through his dinner like a man who swung a pick and used a shovel rather than sitting behind a desk in his hotel and issuing orders to the foremen.

When Morgan spoke to Louis, she managed to secrete the knife into the fold of her skirt. The remaining dishes were removed, berry cobbler served. Morgan declined. It was unnerving to have him watch her eat, but she pretended not to care. When she finally couldn't eat another bite, she dabbed her lips and folded the napkin over the fine porcelain plate and gave him her full attention. "I haven't had a five-course meal since being cast out of Boston."

"I'm glad you enjoyed it." He smirked. "Now, put the knife on the table, Kathryn. It's poor manners to steal the silver."

She did as she was told.

Pushing his chair back, Morgan stood. When he came to her and drew her chair out, she felt a shiver of apprehension. Desperate, she said the first thing that popped into her head. "Someday, all the valuable ore will be gouged, blasted, and hauled out of the mountain. Then what happens to Calvada?" She could tell him his mansion would stand as an empty monument to his arrogance and pride—worthless, abandoned, rotting away, or razed to build other structures elsewhere. What good would all his machinations do him then?

He stood close. "I don't care what happens to Calvada. I'll have sold for top dollar long before the ore plays out." He nodded his head, a command for her to precede him out of the room. He put his hand at the small of her back as they entered the hallway.

When they neared the staircase, she tensed, ready to run for the door, but he took her arm firmly and spun her toward the stairs.

"What do you think you're doing?" she cried out, trying to yank free.

"I'm going to do what I've wanted to do for months. After tonight, you'll know you're mine." He pulled her up the first few steps.

Kathryn fought in earnest then. She managed to twist out of his arms. When he tried to grasp her around the waist and lift her, she raked her fingernails across his face and almost gained her freedom. He called her a foul name, his fingers digging into her hair as he raised his hand to strike her.

The stairway rolled under her feet and she cried out.

Morgan, hand still raised, looked up in alarm as the chandelier rattled violently. His fingers loosened and Kathryn pulled free, falling down three steps to her knees. The servant shouted, ran past her, and threw open the front door. Kathryn scraped to her feet, grabbed up her skirt, and fled right behind him.

As she raced down the front steps, she almost fell again. Grasping the rail, she tried to regain her balance, but the very ground was shaking. What was happening? Had there been an explosion at the Madera?

"Earthquake!" someone screamed in the street. A carriage had been passing by, the horse now rearing in harness.

"Kathryn!" Morgan roared, his face livid, as he came after her. She pushed through the gate. The terrified horse whinnied shrilly and reared again. Kathryn darted around it. Its hooves came down hard, blocking Morgan from pursuit.

The tremor didn't last long, but the horse sidestepped and almost tipped the carriage into the ornate iron fence along Morgan's front yard. Morgan cursed loudly. "Get that horse under control!"

Kathryn made it to the corner. Gasping for breath, she slowed, a hand against her stomach. Glancing back, she saw Morgan holding the horse's harness, his face rigid, his eyes fixed on her, black with fury.

Heart pounding, Kathryn kept walking at a fast pace. When she reached Paris Avenue, she gave in to the fear she'd battened down for the last two hours, lifted the hem of her skirt, and ran.

Matthias stood outside in the middle of the street. The earthquake had rattled buildings, shattering a few windows, only one poorly constructed building down the street toppling. He saw Kathryn racing down the boardwalk. Where was she coming from? She looked terrified. Opening her door, she rushed in and closed it quickly.

He crossed over and knocked on her door, concerned. She didn't answer. She didn't even peer through the curtain. "Kathryn! Are you all right in there? Any damage done?"

"Everything is fine. Thank you." She didn't sound fine. She sounded breathless and scared.

"It was an earthquake. It's over. There might be some tremors, but less severe." He paused. "Are you sure you're all right?"

"I'm grand. Just grand." There was a hitch in her voice.

He tried to lighten the moment. Leaning against the door, he spoke more softly. "What do you say to a June wedding?"

"*Go away!*"

Matthias straightened. He'd never heard that shrill tone out of her before. Bandit scratched at the door. "Better let the dog in."

"Which dog do you mean?"

"The one that barks."

"Every man in this town is barking mad!" The door opened just enough to allow Bandit to slip inside, then closed firmly. The bolt slammed into place.

———————

Kathryn didn't come out the front door of her house for three days, though her lantern burned through every night. She opened the door each morning to let Bandit out. He spent the day marking posts, sniffing for rats, and howling at the screeching fiddles in the fandango hall. When Kathryn opened the door each evening, he slipped in and didn't come out again until the next day.

Axel told Matthias that Morgan Sanders had been at her door the night before. "I heard Bandit making a racket and went down to see what was going on." Sanders had left.

Worried now, Matthias asked Ronya if she'd seen her.

"Not since Wednesday morning when she had breakfast. Neither has Amos. He said he knocked, and she said she'd let him know when she was ready to talk about the mine. I sent Ina Bea over to check on her. We've been feeding Bandit. I don't know what she's been eating. Maybe she's working on another issue of the *Voice.*"

Last time Matthias had seen Kathryn, she'd been running along the boardwalk as though the devil was after her. He assumed she had been shaken by the earthquake. Now, he wondered what else might have happened that day. Unable to sleep, Matthias decided if Kathryn didn't show up at church, he'd be knocking on her door again, and if she didn't open it, he'd kick it down.

Matthias dressed early and in his finest. The Closed sign hung in her window. It had been there since Wednesday afternoon. It was another hour and a half before church started. Unable to wait, he put on his hat, crossed the street, and rapped on the door. "Kathryn!" No answer. When he tried the door, it opened. His heart dropped like a barometer warning of a storm when he found the house empty.

Closing the door, he strode up the hill, praying she was at the church. He felt a surge of relief and then a quickening pulse when he saw her sitting inside the sanctuary. *Thank You, Jesus.* She wasn't in her usual place, but near the back, on the right side next to one of the tall windows. Right where he'd sat for the last few services. Her head was bowed, her eyes closed. Was she praying or thinking? As he stood looking at her, a beam of sunlight came through the window, and shone on her. Matthias felt a punch of emotion. If he hadn't found her sitting in the church, he would have gone searching for her.

Letting his breath out slowly, he moved into the pew and sat next to her. Kathryn's body gave a slight flinch. She didn't look up, but her eyes opened. "You're early this morning, Mr. Beck."

"Yes, I am, Miss Walsh. I hope I'm not interrupting your prayer."

"I've been here a while."

Reverend Thacker appeared at the end of the pew. "Good morning, Mr. Beck. You're both early this morning." Matthias greeted him. Sally came down the aisle carrying a vase filled with bright-yellow daffodils. She paused and greeted them, faint speculation in her expression as she walked on. She set the flower arrangement on the altar. Reverend Thacker shuffled through notes at the pulpit, then spoke to her in a low voice, and they went out through the side door to his chamber.

Kathryn sat silent. However long it took for her to speak, Matthias would wait. Minutes passed and he found himself praying that whatever troubled her so deeply, God would give her clear direction. She released a long sigh and looked up at him, her green eyes clear as a mountain meadow after a rain. "I'm glad you're here, Matthias."

Was she beginning to realize they belonged together? Doubtful. But she trusted him. That was a big step in the right direction. "What have you been up to for the last three days? Your friends have been worried about you. I've been worried about you."

She winced. "I'm sorry. I was . . ." She shrugged. "I've been writing. Thinking. Making decisions."

He gave her a wry grin. "Uh-oh."

She laughed softly. "Yes. Well. I know what to do with the mine." She spoke with confidence.

"Sell?"

"No." She looked at him again, an impish smile taunting him. "Just an idea I have. An experiment, if you will."

He felt immediate misgivings. "Do you care to elaborate?"

"Not yet. Can I meet with you and discuss renting the town hall?"

She was full of surprises. He hoped that wasn't the only reason she had sat where he normally did. "Anytime, your ladyship. My office or yours?"

"Yours. Does tomorrow morning, ten o'clock, fit your schedule?"

So formal. So businesslike. No matter what was on his schedule, he'd make time for her. "Yes."

Others were coming into the sanctuary. Kathryn seemed less at ease. She looked over her shoulder and then smiled a warm greeting. Glancing back, Matthias saw Fiona Hawthorne, Monique Beaulieu, and three others slip into the last pew on the left, closest to the door. Matthias felt Kathryn tense. She turned away, eyes straight forward.

Morgan Sanders came down the aisle. Matthias knew he was looking for Kathryn when the man glanced at the empty pew across from his usual seat, then looked around. His expression darkened when he saw where she was sitting. Kathryn didn't move. She didn't breathe. Matthias felt her body trembling. He met Sanders's eyes, a hot surge of bloodlust inside him. Rather than step into the pew and sit, Sanders strode back up the aisle, ordered someone to get out of his way, and left the church. Matthias heard Kathryn's soft exhalation. She lowered her head, but not before Matthias saw how all the color had drained from her face.

What had Sanders done to her? He started to rise, intending to go after Sanders and find out, when Kathryn put her hand on his arm. Controlling his anger, he took her hand and found it cold and shaking. "Does he warrant a bullet?" His voice came out frigid and gruff. She didn't pretend to misunderstand.

"No. He's less a fool than I've been." She cast him a smile. "Though I may buy a gun."

Matthias knew she meant it to lighten the tension, but his heart hammered. "Do you want to move back into the hotel? I guarantee your safety."

Her mood lightened. "Oh, no. I don't think that would be a good idea."

Matthias gave her a wounded look. "I thought you were beginning to trust me, your ladyship."

Kathryn regarded him gravely. "I trust you more than any man in this town, Matthias." She held his gaze for a few seconds, then slipped her hand from his and looked at Reverend Thacker, who was welcoming everyone to the service.

21

MATTHIAS WAS STANDING ON THE BOARDWALK in front of his hotel, talking to Henry, when Kathryn came outside, stunning in Boston finery. Half a dozen men stood like poleaxed bulls staring at her, including him. Was her attire a sign of war or a softening of her heart? The dog came with her. Matthias counted himself lucky he had made friends with the animal.

Kathryn came up the steps and greeted both him and Henry. Matthias nodded to Bandit. "I see you've brought your bodyguard with you."

"Go on now." She waved the dog away, then asked Matthias if he was ready to talk business. He escorted her into the hotel. Her companion stuck to her like a burr. "Shoo, Bandit." She frowned at him, but the animal remained at her side. Bandit had been left in the house when Kathryn was picked up by Morgan Sanders's driver. A pity the dog hadn't followed. Morgan wouldn't have let him, but that animal would have started a ruckus if he sensed any threat to his mistress.

Kathryn tried again. "Go outside, Bandit." The dog flopped down, put his head on his paws, and looked up at her. Matthias laughed.

Kathryn gave him a pained look. "I'm so sorry. He doesn't mind very well."

"He knows where he wants to be." She took the seat he offered, a table between them with coffee service just delivered. Pouring, he asked if she wanted cream or sugar. She declined both. He handed the cup and saucer to her, then poured black for himself as well. Her rigid posture told him she was nervous. "You mentioned wanting to use the town hall."

"Yes. For a meeting."

He raised his brows, waiting for her to elaborate. She sipped her coffee and ignored the silent probing. Setting the cup back in the saucer, she met his gaze. "As soon as I know I've secured the hall, I'll put an announcement in the *Voice*."

Maybe she didn't trust him as much as he thought she did. Curiosity roused, he tried again. "You're not going to give me a hint?"

She considered before answering. "It's about the mine."

"I assumed that much." He could see her debating whether to tell him anything more.

"I want to present a new business venture to the out-of-work miners from the Jackrabbit Mine." She set her cup and saucer on the table. "The town hall might not be big enough. The whole town will probably want to come just to see me make a fool of myself. Perhaps I should ask Carl Rudger if I could hold the meeting at his lumberyard."

Carl Rudger was a bachelor and would be only too happy to do anything to please Kathryn, which she undoubtedly knew. "You could, but he'd have to shut down his business to accommodate you. Unless you had a nighttime meeting, which wouldn't be wise."

"Oh. I hadn't thought of that." She frowned. "I don't want to cost him money. Should I go before the town council and plead my case?"

"You're not on trial." What irony that Kathryn thought she'd have to plead to use the town hall she had inspired. The lady didn't expect any favors. Even so, the council would want to charge a rental fee. And it would be too much for her to afford.

"You can have your meeting at the hall, Kate. Gratis. If any questions are raised, tell them to come to me."

Kathryn laughed softly. "Oh, I'm certain there will be questions." She shrugged. "And probably a lot of laughter as well."

Laughter? He'd like to spare her public ridicule. "What's your idea, Kathryn?"

She gave him an impish smile. "Come to the meeting and you'll hear all about it."

Thanking him, she rose. He'd never seen her look so relaxed and hopeful. "I considered discussing it with you, Matthias, but I thought you might try to talk me out of it."

That gave him pause. "Should I?" They walked down the hall side by side.

"It's best you hear what I hope to do with the mine at the same time everyone else does."

Matthias planned to get there early, knowing there would be a crowd.

Of course, both Amos and Scribe tried to talk her out of her plans for the mine. They started with gentle advice, as though talking to a child, but soon fell into heated argument. Amos said it was folly. Scribe said worse. They both thought she was inviting disaster.

"You might as well sell to Sanders!" Scribe growled.

The two took turns telling her that she was just a woman who knew nothing about mining or any business, for that matter, both apparently forgetting she ran the *Voice*. Amos said she should leave him to organize and do the hiring. Kathryn remained silent and let them yammer, knowing she would face all these same arguments and insults at the meeting. She might as well be prepared for the assault.

Scribe finally noticed her silence. "Aren't you going to say anything?"

"Yes." She stood. "Thank you both for your strong opinions. The fact remains: the mine belongs to me and I can do with it whatever I see fit." Both Amos and Scribe opened their mouths once again, but she raised her hand. "I've listened to your opinions for the last hour. Now, give me the courtesy of allowing me to finish one sentence without interruption." Perhaps some of her anger had seeped through, for they stood silent.

"I love you like a younger brother, Scribe, and I have great respect for you, Amos. But I have made my decision." Her plan did sound a bit mad the way they presented it, but she believed it could do great good and be highly successful. They just had no faith in her. Or in the men, for that matter.

"You can stand beside me or you can walk away. I will respect whatever decision you make." She told them when and where the meeting would take place, walked to the door, and opened it. "Good day, gentlemen."

They walked out the door as though a judge had just given them a twenty-year sentence to hard time in a desert jail.

The next issue of the *Voice* had several well-written articles, including **COBBLER HAS SHOE IN FOR CITY POST** and her popular column. Matthias scanned Bachelor Arts. This week's focus was on the proper manners for courting a lady. But it was the quarter-page announcement that caught Matthias's full attention: . . . *a meeting at town hall Thursday next at 2 p.m. regarding a new and unusual opportunity for men experienced in mine operations . . .* She might as well have waved a red blanket in front of the town bull, Morgan Sanders.

Men started shooting questions at Matthias. "What does she mean by *unusual*?"

Matthias wished he knew. "Your guess is as good as mine."

"She didn't tell you?"

"No, she didn't tell me."

"You're gonna marry that gal, ain't ya? Working your tail off to win her, ain't ya? Ya oughta know sumthin' about what she's thinkin'."

Matthias gave a bleak laugh. "I've yet to figure out the workings of that female mind."

Wiley Baer bellied up to the bar. "He ain't interested in her mind, idjit." He winked at Matthias. "She's the best-lookin' woman this side of the Rockies."

"With the tongue of a wasp!" someone shouted from the back.

"And sticking her nose into everyone's business," Herr grumbled.

"Because Stu Bickerson doesn't have the guts to print the truth!" a new voice called from the back. Scribe.

"What does she want miners for, anyway?"

Wiley watched Brady fill his shot glass a second time. "City had that old claim. Could be she'll end up with somethin' more than a Washington handpress."

The men all started talking at once. Wiley downed his whiskey and meandered his way through the crowd, raising his hand in a farewell salute as he went through the swinging doors. Matthias left the jabbering men and followed him outside. "You know something about all this, Wiley?"

"Maybe. Maybe not."

Axel came along the boardwalk. "What's going on?" He jerked his chin toward the rowdy men in Brady's Saloon.

"Speculating about Kathryn's town hall meeting."

"Should be interesting."

Interesting was a lukewarm way of describing what would probably turn into a volcanic eruption.

Kathryn waited in the front office, wondering if Amos and Scribe would show up. She hadn't talked with them since their heated exchange.

Checking her watch, Kathryn saw the time had come. She felt a wave of despair. Perhaps she had put too much hope in her friends.

Nervous, she adjusted her hat one last time and opened the door. Amos and Scribe stood outside, bathed, combed, and neatly dressed in their best. "Thank God," Kathryn murmured under her breath.

Scribe's mouth fell open as he looked her up and down.

Amos blinked, blushed, and stammered. "M-miss Walsh . . . you look beautiful."

"A woman's armor." Kathryn smiled. "May I assume you have come to accompany me to the meeting?"

"Yes." Amos spoke simply, tiny beads of perspiration on his brow. Was he that worried about what might happen?

Scribe winced. "I've looked the place over and we can get you out the back door if things go badly."

Comforting words. She lifted her chin in a show of courage she was far from feeling. "Shall we go, gentlemen?"

When Kathryn saw the crowd at the town hall, her heart went into a panic rhythm. She wanted to flee. Perhaps the hall hadn't been opened yet, and that's why so many men stood outside. Men turned when she came down the boardwalk. They stared and then made room for her. Some removed hats and gave a respectful nod. As she came closer, she saw the doors were wide-open, the hall packed tighter than the nights of a recent traveling troupe's performances. The room stank of whiskey and men's sweat. Every chair occupied, men filled the aisle and stood along the walls.

Kathryn gulped and strove to calm the wild horses galloping in her chest as she made her way down the central aisle, Amos ahead of her, Scribe behind. Chin up, shoulders back, she kept her eyes straight ahead, hearing the murmurs of the men. Amos opened the gate at the front and she went through, stepping up to the dais and taking her place behind the table where a judge would sit, if one ever happened to get lost and end up in Calvada.

Laying out the forms she had prepared, Kathryn tented her fingers on the table to keep her hands from shaking. She took in a deep breath and exhaled slowly, then looked out at the crowd of men staring at her. Her mouth went dry. The rumble of voices died down as she waited for silence, praying they couldn't see how she trembled, praying her voice wouldn't crack. Amos stood to her right, Scribe to her left, more sentinels than partners. Scanning the crowd, she recognized many of the men she had seen around town, mostly going in or out of saloons, or hanging around outside the fandango hall next door to her little house. She didn't realize she was looking for one specific man until she spotted Matthias standing far back near the door. He smiled slightly and gave a nod. For some reason she didn't want to analyze, his presence steadied her.

"Gentlemen, thank you for coming today. I am going to present a business plan for my uncle's mine. I ask that you withhold any comments or questions until I have finished speaking." She paused, waiting for the grumble of assent. They all stilled and stared at her.

"City Walsh had a mine, which, for some reason, he worked only enough to keep the claim active. I took samples from that mine and had them examined in Sacramento, where I gave them to Hollis, Pruitt, and Stearns Assayers . . ."

Men's voices rumbled low in excitement.

Kathryn waited until they quieted. "Mr. Stearns hand-delivered the report in the hope of examining the mine himself, which he has done. He has confirmed copper, silver, and a visible vein of gold . . ."

The rumbling grew louder, some talking excitedly among themselves. Others shushed those muttering and whispering. Some called out questions. Was she going to sell to Sanders? Was Stearns buying? Was he going to head up the mining operation? How many men did Stearns need? She stood silent, hands loosely folded, waiting.

A piercing whistle silenced everyone. "Let the lady speak!" Matthias spoke from the back.

"Thank you, Mayor Beck." Kathryn went on. "In answer to a few of your questions, gentlemen, I assure you I am not selling. I intend to begin operations as soon as possible. Mr. Stearns has agreed to loan me seed money to start, money we will pay back as soon as possible so the mine will be free and clear of any encumbrances."

"Who's *we*?" someone shouted from the back. "You and Stearns?"

"Shuddup!" several hollered at him.

When it was quiet again, Kathryn continued. "I have a plan whereby those who work the mine will share in the profits. Those who agree to my proposal will enter into a contract with me. I need men who are honest, willing to work hard and help me build a mining operation, perhaps those who now find themselves out of work since the closure of the Jackrabbit Mine. The men must be willing to take the same risks I am in making City Walsh's mine a profitable venture."

Kathryn spotted Wiley sitting near the front. She met his gaze, and he lowered his head. When he started to slip from the seat and make his way out of the hall, she spoke impulsively. "Wiley Baer, I'd like you to be the first to sign up." He stopped and looked back at her in surprise.

"Why Wiley?"

"Wiley Baer has been mining since '49 and knows more about what's in these mountains than most in this room. He and City Walsh came west on the same wagon train. If not for Wiley, my uncle wouldn't have made it to California. My uncle owed Wiley Baer his life."

Head a little higher, Wiley sat down. She smiled in thanks.

"How many men do you need?" someone shouted.

"Twenty, to start. And they will have to be willing to work for a woman."

Half the men left, talking loudly, some laughing, some grumbling about scolds who knew everything about spending gold on fancy clothes and hats, but nothing about mining it. Kathryn didn't dare look at Matthias, imagining his disdain, or worse, amusement. She saw Sanders's carriage driver pushing through the men to the door, undoubtedly on his way to report everything she had said to Morgan. It didn't matter. Everyone would know soon enough, for she had already written out her plan in detail and intended to publish it in the next issue of the *Voice*.

As the crowd thinned, men from outside pressed in, asking questions, desperate enough for work to listen to her answers. Everything Amos and Scribe had said a few days ago was being said again.

"Why should we believe you'd keep the contract?"

"I give you my word of honor."

One man gave a harsh laugh. "What honor? You ain't kept your word!"

Kathryn stiffened. What on earth was the man talking about? And then she knew. Her gaze shifted to Matthias and quickly away. Surely *that* subject wasn't about to be aired in public!

"You ain't married Beck."

"God help him if she does!" someone else shouted, and laughter followed.

Kathryn's face flamed. What could she say? "I . . . He . . . We . . ."

"He's done your dang list, ain't he?"

Men laughed raucously. "You say you can keep your word? Then marry Beck!" It became a chant. "Marry Beck! Marry Beck!"

Kathryn spotted Axel Borgeson, grim-faced and ready for a fight, making his way through the crowd. Horrified, she realized she might unwittingly become the cause of a brawl. Scribe had hold of her arm and was telling her they had to get out by the back door. She pulled free.

A second piercing whistle caught everyone's attention. Matthias Beck left his post at the back and headed toward her. Men moved back like he was Moses parting the Red Sea and Kathryn was the Promised Land.

Kathryn gulped when he came through the gate and turned to the men, standing like a shield in front of her. "Miss Walsh is a woman of her word." When he glanced back at her, Kathryn felt the full impact of that glinting look of devilish amusement. "When I've completed my agreed-upon obligations, she will fulfill hers."

Kathryn didn't dare argue the point now.

"Those who are interested in Miss Walsh's proposal should stay. The rest of you gentlemen are dismissed."

Axel joined in, reiterating those instructions, waving several grumblers out of the hall.

The room felt empty with the few remaining men. Only eleven had stayed, far fewer than she had hoped.

Matthias turned and spoke in a quiet voice the others couldn't hear. "Twenty men, you said? Sorry, Kathryn; I think you're looking at your crew." His enigmatic expression gave her no hint of his opinion of her experiment. He went back through the gate. "Good luck, gentlemen." She watched him walk out the door.

Kathryn explained her plan further. When she finished, she stepped down from the dais, came through the gate, and handed each man a sheet to fill out. "If you can't read or write, Amos and Scribe will help you." She knew there would be men too proud to admit to illiteracy. It took some time, but she collected eleven papers before the men began filing out with Amos and Scribe. She knew Scribe was headed for Brady's, where he still worked part-time, the others following to order a drink or two and talk more with Amos.

Another man stood in the shadows against the back wall. He came forward slowly. Kathryn felt a jolt of recognition when he took off his hat. She had been looking for him for months, finally assuming he had left town.

"Can you use one more?" The tone was respectful, the voice devoid of hope, not filled with hatred as it had been when she heard him plotting murder under the bridge. She could see in his eyes that he knew she recognized him. Shifting, he let out his breath. "I thought you might remember me."

Should she lie to protect herself? Fear was a terrible master, and she would not be a slave to it. "You're a hard man to forget. I'm not sorry things didn't work out as you planned." Strange that she felt an inexplicable calm now that she was face-to-face with him and looking into his hazel eyes. He didn't look like a monster.

His mouth tipped. "You kept me from doing something that would've had me hanging from the end of a rope." He turned the hat brim in his hands.

Would he confess to more? "Did you throw a brick through my window?"

"Yes, ma'am. I thought about putting a torch to your house, too, but didn't because I knew the whole town would catch on fire." Chilled, Kathryn could only stare at him. The confession cost him. She could see that. He sighed and went further, as though he wanted to purge himself of guilt. "Good, too, that you warned McNabb. He was my friend. Anger does evil work on a man. I'm not proud of what I planned or what I did. Men say and do stupid things when they're pushed too far. You didn't do the pushing, but you got the brunt of the wrath stored up against the man who did."

Morgan Sanders.

The man took firm hold of his hat as though about to put it back on. "You've no reason to trust me, Miss Walsh, and I don't blame you that you don't. But I thought I'd ante up and try to get in the game. Good day to you, ma'am." Turning away, he put on his hat and headed for the door.

A war went on inside her, and the quiet whisper won. "Just a minute, please." She took a few steps toward him, the eleven papers in her hand. "What's your name?"

His eyes flickered. "And if I tell you?"

Did he think she meant to report him to Axel Borgeson? What could the sheriff do? "No crime was committed."

"The brick."

"Forgiven.

"Wyn Reese."

"Are you still working for Morgan Sanders, Mr. Reese?"

"I'm one of his foremen."

Had Wyn set his mind to kill Sanders, he could have done so by now. "And now you want to work for a woman?"

"No, ma'am. I want to work for *you*. You were smart enough to get City's newspaper up and running again. That was no easy task, and you're close to putting Bickerson out of business, if you didn't know. Even City couldn't manage that. Maybe you'll surprise everyone with your ideas of how to run a mine." He gave a bleak laugh. "I know how Sanders runs his. I've been part of keeping things under control, and I've lost the stomach for it. His men aren't much better off than slaves."

"And you?"

"Not much better than they are, though I'm not in debt." He hesitated. "I know you don't trust me. But if you give me a chance, I'd like to go to work for an operation that takes care of its own rather than putting all the profit in one man's pocket."

"Can you tell me a little more about yourself?"

"Parents died when I was a boy. I know you're a Christian lady, Miss Walsh. And I'll tell you, faith left me a long time ago. My granny took me to church, and I believed until I was old enough to go north to try to make something of myself. I worked in the factories and then came west and ended up in the mines." He shook his head. "Hard to believe there's a God who cares when you work for a devil in the pit of hell."

Kathryn understood pain and disillusionment. She also knew even the smallest seed could grow into a mighty tree. "We had eleven men, Mr. Reese." She held out her hand. "Now we have twelve."

"The Twelve" Kathryn hired went straight to work, putting their combined experience and expertise into practice. Matthias had been surprised and worried when she took on Morgan Sanders's head foreman, Wyn Reese, a man tough enough to kill a cougar with his own teeth. When Sanders found himself short one foreman and saw others not indebted to him casting envious glances at the profit-sharing venture, he raised wages. The trickle of men leaving Sanders's mining operation continued, slowing progress in his mine, while Kathryn had men lined up and wanting to join. Stearns's prophetic assertions were proving true; City Walsh's mine was a bonanza. Everything Reese and the other miners knew went into their work, and the harder they worked, the more money they made.

Stu Bickerson had attended the town meeting and cornered her on her way out. She had named the mine Civitas, but Bickerson, having no knowledge of Latin, spelled the word phonetically in his headline the next day: **WALSH OPENSE KEEWEETOSS MINE**. Matthias laughed when he read it.

Kathryn quickly wrote an editorial on the Civitas mining community and her profit-sharing vision to lift living standards of miners who would bring prosperity to Calvada. It didn't matter how many times she printed Civitas, Keeweetoss stuck. In the next issue of the *Clarion*, Bickerson claimed the daughter of the great warrior Chief Keeweetoss sacrificed her life by jumping off a cliff into white water, thus ending the war between neighboring tribes.

Sunday was the one day a week when Matthias knew he would see Kathryn. She had made one firm rule at the mine: *Sunday is a day of rest*. Not everyone shared her faith, only a few following her example and attending church, but most appreciated the day off.

The young lady certainly had a mind of her own, and a good one at that. No one in town had been more surprised than he when her ladyship put on a button-down shirt, denim pants, and boots so she could go down into the mine and see for herself what was going on. Apparently, she was interested in every job, asking the miners a hundred questions, and spending hours in Amos Stearns's company. Matthias had overheard them talking at Ronya's Café. How the man could drone on and on about processing copper and silver! Rocks were his bailiwick, and it irritated Matthias to watch Kathryn soak in every word.

She might not know much about mining, but she had keen business sense. She ordered extra safety precautions, including stronger beams for tunnel support. She ordered a cold room dug and ice brought down so the miners could take cooling breaks from the intense heat. She advertised in San Francisco and Sacramento papers for a much-needed doctor. When Marcus Blackstone, MD, arrived, she made an agreement with him to attend to any needs of the mine employees and their families. All medical expenses were paid out of the Calvada Keeweetoss Mine Company.

The men grumbled that such extravagances would eat into their profits. Why should women who weren't working receive any benefits from the men who did? Kathryn answered with an impassioned editorial on the rights a woman lost when marrying.

Some men expected Kathryn to provide housing. She put it in print that she believed it was up to the individual miners to decide how to spend their share of the money. She had no intention of becoming a landlord or company store owner. She listed merchants in Calvada who could be trusted to have fair prices and fair credit should it be needed. Matthias was gratified to see Walker's General Store at the top of the list. Most surprising to the male majority in Calvada: Kathryn kept her word about shared profits.

Kathryn Walsh was working from dawn to dark to turn the town right side up and into a thriving community. Matthias felt a similar drive. Falling in love with her had shaken and then inspired him. Now, he found himself admiring and respecting her abilities. He'd never met anyone with such a driving passion to do what she believed to be right. He had been half-joking when he forced her to make a list. Now that he was near the end of fulfilling it, he felt cornered by it. He didn't want to win the bet. He wanted to win Kathryn Walsh's heart.

She'd given him hope when she sat by him in church and allowed him to take her hand, for that one Sunday morning. Whatever had happened between her and Morgan Sanders, she'd welcomed his protection. It was a move in the right direction.

Patience was proving to be a lengthy season fraught with frustration. He kept an eye on the lady, but his responsibilities mounted. The more Matthias worked, the more he saw other things that needed to be done to make the town safe and prosperous. God willing, he would be able to accomplish more than half a dozen projects before his term as mayor was up. Then he'd have to decide whether to move to Sacramento or stay in Calvada. Everything depended on the one project he had yet to complete.

Matthias intended to warm up Kathryn's cold feet.

22

KATHRYN GAVE THANKS when she awakened and remembered it was Sunday morning. It had been a long, hard week of unending work between putting out an issue of the *Voice* and staying informed as to what was happening at the Keeweetoss Mine. Chump Street was deserted this early in the morning, summer heat rolling in. Last night, the fandango hall had been packed with merrymakers until well past midnight, but Kathryn had become so accustomed to the noise, she slept through the music, then awakened to the silence.

She walked past Ronya's Café, where the door stood open, a few patrons sitting by the windows, having breakfast. Bandit darted to the back door, and Ina Bea set out a pan of leftovers for him. Another block up and Kathryn stopped in pleased surprise. The new schoolhouse was finished and quite charming with red walls and white trim, complete with belfry and white picket fence around the yard, the gate now closed and latched.

"I thought you'd come into Ronya's for breakfast, and we'd walk up here together."

Her heart did a fillip at the sound of Matthias's voice. He looked handsome in his Sunday best. "I fix my own breakfast most mornings."

"You can cook?" He raised his brows.

She laughed. "Well enough to survive."

Matthias nodded toward the schoolhouse. "So? What do you think, your ladyship? Does it meet your approval?"

"It's marvelous! You're to be congratulated, Mayor Beck. It was only framed last Sunday. How did you manage to get it all done this week?"

"Motivation." His smile and the look in his eyes sent her pulse racing. He chuckled. "And I had a good crew. The bell is on order. Henry will bring it up when it arrives in Sacramento."

"And bring Charlotte with him, I hope."

"I'm sure he will."

"We should have a grand opening!" She admired the building again. "What about a teacher?"

"Already hired Brian Hubbard to start in the fall. He was a schoolmaster in Connecticut before he got gold fever. He's had enough of mining." Matthias opened the gate. "Want to take a look inside?"

"Yes! Please." When the gate clicked shut behind her and Matthias fell into step with her, she felt warmth stirring. Anticipation that had nothing to do with the schoolhouse. Scolding herself for romantic nonsense, she went up the steps. He opened the front door for her.

Other than a potbellied stove, the room was empty.

"Rudger has several men building desks." Matthias walked into the center of the room and faced her. "They'll be finished before school opens. A large chalkboard will be mounted up front by end of the week; smaller slates will be provided. Primers and textbooks are coming from San Francisco."

His attention on her was so intent, Kathryn found it difficult to breathe normally. She walked around the room, imagining the school full of lively children eager to learn. Silent and relaxed, Matthias watched her, a faint smile curving his mouth. Ignoring the man was impossible! "It's wonderful, Matthias. You're exactly the mayor Calvada needed."

"Something worrying you, Kathryn?" His tone was provocative.

Many things bothered her, not the least of which was this man who could get under her skin so easily. One look made her heart pound. The memory of one kiss kept her sleepless, her body restless for more. He knew very well that wretched list wasn't a formal contract, even if he had put Stu Bickerson up to announcing their supposed engagement. She tipped her chin. "Why would I be worried?"

"Why, indeed?"

She remembered the town meeting and men shouting about women who couldn't keep their word. They were all going to expect her to marry Matthias now that he'd completed everything on the list Stu Bickerson had printed. She fumbled her watch fob, looking at the time. "Church will be starting soon."

"We're going to have to talk about it sometime, Kathryn." Matthias closed the door behind them. "You do know everyone in town is going to be watching us now, waiting to see if you'll keep your word."

Kathryn stopped and faced him. "About that . . ."

"I have no intention of pressing you, Kate, but that doesn't mean Calvadans don't have certain expectations about what happens next. We should talk about it. After all, your reputation is at stake." He gave a casual shrug. "I could tell Gus Blather that all I feel for you now is brotherly affection."

Kathryn was unnerved by how much that statement hurt. Brotherly affection? She looked away. "Well, thank you for that. It would solve the problem." She wished she only had sisterly feelings for him.

Several parishioners passed by, glancing at them with far too much interest. Matthias put his hand lightly at her elbow. She had been the one telling everyone she had no intention of marrying Matthias Beck—or anyone, for that matter. And she meant it. Even if, on occasion, she had wondered what it would be like to be Matthias's wife. His kisses had left her breathless, her heart racing, her body hot and trembling. He had only to glance at her, as he was doing now, to stir her emotions into a confused mess.

Good grief! No wonder her mother had warned her against passion. Logic seemed to fly right out of her head where this man was concerned.

"I have a buggy reserved and Ronya has made us a picnic lunch. We'll talk about all this later this afternoon."

A flush of excited pleasure came at the idea of spending a sunny Sunday afternoon with him, before common sense stepped in. Alone with Matthias? On a picnic? One kiss could be her Waterloo! She was about to make an excuse when someone called his name. A flicker of irritation crossed his face. "You should go," Kathryn told him, before stepping around him and moving through the gathering congregants. She went up the steps and into the church. She didn't breathe easily until she was seated.

"Mind if I sit with you again, Miss Walsh?" Wyn Reese stood hat in hand at the end of the row. She smiled a welcome. Other Keeweetoss miners came in, joining them until the row was filled. She felt bolstered and protected by their presence. When Matthias entered, people looked at him and then back at her.

Reverend Thacker moved to the middle of the dais, led the opening hymn as Sally played the piano, and dove into his sermon. Kathryn tried to concentrate, but her mind kept circling back to Matthias. They did need to talk over the situation, but how many tongues would wag if they saw her going off in a buggy with him? And why should she care if gossip did follow? No matter what she did, it always raised a ruckus!

Her head ached as she went back and forth. She'd already made up her mind to keep a distance from the man, hadn't she? She rubbed her temple. Reese gave her a questioning look. Folding her hands in her lap, she lifted her head. What on earth was Reverend Thacker rambling on about? She had no idea.

When services ended, Kathryn joined the ladies serving refreshments. There were still some who spoke to her. Her eyes kept drifting to Matthias, deep in conversation with Carl Rudger, Amos, and Wyn. Axel and Ina Bea stood close together talking. A few children ran among the parishioners while their parents chatted with new and old friends. The schoolhouse would soon be in operation and filled with boys and girls.

Matthias broke away from the conversation and headed her way. She felt her pulse increase with his proximity. She lifted a plate of cookies like a shield between them. He declined. "Save your appetite for our picnic. I'll come for you at two." Stepping back, he made room for two children pressing through for a molasses treat. Heart hammering, she watched him walk back to the men and rejoin the conversation.

One of Axel's deputies came up the hill. He took Axel aside. Whatever it was about, both men looked grim. The deputy left. People had already begun dispersing. Women collected empty plates, folded tablecloths.

Axel approached Kathryn. "I'm walking Ina Bea to Ronya's. Walk with us." It sounded more a command than request. Her first thought was that someone had vandalized the newspaper office again. Without another thought, she looked for Matthias.

Matthias had seen Axel and the deputy talking. Something was wrong. But why had Axel headed straight for Kathryn? When she looked around, he knew she was looking for him. She and Axel rejoined Ina Bea and headed down the hill. Matthias excused himself from a conversation. It didn't take long for him to catch up. Axel's warning glance told him not to ask any questions. He took Ina Bea's hand and said something to her before leaving her at Ronya's door.

Kathryn glanced across at her house. "Everything seems to be all right." When Axel indicated she was to stay with him, she seemed perplexed. "What's happened? Where are we going?"

"Morgan Sanders's house."

She stopped. "Why do I need to come along?"

Axel faced her, expression enigmatic. "I'll have some questions to ask you when we get there."

Kathryn paled and turned to Matthias as if he might know. "What's this all about, Axel?"

"Let's go, Miss Walsh." Axel gave Matthias a quelling look. Borgeson never did anything without good reason.

Sanders's front door was wide-open, one of the deputies

standing outside. Kathryn hung back, her face wan. "I don't want to go in that house, Axel."

"Why not?"

"I don't want to explain. I can't."

"You've been inside before."

Matthias shot a look at Kathryn and saw it was true.

"Once."

"Only once?" Axel's face showed nothing. "Are you sure about that?"

"If she said once, it was once!" Matthias snarled.

Kathryn looked sick. "What are you implying?"

Axel lifted his hand, and she followed the silent command. She hesitated again in the entry hall, clearly upset, then followed Axel into the parlor. She hadn't gone more than a few feet when she drew in a shocked breath. Morgan Sanders lay on the floor near a settee, his face unrecognizable, blood staining the carpet.

Matthias caught Kathryn up in his arms as she crumpled. Furious, he glared at Axel. "What were you thinking?"

"Witnesses said a woman who looked like Kathryn was seen running from the house last night."

"You think she murdered him?" If his hands had been free, he would have grabbed Axel and throttled him.

"Easy, friend. I needed to see her face when she looked at Sanders's body. I don't think she had anything to do with it."

"You think?" Matthias growled and carried her out of the house. She was coming around before he reached the bottom step.

"Put me down, Matthias." She struggled, weakly at first, then desperately. "Put me down! Please!" When he did, Kathryn took one faltering step and bent over the low boxwood hedge. Standing behind her, Matthias slipped a supportive arm around her waist as she retched. "I'm sorry you saw that," Matthias whispered, cupping her forehead. She was clammy from shock.

Kathryn leaned back against him, trembling violently. "Why did Axel make me see that?" She uttered a gasping sob. Matthias told her.

She turned, her face ashen. "He thinks I did it?" Her laugh verged on hysteria. "Quite a story for the *Clarion*. I can see Stu's headline. 'Editor Suspected of Murder.'" She put the back of her hand against her mouth, her eyes filling with tears. "Morgan wasn't a very nice man, but I wouldn't wish a violent death on anyone." Matthias could see the jumble of emotions, her mind whirring. "Is that how Scribe found my uncle?" She sounded horrified.

Matthias wasn't going to answer that question. And it wasn't time for him to start asking his own.

"Let's get you out of here, Kate." Word spread fast in Calvada, and it wouldn't be long before a crowd showed up. When he took her hand, it was cold, and she didn't pull away.

Seeing Sanders lying there had made him think of City Walsh. His murder had shocked the town. Men had grieved City's loss. Far too many would see Morgan Sanders's death as cause for celebration.

Word spread quickly through Calvada that Morgan Sanders had been brutally murdered. Some men did celebrate, especially those who could barely afford to pay rent on his shacks and had tabs at the company store they'd never be able to pay off. But any hope of gain died when signs were posted that the mine was closed. On Reese's recommendation, Kathryn and Amos hired a few of Sanders's miners, but most of the unemployed packed up and left town before new management could arrive, if it ever did. Matthias couldn't help but wonder if the murderer was among those who left.

One of Axel's deputies collected all of Sanders's files. No will turned up in the initial search, nor any information linking Sanders to any relatives who would benefit from his considerable assets. It would take months to read through all the papers and documents. In the meantime, Axel questioned the carriage driver and the servant whose daughter had done the housekeeping and delivered laundry to Jian Lin Gong.

Matthias only heard rumors about Axel's inquiries over the first two days. He stayed clear of the mess until he saw the sheriff sitting at a table in Brady's bar, having a beer after doing his rounds. Matthias joined him. "How's the investigation going?"

"Sanders had a lot of enemies." He scoffed. "The deeper I dig, the more I wonder why I'm working so hard to solve his murder."

"It takes a hard man to run a mine."

Axel gave him a wry look. "The lady seems to be doing very well without brute force and debt bondage." He gave a slight laugh. "But then that's probably because half the men in town are in love with her."

Matthias didn't find that funny. "Men hated Sanders, but I don't know how many would go so far as to murder him in cold blood."

"Not cold blood, and I think it was a woman." He sipped his beer. "The killer didn't stop with a blow to the head."

Matthias hadn't noticed; his concern had been fixed on Kathryn. "I did hear you talked to Monique Beaulieu. Wondered about that."

"It was pretty well-known that she was Sanders's mistress. He wanted the best, and she is the most beautiful soiled dove in town. Whenever he sent the carriage, she got in it. She said things cooled after Kathryn arrived."

Matthias leaned forward. "Now, wait a minute!" He didn't want any misconceptions about Kathryn's strong moral fiber.

"You hold on and hear what I'm saying. Monique admitted she strayed a few times. A girl in her profession has to look out for herself. She was with Wyn Reese the night Sanders was killed. Reese confirmed it. He said she was still in bed when he left for the Keeweetoss at six in the morning."

Matthias wondered where this conversation was going. Axel usually kept information like this to himself, but he'd dropped Kathryn's name and made an insinuation Matthias couldn't let pass.

Axel sipped and kept talking. "Monique said Sanders sent for her four to five times a week until Kathryn arrived. Then only once a week. She said he was a man with a healthy appetite, and she assumed he was finding his needs met elsewhere."

"You know her." Matthias glared at him. "Nothing was going on between Sanders and Kathryn."

Axel finished his beer and fixed Matthias with a steely gaze. "Sanders made no secret of his interest in Kathryn. Two powerful men in town wanting the same woman. Could be something there."

Matthias leaned back and gave a low laugh. "You think *I* killed him."

"I did wonder, but there are a lot of people on my list of suspects. I eliminated you straightaway. You were in a meeting the night Sanders was killed. I talked to members of your civic improvements committee, and they all confirmed you were there from start to finish."

"Thanks for your vote of confidence, Sheriff."

"Asking questions is my job, Matt." Axel raised his empty

mug and Brady sent a helper to fetch it. Matthias had never seen Axel have more than one. He had something stuck in his craw. How long would it take to spit it out?

"What's bothering you?"

Axel slid him a hard look. "Everyone in town knows where you are most of the time, Matthias." Leaning forward, he spoke quietly. "Even when you don't think people are watching, they are. You should keep that in mind, my friend. Especially if you have real regard for Kathryn Walsh."

Matthias felt flush with heat. "What are you trying to tell me? Just say it."

"You've been seen going into Kathryn's house. At night. And staying."

Matthias went hot. "One time. Not all night. And nothing happened."

"Knowing the lady, I believe you, but then what I think doesn't matter much, does it? She admitted going into Sanders's house. Worse luck, she was seen going in." He lowered his voice to a near whisper. "Oliver Morris picked up Kathryn and brought her to Sanders. Just like he did Monique. For a private dinner, he said, but it was clear what he thought, especially when Sanders told him to take the rest of the night off."

Matthias was having trouble staying in the chair. "She wouldn't be going up there for the reasons you're implying."

"I'm not implying anything."

"Aren't you? And I know the day and the hour."

Axel leaned back, relaxed. "How?"

"It was the day we had the earthquake. I saw her running like the devil was after her. I thought the earthquake terrified her."

Axel gave a low laugh. "It terrified a lot of people, including me." He tilted his head slightly, eyes narrowing. "Did Kathryn ever tell you what happened? Longwei said she was in the house for two hours. A lot can happen between a man and woman in that amount of time, even if a woman is unwilling."

A rush of hot fury swept through Matthias.

"Matt." Axel spoke quietly, frowning.

Matthias tried to get past the anger and think clearly. "She stayed in her house for three days. I knocked on her door a few times. She said she was fine." He remembered being surprised at how she'd screamed at him to go away and leave her alone. "People were coming to me for help. We were putting things back together. She wouldn't even let Scribe in. I saw you stop by. Every evening on your rounds. Like clockwork."

"You keep a pretty close eye on her."

"I care about her. She tends to get into trouble."

"You care about her." Axel smiled, amused. "Everyone's waiting to see what happens now that you finished everything on her list."

Matthias swore. "I wish I'd never made her come up with it."

"How did you?" Axel chuckled. "Never mind. It's none of my business." He grew serious again. "I need to ask her some more questions, and they're not going to be easy ones."

"If you're going to talk to her, send her a message to come to my office." Matthias downed his whiskey and slammed it on the table. "And I'm staying in the room." He'd wanted to ask a few questions about that night himself, questions he probably should have asked long before now. He'd hoped she would trust him enough to tell him what happened. When she didn't, he chose to respect her silence. Kathryn hadn't mentioned Morgan Sanders, either in print or in conversation, since the day the man saw her and Matthias sitting together in church and walked out.

Kathryn had looked upset when he'd seen her running, but not harmed. But then, how could he be sure? He hadn't pressed her. Maybe because he knew that if he learned Sanders had laid even a finger on her, he would've killed him himself. With his bare hands.

When Kathryn entered Matthias's office and saw Axel, she knew she faced an interrogation. Matthias ushered her to a wing chair, and he and Axel sat in straight-backed chairs facing her. She was certain she was going to be asked about her relationship with Morgan Sanders. Folding her hands in her lap, she looked at Axel, trying to block out Matthias's presence. If she had to tell these men everything, Matthias would never see her the same way.

Axel got straight to the point. "Tell me everything that happened on the day of the earthquake, from the time Morgan Sanders's driver picked you up until you were seen running along the boardwalk after the earthquake."

Heat surged into her face as she wondered what Axel might be thinking happened. She didn't have to look at Matthias to feel the tension radiating from him. Maybe she should have told him, but how could she? The whole episode had been mortifying. It was her own fault for being so foolish. She worried her lip and cast Matthias a glance. "Couldn't this questioning be done in private?"

"Pretend I'm not here." Matthias spoke gruffly.

Tears burned and she fought them back. "That's difficult to do."

Matthias leaned toward her, hands clasped between his knees. "Kate . . ."

She couldn't bear it. "I didn't kill Morgan." She met Axel's eyes. "I did . . . I did claw his face."

Her heart jumped when Matthias stood, muttering something under his breath.

"Go on, Kathryn," Axel encouraged her, but she was too intensely aware of Matthias moving restlessly around the room. She looked at Axel, eyes pleading. He turned his head. "Matt, sit down or leave."

Matthias rubbed the back of his neck, came back, and sat.

"Morgan sent a message telling me there was a meeting of the mine owners and he thought I should be there." She heard Matthias make a sound of derision. "When I arrived, there was no one else in the house but his house servant and his chef. I felt as though I'd walked into some kind of trap."

Matthias sat still, tense, and silent. Axel nodded at her to go on. Clearly, she wasn't going to get away without telling everything. Why must she be humiliated a second time? "He said we had things to discuss. When I tried to leave, he blocked my way. He . . . he made me sit. He wanted to know about the mine. He knew Amos Stearns had brought me a report." She gave a laugh that sounded odd in her own ears. "Of course, everyone in town knew. Everyone knows everything in this town. Except who murdered City Walsh."

"And Morgan Sanders," Axel added.

Kathryn glanced up. "Are the murders linked?"

"Let me ask the questions." Axel's tone was gentle, but pointed. "What else happened?"

She kept her head down, unable to look at either man. "He wouldn't let me leave. He made me stay for dinner. He said I would marry him." She gave a bleak laugh. "Everyone knows how I feel about marriage." Her voice broke softly. "He tried to force me up the stairs." She covered her face, hiccuping a sob. When Matthias said her name in a pained tone, she couldn't speak.

Axel leaned forward and put his hand on her shoulder. "What we say in this room stays in this room, Kathryn. You have my word on that."

She lowered shaking hands. "I fought. I kicked. I scratched." She gave a mirthless laugh. "I was going for his eyes. He raised his hand and then everything was shaking. The chandelier, the floor felt like it was rolling under my feet. The servant was screaming. He ran right past us and out the door. Morgan's hold loosened and I broke free and ran. And I ran and ran." She started to cry. Mortified, she covered her face again. "I was stupid, so stupid."

"Kate . . ."

"Everyone warned me about him, but I didn't listen. He came to my house. The night after it all happened. Bandit started growling, and when Morgan spoke, he lunged at the door, barking like he'd gone crazy."

"And you never saw him after that?"

"At church. He saw me sitting with Matthias." She met his eyes, praying he understood. "I felt safe with you."

His expression softened. "You'll always be safe with me."

Axel pressed again and she wanted done with it. "I saw Morgan around town after that, but I never spoke to him again. I kept my distance." Her emotions were appallingly close to the surface. "He told me there were three things he wanted: wealth, a cultured wife, and a son to inherit his empire. He said I was the second and would provide the third. But I think he really wanted to force me into marrying him so he could gain control of the Keeweetoss."

Trembling, Kathryn lifted her head and looked between Matthias and Axel. "May I go now?" She wanted to be home behind a locked door.

Axel stood and held out his hand. "I'm sorry for putting

you through this. I needed to see if your story confirmed what others have said." He looked at her with apology. "I was sure it would." She took his hand because her knees were shaking too much to stand.

Matthias stood and moved closer. "I'll see you home, Kate."

She gave a light, broken laugh. "You might think twice about being seen with me, Matthias. What will people say about me now when word gets out?"

"I gave my word it wouldn't," Axel reminded her.

"In Calvada, even the walls have ears."

She felt Matthias's hand spread against the small of her back. "Try not to worry about things that don't matter."

23

THAT EVENING, the town council members came to Matthias's office for another meeting. Hall and Debree had hired another man, but there was still a lot of trash to clear out from behind buildings. Gravel would continue to come from the abandoned Jackrabbit Mine. Most of the town's financial reserves were being put to good purpose, but money was growing short fast, and progress would have to slow down until more came in.

Rudger stretched his legs and leaned back in his chair. "It's beginning to feel like a real town around here." Kit Cole from the livery stable agreed.

The meeting adjourned at ten and Matthias walked out with them. They talked more on the boardwalk. Kathryn's front office lantern was still lit. Matthias wondered what she was doing. Writing another editorial or a column on bachelor arts? Maybe she just couldn't sleep with the fandango hall in full swing.

The council members kept talking. Matthias saw Axel stop at Kathryn's door. She opened it, they spoke briefly, and the sheriff moved on. Matthias lingered as the council members left. Kathryn's lantern went out. He stood a while longer, thinking about her, tempted to go over and tap on her door. She couldn't possibly be asleep yet with all the racket coming from next door. Her door opened and she slipped out wearing her cloak. She pulled the hood over her hair and started down the boardwalk. There was a furtiveness in her movements.

Matthias muttered a curse under his breath. *There she goes again. Trouble on the move.* Stepping off the boardwalk, Matthias crossed the street and followed.

Kathryn walked quickly down the boardwalk, keeping her head down. When she came to the end of Chump Street, she turned right onto the street that had no sign, but which everyone called Gomorrah. Shabby cribs where prostitutes lived lined the right side of the street. Farther down was Fiona Hawthorne's two-story house with a picket fence around the front yard.

The brutal murder of Morgan Sanders had brought the still-unsolved murder of Kathryn's uncle back to the forefront of her mind. For some time, she had wished she could speak with Fiona about City and their relationship. Finally she decided she could put it off no longer. She had to find out anything that might help her understand her uncle and why someone had wanted to kill him.

The windows upstairs and down glowed warm welcome. After a quick look around, Kathryn hurried through the gate and up the front steps. She knocked lightly on the door. Though she could hear women's voices, no one answered. Swallowing her nervous tension, she knocked again, firmly this time.

The door opened and Monique Beaulieu stood before her, finely dressed and coiffed. "Miss Walsh!"

"*Bonsoir*, Mademoiselle Beaulieu." Kathryn continued in French, asking to speak with Mrs. Hawthorne. Following Monique into the parlor, Kathryn inhaled the scent of perfume. She recognized the three women and greeted each by name while Monique left to make the request. Kathryn hadn't known what to expect inside a brothel, but found the room quite comfortable. Painted hurricane lamps and the fire in the hearth gave the room a warm glow. Framed landscapes hung on white walls, and a red Kashan rug evoked a richness uncommon to Calvada.

Hurried footsteps approached and Fiona Hawthorne appeared in the doorway.

"What are you doing here, Miss Walsh?"

"I'm sorry to intrude, Mrs. Hawthorne, but I must speak with you."

"Look outside, Carla, and see if anyone is coming." Fiona gestured at Kathryn. "We must get you out of here. If anyone sees you, your reputation will be ruined!"

Kathryn gave a soft laugh. "My reputation is hardly as glowing as you seem to think. I'm not going anywhere." She removed her cloak and hung it on the hat tree.

"Someone's coming up the steps." Carla closed the front curtain. "For Monique, I think."

"Come with me." Fiona walked to the end of the hall and motioned for Kathryn to enter the room. It was furnished with a big brass bed, a mahogany armoire, and a large brown mohair chair nestled in the corner with a small table lamp and book on a side table. One lace-covered window opened to black night behind the house. Fiona looked furious. "You should have more sense, Miss Walsh!" She waved her hand toward the mohair chair in the corner. "Sit and ask your questions. I can't promise to answer all of them."

Kathryn sat on the edge of the chair, hands folded on her knees. "Did you know my uncle had a mine?"

"Yes."

Hoping for more, Kathryn waited, but Fiona sat silent. "Do you know if he knew how valuable it was?"

"He knew. It came too late to matter." She looked away. "He called it the Bitter Reminder."

"Reminder of what?"

"You should leave some things alone."

"I can't. I won't. He's the only blood relative I have besides my mother and half brother. I want to know everything about him. I've read his journals. He mentioned you often. I think he loved you."

"Perhaps." Fiona's eyes filled with sorrow and pain. "Be that as it may, I don't know if City would want you to know his story."

"I won't leave until I do."

Fiona searched her face, and her expression softened. "I knew who you were the minute I saw you. You have his ginger hair and green eyes. I wonder what he would have said to you if he'd had the chance to meet you face-to-face."

"Scribe and Matthias said you were closer to my uncle than anyone. Sally Thacker said you cried the day my uncle was buried, and I've seen wild red roses on his grave several times. You loved him, didn't you?"

"Yes. I did. We talked of marriage once." Shaking her head,

she looked away. "He told me he'd marry me if it weren't for . . ." She closed her eyes.

"For what?"

Fiona looked at her. "An impediment."

"Impediment?" When Fiona said nothing, Kathryn decided to change course. "How did you meet him?"

Fiona laughed bleakly. "I own a brothel, Miss Walsh. One evening, Monique made City wait. She plays that game with men sometimes, believing she means more to them than she does. He and I talked and found we had a great deal in common." She smiled slightly. "Hard beginnings, tragic ends, getting by the best we could. He never asked for Monique again." Fiona met Kathryn's quizzical gaze. "Contrary to what most good women believe, men don't always come to a brothel for sex."

"Oh."

Fiona grimaced. "I'm sorry, Miss Walsh. I see I've embarrassed you with plain talk."

"Not enough to make me leave."

"I could tell you to mind your own business."

"My uncle is my business. And considering your relationship with him, you're as close to an aunt as I shall ever have."

Fiona blanched. "Don't ever say that again! You're a lady! My relationship with City hardly makes me part of your family!" She stood, agitated.

Kathryn felt quick tears at Fiona's harshness. "Had he done right by you, it would have."

Fiona flashed her an angry look. "City always did what he felt was right." She pushed the curtain aside and stared out into the darkness. "No matter the cost." She came back and sat facing Kathryn. "All right. I'll tell you what I know."

Her tone warned Kathryn of coming revelations she might find difficult to hear.

"City and I both arrived in California in '49. I'd lost a hus-band. He lost a brother. Life on the streams is hard. City gave up prospecting and found work in the mining camps. When he came up here, he bought the press. He won the claim in a poker game. City used the mine as a hiding place whenever he wrote something that stirred up trouble."

"How often did that happen?"

Fiona smiled slightly. "More often than I liked." She sat silent for a moment. "Wiley Baer came through town looking for work. They had come across on the same wagon train. Wiley pulled him out of a river and saved his life once. City took him up to the mine and let him work it. He never took much." She shook her head. "Just enough to make people wonder."

Wiley's secret mine.

"What was my uncle like?"

"Compassionate and hard, volatile occasionally, quiet more often, a truth teller, loyal . . ."

Kathryn leaned forward. "Can you tell me why he left every-thing to my mother? Was he paying penance for talking my father into leaving her for the goldfields?"

"Penance?" Fiona lifted her chin. "Is that what you were told? That he abandoned her?"

"Yes! My mother defied her father when she ran away to marry him. She'd lived a pampered life. She didn't know any-thing about cooking or laundry or bartering, things the wife of a poor man needs to do. When word of a gold rush spread, his brother talked him into leaving for California. My mother was afraid to go. He sent her home, told her to make up her mind about what mattered most. She wrote to him a few days later, pleading—"

"Your mother wrote to him?"

"Several times, but she never heard from him again. The

first word she had was from my uncle, informing her that her husband had drowned while crossing the Missouri River . . ." Kathryn hesitated. *Wiley Baer . . .*

"Did she grieve?" Fiona asked, a hint of derision in her tone.

"Yes! She grieved so much, she became sick. My grandfather called in a doctor. That's when she found out she was with child. After I was born, my grandfather arranged her marriage to another man, one he approved of." Pausing, Kathryn smoothed her skirt. "My earliest memory is of my stepfather telling me I was not his child and not to call him Papa ever again." She gave a breathy laugh and shook her head. "My red hair and temperament reminded both my mother and stepfather of Connor Walsh. He was the love of my mother's life and the bane of my stepfather's."

Fiona looked troubled. "Oh, what webs we mortals weave."

Confused, Kathryn glanced up. Why did Wiley keep coming to mind? What had Scribe said in her uncle's mine? Oh! She gave a soft, nervous laugh. "It seems a strange coincidence that both brothers fell in a river . . ."

"Both brothers made it to California."

"Both?" Kathryn's heart began to pound.

"City's brother died of pneumonia after they arrived."

Kathryn tried to take in what her heart wanted to reject. "If my father drowned in the Missouri, how did two brothers end up in California?"

Fiona had a defeated air about her. "City told me he wrote several letters to his wife and never received an answer."

Kathryn felt the blood draining from her face and sensed what was coming, afraid to believe it. "City's wife?"

"Elizabeth Hyland Walsh."

"No . . ." She felt her heart breaking.

"City believed your mother regretted the marriage. I imagine

375

your grandfather intercepted their letters. He did almost drown in the Missouri. Wiley Baer threw him a rope and pulled him back onto the barge. That's when he came up with the idea he had to live with for the rest of his life. He told his brother to write a letter saying he'd drowned. As a widow, Elizabeth could marry again, someone from her own class, someone who could make her happy and give her the life to which she was accustomed. But in his mind, he still had a wife."

Kathryn let the words sink in, understanding, and feeling a depth of loss she'd never known before. "City was Connor Walsh. My father." Agitated, Kathryn stood. "I should write to my mother."

"Why?"

"She believes he abandoned her! She should know how much he loved her!"

"What good would that do now? If she's content with your stepfather, what purpose would it serve?" Fiona spoke gently. "It was right for the inheritance to go to family, Miss Walsh."

Kathryn turned. "Then everything should have gone to you and Scribe. You were his family. You meant so much to him, Fiona!"

"Oh, my dear. I've been making my own way for years. I didn't need an inheritance." Fiona stood and stopped Kathryn from pacing. "As for Scribe, City saw to his education, provided him with a skill, treated him like a son. From what I've heard, you treat him like a brother."

Heavy footsteps crossed the floor upstairs, the door opening. As soon as it closed, Kathryn heard weeping. She looked at Fiona in question and concern.

"Elvira." She shrugged. "Few women choose this life."

Kathryn's throat closed tight and hot.

"Have I answered all your questions?"

She nodded, unable to speak. Fiona had answered questions she didn't even know she had. "I wish I'd known him." Her voice broke.

"I see him in you, Kathryn." Fiona held up a hand. "Stay here until I make sure it's safe for you to go." She opened the door and went out.

Kathryn held herself together, pent-up anguish strangling her. When Fiona came back, she draped the cloak around Kathryn and pulled up the hood. "Keep your hair covered and your head down." A finger to her lips, Fiona led her to the front door.

Kathryn embraced her. "I want us to be friends." She clung. "You knew him . . ."

Fiona held her tightly for a moment and then withdrew. She touched Kathryn's cheek tenderly, eyes moist. "Go on now, back to where you belong." She pressed Kathryn forward. "Get away from this place as quickly as you can, and don't ever come here again." Fiona closed the door firmly. Kathryn heard the bolt set.

Shaking, Kathryn went down the front steps. Her legs felt weak. Head down, she crossed the street and hurried toward Chump Street. She'd almost reached the corner when she bumped into a man. "Oh!" She stepped back, startled.

"What in blazes are you doing in this part of town?"

Matthias! With a sob, Kathryn went into his arms as though that were the most natural place to be when her world had been turned upside down and inside out.

Matthias held Kathryn close, her body shaking with sobs, her fingers grasping the front of his shirt, holding on to him as though she couldn't stand without his support. He cupped the back of her head and whispered comfort, all too aware they couldn't remain here on Gomorrah where someone might see them. His own heart broke, listening to her.

"Let me get you home, darlin'." The endearment escaped, and he expected her to pull away, but she stayed nestled tightly against him. Withdrawing, he slipped his arm around her waist. "We need to get away from here, Kathryn." She stumbled once, but he kept her up as they went around the corner to Chump Street. A block down, Matthias spotted Axel checking the doors of Aday's General Store. He looked their way. The man didn't miss anything.

Opening the door of her small house, he let her slip by him and followed her in. She went straight to the settee and sank. Covering her face, she went on weeping. Matthias lit the lantern. He wanted to ask what happened to put her in this state, but knew she didn't need an interrogation right now. Seeing Kathryn in tears shook him. He wanted to do something, *anything*, to fix whatever was wrong.

The lady would probably want tea. Matthias went into her apartment, added wood to her potbellied stove, and put the kettle on. She kept everything clean and tidy, books in neat rows, bed made, the tin tub set back in a corner. He picked up a dish towel and took it into the front office, dropping it in her lap. Murmuring a watery thank-you, she blew her nose. He sat beside her, putting his hand on her back. He felt the wrenching sobs, the gasping breath, the hard beating of her heart. Gradually, her shoulders stopped jerking and she wilted, exhausted.

Pushing the hood back, Kathryn looked over at him with reddened, grieving eyes. "City Walsh was my father." She started to cry again, and then hiccuped. "Excuse me." She hiccuped again.

Was the thought of City so appalling? Was she ashamed of him? "He was a good man, Kathryn."

"Everything I've ever heard about him since coming to Calvada made me wish I'd met him. And now, it hurts even more that I never had the chance. My father was alive! All these years . . ." Her mouth trembled.

"What would you have done if you'd known?"

"Come to California!" She tried to stand and sank back. "He never even knew he had a daughter! Fiona said she knew who I was the first time she saw me." She shrugged and started to cry again. "I understand why I was such a thorn in the judge's side."

"Tell me what Fiona said."

"Oh, Matthias, it's a long story . . ."

"I'm not going anywhere."

Kathryn talked and Matthias soaked in more about her life than he'd been able to glean over the months she'd been in Calvada. He learned about her mother's scandalous marriage to an Irish rebel and why he'd sent her home.

Her mother had told her about Connor Thomas Walsh, the Irishman who'd captured her heart. She'd been so in love with him, she'd cast aside family, friends, social position, a life of luxury to be with him. "She said I was like my father. Rebellious, passionate, wanting to change the world. She said her life would be much easier without me. And I knew it was true."

Matthias felt a rush of anger and empathy. She *was* like City. She didn't make life easy on those who loved her. But she was worth it.

Kathryn went on, telling him about Wiley saving City, City seeing a way to free his wife so she could marry again, his love for Fiona, and why he never married her. Wiping tears from her cheeks, she sighed, spent. "Well, I've certainly talked your ear off."

"I'm honored." Matthias got up.

She straightened, her expressive eyes melting his insides. "Are you leaving?"

"Just making tea."

She giggled. "Matthias Beck making tea. That should be a headline."

He grinned back at her. "No one would believe it."

Matthias brought her a mug and sat on the edge of the settee, leaving some space between them. She looked up through her lashes as she sipped. "I think I've told you everything about my life. Well, almost. I was expelled from three boarding schools, the first because I punched a girl in the face for calling me a mick, and the second because I argued with a teacher. The last one accused me of 'unladylike behavior.'"

Matthias stifled a grin.

"Oh, and I went to a rally with several other suffragettes. That was the final rebellious act that earned me a one-way ticket across the country. The judge said he wished Casey had made it to the Sandwich Islands."

Matthias laughed. "Well, I'm glad City didn't go any farther than Calvada." He brushed a tear from her cheek. "Everything you've said stays with me, Kathryn."

"I believe you." She still seemed troubled.

"What is it?"

She gave him a probing look, her cheeks gaining color. "Why were you there? On Gomorrah."

When he looked into her eyes, she glanced away, embarrassed, and he knew what she was thinking. "I saw you leave your office, cloaked and practically sneaking toward the end of town. I thought I'd better keep an eye on you." He smiled wryly. "What did you think I was doing?"

She shrugged. "It's really none of my business."

Matthias wanted things clear between them. "There's only one lady I want, and I'm looking at her."

Her cheeks flushed and she gave a soft, teasing laugh. "Back to that again, are we?"

He saw more in her eyes than she might want him to know.

Kathryn held the mug in both hands, head bowed. "Sometimes love isn't enough. And passion clouds the mind."

He frowned. "You sound like you're quoting someone."

"My mother."

Did she realize she'd just told him she loved him? His pulse quickened. "You're not your mother, Kathryn, and I'm not City Walsh."

She took another sip of tea, eyes lowered. He could see her mustering her defenses. He knew he could breach her walls right now. Tempted, Matthias stood, not wanting either of them to have regrets later. She was vulnerable tonight, too vulnerable to touch. "Did City know how valuable the mine was?"

Kathryn glanced up, bemused. "The mine?" Her eyes cleared. "Yes. He knew it was valuable."

"Why didn't he work it?"

"He called it the Bitter Reminder." She set the mug aside. "Maybe it reminded him of why he left my mother and came west. He wanted to get rich so he could give her the life she'd had. As if that was what mattered most to her. He never knew how much she loved him, or that she couldn't follow because she was ill and carrying his child." She grew distant for a moment, thinking. "My father stopped looking for gold when his brother died. He won the claim in a card game. He went up and worked when one of his editorials stirred up trouble."

Matthias chuckled. "He did disappear a few times that I remember."

She smiled. "I've felt like hiding out occasionally myself."

"I'll bet you have." He wanted to tuck a stray tendril of curling red hair behind her ear.

Kathryn met his eyes and looked away. "When City realized what he had, it must've been a cruel reminder of the dream that brought him to California. What good was gold when he was already dead to the woman he loved? He couldn't resurrect himself and reclaim her."

"And her father would have long since arranged a marriage he deemed suitable." Matthias understood.

"No amount of gold could undo the decision he made. He probably thought my mother happily remarried with children . . ." Her eyes welled again. "What a tangled mess men make when they try to play God."

"He did what he thought best for your mother, Kate."

"If he'd only gone back for her! If he'd been willing to wait a year. I would have been born. We all would have come to California together."

"You're sure of that? Your mother would have been willing to undergo the hardship of a three-thousand-mile journey across country in a wagon with a baby?"

A frown flickered. "She might have."

Matthias knew she doubted it.

Kathryn was silent for a moment. "I suppose it does no good to wonder. What if . . . if only. We'll never know, and it only hurts to wish."

"Things work out according to God's plan." That caught her attention. His mouth tipped. "My father's rejection sent me wandering. Why did I end up here?" *For you,* he wanted to say. *So I'd be here when you arrived.*

She closed her eyes. "'Even if my father and mother abandon me, the Lord will hold me close.'"

Psalm 27. He knew the verse.

Opening her eyes, she looked up at him and laughed. "Look at us, quoting Scripture."

Matthias loved the warmth in her eyes. "My father was a preacher, but it was my mother who taught me the Bible." He tucked the strand of hair behind her ear. "Never underestimate the importance of the woman who rocks the cradle."

24

THE NEXT MORNING, after asking Ronya to prepare a picnic basket, Matthias knocked on Kathryn's door. "Do you want to get out of town for a few hours? I've got a buggy outside."

"Oh." She paused. "Yes. I think I'd like that. Thank you. I'll get my shawl."

Surprised, Matthias waited in the front office. "I thought you'd say no."

Kathryn came back with a hat that didn't match her dress, a sure sign trouble was on the horizon. Jamming the hat on her head, she tied the silk ribbons under her chin. Bandit barely managed to dart out the door before she closed it. "I want to drive."

"Sorry. No deal."

Mutinous, she glared at him. "Why not? Because I'm a woman?"

"Because you look like you're about to explode. You can handle the reins on the way back when you've calmed down."

She surveyed him and then let out a sharp breath. "You're right."

"That's a first."

She climbed into the buggy before he could assist. Matthias came around and sat beside her. "Bad news?" He took up the reins.

"A letter from home." Eyes snapping, cheeks flushed, she sat rigid, every muscle in her body tense with rage he knew wasn't aimed at him. Her mind was elsewhere. He decided to keep quiet while she boiled. Relaxing, he enjoyed her company, despite her mood and wandering mind. The ride out of town gave him plenty of time to daydream about future possibilities. The only sounds that broke the silence were the clop of the horse, whispers of wind, and birdsong.

Matthias turned off the road. Axel's interrogation, everything she'd learned from Fiona, and now the cursed letter made him certain his personal quest would have to wait, but at least she was sitting beside him. Stopping the buggy near some pines, he came around to lift her down.

"Where are we?" Her hands rested on his shoulders.

"A couple of miles outside town." He set her on her feet, but didn't let go. When her eyes met his, she drew in a soft breath and stepped back.

Matthias watched her as he removed the harness and hobbled the horse. Taking the basket from beneath the seat, he approached. "This way to paradise, your ladyship." He led the way down a deer path to a bower overlooking the rapids.

"It's beautiful here. How did you find this place? It's so tucked away."

He'd searched for a private nest where they could talk without prying eyes watching. "There are places like this all around these mountains."

Closing her eyes, Kathryn inhaled. "It smells like heaven."

"A whole lot different than Calvada, you mean."

"Most assuredly." She smiled at him as she took the cloth from the basket. Opening it, she spread it on the grass while Matthias stood by watching. His second surprise of the day. Instead of telling him it was improper for her to be alone with him, she took charge. As his gaze drifted over her, he spotted a wadded paper on the grass.

"What's this?" He stooped to pick it up.

"The letter Mr. Blather gave me. From my stepfather. The judge." Her eyes flashed again, and Matthias wished he'd left well enough alone. "Go ahead! Read it!"

He'd only managed to read the greeting before Kathryn snatched it from him, wadded it again, threw it on the ground, and stomped on it. "Apparently, my mother told the judge about the mine and my plans for it. He says my motives are *admirable* and suggests it would be wise to look at *alternatives* and suggests sending *Freddie*, of all people, to manage the mine."

Angry tears filled her eyes as she paced, furious. "Just because a woman is unmarried doesn't mean she's incapable of handling her own affairs! He certainly felt I was up to it when he gave me a one-way train ticket out here."

Shaking with anger, she ranted. "He wants to take over. Unfortunately, it's his legal right to do so. Oh, he knows me well enough not to say it in those words, but it's all there, cloaked in his *concern* for my welfare and future." She harrumphed. "Now he refers to me as his *daughter*. I'm no more his daughter than that horse is your brother!"

Matthias withheld a smile. His little general looked battle ready.

"The judge says he wishes to act in my best interests. *Bullwhacky!*" She stamped her foot. "I've a good mind to tell him he made my mother a bigamist when he married her." She paused, frowning. "No, I can't." Wilting, Kathryn sat on the checkered cloth. "It's not fair."

Matthias took it all in, but wanted to know one thing. "Who's Freddie?"

Kathryn looked up at him in surprise. "Is that all you heard?"

"Oh, I heard all of it. I just want to know who he is and what he is to you."

"No one you need ever worry about."

He liked the way she said that, but she hadn't answered the question. "An old beau you left behind?"

"Frederick Taylor Underhill is the obnoxious son of a factory owner who thinks there is nothing wrong with employing children as workers. Who cares if they never see the light of day? Who cares if they get crushed in the machinery? Profit is all that matters!" She avoided looking at him. "Someone my stepfather and mother wanted me to marry. Freddie proposed to me once and I said no. Emphatically! And now, my stepfather suggests he might send him out here to help me attend to business? I know exactly what he's plotting."

So did Matthias, and the idea irked him. "I suppose you could marry Freddie. That way you'd retain some say in how the mine is operated."

Kathryn gaped at him. "You can't be serious! I wouldn't marry Freddie if he were the last man on earth and the only means to increase the population!"

Matthias laughed, pleased to hear it. "Poor Freddie."

"It's not funny, Matthias! I know what he'd do. The same thing his father has done in the factories he owns. The miners won't have decent salaries, let alone a share of the profits. They'll be lucky to get subsistence pay. They'll end up living in shanties and buying supplies from a company store! The Keeweetoss would become worse than the Madera!"

She looked anguished, her every thought fixed on the future of her employees, not one thought on her own crushed hopes and plans. Her heart might be pure, but she was poised for battle.

"Print your side of the story. Once the men read it, they won't blame you for what happens."

"They have every right to blame me if I let it happen." Her eyes shimmered green fire. "I won't!" She kicked a rock and winced. "Oww . . ." She hopped and hobbled back to the blanket. She had worn her pretty leather shoes rather than her mining boots. Sinking down, she clasped her foot. "Can things get any worse? I think I broke my toe."

Matthias hunkered down. "Let me have a look."

"Oh, no, you don't."

"Then stop whining."

Removing her shoe, she massaged her toes. "It's unjust, Matthias. Women should have some rights." She glared at him. "Unfortunately, men write the laws."

Matthias had full confidence Kathryn would send Freddie packing before he had both feet off the stage. "Women like you will eventually convince us to do what's right."

Kathryn laughed. "This from the man who didn't think a woman should be running a newspaper."

"My apologies to the lady." He inclined his head. "I stand corrected."

"You never cease to amaze me, Matthias." Untying the ribbons, she removed her hat and tossed it aside. Bright-eyed and glowing, she smiled up at him, a soft breeze stirring the tendrils of red hair.

Matthias felt a surge of desire. "Watching you in action has changed the opinions of quite a number of men I know, or hadn't you noticed how many hop to when the lady sends down orders from on high?"

She grinned. "It is rather nice being in charge."

When hadn't she been? "If you behave, I might let you drive back to town."

"What do you mean by behave?"

Was she flirting with him? He sat and stretched out on his side. "What do you think would happen to anyone who came out here and tried to take the mine away from you?"

Her gaze drifted over his body as she sat quiet for a moment. When she met his eyes, he saw something in hers that set his pulse racing. She blinked, looked faintly disturbed, and then frowned. "What did you say?"

The afternoon might have possibilities, after all. "We were talking about Freddie and the mine."

"Oh."

"Your Twelve won't let anyone take it from you."

"No, I don't suppose they would." She gave him a quick glance and busied herself. "I'm starving, aren't you? We should see what kind of feast Ronya prepared for us." She set out fresh baked bread, sliced ham wrapped in cheesecloth, a small jar of butter, another of pickles, and squares of sugared shortbread. She held up a bottle. "Apple juice! Ronya even packed plates, cups, and a knife."

Good old Ronya, ever the matchmaker. Kathryn didn't seem to have a thought for what else her friend must have in mind for today. Matthias watched Kathryn prepare their sandwiches. She put one in front of him like an offering and filled their cups. He took one sip and knew it wasn't juice.

"This is delicious." Kathryn had already taken a sip.

The girl had been far too sheltered. "You might want to go easy on that. It's hard cider."

They ate in companionable silence. Matthias could see her mind working again. Something serious. He hoped it wasn't the mine or Freddie. She finished her sandwich and swept the few crumbs from her skirt. Taking a breath, she folded her hands and looked at him. "I owe you an apology, Matthias. I've misjudged you. Not that you haven't been a thorn in my side. I think you take pleasure in provoking me at times."

"And you don't?" He mentioned several editorials. She looked unrepentant. And distracted. "What's on your mind, your ladyship?" Besides the mine and Freddie . . . and everything she'd just learned from Fiona.

"It's been a surprise to find out we have so many common goals."

Why not get to the point? "You mean our lists." It was time to put his cards on the table. "I counted Calvada a lost cause and was ready to sell out and move on. And then you got off the stage."

"Oh."

There was that look again, melting his insides and making his heart quicken. "I didn't play fair the night I got you to make your list, but I'm not sorry."

"You were rather . . . overwhelming." She glanced away as though the intensity of his feelings unnerved her. "You certainly gave me something to think about that night."

"Did I?" he drawled, noticing the heightened color in her cheeks, the darkness of her eyes.

"I never intended to marry. Because I've never met a man I could trust." She raised her head slowly. "I trust you, Matthias."

Stunned, Matthias felt like he'd been playing high-stakes poker and just won the biggest pot of his life. Then their earlier conversation came back with a punch. His eyes narrowed. "Hold on." He sat up, annoyed. "Does this sudden change of heart have anything to do with the judge, Freddie, and your mine?"

"What? No!" She looked aghast, then frowned, her eyes flickering. "I hadn't thought of that."

And he'd just planted the idea in her head! Matthias got up and moved away.

"I only meant to say . . . I . . ."

Turning, he looked at her sitting there, hands folded tightly in her lap. "You what?"

"I like you."

"*Like* me?"

Annoyed, she turned away. "I meant it as a compliment!"

"Thanks."

Kathryn sighed. "I'm beginning to understand how Freddie felt when I left him on one knee in the rose garden."

Matthias wasn't sure he'd heard correctly. "So, you're proposing to me? Is that it?" He laughed at the very idea.

She blushed, eyes fierce. "I did give my word when I gave you the list, and you fulfilled your part of the bargain."

She'd been serious! "And that'd be your only reason?"

"I thought it only right that I be the one to bring it up, considering what I've put you through." She shook her head, clearly regretting everything. "Why am I even trying to talk to you about this? My mother warned me."

"About what?"

"Allowing passion to overrule the mind."

Matthias wondered if she knew what she'd just admitted, and when she lifted her chin, saw she did. "Say it, Kate."

"Say what?"

"You love me."

"A lot of good it'll do me!" She emptied the bottle of hard cider into the grass. "Ronya and her bright ideas."

Matthias grinned. "Ah, your ladyship, you've given me cause to celebrate."

"Go ahead!" Her eyes shimmered with tears. "Laugh!"

Pulling Kathryn to her feet, he cupped her face tenderly. "We will laugh, darlin', right up until we're both old and gray and have a dozen grandchildren." He kissed her firmly. "The answer is yes. I'll marry you." He grinned and kissed her again. When she responded, he didn't stop until they were both breathless and shaking. He put his forehead against hers. "We'd better pack up and head back to town." She gave a soft moan that almost made him change his mind. "Don't sound so disappointed. We'll come back. Right now, we're going to hunt down Reverend Thacker and set a date."

"The end of summer . . ."

"Oh, no. We're not waiting. We're getting married the first day the church is available."

Kathryn blushed. "Reverend Thacker will wonder at our haste."

"He'd be the only one. Everyone in Calvada is wondering why we've taken this long."

⸺⸺⸺⸺⸺⸺⸺

The entire town turned out for Kathryn and Matthias's wedding, and everyone was talking while they waited for the bride to come down the aisle.

Matthias always was one to attract trouble.

May the Lord God Almighty please bring this union to pass!

Maybe with Beck in charge of her, we'll all have a little peace around here.

One man said Calvada wouldn't be what it was but for the list Kathryn Walsh had given Matthias. Others longed for the old days when there were eighteen saloons, a dozen cribs, and three cathouses lining Gomorrah, not to mention the three fandango halls where men could kick up their heels well after midnight. Now, there were a mere eleven watering holes, three houses of ill repute, and one dance hall remaining. "If that woman has her way, Chump Street will be lined with stores and half the population will be women!"

Charlotte kissed Kathryn's cheek just inside the door of the church. "You're a beautiful bride. I'm so happy for you." She headed up the aisle.

Ronya, her matron of honor, stood waiting, looking regal in blue, her graying-blonde hair braided in a crown. She touched Kathryn's cheek. "Are you ready, dearie?"

"As ready as I'll ever be."

Smiling, Ronya's eyes lightened as she squeezed her hand. "Matthias will have his hands full with you."

When Kathryn stood at the end of the aisle, Sally began Mendelssohn's wedding march. Pews creaked and a rustle of sound filled the church as everyone stood. Kathryn saw friendly faces on both sides of the aisle. Tweedie, Ina Bea and Axel, Carl Rudger, Kit Cole, the Mercer family. Her eyes welled with tears at their encouraging smiles. Up front, Scribe stood next to Henry Call. The boy looked like a young man in his fine suit.

Gathering her courage, Kathryn finally looked at Matthias. He was devastatingly handsome in his dark suit and white shirt. His gaze was fixed on her, his expression one she couldn't decipher. When she reached him, he offered his arm and she slipped trembling fingers into place. They went up the two steps together and stood before Reverend Thacker in his formal black vestments.

The cross loomed on the wall behind the altar, a reminder of where she was. *"Where two or three gather together as my followers, I am there among them."* Jesus was inside this church.

Kathryn's heart pounded. *Oh, God, oh, God. I'm about to do something I swore I never would!* Matthias looked down at her. She wondered how she had come to be standing here beside him. *I am doing this for Keeweetoss and the miners.* Wasn't that true? She looked at the man standing beside her. She loved him. *How did I let that happen?* There was no way out now, but to run and humiliate herself. And Matthias, whom she had come to respect.

Reverend Thacker wasted no time starting the ceremony. Every word he spoke describing God's plan for marriage sounded wonderfully romantic, until she remembered her mother's warning. *Guard your heart, Kathryn.* She feared it was already captured. Every little girl dreamed of marrying her Prince Charming. Kathryn had, too, until she was old enough to learn how much women gave up when they said *I do*, and how easily a prince today could become a tyrant tomorrow.

Doubts attacked, but what could she do now that she was standing before the altar, the entire town watching? Matthias's attention was fixed on Reverend Thacker, and she found herself praying frantically. *Oh, God, please let Matthias be the man I hope he is.* In another half hour, she wouldn't be Kathryn Walsh anymore. She would be Kathryn Beck, and Matthias would have legal rights over everything that belonged to her, and to her person as well.

When Reverend Thacker came to the vows, Matthias

turned to her. Trembling, she faced him, thankful for the gauzy veil. Matthias took her left hand gently in his. He didn't wait for Reverend Thacker's prompting, but recited the vows. "I, Matthias Josiah Beck, take thee, Kathryn Lenore Walsh, to be my wedded wife." He slipped a gold band on her finger. "To have and to hold from this day forward, for better, for worse, for richer, for poorer, in sickness and in health, to love and cherish till death do us part." He looked at her then, eyes aglow, and her heart raced. "According to God's holy ordinance, and thereto I pledge thee my troth." He lifted her hand and kissed it.

The magnitude of the vows shook her.

Matthias's expression softened. "Ah, Kate." He spoke so softly no one would hear. "Don't turn coward now."

Kathryn's back stiffened at those words.

Reverend Thacker had turned to her and begun prompting her to say her vows. Swallowing hard, Kathryn spoke in a soft, shaky voice. "I, Kathryn Lenore Walsh, take thee, Matthias Josiah Beck, to be my husband . . . to have and to . . . hold . . . from this day forward . . . for better, for worse, for richer, for poorer, in sickness and in health . . . to . . ." She stumbled along, knowing she would have to keep these vows for the rest of her life. She could barely breathe past the pounding of her heart. ". . . love . . . cherish . . . and . . ." She fell silent, casting Matthias a wary look. He stood steady, a faint smile touching his lips.

"And obey," Reverend Thacker repeated.

She hesitated, then shook her head. "I can't say that."

A rustle of whispers spread through the congregation. "Told you, didn't I?" One man spoke up. "You owe me ten bucks."

His companion muttered loudly. "It ain't over yet." People shushed the men.

Shocked, Reverend Thacker stared at Kathryn. He uttered a nervous cough. "You must say it, Kathryn."

"I won't say it." She leaned close, whispering firmly. "I cannot make a promise before God and all these witnesses that I know I will be unable to keep."

Someone in the front row spoke aloud. "God help us all!" Twitters of laughter as well as disappointed groans were heard.

Reverend Thacker looked at Matthias for help and guidance. Matthias shrugged, seeming not the least bit surprised or put off by her refusal. "Just omit *obey*, Reverend." He grinned at her. "Leave me to deal with her rebellious nature."

What did he mean by that veiled threat? Kathryn knew it would be within his rights to beat her. But would he? She couldn't believe it of him, but his expression told her he had expected her to balk and already had a plan of what to do about it. She finished the vows without raising further objections. Reverend Thacker gave an audible sigh of relief.

"Matthias—" Reverend Thacker gave a nod—"you may kiss your bride."

Matthias lifted the veil. Kathryn took an instinctive step back. Looping an arm around her waist, he yanked her fully against him. When she opened her mouth to protest, he cupped the back of her head and kissed her. It wasn't the usual chaste kiss, but one of passion. An audible gasp spread through the congregation. She struggled weakly, then gave up, her body going warm and soft.

Oh, Mama, was this what you warned me about?

Matthias raised his head and looked into her eyes, his own glowing with mirth and triumph.

"That's one way to shut her up, Beck!" some man shouted from the back. Others laughed. Most sat stunned and silent.

Matthias turned her around so that she faced the entire congregation, his hands firm at her waist, locking her in place. Women stared round-eyed. Men chortled and nudged each other. "L-ladies and gentlemen," Reverend Thacker stammered, "I present to you Mr. and Mrs. Matthias Beck."

Everyone surged to their feet and cheered. Men laughed; women sighed. As word spread that the deed was done, hoots and hollers could be heard from outside. Someone fired a few shots into the air. Axel headed for the door.

Laughing, Matthias secured her hand in the crook of his arm. "It's a done deal, your ladyship. No backing out or running now." He took her down the steps and quickly along the aisle. "Time to greet the mob."

Ronya had made a three-tiered wedding cake. The ladies of the church made sure the long sawhorse and plank tables were cloth-covered and laden with casseroles, biscuits, apples, grapes shipped from Sacramento markets, baked beans, and ham. Overwhelmed by the town's generosity, Kathryn felt teary, but had no appetite. She nibbled at this and that, pushing her food around on the plate and hoping no one noticed.

Matthias took her hand beneath the table. "Try not to worry, Kate. You'll get through it."

Through what? She hated feeling so vulnerable. "Will we be staying at the hotel tonight?"

Matthias gave her a look of comprehension. "We'll go home for our wedding night."

"Home?" That announcement caused her stomach to flutter. "At the newspaper office?"

"Enjoy the party, Kathryn. We'll talk about what comes next."

The fandango band showed up with fiddle, harmonica, banjo, and a drum. Matthias caught Kathryn around the waist and pulled her into a dance. She'd never seen this side of Matthias and found herself charmed. How long had it been since she had danced?

Hours later, Matthias stood with her on the church steps and thanked everyone for a grand wedding and reception, especially on such short notice. Charlotte hugged Kathryn at the bottom of the steps. She giggled. "Try not to look like you're going to the guillotine."

Ronya was next in line to wish her well. "Marriage is what you make of it, Kathryn. Matthias is a good man. You'll make him better." She drew back and cupped Kathryn's cheek in a motherly gesture. "Be brave."

A few followed them down the road into town. Rather than head for the *Voice* and her little apartment, Matthias turned right. They walked several blocks and went up a slope where new homes had been built, each with plenty of space around them. He took her up the steps and onto the porch of a small, freshly painted yellow-and-white house.

"Your new home, your ladyship." He opened the door and swung her up in his arms, carrying her over the threshold. He set her back on her feet in the middle of the entry hall.

A wide doorway to the right opened into a parlor furnished with a settee, two cushioned chairs, and a low table in front of a stone fireplace. A library was at the back with City Walsh's bookcase and books. There were even white lace curtains covering the front windows. To her left was a dining room with a pantry at the back that opened into a kitchen with a new woodstove and icebox. The cabinets smelled freshly coated with linseed oil. The shelves were bare.

Leaning in the doorway, Matthias watched her. "You can pick up what you need at Walker's."

She looked back at him, perplexed. "You couldn't have done all this in a week. Not even with two good crews."

"It's been ready for a while."

"What do you mean by *a while*?"

Matthias just smiled. She felt tears welling. "It's far more than I expected . . ."

"I know. You thought we'd end up at the hotel."

She felt overwhelmed that he would take such care in making a place for them.

Matthias straightened and stepped back. "You haven't seen the rooms upstairs."

Mustering what little courage she had left after the momentous, life-changing day, she followed him. There were two small, unfurnished bedrooms and another large enough to hold a double bed with carved head- and footboards, a dresser with a large mirror, her father's armoire, and her Saratoga trunk.

"When were my things moved over here?" She was embarrassed at how her voice quivered.

"Right after the wedding. I wanted to make sure you didn't bolt for the livery stable, steal a buggy, and make a run for Sacramento." He moved closer. "I've never taken you for granted, Kathryn, and I won't start now." He made it sound like another promise. When he ran his hand over her shoulder, a shock of intense feelings went through her.

"Oh, Kate." Matthias cupped her face. "You look so scared. Please trust me. It won't be as bad as you may have heard."

That was the problem. "I haven't heard anything." No one had told her a thing about what happened from here forward.

Matthias frowned. "Nothing?"

"Some subjects are never discussed. My mother said . . ."

"Forget what your mother said." Searching her face, his expression softened. "Remember, God created Adam and Eve, and what comes next is all part of His plan, not just for procreation, but also for our pleasure." He kissed her again and took his time. When he raised his head, she found it difficult to breathe. His eyes were so dark and sultry as he removed pins from her hair. She could feel her hair loosen and slip down over her back. He took a step back and unbuttoned her high collar. "What do you suppose Adam thought the first time he saw Eve in all her glory?" Matthias smiled wryly. "Of course, he didn't have to deal with all these buttons."

Kathryn didn't know what to expect, but her anxiety melted as Matthias introduced her tenderly to the intimacies of married life. When it was over, Matthias lay on his side, relaxed, running his hand over her body, exploring every curve. "You are wonderfully made, Kathryn Beck."

Kathryn Beck! Her new name gave her a slight start, but the fear of what she might lose didn't seem so important anymore. That alone gave her pause to wonder what great shift had taken place inside her. Sighing, she looked at her husband and felt this was only the beginning of new discoveries. "The day we went on the picnic, I watched you run your hand over the carriage horse and wondered if you'd treat me as kindly."

"As a horse?" He laughed.

"Well, men break horses, don't they?"

"Oh." He thought about that. "I suppose some men treat women that way."

She made a soft sound of pleasure and rolled toward him. "I'm glad you're not one of them."

"I'm glad you've learned that much about me."

"I have been rather judgmental, haven't I?"

"Since we're confessing our sins, I thought you were a spoiled rich girl who assumed she was better than everyone else. Even then I knew we'd end up together."

"Did you?" She'd felt the magnetic pull of him that first day, too, but that attraction had been weak compared to now.

"I promise you, I am not going to crush your spirit, Kate. Why would I, when that's what I love most about you?" He kissed her forehead as though she were a child.

Oh, yes, she loved him. She had loved him even when he was an irritating rogue taunting and tormenting her. She'd avoided him because she knew she was losing her heart to him. Well, so be it. Losing her heart didn't mean she'd lost her mind. Did it?

"Don't look so downcast." Matthias propped his head up on his hand, gently wiping the tears from her cheeks. "You have no idea the power a good woman has over a man. You made me think about the faith I thought I'd lost." He gave a low laugh. "You got me back inside a church. And, if all that isn't enough . . ." He took her hand, kissed the palm, and pressed it flat against his bare chest. She could feel the hard pounding of his heart. "Does that make you feel safer?"

She spread her fingers against the full, hard muscles. "A little." She loved the feel of his skin. As she ran her hand over him, he caught his breath. Women did have a certain power. But she couldn't help but wonder how long this kind of hunger and wanting lasted after the wedding vows.

Matthias gave her a hard kiss. "I love you, Kathryn. You have your press. You have your mine. No one—not even your husband—is going to take anything from you. But I hope those aren't the only reasons you married me."

She softened at the look in his eyes. A strong man could be vulnerable, too. He had maneuvered her, but then, he hadn't succeeded without her cooperation. "Other reasons." She pretended to ponder. "Well, I suppose there are a few." She combed her fingers into his hair and pulled his head down while rising up to kiss him.

Matthias raised his head, his breath labored. "What do you say we make a new list?" He rolled her on top of him. "One we'll enjoy working on together."

25

THOSE WHO THOUGHT Matthias Beck would keep Lady
Kathryn housebound, cooking and cleaning, soon saw new edi-
tions of the *Voice*. If anything, she had a renewed fire for civic
improvements to *make Calvada into a town where people can find*
work, marry, have children, and live the good life. Men groaned as
they read. Why couldn't women leave well enough alone?

With the booming Keeweetoss Mine, men poured into
town, and trouble came with them. Kathryn advocated hiring
additional deputies to assist Sheriff Borgeson in keeping the
peace. *One sheriff and one deputy are not enough to handle the*
mischief of an increasing population of single men. We could use a
few more troops to keep men in line.

Alarmed males bellied up to the bar. "What does she mean by keeping men in line?" Surely two lawmen were enough for a town of two thousand! Most liked the odds. Why not let men duke out their differences in the street?

Town council meetings started drawing crowds. The men knew the lady would be there, and bets were on as to who would win the battle of the sexes: Beck or bride. There was considerable consternation when council members reached a compromise: one new deputy would be hired and stiffer fines and penalties of community service sentences would be issued to anyone who disturbed the peace.

Scribe came up with the headline: BECK AND BRIDE TURN THE TIDE. His first editorial earned him a broken nose and a visit to Dr. Blackstone's office, where he met pert and pretty Millicent. With Doc away, it was left to his able sixteen-year-old daughter to straighten things out, and with a firm snap she did. Scribe was so taken, he barely let out a howl. She handed him a rag to stanch the flow of blood and gave him a smile that curled his toes and made him want to follow her around the way Bandit followed Kathryn.

"It's *Millie this* and *Millie that*," Kathryn told Matthias with a laugh and a shake of her head. "He's so preoccupied, he had to reset two lines of type yesterday."

"The poor boy is in love."

"Poor boy. Did you suffer?" she teased.

"What do you think?" Matthias gave her a smile that made her wish they were at home and not in Ronya's Café. Over the past weeks, she'd learned a great deal about how enjoyable marriage could be. She'd even started thinking about cooking and doing his laundry, but came to her senses.

Matthias glanced at her plate of bacon and eggs. "Not eating again?"

She shrugged, feeling slightly queasy. "No need to worry, Mr. Beck. I'm always famished by noon." On the way out of the café, Matthias kissed her cheek before they headed off, Matthias to his office at the hotel and Kathryn to the *Voice* first and then the Keeweetoss.

Kathryn awakened in darkness, disoriented and groggy. Was someone pounding on their door? She heard shouting. Swearing, Matthias pulled on his pants and headed into the front room barefoot. "Hold your horses!" Kathryn heard Axel talking fast, but couldn't make out what he was saying. She was too tired to care, and almost asleep when Matthias came back in a rush. Throwing the covers off her, he pulled her up. "Get dressed! Fast!"

Bleary-eyed and confused, Kathryn sat back on the edge of the bed. "What's happened?"

"The southeast side of town is on fire! And it's coming this way!"

Pandemonium reigned outside the house. Kathryn's eyes burned from the smoke. Coughing, she had to turn away to catch her breath. All the shouting just exacerbated the situation.

"The fire's coming fast!"

"Fill buckets!"

"Hurry!"

"Get out while you can!"

"Where do we go? Oh, God, help us!"

People shouted to one another, running in and out of their homes, dragging and carrying as many possessions as they could manage with each trip and dumping everything in the middle of the street.

"Look! I can see flames!"

"Fire is coming this way!"

A house a few doors down from Matthias and Kathryn's caught fire, embers floating to the roof of the next. The night breeze that was usually pleasant and welcome now fanned the conflagration. Everything was summer dry, a tinderbox.

Matthias closed and latched Kathryn's Saratoga trunk.

"Leave it!" Kathryn shrugged into a shirtwaist and stepped into a blue skirt, no time to lace up a corset or bustle. She shoved a foot into one of her boots. "My father's journals and notebooks are more important!"

Stacking two boxes, Matthias headed for the front door. "Come on, Kate! Let's go!" When he dropped the boxes in the middle of the street, he realized Kathryn hadn't followed him out. Alarmed and furious, he headed back. *"Kathryn!"* The house next door caught fire, and it wouldn't be long before theirs was in flames. Running back inside, Matthias found her filling a laundry basket with books. "What do you think you're doing? We have to get out of here!"

"I want the books."

"Leave them!"

When she didn't go, Matthias caught hold of her. She jerked free. "I can't leave them!"

Not bothering to argue, he swept her up in his arms. Despite her protests and wriggling, Matthias carried her out of the house. When he set her on her feet, she tried to go back. Catching her arm, he spun her back, and locked his arms around her so that she saw the roof had caught fire. Her resistance wilted.

"All of my father's books." She stepped back from the heat when the side of their house caught fire. "Oh, Matthias, our beautiful home . . ." She wept. "All the work you did . . ."

Pulling her close, Matthias rested his chin on the top of her head. "Books can be bought. A house can be rebuilt, darlin'. You can't be replaced." She turned and pressed against him, her body jerking with sobs.

Glowing embers floated everywhere on the night air. Soon the whole block of small homes would be burning. Across the way, people were still hauling out whatever they could salvage. "Stay put. I want to make sure everyone is out of their houses." Matthias set Kathryn away from him and headed up the street.

At the first cry of "Fire!" many managed to haul out furniture, pots and pans, chairs, and supplies. One neighbor told Matthias the fellow next door drank himself into a stupor every Friday night. "We haven't seen him out here." Matthias went in and found the man sprawled on his bed, snoring. When Matthias couldn't rouse him, he pulled the man up and over his shoulder and carried him out. Laying the drunk in the middle of the street, Matthias went to help others frantically heaving things through the front doors of their houses.

Kathryn wasn't where Matthias had left her. Swearing, Matthias looked around. *"Has anyone seen my wife?"* Several pointed toward downtown. He should've known better than to leave her on her own! The sky to the east was lit with orange-and-yellow flames, telling him half the town was gone already. Wherever the fire had started, Calvada would soon be in ashes. A fire of this size couldn't be doused with buckets. It would take God sending a rainstorm!

Matthias knew the first place Kathryn would go and ran down the hill toward Chump Street. He was out of breath by the time he arrived, but there she was. By the grace of God, the building hadn't caught fire.

Merchants were getting everything they could out of their stores before the flames took all. The roof of Aday's General Store was on fire. Nabor carried out a crate of oranges, shouting over his shoulder for Abbie to hurry up, *hurry up*. She appeared, bearing the weight of half a dozen bolts of cloth. Buckling, she fell to her knees. "Get up, you lazy cow!" Nabor kicked her in the side. "Get up and get back in there. Fill the wheelbarrow." Putting his crate down, he hauled her up and shoved her toward the door, where smoke was already billowing. "Hurry up!"

Furious, Matthias left what he was doing, but Kathryn was already running toward the store. "Abbie! Don't go in there!"

Bandit barked, sticking close to her, sensing trouble.

Matthias strode past Kathryn. "See to the others." When she didn't stop, Matthias blocked her way. "I'll handle it!"

Bandit cowered at Matthias's tone, tucked tail, and retreated. Kathryn did not. "Where you go, I go, and let's not waste time arguing because she's gone back in that store! Oh, Lord . . ." Lifting her skirts, Kathryn ran. *"Abbie!"*

Nabor picked up the crate of oranges, shouting at his wife to get the denim pants at the back of the store. He didn't notice Matthias until it was too late. Kicking the oranges aside, Matthias grabbed Nabor by the back of his neck, hauled him up onto the boardwalk, and sent him flying into the store. "Pack your own wheelbarrow!" He followed him inside. "Kathryn!" She came out, an arm around Abbie. "You two stay out here! I'll help that sorry excuse of a man get his precious dungarees."

When Nabor tried to escape, Matthias swung him around and shoved him. "The dungarees, you said. Go get 'em! I'm right behind you." Wide-eyed in fear, whether from the encroaching fire or the one burning in Matthias, Nabor flung a stack of Levi Strauss jeans into a wheelbarrow. They managed to fill and bring out two wheelbarrows full of merchandise before it became too dangerous to go back inside the store.

Matthias grabbed Nabor by the front of his shirt. "If I ever see or hear of you mistreating your wife again, I'll kick you to kingdom come!"

"Matthias." Kathryn's voice was plaintive. "The hotel is on fire."

"I saw. Nothing we can do about it." Matthias had known before he'd headed for Nabor that the hotel would be a total loss. Brady's Saloon had already collapsed, flames and charred bits exploding. Farther down the street, Ronya and Ina Bea stood outside the café, watching it burn. He headed their way, Kathryn catching up and grasping his hand. When they reached the women, Kathryn let go and embraced Ronya, who seemed quite calm despite the scene of lost hope in front of her. Ina Bea and Tweedie stood with her.

"Thank God, you're all right." Kathryn let go of Ronya.

Matthias took her hand again and held it firmly, wanting to make sure she didn't run off to check on someone else and leave him frantic with worry about where she was. "Glad you're all safe and unharmed. I'm sorry about your café, Ronya."

"I smelled smoke and saw the glow coming from Slag Hollow. A breeze was coming this way and I knew it wouldn't take long before it reached town. I got a few things out." She waved her hand toward a pile of pots and pans and boxes of supplies. She shrugged. "It's the third time I've been burned out." She drew her shawl tightly around her shoulders and shook her head. "Nothing to do but start all over."

"Our house is gone." Matthias sighed. "Sometimes you win, sometimes you lose." Almost everyone standing in the middle of Chump Street had lost something tonight. "We'll get back on our feet."

The wind changed, burning Chinatown to the ground, including Jian Lin Gong's new house, built on earnings from Keeweetoss as one of the original partners, a specialist in explosives. He had turned his laundry over to his wife and son. A section of downtown was spared, including City's little house and Barrera's Fandango Hall. It would be hours before they would know how much of the town would be left, and how many might have died.

Matthias found himself praying for rain, knowing even if it came, it would be too late to save Calvada.

The fire swept up the mountainside toward the Keeweetoss Mine. Because trees had been cut down and used for shoring up the underground tunnels, enough underbrush and smaller trees had been cleared so that the fire died down. Men formed a line and threw shovels of dirt, making a firebreak between the office building and the cabins of Amos Stearns, Wyn Reese, and several others. When the fire shifted again, the cabins were spared. The fire raged through the brush, coming up against a rocky incline. Finally it died down, leaving a blackened landscape behind.

Miraculously, no one in Calvada died. People started asking how the fire got started. There hadn't been any lightning storms. Some thought it had started in Slag Hollow.

Barrera's Fandango Hall, Fiona Hawthorne's Dollhouse, and Walker's General Store survived, along with two saloons and most of the big houses on Riverview, including Morgan Sanders's house, which was quickly turned into a shelter for the dispossessed. Though Matthias and Kathryn were offered the master suite, an honor felt due the mayor, she refused to go inside.

"I'd rather live in a saloon than be inside that house ever again!"

"How about the fandango hall?" Matthias told her Jose Barrera had offered to shelter as many as the place could hold.

"Just you and me and fifty men on the wood floor—or sixty, depending on how many of us can squeeze in together." Matthias laughed at her horrified expression. "I thanked him for the kind offer and told him we already have accommodations."

"We do? Where?"

"Scribe offered City's house." Bandit would also be welcome, unless the canine preferred the outdoors where he could search for tasty barbecued raccoon or opossum, courtesy of the Calvada fire.

The back apartment was spotless, everything in its place, the sheets and blankets clean, the bed remade. Kathryn grinned. "Either you've changed your habits, Scribe, or Millicent Blackstone took charge."

He smiled slightly. "It was Millie."

Matthias chuckled. "You should marry that girl before someone else sees her worth."

Scribe blushed. It seemed the idea had already occurred to him. "Yeah, well, we're talking about this winter. She'll be seventeen in December, and she thinks that's a good month for a wedding."

Kathryn looked surprised. "She's so young."

"She has a mind of her own, that's for sure." Scribe shrugged.

Matthias grinned at Kathryn. "Sounds like someone else I know." He extended his hand to Scribe. "Congratulations. It's a good thing, kid. The best decision a man can make is to marry a smart woman." He winked at Kathryn.

Axel Borgeson came into the *Voice* office the next day. "Kathryn? I need to speak with you." She followed him outside. "Fiona sent word to me that one of her girls is sick and asking for you."

Kathryn was confused. "Why didn't she just send a messenger?"

"She asked me to come too."

"Did she say why?"

"She said Monique keeps asking for you. She's raving in French. And she said something about a murder in San Francisco." He shrugged.

Kathryn went back inside to tell Matthias she'd been called away and didn't know how long she'd be gone. Then she and Axel headed for Fiona Hawthorne's Dollhouse.

Elvira Haines opened the door. She kept her head down as she stepped back, allowing them into the house. Kathryn felt regret that she hadn't found a way to spare Elvira from this life. Elvira seemed weighed down by shame. "Fiona is with Monique. They're upstairs. Second door on the left." She turned away without raising her head. "I'll be in the kitchen."

Monique looked awful, eyes sunken, lips dry and cracked. A half-empty bottle of laudanum was on the side table.

Fiona glanced up at Kathryn, stricken with grief. She shook her head. "Doc Blackstone said it's a malignancy. There's nothing that can be done but give her laudanum."

Monique moaned and moved restlessly. The once-beautiful young woman appeared wizened and old, face twisted. She looked up at Kathryn, her eyes fierce. She spoke in French, and Kathryn drew back, understanding.

Axel looked at her. "Do you understand French? What did she say?"

"'I killed him. I smashed in his head. And I'd do it again.'"

Monique raised her head, eyes crazed, spewing French at Kathryn.

"'I'd kill them all if I could . . .'" Kathryn translated, as Fiona tried to offer her a drink of water.

Sinking back, Monique shook her head, crying now like a broken child. "I thought he loved me . . ." Her chest heaved with sobs. "He did!" Angry again, she glared at Fiona. "He would have married me if you hadn't interfered." She called Fiona a name that Kathryn couldn't translate, but which sounded vile.

Fiona straightened, staring down at the dying girl.

Axel stepped closer, looking intently at Fiona. "Is she talking about you and Morgan Sanders?"

"I don't think so." Fiona leaned over Monique for a moment and then drew back, comprehending. "Oh, no, Monique. Oh, you didn't . . ."

"He always wanted me. I couldn't bear seeing him go into your room." Monique's breathing grew ragged. She cried like a child again. "I only went with Morgan to make him jealous. I went to him and told him that. I promised never to do it again."

Confused, Kathryn looked at Fiona. Who was Monique talking about? She felt a sick premonition.

Monique's shoulders heaved as she cried. "He said it was all right. He said he had no claim on me."

Glaring at Fiona with glazed eyes, she kept on. "I did it. I hit him."

Axel stepped forward, but Fiona pressed between him and the dying woman. "You killed City."

Monique's face contorted with hatred. "Yes. I killed him."

"Why?" Fiona cried out.

"He turned his back on me like they all do." She raised her head. "I hit him with the handle of the press he loved so much." She sank back, body shaking. "I loved him! And then I hated him. I wanted him dead! I want them all dead! They all turned their backs . . ."

Fiona fled the room, weeping. Tears flooded Kathryn's eyes at Monique's confession.

Axel stepped close to the bed. "Did you kill Morgan Sanders, Miss Beaulieu?"

Monique looked at him in confusion. Her cracked lips curved in a seductive smile that altered into one of satisfaction, her expression twisted by madness. The horrifying transformation made Kathryn step back.

"Monique?" Axel spoke again. "What about Morgan Sanders?"

Monique glared at Kathryn. "He said he was going to marry you. He'd still send the carriage for me whenever he wanted my company. Then he turned his back and poured himself a glass of wine. I took up the poker and hit him."

"What's she saying?" Axel demanded.

"Il avait l'air tellement si surpris." Monique gave a soft laugh, her body relaxing.

"Kathryn!"

"She killed Morgan Sanders."

Axel frowned. "What about Wyn Reese? Did he lie for you? He said you were with him all night."

"He thought I was." She giggled. "I put laudanum in his whiskey. He never knew I left." Her face was white and blank. "He didn't even move when I got back into bed with him." As her breathing slowed, she seemed to shrink into the bed.

Axel took Kathryn by the arm. "We'd better go."

"I can't leave her alone."

"She murdered your father. She murdered Morgan Sanders, and maybe even others, if her confession is to be believed."

"Whatever she's done, Axel, she's still a human being." Kathryn felt compassion come upon her that was beyond her understanding. Surely, even now, there was hope for Monique's tortured soul.

"Matthias will have my head for bringing you here in the first place. I can't leave you—"

"You didn't bring me, Axel. I was called here."

"You can't save everyone, Kathryn." He went quietly out of the room. Neither Fiona nor Elvira returned.

Monique turned her head and looked at Kathryn. "Everyone leaves me . . ."

"I won't leave."

Wringing out a cloth, she took the chair Fiona had occupied and wiped Monique's brow. The laudanum had taken effect. Could Monique be reached in such a state? Whatever happened, Kathryn knew what she must do. Leaning forward, she spoke truth tenderly into Monique's ear and prayed the hope and saving grace it offered would reach the dying girl in time.

Kathryn prayed softly in French until Monique growled bitterly that she hated God and couldn't stand to hear another word. It was a long, difficult night as Monique mumbled incoherently, cried in pain, and battled for life. In her last moments, a look of terror came into her eyes. She uttered a soft cry before she died, shrinking as her lungs expelled air. Filled with pity, Kathryn closed her eyes, covered her with a sheet, and blew out the lamp.

<hr />

Matthias rounded the corner of Gomorrah and saw Kathryn coming out of Fiona Hawthorne's house. "Kate!" He ran toward her, pulling her into his arms when he reached her. "Axel told me about Monique."

"She's gone."

"God's mercy." He let out his breath, relieved that he had his wife in his arms. "If she'd lived, she would've stood trial for two murders and been hanged." He felt Kathryn trembling, no doubt the aftermath of what Monique had confessed about City

Walsh. He held her at arm's distance, studying her. "You look wrung out and hung to dry."

She gave a soft laugh. "Thank you very much." She felt dead on her feet. "She was so lost, Matthias. I couldn't leave her."

He tucked a tendril of hair behind her ear. "Axel said you were speaking to her when he left."

"I don't know if she heard anything I said to her."

"You did what you could, darlin'."

26

CITY'S BED WASN'T BUILT FOR TWO. Matthias lay on his side, head propped up, one arm around Kathryn's waist. She wiggled over onto her back, pensive. "I wonder what made Monique the way she was."

He moved his hand to her hip, keeping her secure. If they weren't careful, they could end up rolling onto the floor. "Some people are bent on evil, Kate." He gave a heavy sigh. "I saw it in the war. Some men loved the battle. You'd see it in their eyes. Something's missing. Or corrupted almost beyond redemption." Like Morgan Sanders.

"Her last moments . . ." Kathryn shuddered. "She hated God."

"Blamed Him, probably. He's often the scapegoat for people who mess up their lives." Hadn't he himself turned his back on the Lord?

Kathryn looked at him. "But did she have a wounded soul—or a seared conscience?"

It was one of the many things Matthias loved about Kathryn. She cared deeply about people, even those who were twisted and relished evil. "Only God knows."

Sighing, she stared up at the ceiling. When she closed her eyes, he thought she'd gone to sleep. Then she spoke again. "I think a hundred people packed up and headed out of town today."

"You can't blame them."

"It just means rebuilding will be harder." She didn't sound happy about it. Rebuilding would be a monumental job.

"Some would rather start fresh somewhere else."

Kathryn turned her head toward him. "I'm so sorry about your hotel, Matthias."

Her eyes were like a spring meadow, her skin like silk. "Our hotel," he corrected her. "Walker's is still standing, and I own half of a thriving drayage company." He didn't want to count his losses, not when he had his greatest blessing lying beside him.

"You aren't thinking of moving to Sacramento, are you?"

"I still have time to serve as mayor."

"You make it sound like a sentence rather than a privilege."

Matthias chuckled. "Depends on how you look at it." He loved the feel of his wife tucked against him. She'd be better off in a big town. Safer, too. With good men running the Keeweetoss, the operation would continue smoothly even without her here. Amos Stearns and Wyn Reese had proven themselves fully capable and trustworthy.

The town would have to be rebuilt from the ground up. It would take time to reframe businesses and homes. More than likely, Calvada would go right back to what it was before Kathryn arrived. Axel said he'd stay, but his two deputies had left town among the caravan of others, and one man might not be able to prevent the place from descending into the rough-and-tumble wild town it had been. But right now, Matthias had other things on his mind than what it would take to recover from the fire.

Kathryn caught hold of his wandering hand. "You are mayor, Matthias, and you can do a lot of good. The sooner we get started, the better."

Matthias groaned inwardly. Knowing his wife, he could expect big ideas. "There's not much of a town left to manage, and even a mayor gets a night off." He nibbled her earlobe.

Shivering, Kathryn pulled away enough to look at him. "There's more to do now than there ever has been. A town isn't buildings. It's people!"

Nudging her chin up, he went for her throat. "Darlin', I know, but Rome wasn't built in a day."

"We're not talking about Rome." She edged away again. "We're talking about a mining town that will be tents until houses can be built. You're the man to see that Calvada comes out of this crisis better than before."

Kathryn was on a straight and narrow road. Matthias put a fork ahead and knew which prong he wanted to take. "You were singing a different song a few months ago about my abilities." He ran his hand up her thigh. When she exhaled a soft sound, his pulse shot up. Success was close at hand.

"Matthias . . ." Kathryn put her hand on his bare chest. "That's before I saw what you're capable of accomplishing." Her mouth was at his jugular. "When you had motivation . . ."

Groaning, he laughed. "Woman . . ." He encircled her waist; he pulled her tight against him. "I appreciate the confidence you have in me, but . . ." When she drew her head back and looked at him again, he knew her mind wasn't following the same path as his. The wheels inside that fertile brain of hers were spinning again. She probably already had a plan of what the future could hold, God willing, and the river didn't rise. A flood! That's all they would need to add to recent disasters, and it wasn't beyond the realm of possibility. Sliding his hand over her hip, he tried one last time. "Are you going to deny your husband his rights if I don't organize the town's rebuilding?"

She batted her eyelashes at him. "I suppose I could make that sacrifice if I knew it was for the good of our neighbors."

"You don't play fair!" Testing her resolve, he kissed her. "I could win this battle, couldn't I?"

Breathless, Kathryn put her hand firmly against his chest. "Do behave, Matthias."

"I am behaving."

She laughed and drew in a sharp breath. "Stop it! Now listen . . ."

"I'm all ears."

"The Keeweetoss is still in operation. We'll need more men. They'll bring families with them."

"If they have families." She needed a reminder how few men had wives, let alone children.

She went on quickly. "Not all of the men who come will be miners. Some will be carpenters, wagoners, lumberjacks, bankers, shopkeepers. We'll put out advertisements . . ."

Matthias made a sound of acquiescence, only half-listening. She threw off the covers and got up. "You have a one-track mind, Mr. Beck!" Scowling down at him, she wrapped a blanket around herself. "There should be rules!"

Propping his head up again, Matthias grinned, unrepentant.

She looked flushed and beautiful. "Oh, no, darlin'. No rules in love or war."

"You can stop looking at me like that."

"What's wrong with the way I look at my wife?" He patted the empty space beside him. "We can talk in the morning."

Kathryn moved to City's old chair near the potbellied stove. A bookcase used to be against the wall behind her, the one he'd moved into their new house. He remembered how desperate Kathryn had been trying to save those books and almost felt sorry he hadn't gone back inside to rescue them from the flames. At least City's journals and notebooks were safe.

Kathryn sat, knees pressed together, hugging the blanket around her shoulders, expression serious. "We need a plan, Matthias. The fire was a terrible disaster, but it could also provide our greatest opportunity. The mountains are so beautiful up here, and all that fresh river water coming off the mountain. We only have a couple of months before winter hits. We could lay out a new Calvada."

"A new Calvada?"

"We could present a plan to everyone. Think of it! A town square, a grid of roads with drainage ditches on each side to direct rainwater and snowmelt. We could design a water system so there wouldn't be any chance of contamination from outhouses. The mine will draw people, lots of people. When they come, we want them to look around and decide this is a good place to sink roots, start families . . ."

She was a dreamer. It was one of the things Matthias loved about his wife, her optimistic spirit. But she needed to face the facts. "When the copper and silver play out, those same people will leave. Calvada is at the end of the road, Kate. The Madera was playing out and is now shut down for lack of leadership. The Jackrabbit is finished. Twin Peaks Mine shut down. Calvada will go from boom to bust in the next few years."

"You can't know that."

"It's the nature of a boomtown. People will leave. People who had little to begin with don't want to start over and have even less. They want to go to Truckee or Reno or Placerville or Sacramento, where they can find work. Even more would head home if they had the money to get there. When this town dies, the buildings will be razed, reusable materials loaded onto wagons and taken somewhere else."

"You're forgetting the Keeweetoss. Amos said there's enough copper to last for years."

"One man's opinion, and a young and inexperienced one at that."

"He's a geologist, and he's talking about the quality of copper they've been bringing out over the last months."

"And they could run into a wall of granite tomorrow. Mines are bonanzas one week and a bust the next."

Kathryn just looked at him with those confident green eyes. "Granite is good, too. It's used to build structures that last."

"Like tombstones."

"Oh, Matthias!" Clearly frustrated, she stood, pacing, blanket tightly wrapped around her. "You've been here longer than I have. You must have some feeling for this place!"

"Sacramento is a hub, and Henry and I have mapped out routes from there. California is going to keep growing, and goods will need to be transported. It was never my plan to stay here forever."

She wilted into City's chair. "But surely you feel some loyalty to the people here."

"Yes. I do. But that doesn't mean I want us to settle here permanently." When his wife's eyes welled with tears, Matthias grew concerned. The tough-minded little editor had gone all soft lately. "Tell me truthfully. When you arrived, did you look around Calvada and say to yourself, 'This is the place I want to spend the rest of my life'?"

She gave a soft laugh. "No."

"Well, then?"

"Over the past year I've seen what this town could be."

"Darlin', I'm not saying we'll get on the stage and leave the day I finish my term as mayor."

Kathryn gave a shuddering breath and wiped a tear away. She had that faraway look on her face again. "It's the people I've come to love, Matthias. I can't bear the thought of leaving Ronya. She's the best friend I've ever had. And Ina Bea will marry Axel in the next few months. Scribe is as close to me as a brother. He'll marry Millicent by Christmas and probably have a baby on the way by January! I want to see their children grow up. And then there's Wiley and Carl and Kit, Herr, and Reverend and Mrs. Thacker, and a dozen others who are our friends. And Fiona . . ." She looked at him with tears flooding her eyes. "And there's Wyn and Elvira . . ."

Matthias could see her winding down. Yawning, she sagged slightly. She looked pale, shadows under her eyes, and she seemed to have talked herself out for the evening. Sighing, she rose and came back to bed without prompting. Slipping under the covers, she remained facing him. "You do make me very happy, Mr. Beck." Her hand slid around him, sending heat waves through his body, but Scribe had told Matthias he found Kathryn curled up on the sofa in the middle of the day. She seemed exhausted, and that worried him. She usually pulsed with life.

Matthias had to batten down his desire. She needed sleep. "Roll over, darlin'." When she did, he tucked her tightly into him, like two spoons in a drawer. "Maybe you should see Doc. Just have him make sure you're okay. What do you think?"

When she didn't answer, Matthias rose up slightly and looked at her. She'd already fallen asleep!

It was a long time before he could.

A few days later, Ronya's Café had risen from the ashes as a large tent with plank tables and benches for customers. Kathryn and Matthias joined others who had lost their homes. She was worried about Fiona. "I haven't seen her since the day Monique Beaulieu died. I want to make sure she's all right." She knew Matthias valued loyalty as much as she did. "And Elvira, too, of course."

He frowned at her untouched plate. "Why aren't you eating?"

"I'm not hungry." In fact, she felt queasy looking at the food on his plate.

"Are you feeling sick? Have you seen Doc Blackstone yet?"

"No, I'm fine. I'm sure it's just that I'm worn-out."

"And no wonder." His eyes lightened. "You were feeling good last night." He grinned. "I'm pretty tired myself this morning."

Blushing, she gave him a stern look. "Do be quiet, Mr. Beck," she whispered, but he just chuckled. Kathryn folded her napkin and put it on the table and got up to leave.

Matthias caught her wrist. "A kiss before you go."

"Not in public, for heaven's sake!"

"The place is empty, and I'm not letting you go until you obey me." He gave her a roguish grin.

"Very well." She leaned toward him. When he closed his eyes, she planted a kiss on his forehead and hurried off with a laughing glance over her shoulder.

When Kathryn came around the corner, she saw Wyn Reese at Fiona's front door. "Wyn! What're you doing in town?"

He swung around, his face going red. "Mrs. Beck. I didn't expect to see you here. I just wanted to check and make sure—"

"Fiona and Elvira are friends of mine."

"They are?" His brows rose slightly. "Well, that's good."

"I'm sorry for your loss, Wyn." He looked bemused, and she went on, uncertain now. "I know you and Monique were . . . friends." She blushed, feeling she'd blundered. He looked ill at ease.

"Of a sort." He sounded grim. "She was trouble. Truth is, I was hoping she'd turn her affections to someone else because—" He shook his head and shrugged. "Never mind." He glanced up at the window, dejected. "I . . . I'd better go. I should be at the mine." His mouth curved. "The boss lady might fire me." He gave a nod. "Good day to you, Mrs. Beck." Stepping back, he put on his hat and walked away.

The door opened and Elvira peered out. "Oh. Mrs. Beck. I thought I heard a knock." She saw Wyn Reese walking away and looked disappointed.

"May I come inside?"

"Oh, no. Fiona said not to let you in."

"Well, I'm coming in." Kathryn stepped over the threshold. "How is Fiona?"

"She's grieving." Elvira looked like a child about to be repri-manded. "She blames herself for City's death."

"I'll talk with her." Kathryn started down the hallway toward Fiona's apartment, but another matter was on her mind. "Do you know Wyn Reese, Elvira?"

Elvira glanced away. "Why would you ask?"

"He was here. Outside the door."

"Oh, well, he comes around sometimes. Monique told the girls Wyn was her beau."

Kathryn felt a chill go through her at those words. "Did you meet Wyn here?"

"Oh, no. I knew him before I came here. He and my husband were friends." Elvira lifted one shoulder in a half-hearted shrug. "I can imagine what he thinks of me now, working in a place like this." Her eyes grew moist and bright. "I'll never forget the look on his face the first time he saw me here." She put fingertips to her lips. "I've never been so ashamed." She blinked her eyes rapidly. "Wyn works at your mine, doesn't he?"

Kathryn saw something in the young woman's eyes that hinted at feelings beyond friendship for the man. "He's my foreman." She intended to go up to the Keeweetoss right after she spoke with Fiona. She put a hand on Elvira's arm. "Life can change in—"

"It's too late, Mrs. Beck. I'm thankful you speak to me at all. No one else does." She walked to the doorway. "You know where Fiona's room is."

Fiona was pale. Kathryn wasn't in the room two minutes before she started weeping. "It's my fault your father is dead, Kathryn."

Kathryn sat and took her hand. "You couldn't have known."

"I knew she was trouble when she first came. She was scared, and then she settled in and I noticed a dark side to her, an arrogance, a possessiveness. I've been thinking back and remembering what she was like after City spent that first evening with me. She was furious. She said some hurtful things. I just never thought . . ." She put trembling fingers to her temples. "And then Sanders. The signs were there. I just didn't see them." She leaned back, looking worn down and depressed. "I've had enough. I'm selling the house and leaving Calvada. There are too many memories here."

"Where will you go, Fiona?"

"Another mining town." She smiled bleakly. "And who knows? I might even try another trade."

"I hope you do, and that you find happiness in it. What about the other women?"

"I'll take them with me."

"Would you be upset if Elvira stayed?"

Fiona gave a soft laugh. "I wish she would. She's not much good at this work. She's so miserable, she makes the clients feel guilty." She cocked her head, studying Kathryn. "Why do you ask?"

"I just had a thought, but I don't want to make any assumptions or give Elvira false hope."

"I feel responsible for her." Fiona walked with Kathryn to the door. "Calvada hasn't been the same since you arrived, Kathryn." Her smile was tender. "It's as though you picked up where City left off. He'd be so proud of you."

Kathryn felt hot tears welling. "Are you sure you couldn't stay and start fresh here?"

Fiona gave a long sigh. "Women like me can't shake the past if they stay in the same place."

Kathryn hugged her. "Thank you."

"For what?"

"Loving my father."

"That was easy. Losing him was hard."

As soon as Kathryn left Fiona's house, she went straight to the livery stable and rented a carriage. When she reached the mine, Amos caught her up on business. She interrupted him and asked to see Wyn Reese on a personal matter. Clearly curious, but not asking questions, Amos sent one of the men into the tunnel to get him.

Wyn came into the office, dust-covered, face grimy with dirt. Amos excused himself and left them alone. Wyn faced

Kathryn as though she had a rifle, and he had a target on his chest. "You sent for me, Mrs. Beck?"

Kathryn knew she was sticking her nose into his business, but sometimes waiting for a man to make up his mind allowed a God-given opportunity to pass by. "Do you care enough about Elvira Haines to marry her?"

He didn't speak for a moment, then let out his breath. "I saw her in Fiona's parlor once and she looked at me like I was . . . I don't know." He rubbed his neck. "I doubt she wants anything to do with me."

Kathryn couldn't curb her impatience. "Wyn! Do you care for her?"

"Yeah. I care. Plenty." His face was set and tormented. "I cared when Walter was alive and treating her poorly. Did my best to keep him away from the house when he'd been drinking, and—"

"You're off duty as of this moment. Get a fresh suit of clothes, go down to the bathhouse, and clean yourself up. Get your hair and beard trimmed. Then go and get her out of Fiona's house."

"I don't know if—"

"*I* know. And that's an order, Mr. Reese." When he stood undecided, she gave an exasperated sigh. "Get moving!"

Wyn looked taken aback, then laughed. "Yes, ma'am. Is this what Matthias puts up with on a daily basis?"

Kathryn smiled. "Mr. Beck gives as good as he gets, Mr. Reese. Now, go on and rescue your lady."

"Well, whatever upset your stomach this morning is gone now." Matthias chuckled, looking at Kathryn's empty plate. She'd eaten a steak, mashed potatoes, summer squash, and had just finished a large slice of apple pie. "You ate more than I did."

"I was hungry!" She finished the last of her tall glass of milk before telling him what she'd been doing all day. Matthias leaned back, looking smug and happy listening to her talk about Wyn Reese and Elvira. He wondered if she saw the irony that a woman once so opposed to marriage was now playing match-maker. Winding down, she told him about Fiona Hawthorne's plans to leave Calvada.

"You like her, don't you?"

"Yes, I do. When I first arrived, she wouldn't speak to me because she was worried my reputation might be damaged, as if I didn't manage that on my own. She's kind and generous. Had she skills like Ronya's, her life would've been much different."

"You look as if you're about to cry."

"Well, I don't want her to leave, but I understand why she must." Kathryn swallowed the lump in her throat, wondering why her emotions were so close to the surface lately. All the losses from the fire, of course. "She's grieving over my father, Matthias, blaming herself for something that wasn't her fault."

Matthias put his hand over hers. "They were good friends."

"Oh, they were so much more than friends." She managed to fight back tears. "I wouldn't know anything about my father if not for her." One tear escaped. She wiped it quickly away. "I don't know what's wrong with me lately."

"It's been a rough spell, Kate. You've been working from early morning until evening."

"So have you. And I don't see you getting teary-eyed."

"I have my moments, but I'm a man, and not allowed to show it." He'd been told he was the right man for the job of mayor, but it had been the crisis that opened his eyes to how much he cared about the people of Calvada.

"Talk yourself out, darlin'?" His tone was teasing, but he looked serious.

"I'm so tired, you might have to carry me." She was only half-teasing.

"I want you to see Doc first thing tomorrow morning."

Kathryn mm-hmmed agreement.

"I mean it, Kate. Tomorrow morning." He took her hand as they walked home, letting her set the pace.

Doc Blackstone spoke briefly with Kathryn and then called in his daughter, explaining that though she wasn't going to medical school due to distance and expense, she knew a great deal already, and what she'd learned in Sacramento would be useful to Kathryn. Perplexed, Kathryn greeted Millie as the girl took the other chair in front of Doc's desk.

Kathryn already knew that Millie was bright and passionate. Like Kathryn, the girl read everything she could get her hands on, and Doc had a sizable library of medical textbooks.

Millie looked at her father. "What are her symptoms?" He read the notes he'd taken on Kathryn's symptoms: nausea for the past couple of weeks, frequently exhausted and taking naps when she never had before, and unfamiliar tenderness.

"Where?"

He blushed. "She didn't say, and I didn't ask."

"Well, I think I know already." Millicent touched her bodice and smiled at Kathryn. "Oh, you've no need to look so worried, Mrs. Beck. There's nothing at all wrong with you that time won't solve." Her father cleared his throat, but her attention was fixed on Kathryn. "You're pregnant! Isn't that wonderful?"

Doc Blackstone scowled. "Millie, that's not a word we use."

"Why on earth not? Does a farmer say his cow is in a family way?"

Kathryn opened her mouth and then closed it. "You needn't be embarrassed, Kathryn. It's not as if you and Matthias have transgressed the commandments. You are married and healthy. It's not surprising you'll make babies together."

Kathryn's face heated even more as she sat stunned, trying to take in the information, while Millie harrumphed at her father's hushed reprimand to have a care in saying too much too soon. Rolling her eyes, Millicent leaned closer to Kathryn. "It's one of the subjects medical schools neglect out of a ridiculous sense of moral delicacy. Good heavens! I ask you! What is more natural than a woman having a baby? It's the most blessed occurrence in her life. I hope Scribe and I will have a dozen."

Coughing, Doc Blackstone stood. "I'm going to leave my daughter to speak with you, Kathryn. She may be young, but she knows a great deal more about your condition than most men in the field of medicine. She helped me deliver several babies while I practiced medicine in Sacramento."

"Which is one of the reasons we came up here," Millicent remarked dryly. "The new mothers didn't object, but there were people who didn't think I should know *anything* about how babies are made, let alone be a midwife at my age. I was something of a scandal."

"You and I have much in common, Millie." Kathryn learned more about the facts of life in the next hour of conversation with Millicent than Matthias had taught her since they'd married. By the time Millicent finished explaining what she knew about how a baby grew, Kathryn sat speechless, in awe.

"Isn't God's plan marvelous?" Millicent took Kathryn's hand and squeezed it. "Women have the privilege of bringing life into the world." She giggled. "Of course, men play their small part . . . so we must be thankful. They take on more responsibility as the child grows up. Or one can hope."

"Why not from the beginning?" Kathryn wondered aloud.

"Can you imagine a man volunteering to change diapers?" Millicent laughed at the very idea. "And they lack the equipment for feeding a baby, don't they?" She patted Kathryn's hand the way an older woman would do to a much younger one. "Try not to worry." Millicent might be full of confidence, but being told not to worry only made Kathryn worry more. "Just pray you don't have twins the first time around!"

That remark shot cold dread through Kathryn's heart. She was still adjusting to the news that she carried a child. What would people say about this, when she had been so public about her intention to stay single? Her mouth twitched.

On the walk back to the *Voice* office, Kathryn swung between euphoria and terror. Despite Millicent's enthusiasm, Kathryn knew women died in childbirth. And she felt ill-equipped to be a good mother. What would Matthias say? Would he want to hide her away the same way Lawrence Pershing had hidden her mother until Kathryn's baby brother was born? She had too much work to do, and she had to be out and around town to do it!

Matthias and three other men were in the front office of the *Voice*, looking over rough drawings. Her husband glanced up and winked. "Want to take a look at what you started?"

Distracted, she shrugged. "I think I need to lie down." Bandit got off the sofa and followed her into the apartment. She closed the door and sank onto the bed. Bandit jumped up beside her and put his head in her lap, rolling his eyes so he could look up at her with canine sympathy. Could the dog sense she was in a family way? She stroked Bandit's head. "Can you?" He lifted his head, ears perked, questioning.

The men talked in lowered voices. The front door opened and closed. Matthias came into the apartment. "What'd Doc say?"

"You'd better sit down." He went white and she saw the fear in his eyes. She wanted to allay his fears. "I'm not sick."

"Then what's wrong with you?"

"Nothing." She blushed. "I'm with child."

Matthias froze, staring at her. Then he let out his breath in relief. "Thank God."

Apparently, Matthias had been thinking she had some dread disease and limited time left on this earth. She waited for the news to sink in deeper.

"A baby." He grinned as though he had struck gold. Taking her hands, he pulled her up and into his arms, burying his face in the curve of her neck. "Praise God!" Withdrawing, he cupped her face, his eyes brimming with joy and a hearty measure of male pride. "We'll have to come up with a name."

"It's a little early, I think. We don't know if it's a boy or a girl." Kathryn couldn't help but catch his excitement.

"Something strong for a boy. Daniel is a good name. And something tender and sweet for a girl . . ."

Kathryn lifted her chin. "Deborah." A biblical prophetess, judge, and military commander. "But then, if we have others—"

"God willing." Matthias tucked a tendril of hair behind her ear. "We'll work on it."

"Will we be giving them D names, too? Damaris, David, Dorcas . . . ?"

"We could start at the beginning of the alphabet. Abigail. Adam."

She frowned at him. "How many children do you want?"

"As many as God gives us." He smirked. "Sages say the best way to handle a woman is to keep her barefoot and pregnant." When she stepped back, he pulled her close. "Don't worry. I'll make sure you have slippers and shoes, and boots, and I'll do my best—"

"Do be quiet!" Kathryn leaned back, poking her finger in the center of Matthias's chest. "Do not think this is going to keep me housebound and subservient."

He captured her finger and bit the end. "Are you going to put the news in the *Voice* or am I permitted to stand in the middle of Chump Street and announce it to the world?"

She felt like her blood was carbonated. A baby! "I suppose we could do both."

At first, the bets had been whether the baby would be a boy or girl. Now, with her increasing size, men were betting whether she'd have twins. Even the miners had picked dates and started building a pot for the winner. Carrying a baby didn't stop Kathryn from going up to the Keeweetoss Mine once a week to meet with Amos Stearns, Wyn Reese, Jian Lin Gong, and several other heads of operations.

This morning, Kathryn had spotted a man climbing the steep slope beyond the mine offices. When Wyn came out to help her up the stairs, she asked about the visitor.

"That's 'Crazy Klaus' Johannson. Jumped ship in San Francisco and came up here to work. Says our mountains remind him of Sweden. He started working night shifts so he'd have days free. Takes him two hours to climb up there, and less than ten minutes to come back down. I've seen men do some crazy things for fun, but watching him come down that mountain looks like a mad rush to death to me."

"I'd like to see what he does."

Kathryn had just adjourned the meeting when one of the workers came in. The Swede had made the summit. "I have a chair and blanket ready for you, Mrs. Beck, so you can be comfortable and warm while you watch."

She didn't remain seated long. Drawing in a breath, she stood at the railing as Crazy Klaus wove back and forth across the white slope, sending up fans of snow with each sharp turn. Midway, he doubled over, tucked the poles under his arms, and came shooting down the steepest part, aiming for a mound at breakneck speed. He soared up and over with an echoing whoop of pure joy, did a backwards somersault, and landed on his feet to the cheer of a dozen men watching the show. Turning his body sideways, he skidded down the last hundred feet and stopped. Removing the boards fastened to his feet, he shouldered them and headed back up.

"Time for one more run," Wyn told her. "He calls those things skis."

Kathryn's heart still raced. "I'm surprised there aren't men lining up to learn how to do that!" She would be if she wasn't expecting a baby.

"There are. Half a dozen fools are carving and smoothing boards . . ."

On the way home, Kathryn had time to think about the future of the Keeweetoss and Calvada and Crazy Klaus coming down the mountain on skis. Matthias was conducting a meeting in the parlor of their newly rebuilt house. The men all stood as Kathryn came in. Matthias's brows rose slightly as he looked her over. "Good news?"

"Oh, yes!" She laughed, pulling off her gloves as she headed for the kitchen, where she kept some writing materials. Throwing her coat over a chair, she went to work jotting down lists of things that would have to be done to put a plan in motion.

A few minutes later, Matthias leaned against the doorjamb,

watching her. "You looked ready to burst when you came in the door."

"I feel ready to burst, but Millie says it will be a few more weeks."

"Men have a lot of money riding on dates."

"So I heard." She rolled her eyes. "They need better things to do with their money than gamble." She grinned.

"Uh-oh. What sort of wild hare plan are you getting us into this time?"

"Just an idea." She chuckled. "An alternate future for Calvada, if the mine ever shuts down."

EPILOGUE

✦

MATTHIAS AND KATHRYN BECK continued to live and work happily for the betterment of Calvada, though they made frequent visits to Sacramento. The Becks eventually had eight children, five boys and three girls. Matthias and Henry Call continued as partners in Beck and Call Drayage. The company delivered goods up and down the state of California, eventually building refrigerated boxcars that sent California produce east by train. Matthias was reelected as mayor for a second term, but declined to run again after that.

Wyn Reese married Elvira Haines, and they had four children. Scribe and Millie had seven children, four sons and three daughters. Though Kathryn continued to write editorials and articles, she turned the newspaper over to Scribe after the birth of her fourth child. The Mercer boys graduated from the Mother Lode School and went to work as reporters for the *Voice*. They both learned to ski, married local girls, and settled down to rear families in Calvada.

The Keeweetoss continued to produce high quality silver and copper for the next two decades. The Twelve who first joined Kathryn's business experiment became wealthy men. Some stayed on with the mine; others used their profit-shared earnings to start other businesses. Jian Lin Gong became a banker in the Chinese community.

Determined that Calvada would not die like so many other mining towns when the mine did eventually play out, Kathryn worked with Crazy Klaus Johannson to develop an alternative source of income for the town. By the time the Keeweetoss Mine closed, the Keeweetoss Mountain Ski Resort was drawing hundreds of tourists each winter.

Kathryn donated the money to build a town square. She laid out the plan: a cross of walkways to the center, where a large gazebo stood. Pine trees were planted to offer shade to families who would gather for concerts and outdoor plays during the hot summer evenings. The gazebo was decorated for Easter, Fourth of July, Thanksgiving, and Christmas. The square became a gathering place for Calvadans. Businesses surrounded the square. Ronya Vanderstrom's Café and Boardinghouse took a sizable space in the middle of one block.

Aday's General Store took up the center of another block on the square. Nabor slipped on an orange peel and broke his neck when he fell on a barrel full of kidney beans. Few mourned his passing, other than sweet Abbie, who then hired two men and continued to run the store successfully. She bought herself a piano, something she had missed from her days as a girl back East.

When the Nineteenth Amendment passed and the presidential election came in November 1920, Kathryn Walsh Beck gave a speech from the Calvada gazebo. When the polls opened, she and her three daughters were ushered to the front of the line, casting the first votes by women in Calvada. After Matthias and their sons voted, Kathryn and Matthias lingered on a park bench in the town square, listening to the band play patriotic songs.

"It's a good life, isn't it?" Kathryn watched people wandering in the square, children laughing and running along walkways. A boy had climbed a pine tree, his mother pleading for him to come down. Families sat on blankets, enjoying picnic dinners.

"Yes, it is." Matthias slid his arm around her. She leaned her head against his shoulder. "Good speech, darlin'."

Kathryn sighed. "Oh, I didn't think people would want to listen for more than thirty minutes, but there was so much more I wanted to say."

"It's always wise to keep a speech short." Chuckling, he kissed her forehead. "That's why God made you a writer."

A NOTE FROM THE AUTHOR

Dear Reader,

COVID-19 hit shortly after my husband and I returned from South Africa and the filming of *Redeeming Love*. All trips on our schedule were canceled, and we joined the masses of citizens ordered to shelter in place. As the weeks at home turned into months, it seemed the perfect time to reimagine and rewrite a story that had been with me for decades, something addressing serious issues with humor and grace. Life had become too somber to add heaviness to it. We all need to laugh, even when days are dark—maybe even more so during those times. And we all want changes for the better and a happy ending.

My stories always start with questions, and several had been on my mind that would work in an 1870s silver mining town with applications for today. Can one person impact an entire community? We've all met and watched people who inspire others. We all know people who follow their conscience no matter the cost. What can we do to make life better for those experiencing homelessness? We see them living in tents and shanties in our towns across the country. Is there a better, more equitable way to "spread the wealth" without stealing from one group to give it to another? The apostle James said, "Pure and genuine religion in the sight of God the Father means caring for orphans and widows in their distress and refusing to let the world corrupt you" (James 1:27). How does that look?

The Lady's Mine is my pandemic book. A love story, it harkens back to my roots as a romance writer. It tells of a displaced Boston suffragette and a disinherited Union soldier who meet in a remote California mining town. But it also explores how one determined individual can impact an entire community. You may have noticed a few nods to both *The Taming of the Shrew* and *Oklahoma!* along the way, too. I cheered for Kathryn and Matthias's romance and had so much fun writing it. I hope you had as much fun reading it.

Francine Rivers

DISCUSSION QUESTIONS

1. One of the questions the author was exploring as she wrote this book was "Can one person impact an entire community?" How do different characters try to influence the community of Calvada, for good or bad? What can we learn from their examples? How would you answer the author's question?

2. Both Kathryn and Matthias are disinherited by their families. What were the reasons? How did they each handle the rejection? When Matthias reveals to Kathryn why his father disowned him, Kathryn responds with "God promises to finish the work in us." What does this mean? Have you ever been rejected by someone you love? How did you handle it? What, if any, future do you see for Matthias and his father?

3. In what ways are Kathryn and City Walsh alike? Do you think personality traits can be inherited from family

members? What was Kathryn able to accomplish that City Walsh was not?

4. Once Kathryn starts up the *Voice*, Matthias tries to warn her against writing inflammatory editorials. Do you agree with his advice that "too much truth at one time can hurt more than help"? Is Kathryn right that following one's convictions and facing trouble seem to go together? Are there ways to create change without agitating others, or does change always cause upheaval?

5. Give some examples of restrictions women were under in 1875. Did any of these surprise you? Are there areas where women's rights still fall short today? Or are there certain expectations or burdens placed on women that men don't carry? In what ways should society strive for equality between genders? Or is it okay to allow for different roles based on a person's strengths?

6. Is Kathryn wise or foolish in her dealings with Morgan Sanders? What signs of warning did she ignore? Have you ever put yourself in harm's way? How and why? What avenue of escape did God give you? Did you use it? What did you learn from your experience?

7. Matthias turns to Reverend Thacker for help in convincing Kathryn to keep to a woman's place in society. What does Thacker say about Adam and Eve? Is his sermon fair? How does Kathryn react? Were you as surprised by her reaction as Matthias was? What does she conclude about a woman's role?

8. As a Southerner who fought for the North in the Civil War, Matthias has a unique perspective on victors and

the vanquished. He muses: "Men lived not by what they were told, but by what they believed." Do you agree with that idea? What does City tell Matthias about what people believe? (See chapter 17.) Where do you turn for the ultimate authority on truth? When you come in contact with those who have different views, how do you choose to interact?

9. Nabor Aday verbally abuses his wife, Abbie. How does she handle it? How do others respond when they observe this couple's interactions? Do you think people today are more or less likely to speak up when they see abuse? What resources are available today for those in abusive situations?

10. Ronya tells Kathryn, "A woman needs to guard her heart and use her head when picking a husband." What makes her say this? Do you agree with it? What other advice would you give?

11. City had a lot to say about regrets, including "Some decisions haunt you. You can change your mind, but you can't go back." Which characters are haunted by regrets? How do they respond? If you can't go back, what can you do to keep moving forward?

12. Kathryn ponders this idea: "What a tangled mess men make when they try to play God." What messes do various characters in this book make when "trying to play God"? Have you seen any examples of this in your own life? How were they resolved?

13. Widows in the past as well as today have many difficulties. Why did Fiona Hawthorne choose the path she took?

What path did she hope to take at the end? Why did it not seem possible to her to stay in Calvada? How would you rewrite the end of her story?

14. As Kathryn learns the truth about City's murder, Matthias points out that some people seem bent on evil. How much truth is there in that statement? What factors (a wounded soul, a seared conscience) might contribute to that? Do you believe everyone can be redeemed?

ACKNOWLEDGMENTS

MY SINCERE AND DEEPEST THANKS go to the following people:

Danielle Egan-Miller of Browne and Miller Literary Associates—my hardworking, multitalented, trustworthy agent, who keeps me free from stress about the ever-changing market and medias. You've always gone far above and beyond what is expected of an agent.

Kathy Olson—my keen-eyed, creative editor, who continues to rescue me from overwriting and linear structure. I love working with you.

Karen Watson—publisher, mentor of new writers—you have encouraged me from the beginning.

Cd'A brainstormers: Brandilyn Collins, Tammy Alexander, Karen Ball, Gayle DeSalles, Sharon Dunn, Tricia Goyer, Robin Lee Hatcher, Sunni Jeffers, Sandy Sheppard, and Janet Ulbright. Talented writers, all of you! You share the joys and frustrations of the writing life. Whenever I've been stuck, you've been there Zooming with ideas and solutions. You ladies ROCK!

My friendly fellow inklings: Claudia Millerick, Erin Briggs, Kitty Briggs, Christy Hoss, Jackie Tisthammer, Lynette Winters. You have inspired and encouraged me from day one.

Early reader and constant encourager: Colleen Shine Phillips, for your insights and wisdom.

My best friend and the love of my life, Rick Rivers. Thank you for patiently listening to me as I talk (and talk) story. And I admit—it is true that I can take forty-five minutes to tell you about a thirty-minute program.

God bless you all!

ABOUT THE AUTHOR

New York Times bestselling author Francine Rivers had a successful writing career in the general market for several years before becoming a born-again Christian. As her statement of faith, she wrote *Redeeming Love*, a retelling of the biblical story of Gomer and Hosea set during the time of the California Gold Rush. *Redeeming Love* is now considered by many to be a classic work of Christian fiction, and it continues to be one of the industry's top-selling titles year after year.

Since *Redeeming Love*, Francine has published numerous novels with Christian themes—all bestsellers—and she has continued to win both industry acclaim and reader loyalty around the world. Her Christian novels have been awarded or nominated for many honors, and in 1997, after winning her third RITA Award for inspirational fiction, Francine was inducted into the Romance Writers of America's Hall of Fame. In 2015, she received the Lifetime Achievement Award from American Christian Fiction Writers (ACFW).

Francine's novels have been translated into over thirty different languages, and she enjoys bestseller status in many foreign countries.

Francine and her husband live in northern California and enjoy time spent with their grown children and grandchildren. She uses her writing to draw closer to the Lord, and she desires that through her work she might worship and praise Jesus for all He has done and is doing in her life.

Visit her website at francinerivers.com and connect with her on Facebook (facebook.com/FrancineRivers) and Twitter (@FrancineRivers).

The Beloved Classic
FROM FRANCINE RIVERS

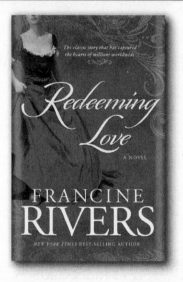

Redeeming Love is a life-changing story of God's unconditional, redemptive, all-consuming love that has captured the hearts of millions worldwide.

Also available in the *Redeeming Love* line of books

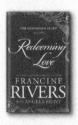

A beautiful keepsake, linen-bound edition.

For group or individual use, inspired by the book of Hosea.

Spend 40 days meditating on the biblical themes of this beloved Christian classic novel.

MULTNOMAH

FrancineRivers.com

CP1765

Connect with Francine online at

francinerivers.com

TYNDALE HOUSE PUBLISHERS
IS CRAZY4FICTION!

Fiction that entertains and inspires

Get to know us! Become a member of the Crazy4Fiction community. Whether you read our blog, like us on Facebook, follow us on Twitter, or receive our e-newsletter, you're sure to get the latest news on the best in Christian fiction. You might even win something along the way!

JOIN IN THE FUN TODAY.

 crazy4fiction.com

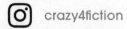 Crazy4Fiction

 crazy4fiction

 @Crazy4Fiction

CP0021

By purchasing this book from Tyndale, you have helped us meet the spiritual and physical needs of people all around the world.